Heart's Desire

by Laura Pedersen

FICTION

Last Call

Beginner's Luck

Going Away Party

NONFICTION

Play Money

Heart's Desire

a novel

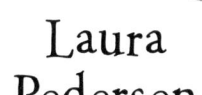

Laura Pedersen

BALLANTINE BOOKS
NEW YORK

A Ballantine Books Trade Paperback Original

Copyright © 2005 by Laura Pedersen
Reading group guide copyright © 2005 by Laura Pedersen and Random House, Inc.
Excerpt from *Full House* copyright © 2005 by Laura Pedersen

Published in the United States by Ballantine Books, an imprint of The Random House Publishing Group, a division of Random House, Inc., New York.

Ballantine and colophon are registered trademarks of Random House, Inc.
Ballantine Reader's Circle and colophon are trademarks of Random House, Inc.

ISBN 0 7394 5719-5

This book contains an excerpt from the forthcoming edition of *Full House* by Laura Pedersen. This excerpt has been set for this edition only and may not reflect the final content of the forthcoming edition.

Printed in the United States of America

Book design by Susan Turner

For all my girlfriends near and far,
from Copenhagen to California.

We lose—because we win—
Gamblers—recollecting which—
Toss their dice again!

—EMILY DICKINSON

Acknowledgments

Special thanks to Carolyn Fireside for her boundless imagination and to Deirdre Lanning at Ballantine Books for her dedication and sharp editorial eye. Ongoing gratitude to my friend and literary agent Judith Ehrlich for her steadfast support, passion, and creative input. Continuing appreciation for my steady helpmates—Willie, Julie, Aimee, Cecilia, and Lucy.

Heart's Desire

Chapter One

SOMEONE CRACKS OPEN THE BEDROOM DOOR. "HALLIE? ARE YOU in there?"

Upon hearing the familiar voice I wake slightly and assume that I'm having weird dreams due to excessive body heat. Lying next to me is my boyfriend, Ray. And on the other side is Vanessa. I push down the blanket.

"Hallie, are you up?" the voice comes again.

Only now I'm definitely *hearing* and not dreaming Bernard's stage whisper. And also smelling the rich aroma of freshly brewed coffee with a hint of vanilla. Wakefulness and reality strike simultaneously. "Oh my gosh!" I shout, and raise my head off the pillow. "What time is it? I have an exam at eight!"

The only thing that's *not* surprising is to find Bernard Stockton in the hallway of my apartment. After all, he's the one who'd saved me when I was sliding down the slippery slope of adolescent rebellion the previous fall by taking me on as a live-in yard person. And now at least one weekend a month he arrives early and cooks us all a big brunch. Only this isn't Saturday or Sunday. It's Wednesday of finals week after my first year of college.

Bernard opens the door the rest of the way and steps inside the room. "It's just after seven," he says. But his voice is hesitant and hoarse, like a record being played at the wrong speed, and I can tell immediately that something is terribly wrong. Normally he would be trilling "Rise and shine!" like Amanda Wingfield in *The Glass Menagerie.* Not only that, he must have awoken at five in the morning to make the one-hour drive to Cleveland.

"What's the matter—I mean, I'm coming. . . ." I start to climb out from my position as pickle in the middle. "Um, could I meet you in the kitchen?"

"Oh, yes, of course. How indelicate of me." His footsteps become faint and then I hear him tackle the mess of dirty pots and pans in the kitchen.

After stumbling around the minefield of packed duffel bags and piles of dirty clothes for a few minutes I finally find a pair of sweatpants to pull on. No surprise to discover a bunch of unpaid bills and parking tickets scattered beneath them. I'll be lucky if the repo man isn't towing my car away at this very moment.

The whole place smells like old pizza and even older laundry. As I pass the living room the sound of loud snoring comes from behind stacks of books and model cardboard buildings that rise in the middle of the floor to form a miniature skyline. A closer look reveals my roommate Debbie and her boyfriend Daniel asleep on the couch, surrounded by notebooks and empty pizza boxes. It's a memorial to unfinished group projects everywhere.

In the kitchen Bernard has lined up his numerous shopping bags on the floor, since there's no available space on the countertops or table. Those are covered in a collagelike mishmash of art supplies, stained coffee mugs, and overdue book notices. Fortunately, he's accustomed to the mess. With four busy young women sharing three rooms and all the various friends and boyfriends hanging about, housekeeping rarely rises above the minimum required for pest control. Particularly during exam time, when everyone is cramming for finals and working like crazy to finish papers and art projects.

I rub the sleep from my eyes. "What's wrong? Is it Olivia?" Though I'd called Bernard's sixtyish mother the night before to ask her a grammar question for a paper I was writing, or at least attempting to write, and she'd sounded fine.

Bernard stops whipping eggs in the shiny metal mixing bowl he brought from home, bows his head, and shuts his eyes as if in pain.

I stop in my tracks and stare at Bernard, waiting for his answer while growing increasingly worried. For he was, as they said of Odysseus, a man never at a loss. Only in Bernard's case, when faced with adversity he was rarely without a witty remark and an audacious plan, though it was oftentimes one he'd seen in a movie.

Finally Bernard exhales for the entire State of Ohio and says, "It's Gil."

Never before have I seen him so grave when referring to his longtime companion. And so of course I assume the worst. "What? Is he *dying?*"

Now that my eyes have become accustomed to the light, I notice how completely wrecked the normally dapper Bernard looks—bags under his eyes, worry lines furrowing his brow, and something I've *never* seen on him before, brown socks with black loafers!

Bernard turns away from me and dabs at his eyes. "I promised myself I wouldn't shed any more tears." He waits a moment to compose himself, takes a deep breath, looks me straight in the eye, and in a trembly voice blurts out, "Gil left me!"

"You broke up?" I'm truly stunned. I'd have voted my parents more likely to break up than Gil and Bernard, and even the thought of *that* is impossible.

"We didn't break up." Bernard starts sniffing again. "Gil *left* me!" He switches to French for greater effect. *"Abandonnement."*

I'm not sure exactly what the difference is between breaking up and one person leaving, but this doesn't appear to be the right moment to ask. Tears begin to stream down Bernard's cheeks. I've never seen him full-out cry like this before, not even when his father died.

As I reach to put my hand on his arm, a hiss comes from the stove and he leaps to adjust the heat on his beloved Calphalon non-stick crepe pan. Then he concentrates on making chocolate crepes and this seems to calm him slightly, to my great relief. Hopefully Bernard is overreacting and he and Gil just had an argument that will eventually be resolved. Perhaps it was about Bernard's antiques taking up the entire garage. In the spring Gil always gets cranky when bucketfuls of pollen land on his car because it has to sit out in the driveway all the time.

"What happened?" I ask. "Did you two have a fight?"

"No. I mean, here Gil is, always insisting that *he's* the *normal* one. Then all of a sudden he goes berserk and announces that he doesn't want to be part of a *committed relationship.* Gil just hasn't been the same since his older brother, Clifton, died unexpectedly last month . . . he became more and more distant and then . . . he said . . . it was over. . . ."

Bernard becomes upset again and uses the dish towel over his shoulder to wipe away his tears. He always brings his own Marshall Field's British icon dish towels when he comes to cook for us.

All of my friends love Bernard. He's like an eccentric uncle who unexpectedly shows up and bakes, helps to decorate, rearranges the furniture, and organizes theme parties. One of my professors had even invited him to guest lecture in a pottery class. Having bought and sold plenty of ceramics for his shop over the past fifteen years, Bernard knows everything about the different schools and designs, and most of all, precisely how much any lump of painted clay you might have lying around your attic is worth. This morning, how-ever, his usual exuberance is nowhere to be found.

Either the noise from us talking or, more likely, the smell of food and vanilla-flavored coffee awakens the couple on the couch in the living room and we hear them carefully making their way toward the kitchen. Design projects in various states of completion are everywhere, transforming the path into an obstacle course.

Bernard says to me, "I can't have anyone seeing me so out of sorts. Now, don't breathe a word to them about this calamity, all right?"

"Mum's the word," I reply. Bernard does indeed have a reputation for inexhaustible zest and witty remarks to protect.

He takes a deep breath, straightens up, and lifts his head high. "I'm channeling Susan Hayward in *Valley of the Dolls* when, after having her wig ripped off, she announces with great dignity, 'I'll go out the way I came in.' "

"I'm sure that's exactly what nine out of ten therapists would recommend," I agree wholeheartedly with his strategy.

Chapter
Two

DEBBIE AND DANIEL APPEAR BLEARY-EYED IN THE ARCHWAY. Daniel is bare-chested, wearing only jeans that hang low on his waist, suggesting an absence of underwear, and Debbie has a mint-green sheet wrapped around her, Statue of Liberty style. I'd rather we were all exhausted from partying, like at the beginning of the semester, but everyone is beat as a result of hitting the books hard all week.

"Hey," they say sleepily, but in unison.

Debbie is accustomed to Bernard arriving early and unexpectedly, though usually on weekends rather than school days. And Daniel is around often enough to have met Bernard a few times as well. They also know that he's very generous with his cooking. Bernard always claims that he's trying out new recipes and needs tasters, as if we're all doing him a huge favor by eating a five-course breakfast.

"Something smells terrific," says Daniel, hungrily eyeing the platter that now contains three crepes surrounded by sliced bananas and dusted with powdered sugar.

"Come on now, I know that everyone is tired and hungry as a result of all these horrible tests!" With forced cheer Bernard digs into his shopping bags and starts taking out cartons of cream, fruit salad, and fresh orange juice.

"Your eyes are all red," Debbie says to Bernard. "Are you okay?"

Bernard looks at me searchingly.

"He was just chopping onions," I quickly supply a plausible explanation.

"It's no use," says Bernard and begins to weep again. "Gil left me and I'm just a wreck!"

Bluffing was never his great strength. At least not like blanching. Bernard crumples into the nearest chair and cradles his face in his hands.

It so happens that Debbie's mother is a rapid-cycling bipolar and as a result she's excellent at dealing with unexpected mood swings. Debbie calmly pours Bernard a mug of the fresh coffee and pulls a chair up right next to his. "That's *terrible!*" She places her arm around him. "Tell us *all* about it."

"Oh, no. You have enough to worry about with exams." Bernard takes a deep breath and immediately begins, "Gil's older brother died a little over a month ago. They weren't on speaking terms because the family had disowned Gil when he came out of the closet. . . ."

Just then I notice the clock on the microwave says a quarter to eight. My exam in motion graphics starts in exactly fifteen minutes. Leaping up from the table I say to Bernard, "I'll be back in two hours. Can you stay that long?"

"*Stay?* I can't go *home!*" He waves the end of the dish towel with the Buckingham Palace guard wearing the big black furry hat at me. "I've driven mother insane the past two weeks with all my keening and wailing. She says that if I can't let go then I need to see a psychiatrist before she'll let me back in. And to make matters worse, she keeps reminding me that Shaw's *Pygmalion* didn't have a happy ending—the Americans added it when the play was made into the musical *My Fair Lady*."

Leaving Bernard at the kitchen table I hurry off to take a quick shower. As much as I love Bernard, his timing couldn't be worse. Not only must I do well on this test, since my grades in the class up until now haven't been that good, but I need to stop at Career Services and figure out how to make some serious money this summer or else I'm going to have to drop out and work full-time for a year. I hated high school so much that I quit at the beginning of junior year, but college is everything that high school wasn't, and I really want to finish and earn a degree. As it is, I'm likely to graduate a hundred grand in debt, a number considerably higher than the starting salary of the graphic designer I'm paying a fortune to become.

As I rush down the hallway, my other roommates, Suzy and Robin, emerge from their small dark cave in the back like crustaceans crawling out of their shells. With eyes half closed they stumble toward the kitchen and the aroma of a real breakfast.

By the time I return, an overly wound Bernard is recounting the Gil saga to them, starting at the beginning.

As I race out the door Bernard interrupts himself to ask me, "Uh, Hallie, that was Steve in your bed with you, wasn't it? But I didn't recognize the woman."

"Actually that was Ray, my latest boyfriend of two weeks. And on the other side was Vanessa. She stayed over last night."

He gives me a curious look. "A ménage à trois. Mother would be so proud!"

"Oh my gosh, no! Vanessa is Ray's neighbor. She's planning on going to school here next year. We ran out of beds."

"Of course. I've forgotten how *loose* everything is at college," says Bernard. "I suppose all that's missing is Toulouse-Lautrec sitting over in a corner painting away and immortalizing us for posterity."

Chapter
Three

TAKING AS MANY SHORTCUTS AS POSSIBLE, I JOG OVER WET LAWNS and across streets until I reach the edge of campus. Fortunately the Cleveland Art Institute doesn't have the same bomb shelter décor as my high school. Ivy twines down the pale cement arches in front of reddish-brown brick buildings with large windows and elegant statuary tucked into the cornices. The library looks like a domed cathedral, with stained-glass windows and a cupola that is home to a nest of storks. And there's plenty of space between the buildings for pedestrian paths, the edges dotted with pretty bluish-gray juniper trees, grassy patches where you can relax or study outside, and strategically placed wrought-iron benches on which to sit while sipping coffee and catching up with friends. It's really wonderful. Though I suppose it wouldn't be a very good marketing strategy to have an ugly art school.

I slump into one of the last seats in the lecture hall just as the test books are being passed out. The tension is so palpable that if you close your eyes for a minute it's actually possible to smell the coffee coming out of students' pores and hear the prayers being sent heavenward to the Grade Gods.

The exam isn't too bad, though mostly because I met someone in a mechanical drawing class who took the course last semester and told me exactly what to study. However, a stop in Career Services afterward doesn't turn out to be as big a success. All the salaried internships were snatched up a month ago and the only jobs left are either in warehouses or as data clerks and receptionists, paying $6.50 an hour.

When I reach the apartment the windows are wide open and it smells as fresh as spring. Bernard has straightened up the kitchen and somehow organized the heaps of junk all over the living room into neat stacks. He appears pale but composed.

"How was the test?" he asks.

"Not nearly as good as your breakfast," I say.

"Now Hallie, I've been afraid to inquire, but what's happening with your summer internship at that art gallery in Buffalo?"

"Oh, I got it, all right. The only problem is that at the last minute I found out they don't *pay anything*. The woman claims that it's a 'résumé builder.' Sounds more like 'slave labor' to me. And I need to make some serious money this summer. Otherwise I'm going to be living in a tent next year and I'll be paying off student loans from my nursing home."

"So I assume that you're declining the position." Bernard appears more relieved than disappointed.

I scowl in the affirmative.

"Thank heavens. Because you *must* come home ASAP. Brandt's busy working on some laboratory project with a professor over at the community college. Apparently the high school ran out of experiments for him to do."

When I left for college, sixteen-year-old Brandt had taken my place as the local adolescent in distress and live-in gardener.

"Quite the budding scientist, that boy," Bernard continues, "but absolutely useless in the garden and the kitchen. Anyway, you simply must resume your role as yard person this summer. The grounds will not survive another season of Brandt!"

Only I get the feeling Bernard has something other than just yard work in mind for me. But at least he seems to have regained a bit of his old enthusiasm.

"And . . . ," I prompt him.

"It will be just like old times," Bernard claims a shade too cheerfully.

"And . . . ," I say again as I watch him grow suddenly grim.

"I need your help getting Gil back." He sounds desperate. "Mother is no use at all with her *live and let live* nonsense. Whereas you're clever about things like this. I *need* you!" he implores.

And now I begin to understand why he's shown up in the middle of the week.

"Of course, you'll receive a raise," says Bernard. "How's fifteen dollars an hour?"

When you're talking about tuition, rent, books, and art supplies, even fifteen dollars an hour doesn't go very far. However, it's not as if I have another job lined up. And there *is* a one-year scholarship being offered to the winner of the annual design competition sponsored by an advertising agency here in Cleveland. Only the entries are due at the end of June and I haven't even begun to think about it.

"All right. But on weekends I have to work on winning this stupid contest. And I'm not doing anything *illegal*. I want to get a fresh start back home." After dropping out of high school, getting kicked out of the local casino for underage gambling, and then the bum rap over some stolen money, I've had enough of being the town miscreant.

"Of course; you'll become a model citizen, earn a plaque, and run for town council—I'll throw wonderful tea parties with cucumber sandwiches like the Kennedy women used to do—and then you'll go on to prosecute all of your old cronies and become the first woman President. Now, when can we leave?"

"This horrible cat food campaign is due at nine o'clock tomorrow morning. And I haven't even started it yet." How did I get so behind? A string of ill-fated romances is how. This is another good thing about college: It teaches you to answer your own questions.

"Perhaps I can help," offers Bernard. "I could think up a jingle, or rather, a little *kitty ditty.*"

"Thanks. But it's computer stuff. And it's going to take all night." This deadline crunch is my own fault. There'd been plenty of time to do the damn thing. My mind has just been elsewhere. On how to lose my virginity in two semesters or less, to be specific.

"Very well, then I'll prepare a fortifying repast for everyone," says Bernard. "You've all been working much too hard. For dinner we need comfort food—meatloaf, garlic mashed potatoes, an enormous spinach salad with hot dressing, macaroni and cheese, creamed corn, and Bernard's Very Berry Crumble for dessert."

"Anything but pizza sounds good to me."

"How many gourmands do you think we can expect?"

"If kids find out that you're cooking, probably around twelve."

Bernard heads out to the grocery store and I hit the books—or rather, the keyboard.

Debbie invites her drawing professor to dinner, who she suspects has a crush on Bernard. A few months ago he drove all the way to Bernard's antiques shop supposedly to see some Victorian pencil sketches. And then he stayed for over three hours.

By the time we all reconvene, everyone appears to be in good spirits. The two men indeed seem to get on well at dinner. The wine flows, the food is delicious, and we stuff ourselves into carbohydrate comas.

Bernard says not to worry about the messy kitchen and waves us students off to finish our projects while he and Professor Harris clean up and then sit around the kitchen talking. The first time I go for coffee I'm actually encouraged. Not only have the men created a tasteful study-break buffet of highly caffeinated beverages, Power-Bars, and Bernard's chocolate chunk cookies, but they're enjoying glasses of sherry and animatedly discussing Victorian wallpaper. From what I can gather, they're both fond of "tripartite treatment with geometric patterns" and believe that "imitation High Style plasterwork is a sacrilege."

However, when I go for a refill, Bernard is tearfully telling the professor about Gil's recent departure. I end up ushering out a flummoxed Professor Harris while making excuses for Bernard. Then I pack him off to the back bedroom, since Suzy left for home after finishing her last exam this afternoon and Robin is having a final fling over at her boyfriend's dormitory.

One thing is certain: Bernard is as theatrical in his sorrow as he previously was in his exuberance. As I settle down to work I can hear him singing "It Ain't Necessarily So" from *Porgy and Bess,* complete with dialect and low rolling bass notes.

Chapter
Four

As the pink glow of early morning creeps across my desk I put the finishing touches on the campaign to launch a high-performance cat food, a product for which your "feline will make a beeline." Where is Olivia when I need a decent rhyme?

Bernard is busy in the kitchen whipping up what he calls a "brain breakfast" of strong Chilean coffee, fresh-squeezed orange juice, fried bananas, and scrambled eggs with red peppers and hot sausage.

After handing in the cat food assignment I pack my bags and call Ray on his cell phone to say good-bye, but his voicemail answers. I hang up since there's really nothing to say. We've made plans to get together in a week, right before he leaves for New York City. And we both know what's supposed to happen then, since Ray's given me the "fish or cut bait" ultimatum about sleeping with him. Which I want to do. At least I think I do.

Finally I climb into the secondhand green Cabriolet I purchased last spring and follow Bernard back to the Stockton homestead in Cosgrove County. He makes no secret of the fact that he's been waiting for me because he's afraid to confront Olivia without backup. Apparently she's threatening to ship him off to Dalewood, the local booby hatch.

In the sky above flocks of geese honk as they make their return, the soft spring sunshine silvering their wings. The light falls in great sheets between the trees along the highway, transforming them into bright green parasols of new leaves as I speed past. It's good to be heading east, toward home. I hadn't been back since the middle of winter. While my roommates spent spring break in Key West, lying on the beach all day and sneaking into bars with fake ID at night, I'd remained at school. The entire two weeks were spent drafting an album cover and T-shirts for an imaginary rock band, and making up three overdue papers for freshman composition. By that point I'd fallen far enough behind to briefly qualify for academic probation.

The problem isn't the work, or even the freewheeling schedule of college life. College itself is terrific. No more bells. No alarm clocks, at least if you don't sign up for morning classes. I was finally free. No Attendance Nazi scouring the student lounge for wayward youth. No dress code. No curfew. No students making out in every hallway and around every corner. Heck, if you ask they'll assign you a bed in a co-ed dorm, to sleep in, or to do whatever else you want in it.

However, what college administrators don't tell you in the acceptance letter is that the first year is entirely about sex. It bubbles through every aspect of campus life like an underground stream. I'm positive that this is the sole reason they give us through second semester of sophomore year to declare a major. Since it's not until then that students start to recover from the initial fornication rampage. And that's just the Baptists, Jews, Lutherans, and so forth. Some of the Roman Catholic and Fundamentalist Christian girls never made it past the first six weeks and had to be taken home, pregnant or else headed for a folding chair in a church basement to attend Alcoholics Anonymous meetings. When I lived on campus the first semester, my resident adviser basically ran a twenty-four-hour Planned Parenthood office, complete with relationship counseling, STD pamphlets, and home pregnancy tests.

There were a few exceptions—those who arrived bohemian, agnostic, or just plain lonely, and through the Soldiers for Christ campus ministry or some other religious organization, found Jesus. But more often than not they lost him again by homecoming weekend.

On the other hand, the sex scene isn't entirely the result of the students' inclinations. The school gives you a list of classes to choose from and tells you to "get involved," which I suppose the parents assume means extracurricular activities. But they may as well just say "sex." Going out for coffee or a drink in the student union is usually a vague, "Will you sleep with me?" A frat guy sidling up to a girl at a party with an extra beer means "Will you sleep with me?" More often than not "What are you doing this Friday night?" translates to "Will you sleep with me?"

College is not at all like high school when it comes to dating. This is the fast track, courtship on crack cocaine. Two meetings, three at the most, people jump into bed together. None of that high school test-driving by going to a dance or kicking the tires with a kissing and fondling session at a make-out party.

Sex is in the air like sweet perfume and freshmen are the bumblebees. You arrive in class the first day and the professor stands at the front of the room discussing the syllabus. Only instead of deciding whether the teacher is any good or the workload is too much, you look around at everyone and make a candidate list. Then you either ask the other person out "for coffee" or else organize to meet at a party. A party is best because kegs can crush nerves and embolden a person to move at an even faster clip. Keg parties also provide a built-in clause to eject after a one-night stand, pretending not to remember the encounter, or in cases of extreme alcohol consumption, not remember it *for real.*

Then there's the handful of sophomores who were too grade-conscious the first year and decide not to make the same mistake twice. So they're like freshmen emeriti who jump into the fray as enablers by planning parties and E-mailing all the frosh girls. Now add in the sophomore guys who already ran through their entire class and are hitting on the new crop of girls, and you have a seven-day-a-week orgy.

Also belatedly diving in are sophomore girls who were faithful to their high school boyfriends throughout freshman year. Weeknights were spent crying on the phone and as soon as classes finished on Friday, they dashed off to catch a train or bus, just when the real fun was starting on campus. Those relationships had mostly gone up in flames after one drunken evening of confessions, usually the result of a female spy reporting illicit activities back to her high school girlfriend.

My high school boyfriend, Craig, and I attempted to avoid that trap by agreeing to see other people when we left for schools eleven hundred miles apart. Everyone we talked to at our respective orientations said the same thing: "Don't come to college with a boyfriend or girlfriend at a different school, especially one more than two hours away." They told stories of promising young lives ruined by long-distance relationships. Even suicides. Plus, with my spending so much time in the art rooms and Craig taking the bus all over the Midwest for lacrosse games, there wasn't any chance we'd be able to visit each other. Best I could tell, he'd ended up playing lacrosse well and playing the field, too, casually mentioning the names of different women friends almost every time we spoke.

The college juniors are mostly in one-on-ones, or else some sensible dating pattern, focused more on pulling their academics together so they don't need a victory lap to make up for lost credits. Basically they've just come off a two-year roller coaster of sex and binge drinking and suddenly realized that a major is exactly that, requiring a concentration of courses, and as of now, they have one from every department.

Meantime the seniors are like old married couples, mostly paired off, having at some point worked out a verbal contract with a significant other. A number of them are engaged and a few have already married. The seniors bear a striking resemblance to grown-ups and it's easy to mistake them for professors or administrative staff. They don't appear to have time-management problems the way the rest of us do—flying across campus at 9 A.M., barefoot and wearing the ketchup-stained sweats we slept in. They can often be seen in dress clothes since they're interviewing for jobs. And some even carry briefcases because they're already working in real offices.

It's a relief to leave the gray slab and brown brick buildings of Cleveland behind and once again see the Ohio countryside with its white clapboard houses and front lawns littered with kids' toys and garden hoses. Spring is everywhere, from the restlessness of birds and squirrels as they dart across the road to the mashed banana sunlight creating dark shadows alongside anything blocking its determined path. The warm winds cause the young leaves in the trees above to flutter, while down below clouds of feathery white Queen Anne's Lace appear to drift through the gullies adjacent to the highway. All that's missing is a soundtrack.

When we reach the sign for Timpany it means that home is just ten minutes away. Only I'm amazed how it's gone from being a town twice the size of Cosgrove to The Town That Charm Forgot, a cement industrial park with sprawling office buildings and factory malls. However, I soon discover a circuit board of new housing developments and plazas on the outskirts of my own town, replacing what was all farmland when I returned to school just five months ago.

Before pulling into the neighborhood I pass the old maximum-security high school, where my younger sister Louise is now finishing her sophomore year. The teachers must be starting to wonder exactly how many of us Palmer children there are. And the answer is, to quote from the SAT study guide, *myriad,* translate: a vast number—or in this case, eight! Next fall the school gets Teddy, and after he graduates there will be the twins, Darlene and Davy. Francie will eventually follow, if the administration hasn't installed a Palmer family quota by then, and in a few years baby Lillian will be of legal torture age. We were fast becoming a public education dynasty. At least budget-conscious Dad must be happy that he's getting his money's worth when it comes to paying local property taxes.

Chapter
Five

WHEN WE ARRIVE BACK AT 48 NUTHATCH LANE IT'S ALREADY
lunchtime. In the afternoon light the old Victorian-style house appears bright and fresh, the coat of white paint I applied last year having held up well throughout the rough winter. Same with the shiny
black shutters. And the gutters don't seem to have broken out with
rust patches. The silvery-white birch trees lining the driveway stand
tall, their papery-thin bark appearing almost too delicate to with-
stand so much as a spring breeze. The gravel driveway is sprinkled
with fallen pink blossoms from the gnarly old cherry tree, making it
look as if a bucketful of confetti has been tossed down from one of
the upstairs windows.

The only visible problems out front are that a recent storm has
pulled up the weather vane atop the cupola so that the arrow is now
stuck into a shingle, and the grass is so overgrown that I can't help
but wonder if anyone has mowed the lawn since last summer.

Inside the house Olivia and her live-in Italian lover, Ottavio, are sitting next to each other at the dining room table enjoying hearty servings of fettuccini.

"Hallie!" Olivia leaps up and with a spirited tilt of the head pulls me to her. "Thank goodness you've returned!" Her soft musical laugh rises and descends like a flute playing a scale.

"Yes, Mother, Hallie has agreed to care for the yard this summer." Bernard seems a bit frosty with her and quickly turns to leave the room.

"Hey, where are you going?" I call after him.

"Bertie's been a slave to unpredictable bowels since the breakup," says Olivia.

Bernard stops in the archway and informs us, "It's *not* a breakup." However, he doesn't dispute the bowel accusation and makes a dash for the stairs.

Ottavio bounds over and gives me one of his enthusiastic Italian greetings, complete with a bone-crushing hug, cheek pinches, and a big kiss on the nose. If this is what I'm entitled to after only five months of being away, I'd be slightly afraid to suddenly show up after ten or twenty years. He'd probably do a full running tackle before trying to feed me all the meals that I'd missed. And though with his slightly rounded body and thinning hair he's not nearly as handsome as was Olivia's husband, who passed away last winter, Ottavio is effervescent, passionate, and loving, and certainly not afraid to be caught demonstrating these capacities.

Olivia has soft fan lines of wrinkles around her eyes but they don't make her appear old. Her blue eyes are not gentle, but silvery clear, and they flash like sapphires with vitality and anticipation. As always, she has the power of suggesting things even more lovely than herself, as the perfume of a single apple blossom can call up the entire sweetness of spring.

"It's a stroke of good fortune that you've returned," Olivia says to me. "Brandt is very sweet but his head is in the clouds with periodic tables and perpetual motion. In fact, Ottavio has nicknamed him Galileo."

Ottavio smiles at the mention of Brandt's nickname and then

hurries off to get another bowl from the kitchen. If Bernard is away at an estate sale or busy down at his antiques shop, Ottavio dives into the kitchen and makes all sorts of northern Italian dishes containing pasta, vegetables, and shellfish. The men appreciate each other's cooking and often exchange notes and ideas, though I've rarely seen them occupy the kitchen at the same time.

Rocky the chimpanzee comes gamboling in from the sunporch and jumps up and down while exuberantly waving his arms as if he's playing charades. Then he lopes over, gives me a big hug with his gangly arms, and plants a loud smack of a kiss on my cheek. A dog barks outside and Rocky quickly turns and scampers toward the front door.

"He's taken a shine to Lulu, the Great Dane from next door," explains Olivia. "A nice older couple with the last name of Shultze moved in last month."

Rocky began as one of Olivia's humanitarian projects, eventually segued to household pet, and is now a full-fledged member of the family. When Olivia first adopted him, Rocky was about to be put to sleep because he'd been specially trained to work with diabetic paraplegics and his patient of many years passed away. Reassignment wasn't an option because it happened that his mistress was an alcoholic and the two of them had been enjoying Singapore slings all day long, Rocky acting as bartender and eventually becoming an alcoholic himself. Apparently there isn't any chimp rehab, and so Olivia stepped in and placed him on a moderation program, since which he's been doing fine, aside from a few setbacks near the beginning.

Bernard reappears in the archway. "I'm tired of having to hide all the leftovers because Rocky's constantly sneaking that hound treats from the refrigerator," he says, and frowns after the excited chimp. "Now Hallie, I thought you could sleep on the sunporch and we'd move Rocky into the den. But Mother feels you'd prefer the summerhouse, so I replaced one of the couches with a daybed and added a space heater, in case it gets cold at night."

"And if all that light bothers you, we can install some blinds," adds Olivia.

"Oh no, I like to be able to see outside," I say. "And light doesn't bother me." At college everyone keeps a different schedule and if you can't sleep with lights on and music playing then you aren't going to sleep at all. I'd become a prime example of how evolutionary theory works on a college campus. Adapt or die.

"I'll go ahead and move your personal effects out there," Bernard announces as if he's a professional bellhop. His lips are tense as wire and he seems anxious to make another escape.

"Why don't you have some lunch first, Bertie?" suggests Olivia.

Bernard haughtily waves her off as if he's dismissing an invisible royal court and then disappears again. Meantime, Ottavio lays another place for me and sets down a bowl of delicious-looking fettuccini with fresh vegetables covered in marinara sauce, along with a salad of tomatoes, mozzarella, and artichoke hearts.

As soon as we hear the front door close, Olivia places her fingers to her temples as if staving off a migraine and the usual gaiety drains from her voice. "You have *no idea* what it's been like around here, Hallie. I mean, of course we all miss Gil terribly, but Bernard has completely lost his grip, and I'm *very* worried."

"*Pazzo in testa,*" Ottavio circles a finger around his ear to correlate with his Italian for "crazy in the head."

"I know my son has always had a tendency toward the melodramatic, but he's now fallen solidly into the operatic," confirms Olivia.

At the word *operatic,* Ottavio places the back of one hand up to his forehead and moans, "Pagliacci," and then rolls his eyes toward the ceiling.

"Who's Pagliacci?" I ask. Has Gil run off with another man? An Italian?

"*Pagliacci* is an opera by Ruggiero Leoncavallo," explains Olivia. "It contains some of the saddest music ever written, especially Act Fifteen." She turns to Ottavio. "Don't worry, darling, I hid the CD while he was off at Hallie's school."

Ottavio appears relieved and offers me more salad as Olivia continues, "Whereas others wear their heart on their sleeves, I'm afraid that Bertie buys airtime. Seriously, Hallie, I never thought I'd hear myself say this, but my son really needs to see a counselor. He's miserable beyond belief, doesn't shop or cook, and hardly sleeps a wink—just watches old movies in his room all night long." Her mouth draws tight and she looks down. "I'm afraid . . . that . . . well . . . he might do something. . . ."

"*No!*" I'm aghast. Because I know how those operas that Bernard listens to can end. And it's terrible to think of the normally bright and cheerful Bernard suddenly identifying with the tragic suicides that accompany all of his favorite arias—Aida wanting to share in her lover's suffocation; Selika inhaling the deadly perfume of the manchineel tree; and his all-time favorite, Tosca leaping to her death after her lover has been shot by a firing squad.

Olivia places her hand on mine. "I didn't mean to frighten you, but I *am* concerned. I've been reading to him from A. E. Housman. *'And now the fancy passes by, And nothing will remain, And miles around they'll say that I, Am quite myself again.'* "

As always, Olivia can produce a verse to suit every occasion.

"What can I do to help?" I ask. But what I really mean is, *Are we truly on a suicide watch?*

"Just be yourself and don't leave any Hart Crane poems lying around the house. Bernard so enjoys your company. Though I do wish he'd give up this notion of winning Gil back, and start moving on with his life—perhaps even get out and meet people. But he'll have to arrive at that in his own good time. Bernard must learn to embrace the shadows, because they indicate there is light nearby. And the deepest shadows result from the greatest illumination."

I don't mention the shadow cast by his recent meeting with my professor, and the resultant round of sobbing, rather than flirting.

Chapter Six

When the front door opens I assume it's Bernard again, but a young man appears carrying a glass aquarium along with some gravel, plastic greenery, and a water-filled plastic bag containing a half-dozen pollywogs. Come to think of it . . . he looks like an older and more handsome version of Brandt.

"B-Brandt?" I stammer with surprise.

"Hey, Hallie! You're home!" He places what is no doubt a science project on the sideboard and comes over and gives me a hug and a kiss. It's only on the cheek, thank heavens. Back when we were in high school together Brandt had the longest-running crush in history on me. He was nice enough, but what a geek, from the safety goggles on his head all the way down to the reflective stripes on his sneakers!

I must admit, however, that like Pinocchio before him, Brandt's turned into a real boy. Almost a man, actually. He's left behind the vague shape of adolescence, with its gangly appendages interrupted by pointy outcroppings, and appears to have developed honest-to-goodness shoulders, and arm muscles, too. There's also a slight shadow above his lip that indicates shaving has become part of his daily regimen. Even the trombone voice, though not particularly deep, has finally steadied and settled into a more or less appropriate octave.

"I was afraid that you were going to take that internship in Buffalo, and I'd be stuck with the yard again," says Brandt. "I can't figure out how to keep the mower from stalling out and I've got an incredible research job at the community college working with a professor on a physiology paper." He nods toward his tank. "I've been accepted at Massachusetts Institute of Technology for fall."

"Congratulations!" I say. Though more out of goodwill than surprise. I mean, if MIT had turned Brandt down they would have had a lot to answer for when he eventually picked up his science prize in Norway.

"Brandt received a full academic scholarship," Olivia adds proudly.

"Yeah, but I can easily work off my rent and books as an assistant in the lab," he quickly adds.

I think how nice it would be if I could work off some of my tuition in a lab. But the only way that is going to happen is if they need a human guinea pig. There *must* be a way to make some real money this summer. At least there was the weekly poker game. At school no one is much interested in poker, unless it's strip poker. Though I'd managed to win a couple hundred bucks playing hearts. Of course, there's always the racetrack. Even though I'm still not old enough to place a bet, they never ask for ID, unlike the sticklers at OTB. And if worse comes to worst, I can call my old friend Cappy the bookie, who's always been impressed with my talent for probability theory and happens to be interested in setting up a rebate shop. These are betting parlors on Indian reservations and offshore locations reached via Internet, where high-rollers receive a small percentage back whether they win or lose. For a brief moment I imagine myself working from a bamboo hut overlooking a gorgeous white sand beach and sipping chocolate Yoo-hoo from a bottle with a brightly colored paper umbrella sticking out of the top.

"Okay!" Bernard appears in the archway and smacks his hands together as if he's leading a motivation workshop and it's time to break into discussion groups. "Old home week is over."

Rocky has returned from outside and enters the dining room frantically waving his arms at Brandt just the way he had done with me. Only Brandt motions back to him, as if they're playing Simon Says. "Rocky says that he's happy you're home," Brandt translates.

"Oh really?" I'm aware that Rocky is glad to see me but I'm skeptical of the word-for-word translation.

"It transpires that Brandt discovered Rocky knows some sign language," explains Olivia. "So he contacted Rocky's former trainer and asked for a copy of his operating manual. In addition to being an accomplished bartender, Rocky apparently learned over fifty signals and can practically communicate like a person."

But it's obvious that at the present time Bernard has no patience for stupid chimp tricks. "Rocky speaks!" he says sarcastically, referring to the hullabaloo made when his beloved Greta Garbo made her first talking film. Bernard has an antique "Garbo Speaks!" movie poster behind the register down at the shop that is clearly marked NOT FOR SALE.

"It's really amazing," says Brandt. "He knows at least forty nouns and enough verbs to express his emotions pretty well."

"Yes," says Bernard. "And if they ever launch Mensa for chimpanzee saloonkeepers, I'm sure Rocky will be the first one admitted. Now, Hallie and I have lots and lots to do!" He takes me by the arm and steers me out of the room.

I know that *I* have to unpack and that *I* have to get started on the yard, but I'm not sure exactly what *we* have to do together.

"Yeah, I'd better get to work," I say. "But be sure to let me know if anyone has a suggestion as to how I can make twenty thousand dollars over the next ten weeks."

"It's such a shame about money," opines Olivia, and then launches into one of her impromptu but frequent history lessons. "Though certainly not a new dilemma. The French political philosopher

Rousseau supported himself by copying music. He had beautiful handwriting. I suppose copy machines do that sort of thing nowadays. A lack of funds meant the British landscape painter Constable couldn't marry the woman he passionately loved until he was forty, and then she died a mere ten years later. And Seneca, the great Roman dramatist and philosopher, supported himself by lending money and trading tax futures. Had he not possessed some solid business sense we might not have *Thyestes* nor *Phaedra,* works that influenced Elizabethan drama and the French playwrights Corneille and Racine."

"Sounds like Mr. Seneca figured it out," I say.

"Hardly," scoffs a Bernard anxious to get a move on. "He committed suicide in the bathtub after his student Nero turned against him."

Olivia and I exchange a wide-eyed look at the *S* word.

"Let us not confuse history with histrionics," chides Olivia.

Chapter
Seven

THE SUMMERHOUSE IS SPARKLING CLEAN, WITH NEW CUSHIONS on the chairs and the aroma of citrus-scented furniture polish rising from every side table. The couches that I used to sleep on have been re-covered in attractive pink-and-green-striped damask, with matching pillows. And there's a new daybed against the far wall, with a pretty white lace coverlet spread across the top.

It's obvious that Bernard assumed I'd be coming home, or else he's been preparing to kidnap me. There are a few more small bronze statues and decorative orange-and-blue Limoges plates in gold stands on the already jam-packed tabletops than I remember, but Bernard is always finding antiques that he loves so much he can't bear to put them up for sale at the shop.

The view from the summerhouse certainly isn't what it was a year ago. I hope that gardening isn't a required course at MIT because the yard is truly a natural disaster, unless Brandt has been using the area to test chemical weapons. A brown tangle of last year's plants and half-disintegrated leaves is spread across the ground like industrial-strength algae. The hedges are growing heads, arms, legs, and even tentacles, like undersea monsters. The lawn is high enough to ripple in the breeze like ocean waves. In fact, it's poised to leap up over the house. And there are tall dark squares of crabgrass scattered throughout like so many corduroy patches. Meantime, the greenhouse we built is completely *empty* except for the plastic planters and potting soil left over from last year.

However, Bernard, who normally loves to have perfect gardens, seems surprisingly unconcerned by this mess and lack of preparation. "Now let me explain my plan to win Gil back," he immediately begins. "People always want what they can't have, right? So—"

"Wait a second," I say, "I thought the two of you just broke up."

"Don't be ridiculous," says Bernard and dismisses this suggestion with a sweep of his arm. "For two people to break up they must both *agree* to break up. And I certainly haven't agreed to any such thing. As far as I'm concerned we're still together." His voice is croaky and his eyes are glassy, as if he hasn't had a good night's sleep in a long while.

It's quickly becoming apparent why Olivia is thinking along the lines of professional help. I'd taken psychology last fall and the first stage of coming to terms with any great loss is denial. Only it's supposed to be followed by anger and then bargaining, until you're finally traveling along the healthy road to acceptance.

On the other hand, Bernard's attitude sounds a lot like mine when this really hot sophomore named Josh was my boyfriend for two weeks during the fall term. The only problem was that Josh never knew anything about the relationship. This certainly made the breakup a lot easier, at least for him.

"I understand that what you're going through is really tough," I attempt to reason with him.

"I've grown accustomed to his face," insists Bernard. "He almost makes my day begin."

Okay, not only is Bernard speaking about Gil in the present tense, but I'm pretty sure he's quoting from *My Fair Lady*. "Yes, I understand it's very difficult right now. But each day will get a little easier, believe me."

However, Bernard isn't hearing a word of my constructive sympathy. "Gil has taken an apartment in downtown Cleveland. I've driven past the place several times. The brick building itself certainly isn't anything to look at. There's a dentist's office on the ground floor. Or maybe it's a periodontist. Anyway, I keep trying to get him to invite me over, because, you know, I could help him decorate and arrange things. But he insists that it's not a good idea right now."

"And does he say *why* it's not a good idea?"

"Well, actually, he won't take my calls anymore. So I'm presuming he wants to settle in first."

Great. Bernard is openly admitting to stalking his ex. Next he's probably going to confess that he's tapped Gil's phone.

"So I want you to call him and see if he'll let *you* visit." Bernard hands me the cordless phone. "I've blocked our number so it won't show up on his caller ID. And afterward you can report back to me with the necessary information."

"What do you mean, *information?*"

"You know—what he's doing, his appearance, how the rooms are arranged."

"Why don't you just hire a detective?" I ask in a tone that's meant to be sarcastic. Although when Bernard seems to be actually considering the idea, I'm obliged to say, "I was only kidding."

But in his sorrow Bernard has lost the ability to laugh easily. Instead, he continues to divulge his strategy. "You and only *you* can get inside to see if he's unpacked everything and plans on staying . . . if he's installed a pole lamp and hung pictures, or if it's all just rather makeshift and temporary-looking."

"I'm not going to *spy* on Gil." I would do practically anything for Bernard, but here I have to draw the line. "It's wrong!"

"So I'll go to confession and say five Our Miss Brooks and two Hello Dollys!"

Bernard lets out a walrus-sized sigh, as if I'm single-handedly destroying all of his carefully thought-out plans. "I'm not asking you to *spy* on him. Simply go visit him and then come back here and tell me about it," he implores.

"Of course I'll go and see him at some point."

"Fine, then." Bernard takes the phone out of my hands and starts pressing the buttons.

He's memorized Gil's new number?

"Ask if you can go over there tonight," he instructs, and hands back the phone.

I click the off button and disconnect the call. "But I just drove all the way from Cleveland after being up all night. I haven't unpacked yet. Or stopped at my house. Or looked in the shed. I'm exhausted from exams and final projects." And from relationships, I would add, if Bernard could go off-mission for a second and listen to me. Not a chance.

"Hallie, this is *urgent*! I'm in *desperate circumstances*." Sounding all too much like Blanche DuBois in *A Streetcar Named Desire,* he retrieves the phone and clutches it to his heart.

"Can't it at least wait until tomorrow?" I plead.

"Who kept you out of reform school last year?" insists Bernard. "*Who* became your legal guardian and arranged it so Mother could tutor you here at the house, thus enabling you to graduate from high school?"

"Point taken," I shoot back. "You've graduated from mentor to *tormentor* in the short space of a year."

Bernard's arms are now flailing above his head like Tippi Hedren in the movie *The Birds*.

"Have I ever asked *anything* of you, other than to read those articles I send you on how to care for your combination skin?" Once again he punches in the number and shoves the handset up to my ear.

I walk outside the summerhouse to talk in private. He follows me. Real close.

"How am I supposed to get Gil back if I don't know whether or not he's seeing anyone?" complains Bernard.

So *that's* what this is about. I'm not supposed to hunt for pole lamps and a captain's wheel coffee table, but for evidence of another *person.* Gil picks up, and following some friendly chitchat, I arrange to go and visit him after dinner. At least this way I can grab a few hours of shut-eye this afternoon.

As soon as I hang up, Bernard hysterically begins making plans. "We'll eat early and then leave at half past six. I'll make a casserole for you to give him since I can't imagine he's been eating properly. Then I'll wait at the diner around the corner while you go in and visit."

"I'm not taking you with me! What if he *sees* you?" By now I'm picturing the mug shot.

"I'll wear a disguise." Bernard says this as if it solves absolutely everything.

Looking directly at the largest vase in the room, I ask, "Are any of these in my price range in case I accidentally drop one on your head?"

"He won't even know I'm there," insists Bernard.

"Do you want the short answer or the long answer?" I ask.

"Short," he says. There's a crazed note of hope in his voice.

"No!" I bang my hand on the bed since just about everything else in the vicinity is an antique and there's no point breaking a thousand-dollar lamp just for emphasis.

"Wait! What's the long answer?"

"No F-ing way!" I say, and give the bed one more hard hit. "Furthermore, I'm not taking sides. Or going on some fact-finding mission. This is getting really weird. It feels as if my parents got divorced while I was in college. It happened to, like, half the freshmen—out of the blue they got calls in early October saying their folks were splitsville, that they'd been waiting the past few years, until the kids left home."

"That's exactly why we must get Gil back! So you're not permanently damaged by living in a broken home."

"Stop saying *we!*"

Bernard studies the dark circles under my eyes and the uncombed hair. "I think you're just tired," he says, as if this explains why I'm not agreeing with him.

"I'm exhausted!" I hurl myself prostrate on the new daybed. "This is a really nice bed, by the way."

"I thought sateen sheets would be a bit much, so I got Egyptian cotton with a very high thread count, a silk blend comforter, and goose down pillows."

"Mmmm," I kick off my sneakers and let my head sink into the luxurious pillow.

"Okay, get some rest while I run down to the shop. It's been incredibly busy ever since this chain of diners and soda bars started buying from me. I send them pictures of 1940s and '50s kitsch and they send money." Bernard bounds out the door, apparently cheered that I'm willing to take on his case, at least within reason.

It feels so good to lie there and listen to the fresh green leaves rustle and the sparrows chirp. The buds on the purple lilac bushes outside my window still look tentative, as if waiting for just one more sign that spring has come to stay for good. My thoughts drift as I head toward sleep. *Working in the yard I can make fifteen an hour and if I work fifty hours a week for ten weeks that's $7,500 . . . not nearly enough . . . have to win that contest and get the one-year scholarship and then use the $7,500 for living expenses . . . can't eat another Ramen noodle as long as I live . . . what about the transformation in Brandt . . . hard not to wonder if he didn't participate in some sort of scientific experiment that made him go from gawky boy to normal guy . . . he's still kind of skinny . . . but it's nothing that a few milkshakes couldn't cure . . . oh dear, I must really be overtired and becoming delusional . . . though I wonder if he still carries that Klingon key chain . . . because maybe if that's definitely gone . . .*

When I hear a female voice calling my name I leap up and look around for a clock, terrified that I'm sleeping through an exam. It's not one of my roommates, however.

Chapter
Eight

THE SUMMERHOUSE DOOR OPENS AND THE SHADOW OF MY mother appears, backlit by bright sunshine with thousands of tiny dust particles swirling through it. I must have dozed off for exactly ten minutes.

"Mom!"

"Oh Hallie, I'm so *glad* that you're back. Mrs. Muldoon said she saw you driving down Main Street with boxes tied to the roof rack."

It's a relief to know that the Cosgrove County grapevine hasn't been experiencing any technical difficulties while I've been away.

My mother's cheeks are flushed pink, her voice is quivery, and her eyes brim with tears, just like when she's pregnant.

"Oh my gosh!" I put my arms around her. "You're pregnant again!"

She bursts into tears and I lead her over to the daybed. To myself I'm thinking, *This will make nine kids! We've just gone from being a sports team to having our own militia.*

But to her I say, "It makes perfect sense that you'd be concerned about bringing another life into this world. How far along are you?"

She dabs at her eyes with a tissue that she's miraculously produced out of the sleeve of her summer sweater, the way mothers of small children are programmed to do in order to catch snot and spit-up before it makes contact with clothing and furniture.

"About two months," she says, and places a loving hand on her abdomen, where the infant in question is not yet visible, but allegedly in residence, rent-free. "I'm absolutely thrilled. You kids are all growing up so fast." She scrolls her eyes up and down my five-foot-eight frame and then touches my almost pimple-free face as if that's all the proof anyone needs.

Unbelievable—a woman who still has six kids living at home is experiencing empty-nest syndrome? But I quickly change course to make sure she doesn't think that I was suggesting she might not want the baby. "That's terrific. Congratulations! I just meant . . . all I meant was . . . you don't look very happy."

"It's Louise!" she blurts out. "Oh, Hallie. She came home late one night last week and I *know* she was intoxicated. I didn't dare tell your father."

"Mom, even Eric came home drunk a few times while he was in high school. It's not the end of the world."

"It's *more* than just that, Hallie. Louise made the varsity cheerleading squad and when sophomore year started they traveled all the time for games. She came home late on school nights and was gone most weekends and I didn't notice anything wrong at first. But then her grades dropped and she started running around with a bad crowd, going off to parties at the University of Akron every Saturday night." Mom starts to sniffle again.

"Mom, most fifteen-year-olds go through that whole rebellious thing."

"But Hallie, she hardly says a word to any of us. And when I ask about her friends or where she's going and what she's doing she gets *so* angry, as if it's none of my business."

"Okay, but I'm not exactly sure what *I'm* supposed to do about it."

"You can *talk* to her. Eric tried during spring vacation but she wouldn't listen to him."

"I don't know anything about cheerleading or traveling on buses to football games."

"No, but you went *through a phase* and now you're fine." She looks up to the shelf with the Greek vases featuring naked people in strange positions, and obviously these make her think twice. "I mean, you managed to graduate and you're in college now. You never got into drugs or alcohol. And those girlfriends, Gwen and Jane, they were always polite when they called or came over to the house. But Louise's friends honk their horns in the driveway until she comes out or else they phone and don't even say *hello,* or *please* when they ask to speak with her. And the *outfits* they wear, if you can even call them that! I mean, where *are* their mothers? Can't the families afford full-length mirrors?"

It appears that Mom is going to start sobbing again just at the thought of young ladies not saying please and hello. Let's not even consider wearing inappropriate clothing.

"Okay, okay. I'll talk to her," I give in.

"Oh, thank you!" Mom gives me her brightest smile, the one normally reserved for toilet training. "Your father grounded Louise for staying out until five o'clock in the morning this past Saturday and so she's home right now."

I think back to when I was grounded, more or less for life, and ended up running away. Dad really needs to add some new stuff to his punishment repertoire. Although in order to take away our allowance I guess he'd first have to start *giving* us one. Dad has this old-fashioned notion that working around the house is your contribution to the family and we should all just be thankful we're not doing chores on a farm like when he was a boy.

"Louise, of all people, is probably going to have to attend summer school," moans my mother, as if this is like hanging a big scarlet letter *S* on the front door. "Why, in middle school she practically had straight A's." Mom may have a lot of kids, but she can always give you a grade-point average.

"So do you want to ride home with me or take your car?" she asks.

"Oh gosh, Mom. I've been up for, like, two days." I rub my eyes with weariness. "Forget about driving, I don't think I can even stand. How about tomorrow?"

"But Hallie, she won't even *speak* to us. What if something terrible happens?"

I assume that "something terrible" is a reference to running away. Or perhaps tackling the rubbing alcohol in the bathroom medicine chest.

The tears begin to flow again and there's no chance of winning an argument with a pregnant woman. "I'll take my own car," I say, and drag myself off the nice comfortable daybed while realizing she didn't once ask me how *I* am. Come to think of it, nobody has. The downside of not being constantly followed around by the police seems to be that people assume you no longer have any problems of your own, and are therefore ready and willing to tackle all of theirs.

Chapter
Nine

My old house hasn't changed except for the eight or ten square feet that it appears to shrink every year as all the kids inside grow bigger and bigger. There's a Playskool lawn mower in the middle of the living room where someone has obviously been giving the stained carpet a good cutting. Though what it appears to need more is vacuuming, especially where the Oreo cookies have been crushed into it. My mom is actually a conscientious housekeeper, but how can one human being keep up with a baby, a toddler, three kids between eight and twelve, and one angry teenager? I move a sippy cup that sits precariously on the edge of an end table while the unmistakable yelling of the twins suddenly rises from the play area in the basement and fills the air like a factory whistle.

Louise is upstairs in our old bedroom, which she now shares with eight-year-old Darlene. The last time I was sentenced to spend a night in here I ended up climbing out the window once and for all. Plastered across the walls are posters of scantily clad teen rock stars, male and female, and beer ads. Dad, who won't even let his daughters wear belly shirts, must *love* this.

"Hey, Hallie." Louise comes over and we give each other a sisterly hug. Darlene is still downstairs fighting with her twin brother, Davy, and so I fall onto my old bed, which is now covered with a Barbie comforter weighted down by ten tons of stuffed animals.

I nod toward a poster of a well-oiled hunk leaning against a surfboard. "You've redecorated."

"You are *so* lucky to be *out of here!*" She throws an evil look in the direction of Mom and Dad's room that I assume is meant for them.

So much for hello and how are you, the point in the conversation where I get to respond that I'm basically living my dream—going into monumental debt and unable to keep a boyfriend for more than two weeks. Make that two days, more often than not.

"Why's that?" I try to sound casual. "Are you the next one to slide down the drainpipe?" That's how I made my getaway. But then, I wasn't wearing the shoes Louise has on—black designer sandals with skinny three-inch heels.

"I wish!" says Louise, and gives a combination sigh and eye roll that only fifteen-year-olds have the lung capacity and muscle elasticity to perform. "You always had money, or were able to make some easily enough."

Yeah, I think, *the good old bad old days back when I was flush.*

It feels as if I haven't seen Louise for five years rather than only five months. She's transformed from an angular girl to a young woman with soft curves and a strikingly beautiful face, deep-set hazel eyes, and perfect bone structure. Her golden chestnut-colored hair falls into soft curls around her face. Only, what happened to the cute cheerleader with the pigtails and pink lip gloss? Now she's wearing Visigoth makeup—thick black eyeliner, maroon mascara, and reddish-brown lipstick. With her scoop-neck black jersey, push-up bra, and the silky strap of a thong peeking above skintight low-rise jeans, she looks closer to twenty. A stunning and slutty twenty. About one trip to the mall away from "Excuse me while I powder my nose ring."

Louise has always been the great beauty in the family, ever since she was a baby. When we were little Mom was twice approached to have Louise model children's clothing for catalogues and be in TV commercials. People tried not to come right out and say how extraordinarily pretty she was when I was around, or if they accidentally did, they'd immediately try to follow up with some compliment for me, too, such as, "And you have such nice . . . you're so good in math." Math gene, beauty queen. Not a hard choice. Except you don't get a choice.

No, there's nothing in fashion magazines about apricot, which is what I am, from tip to toe. My hair is sometimes described as "strawberry blond," but you can tell it's more of a question than an expression of admiration. Beauty is about the dramatic splendor of nature—having yellow sun-drenched locks or a cascade of hair as dark as night, rose red lips, and blue eyes the color of forget-me-nots or deep green like the ocean. It is *not* about nature's fruit. Not strawberries, and especially not apricots. Or freckles the color of Granny Smith apples.

"Hey!" Louise's eyes widen so much that I can actually detect patches of white through all the eyeliner and mascara. "Maybe you can teach *me* how to play poker. All I get is a few bucks for baby-sitting and Dad even begrudges me that. He says that I should do it for free because they're my own brothers and sisters. As if!"

"Actually, I have a few things you can add to your list of grievances. Mom doesn't like your friends, she's worried about your grades, says you have to attend summer school, and that you came home drunk."

"That's *such* bullshit!"

"And she's sent me on a mission to turn you back into the sweet little girl she gave birth to," I add.

Louise flashes me a hostile look that basically demands to know, *Whose side are you on?* "It's all because that attendance asshole Dick

Collier called Mom and Dad after he caught me hanging out with some friends in the parking lot during gym class."

"I have to agree with you that this is one case where Dick isn't just a nickname," I admit wholeheartedly. "But it doesn't sound as if that's *everything*."

"My friends just happen to be cool, that's all. They're older and they have cars. And that way we can get out of this hick town."

Yes, it's obvious Louise isn't going to be bicycling anywhere in *that* outfit.

"Well, Louise, I think Mom has a point about college guys. It's a slightly different scene."

"Oh, fuck you! Just because you graduated early and go to *college* you think you're some big shot and want to give me all kinds of older sister crap. *Puh-leeze,* Hallie, I remember when you were the local juvenile delinquent being accused of robbery, truancy, underage gambling, and God knows what else! Not to mention those lunatics you live with, including the high school geek."

I deduce from her remark that despite Brandt's starting to look and sound normal, a perceived behavioral and social gap still remains between him and most of the adolescent world.

From the way Louise turns away from me in a huff it's obvious that she'd like to storm out of the room in order to finish making her point. But since she's grounded and not allowed to leave the house, exiting will only lead her directly into the grubby hands of the little kids and possible assignments of table setting or laundry folding. So she turns to her computer and pretends that I don't exist.

That talk went really well, I think. *Maybe I should be studying international diplomacy rather than graphic arts.* I flop down on my old bed, pull Darlene's stuffed Tigger to my chest, and fall into a deep sleep. In my dream Tigger becomes the perfect boyfriend—devoted, considerate, and incapable of sending mixed messages, giving ultimatums, or playing mind games.

Chapter
Ten

When I awake Darlene is poking me in the stomach with a baton and the red and white plastic streamers flying off the ends scrape across my face. She hits a portable CD player and a loud march fills the room. I'm treated to her entire twirling routine, which concludes with a toss that puts a dent in the ceiling and almost takes out the overhead fixture.

I clap my hands in appreciation. Louise is now cleaning out her drawers, acting as if both Darlene and I have ceased to inhabit the land of the living.

Darlene grabs my hand and lisps, "Hallie, come thee the doll houthe that me and Franthie built." I assume she means Dad built it and they play with it.

Some dark grammar force buried deep within my DNA leaps to the surface and corrects her. "It's Francie and I."

Louise gives me a disgusted look as if I have indeed turned into *one of them.* I shrug and go back downstairs, convinced that I've officially passed the torch to the new black sheep of the family, or at least to the sheep with the most black clothes and makeup.

Back on the first floor I observe that Mom has re-covered the couches in something that's not so much fabric as the indestructible material you find on seats in commuter trains. And the new floor covering has the distinct coarseness of indoor/outdoor carpeting, or better yet, Astroturf.

Mom is busy preparing dinner and appears relieved that I was upstairs so long. "How did everything go?" she asks, wiping her wet hands on her apron. Mom possesses the eternal hopefulness of a full-time wife and mother and perennially pregnant woman.

"Not that great. Let me think about it." Frankly, I'm stymied. Perhaps Officer Rich has a line on some sort of scared-straight program through the county jail system. At the end of the day he's a good guy and doesn't always assume the worst about teenagers, like so many grown-ups around here do. When I ran away he even offered to let me sleep in the jailhouse so I wouldn't freeze to death.

I hold baby Lillian while Mom sets the table and experience this weird moment where I feel as if I'm looking into my own eyes. Mom's maternal radar system picks up on this and she says, "She looks exactly like you did at that age. Look at that mop of strawberry-blond hair!"

"You mean apricot," I say. "Just think of the third-degree sunburns and lime green freckles she has to look forward to."

"Oh, Hallie! Why do you always act as if your coloring is some sort of handicap, when it's so much more *interesting* than blond hair with blue eyes or dark hair with dark eyes."

"Interesting, huh," I say doubtfully. "Maybe Lillian and I can start a support group for the differently hued."

Five-year-old Francie has come up from the basement and clings to my jeans, beaming up a big gap-toothed grin and trying to show me everything she's ever drawn.

To Francie I'm more like a fun aunt who occasionally comes to visit and performs card tricks. She doesn't remember back to when I lived at home—all the fighting and the doors slamming. And even

I have to admit that I didn't exactly find the little kids very amusing back then. However, now that I'm a visitor who can escape at any time, and no longer an inmate, I think they're pretty cute.

"Isn't she a little young to be losing her teeth?" I ask Mom, though I'm no expert on child development.

Mom shakes her head. "She knocked the front two out while trying to ride Darlene's bike last week. The dentist said the only thing to do is wait for her adult teeth to come in and that we're lucky it wasn't those."

Dad walks in, still as square and sturdy-looking as ever, just like whatever house or car he inhabits. But it also appears as if he could use some sleep. I'd say about a year's worth. First he kisses Mom on the lips. Then there's that awkward moment where neither of us are sure if we should hug and kiss. Dad isn't emotionally withdrawn. In fact, he's very affectionate until you're ten—lots of piggyback rides, kisses, and tickling. However, after his daughters are in training bras Dad doesn't want to be perceived as being involved in anything unChristian. So now it's a quick self-conscious hug and a drive-by kiss. With the boys he transitions to handshakes when they start school so it doesn't appear as if his sons have been raised to be soft or unmanly.

"You look terrific!" Dad announces with a proud smile. This translates to: You're wearing little or no makeup and you're not drunk or pregnant. Also, Dad prefers long hair on girls. Only I don't keep mine long to make him happy but rather so that I can braid my unwieldy mane or pull it back into a ponytail. Ever since reading *The Elephant Man* in ninth grade I've been convinced that an escaped zoo lion frightened my mother while she was pregnant with me.

"Congratulations on the new baby," I say.

"Well, why wouldn't I want lots more children just like my Eric and Hallie?"

What a difference going to college instead of a casino makes. I'd transitioned from reprobate relation to the family hall of fame, right up there with my knightly older brother, Eric, Sir Football Head, who can do no wrong.

"We're driving down to Indiana next weekend to watch Eric play in the end-of-year game that raises money for local charities. Why don't you come along? He'd love to see you."

No way! A half-hour visit with the family is one thing. A ten-hour car trip is another altogether. If there were a scholarship offered for playing license-plate bingo, believe me, I would have applied for it. And having people at rest areas stare at your ten-member family exiting a station wagon like circus clowns pouring out of a Volkswagen gets old pretty fast.

"As much as I'd love to, I'm pretty sure that I have to work." Dad never minds if you skip something for a job, unless of course what you're ditching is church or schoolwork. "In fact, that reminds me, I'd better get going. The Stockton's yard is a total mess. And they gave me a nice raise."

Dad beams. His favorite words are: *scholarship, raise, perfect attendance,* and *it's not broken.*

I say good-bye to everyone, promising the little kids that I'll come back to visit soon and play Old Maid with them.

Out in the front yard Teddy and Davy are tossing a Nerf football, though Davy is too small to catch it and has to chase the ball down after every throw. "It's never too early to think about sports scholarships. If not football there's always swimming. Or cross-country," I encourage them. Teddy is still skinny as a fishing pole. He throws the ball at my head but I catch it and then run over and tickle him until he collapses onto the ground. Davy piles in, shrieking with delight.

It'd be fun to hang out with them, but I know Bernard will be biting his cuticles off if I'm not home in plenty of time for tonight's mission. Backing out of the driveway I notice that Teddy is wearing one of Eric's old football jerseys and recall how I always made fun of my older brother's devotion to being a jock. And now the joke is certainly on me. Not only does Eric get free tuition and board, but his football scholarship even gives him an allowance for books.

Mom and Dad give me $2,000 a semester, and that's a lot for them. But tuition is $24,000 a year, not including books and art supplies. It's another $5,000 for housing. Second semester I'd moved to an off-campus share because it was half the cost of dorm living. It also put the "off" in "off-campus." With so little parking near the main buildings it's basically a one-mile hike to class or the art rooms. And without the meal plan, we tended to subsist on pizza, Ramen noodles, care packages from Suzy's mom, who owns a restaurant, and Bernard's weekend brunches.

Obviously I can't ask my folks for more money. They have another six kids to educate—whoops, make that seven soon—and tuition is only going up, up, and up. In fact, if you can't be really rich, then you're better off being *really* poor. Because if you're in the middle, like my family, then you get screwed—no breaks and hardly any financial aid. The aid office conveniently counts our home as a "liquid asset," fully expecting Mom and Dad to sell our house that's worth about seventy thousand dollars, turn that over to the college in order to cover partial tuition for one child, and then move to a public park with their six younger kids. What they give instead are big fat student loans that cause you to graduate a hundred thousand dollars in debt. Meantime, entry-level jobs for graphic designers are hard to find, especially without a résumé full of internships. But if you're working during vacation, then you don't exactly have time for internships.

Now I understand why Dad gets so cranky when the bills pour in—car payments, mortgage payments, insurance premiums. And that doesn't start to take into account food, clothing, sippy cups, and school supplies.

Maybe it's time to reconsider my bookie pal Cappy's proposal regarding the rebate shop, even if I just set it up and then when school starts again in the fall he finds someone else to take over. Living clean hasn't done a thing for my solvency. What was going through my head when I passed on his offer to make a hundred grand a year, honestly? Or dishonestly, such as the case may be. And whatever was I thinking when I kept avoiding losing my virginity throughout the school year? Did my parents' and Sunday school teachers' hammering away about sin during my formative years suddenly take hold? Because if so, there's still time to consider Pastor Costello's invitation to be a counselor at Bible camp this summer. Sure, the pay isn't so good, but there's lots of Bible bingo for those bitten by the gambling bug, and plenty of nice Christian boys who won't lay a hand on a girl, even if it's just to slap a mosquito.

It's official. I'm losing my mind. It's definitely time to talk to Cappy.

Chapter
Eleven

DRIVING DOWN MAIN STREET YOU DON'T CROSS A RAILROAD track to reach the run-down section of town, but go over a bridge built above a trickle of a creek. A few blocks along on the left is where Cappy maintains his "downtown office." It's actually a small room at the back of Bob's Billiard Parlor. Cappy's "suburban satellite" is next to the starting gate at the racetrack a few miles out of town, which is where I'd first met him.

Learning poker from the janitor in elementary school had quickly led to studying the odds for other games, like blackjack, and then when I saw a horse race on TV and the winner was a long shot paying fifty bucks on a two-dollar bet, I started riding my bike to the track at age twelve. Of course, it was illegal for me to place a bet, and so I had to find a guy who didn't look like he'd mind helping a kid get ahead in the world, and that patron of the underaged happened to be Cappy, a regular fixture during the racing season. By the time I was fifteen and could see over the counter, the people working at the betting windows no longer bothered turning me away, and Cappy decided that I'd learned enough about the business to act as his assistant in exchange for some tips on how to play the odds rather than the horses.

It's not hard for me to find a parking spot in front of Bob's Billiards during the daytime. This particular dilapidated block is primarily home to a long wooden storefront that used to sell farm implements in the first half of the 1900s. The old building is falling apart but somehow the owner rents space to a start-up software company and a guy with a recording studio. Bob's is across the street, next to Nolan's Irish Pub, which isn't the kind of place young people gather to socialize on weekends so much as where a married woman might search for her husband if she hasn't seen him for a few days. When my mom refers to the "iffy" part of town, this is exactly where she's talking about.

From the street, Bob's Billiards looks as if it went out of business about ten years ago, when Old Bob died, and shortly afterward Middle Bob became Robert and moved to Los Angeles to design costumes for TV shows. Only, Young Bob, who is just a few years older than I am, keeps the place going without new investment, aside from refelting the pool tables and changing the lightbulbs. Though changing the lightbulbs is rather important, being that Bob's is open to the public but closed to the sunlight. Otherwise the players don't seem to care how chipped the paint is or how many tiles the ceiling is missing, and so Bob the Younger is able to scratch out a living by renting tables to individuals, pool leagues, and tournament organizers.

And then there's the trickle of rent from Cappy, whose office is in the rear, one door past the men's restroom. Though there's nothing inside there that the police would be interested in—just a bunch of yellowed sports pages and stacks of old horse-racing news. According to Cappy his bookmaking business isn't illegal so much as extralegal, in that the cops would have to work *extra* hard making any sort of charges stick to him. Then there's the fact that another guy would pop up in his place overnight, and not a local who everyone knows and trusts, at least as far as it goes.

Cappy offers the popular service of allowing people to bet on horse races and sporting events by making a phone call. He accepts customers who may not have credit elsewhere and offers complete confidentiality to those citizens who may desire to keep their wagering quiet (or as Cappy prefers to say, "be able to surprise their families when they win"). He can also steer a person to a clean poker game in most any city in the US or Canada. And I have reason to believe there are a few other dilemmas that Cappy can solve for a client willing to pay his service fee, though I'd rather not know about them. In fact, Cappy doesn't even like to be referred to as a bookie. He describes himself as a "problem solver," which in his eyes is more akin to being a management consultant or a social worker. And from the way Cappy set his son up with a car dealership and put his daughter through medical school, it would appear that he's solved a lot of problems in his day.

Knocking gently on the closed door I call out, "Cappy, are you in there?"

"Come in," says a youthful voice from inside.

Using my shoulder I force open the warped wooden door, which always sticks when the humidity is bad. Cappy's place is cramped, poorly lit, and reeks from a toxic mixture of day-old cigar smoke and month-old tacos. The décor consists of dark green walls plastered with newspaper clippings featuring some of the greatest upsets in betting history, particularly those that had also served to help the proprietor separate a large number of wagerers from their wallets.

I'm surprised to see his grandson Auggie sitting at the rusty metal desk. I'm surprised for two reasons. This first is that Cappy has always vowed that *no one* in his family will ever go into The Business, which I of course take to mean the problem-solving business. And the second is that the last time I saw Auggie was about three years ago, when he was visiting from Dayton and tagging along behind Cappy at the racetrack like a worshipful puppy dog.

Only back then he was sporting a Catholic schoolboy uniform with an ugly blue plaid tie, silver braces with green and black rubber bands on his teeth, and wire-frame glasses, all topped off with a crew cut. And although Auggie was a grade ahead of me in school at the time, he looked about twelve instead of fifteen.

When Auggie stands to greet me it becomes apparent that he hasn't grown much taller, since we're about the same height now, but otherwise he's filled out in all the right places. And the crew cut has turned into gorgeous dark brown shoulder-length hair that hangs loose about his face. Auggie's soft brown eyes are set deep in strong arches and he looks up at me quizzically from underneath thick lashes, as if trying to determine how we might be acquainted with each other. Around his neck is a leather-and-bead necklace that I like, but most guys around here would be afraid to wear something so blatantly unisex. In his Creed T-shirt from the *My Own Prison* concert tour, tan cargo pants, and black leather sandals, I find the overall effect to be that Auggie is not only cute but also cool.

"Hi," I say. "I'm Hallie Palmer. We met once at the racetrack a few years ago."

"Oh my gosh!" Auggie reaches across a metal filing cabinet to shake my hand. "You're the famous Calculator Kid—my grandpa talks about you all the time and how you can do probabilities in your head on the spot!"

Wow. A person forgets how nice a little flattery feels after living as a constantly broke B-student for a year. "It's not that I really do them all in my head," I modestly explain. "In most games there are a certain number of combinations that regularly come up and after a while you simply start to remember them all."

He flashes me a metal-free smile and I decide that Cappy indeed got his money's worth on the braces. "I wish that I could do all that stuff in my head. I can't even do it with the help of an adding machine." He nods unhappily toward *The Daily Racing Form* spread out on the desktop, which is all marked up with a pencil and the red rubber flecks of countless erasures. "I'm supposed to figure out the payoffs on a hundred-dollar bet for all of these horses."

Moving closer to the track newspaper, not unlike a moth being drawn toward an old flame, I look to see if there's anything tricky about the project. Maybe Cappy has asked him to do hypothetical odds based on practice runs. But no, it appears to be a straightforward case of dividing the numerator by the denominator and then multiplying by a hundred. Picking up the pencil I quickly perform one calculation for him.

"Way cool, thanks," Auggie says and studies my notation. "The ones with plain numbers, like odds of two-to-one made sense, but I couldn't figure out what to do with six-fifths and the one and one-eighths. Sounds like an amount of scotch or something, huh?" He laughs good-heartedly at his own misunderstanding.

Meantime, I'm thinking that a person unable to do basic math cannot possibly be any grandson of Cappy's. He must be adopted. This is further evidenced by the stack of books on the desk that are *definitely* not Cappy's—F. Scott Fitzgerald, Eudora Welty, Truman Capote, and Carson McCullers. But no, there's too big a family resemblance, especially around the forehead, and I notice that he's also left-handed like Cappy.

"You like to read?" I ask.

"Oh yeah," he says. "And write, too. There's not a lot to do until the local track opens next week so I've been catching up on my American authors."

"What do you write?"

"Short stories, mostly about death. And I'm outlining this novel about a young guy who goes to work for a relative, like an uncle or something, who's involved in gambling. I guess it sounds autobiographical but it really wouldn't be."

"No, of course not," I say.

Auggie points down to a horse on the list named Prairie Gary and says with all the innocence of a happy novice set to lose his entire purse, "Look, Hallie, if that horse had won with those odds of twenty-to-one, you would have made two thousand dollars on a hundred-dollar bet!"

"Huh?" I don't know what it is but I keep losing my train of thought. The necklace crosses his Adam's apple and a large red bead bounces up and down when he talks. Perhaps I'm being hypnotized.

"If Prairie Gary won, he'd have paid out two grand!" exclaims Auggie.

I quickly scan the page to see what kind of race it was and the other horses running. "But there really wasn't any way he could win, because Prairie Gary is a turf horse and it was a dirt track. Ever hear the expression *horses for courses?* Well, that's where it comes from."

"Wow." He looks at me with the kind of admiration that parents and teachers and pastors, especially pastors, rarely employ when they discover that you have more than a passing familiarity with gambling. "You really do know your stuff!"

Yeah, but is this what I want—to sit in some airless cave in the back of a grungy pool hall, multiplying and dividing all day long, waiting for the results to come in and figuring payouts? Then there are the occasional out-of-towners asking where they can find poker games and call girls, and not always in that order.

"So I guess you came here to see Cappy," says Auggie.

"If he's around," I reply. "But it's nothing urgent." Cappy had apparently just hired Auggie and so it's doubtful that he needs *two* assistants.

"He took a ride up to Great Lakes Downs in Michigan to talk with some of the trainers and jockeys. You know Cappy, he doesn't trust anyone until he looks them in the eye, including the horses." Auggie gives me a knowing wink and from the way he grins it's obvious that he idolizes his streetwise and well-connected grandfather. "Is there something I can help you with?"

"Oh no, I—I just stopped by to say hello." I start to back out of the room, because it's getting awfully hot in here, or else I'm having my own personal summer. The place never felt quite this cramped or crowded before. "Did Cappy change the office around?"

Auggie nods toward the gray metal filing cabinets precariously stacked on top of each other against the far wall. "I cleaned out the storeroom last month so Grandpa can sell seats to a Friday night poker game."

"Cappy's running a game right *here?* On Friday nights?"

"Yeah, that's one of the reasons he hired me to help out. A bunch of rich guys want to play this new kind of poker from Tennessee or somewhere."

"Texas Hold 'Em?" I don't bother trying to hide my excitement. It's a game where knowing the odds and how to play them can make or break a person.

"Yeah, that's it," says Auggie. "I even bought some really cool black-and-white-checked cards. But Grandpa said we couldn't use them." His frown indicates bruised feelings as he points to a deck that looks like a stack of miniature M. C. Escher paintings.

"You really want to use red diamondbacks in a clean game or everyone will think it's a marked deck," I say.

"That's *exactly* what Grandpa said!" Auggie appears briefly mystified.

"Did Cappy say anything else about the game?" I ask.

Auggie thinks for a moment, apparently sorting through all the new terminology he's been hearing. "Oh yeah, that it's nickel-and-dime poker."

"Wow!" I say. "He must be attracting some out-of-towners."

"Who doesn't have fifteen cents to bet?" asks Auggie.

"*Nickel* means five hundred and *dime* means a thousand," I explain in a nice way.

"Oh right—*high-rollers.*" Auggie demonstrates that he is indeed working on his lingo. "Anyway, if you want to place a bet or something, Cappy's going to phone in soon and—"

"Thanks, but actually no." I unconsciously wince at the idea of going to a bookmaker to place a bet. I mean, hitting the racetrack or playing in a friendly game of poker is one thing, but being one of those people constantly on their cell phones laying action and then more often than not trying to hide losses from their families isn't exactly the life I've envisioned for myself. Because if you're on the betting end, and not the booking end, eventually the percentages are going to get the best of you. Or as Cappy likes to say in private, "You may as well waste your time voting."

"Over the winter Cappy called me about setting up a shop to offer rebates on bets," I explain. "But I'll catch up with him when he gets back."

"Okay," says Auggie. "He's coming home tomorrow night. But maybe you want to leave me some digits in the meantime."

Digits? As in a finger or two? Certainly Cappy hasn't gone into *that* end of the business? And besides, *I* certainly don't owe him any money.

Auggie quickly notices my confusion. "You know, a phone number."

"Oh right, *digits*!" I can't tell if I've been away from the pool hall too long, or more likely, that Auggie doesn't sound very convincing slinging his grandfather's slang.

"Cappy's got my *digits*," I say. "Tell him that I'm back staying with the Addams Family." At least that's how Cappy refers to the crazy assemblage at the Stockton place.

Auggie moves a step closer and says, "Uh, well maybe I could have 'em, too." He flashes that stellar and completely paid-for grin and his brown eyes sparkle. "I'd love to take you to dinner some night."

"Oh! Sure then, okay." I write the Stocktons' number down on his scratch pad and head back out through the poolroom a little lighter on my feet. A man in a cowboy hat practices alone at a table near the door and it's pleasant to hear the solid crack of a good break followed by the low thunk of balls dropping into pockets.

And why not go out with Auggie? Ray and I never said anything about not seeing other people. In fact, I'm pretty sure that Ray *does* date other women. He always made it clear that some Saturday nights he had "business" to attend to and wasn't interested in being asked to elaborate on what exactly that might entail. And since I hadn't yet decided to sleep with him I didn't exactly feel that I had a right to request monogamy.

Besides, Auggie is cute. And he can't be stupid if he's reading those books. Not everyone is good at math. Yet he doesn't seem like the kind of guy who would be threatened by a woman figuring out the gratuity in a restaurant. Macho Ray can never work out the correct tip without a calculator and so he just leaves way too much, in cash. Of course, this also serves to make him look like a big shot, which I think he rather enjoys.

Chapter
Twelve

I take off for Cleveland to visit Gil just as dusk is falling. The mellow sunlight casts a honeyed glow over the houses in the neighborhood and the breeze sinks to stillness. A few days of hot weather has hurried the tulips, violets, marigolds, and cherry blossoms into bloom, and under the pink tissue-paper sky it appears as if rainbows quiver on the front lawns.

Gil throws open the door like he's been waiting for my knock. "It's great to see you!" He puts his arms around me before I'm even inside the door. Though he's careful not to clunk me with what appears to be a fresh white plaster cast on his right wrist.

"It's terrific to see you too," I say, and hug him back.

"Come on in!" He waves toward the tiny entry hall. "Of course, I haven't finished settling in yet."

Aside from the busted-up wrist Gil looks pretty much the same.

Though in his mid-thirties, of medium height and weight, and now slightly disabled, he still moves with the ease and grace of an athlete. Otherwise the only difference seems to be that his hairline has receded perhaps just a bit farther back than I remember it, as if it's currently at low tide.

We move into the cramped hallway and I'm careful to wipe my feet on the mat. The new apartment is shaped like a railroad car, with a long corridor down the middle and four small square rooms going off to the sides. There are still boxes lining the walls and I can only hope the nubby yellow couch and director's chairs of blond wood and maroon canvas came with the rental.

Gil stares at me for a moment and says, "You look so . . . so grown up!" However, he seems slightly preoccupied and doesn't bother to ask how I'm doing, same as everyone else these days. A year and a half ago all people did was chase after me asking, "What's wrong?" A few even managed to make it into a full-time job. And to think I actually resented them for it. Now *nobody* asks. Not Mom, Dad, Louise, not even Bernard. It makes me suddenly realize that even though I'm only three months shy of eighteen, they must all figure that I've *had* my crisis. One per customer.

So this is what it's like to be an adult—if you look okay and don't have a bag of stolen money in your hand then people automatically assume everything is hunky-dory. Of course, there's plenty to ask Gil, since he's the one who has moved into a new place and also the one whose arm is in a cast. I find myself hoping the injury didn't have anything to do with Bernard. Especially since it would be just like him to leave out a minor detail such as a recent brawl.

"Looks as if I'm just in time to sign your cast," I say.

Gil glances down at the wrist as if he'd forgotten all about it. "Oh that. I was demonstrating a trust exercise at a training seminar and they didn't catch me."

"That's not very nice," I say.

"They thought *demonstration* meant that they weren't supposed to do anything. I guess I didn't explain it very clearly."

Gil organizes seminars that are supposed to help employees

work together in teams and be more productive. At least that's what the companies claim. Gil says that in actuality it's supposed to make them feel better about doing more work for less pay. It's no secret to me that he hates his job, but it pays the bills and they like him, so he must be pretty good at it.

We navigate our way around towers of unpacked boxes and he offers me a glass of milk or water. "Sorry, I meant to stop and pick up some Yoo-hoo. Maybe you'd like wine or a beer."

"Coffee is great if you have any. I've become a caffeine fiend at college." Also, my power nap wore off about four hours ago. And a holiday from alcohol may not be a bad idea for the summer. Getting drunk at keg parties almost every weekend obviously hadn't achieved the desired effect of making me irresistible to Mr. Right.

Gil rinses out two mugs and heats up water in the microwave for instant coffee. Then he takes a bag of Milano cookies off the countertop and places it on the table between us. Bernard would die if he knew about the instant coffee and store-bought cookies. Which reminds me of the box I've set down in the front hall. "There's a casserole and some other stuff in that box I brought up."

"Oh Hallie, that was very sweet of you. But I'm doing just fine as a bachelor." He toasts me with a mug of watery coffee.

"Actually, it was Bernard's idea."

From the pinched look on Gil's face I gather that he now has mixed feelings about the offering. "I see," he says.

We make small talk about work and school but the conversation feels forced, like talking to your parents from your college dorm room while just two feet away some kids are getting stoned. It's as if neither of us wants to mention *it*.

He finally breaks the ice. "So how *is* Bernard?"

Bernard has of course coached me for at least an hour on exactly how to answer this question. And though I hadn't promised to stick to the script, which is basically to say how fabulous he is, I really do feel a loyalty to Bernard, at least in so far as omitting how upset he's been.

"Oh, fine. You know, listening to opera, buying Egyptian cotton sheets. And the antiques business is going gangbusters now that the economy has picked up again. He's selling old-fashioned Coke signs and soda-fountain stools to some retro diner chain."

Gil doesn't appear disappointed but he doesn't look thrilled, either. Like he would have been happier if I'd worked in at least one negative.

"And what about you?" I ask. "I was sort of surprised . . . you know . . . kind of sad that the two of you . . ."

"Yes, I meant to phone you." He stares down at the tangerine-colored Formica tabletop, which I will *not* be telling Bernard about. "But it was hard to find the right words. And I guess . . . I guess you sort of belong over there, with them. I—I didn't know if you'd want to see me. . . ."

"Of course I want to see you! We'll get together and do stuff." Only it sounds like a lame plan made by friends moving to opposite coasts.

"Yes, of course we will."

It suddenly dawns on me that I'm not even exactly sure *why* they broke up. "I didn't ask Bernard, but, I mean, I'm not sure exactly why . . ."

"Oh!" Gil looks surprised. "I thought he explained."

"No, not really." I don't want to say how Bernard implied that Gil had a nervous breakdown or a midlife crisis.

"My brother died very suddenly last month. A heart attack."

"Yeah, Bernard told me that. I'm sorry I didn't hear sooner. I'd have called or something. I mean, actually I didn't remember that you had a brother. . . ."

"Oh, don't worry about it. I'm sure you're aware that my family disowned me when I came out of the closet. I hadn't spoken with Clifton in years. I wouldn't have even known about the funeral if Aunt Theodora hadn't called. Anyway, I saw the family. My dad's grown so old. And my sister, Kathleen, and her husband don't have any children. I went back to the house afterward. It was nice to be with them again. And I felt sorry that I hadn't seen my mother before she died, and didn't go to her funeral."

Gil looks morose and stares at the bank calendar tacked onto the wall with a pushpin. "We're all getting older," he continues. "I just started to think about changing my lifestyle."

"Do you mean that you're tired of living in a small town, with people scrutinizing your every move?" I ask. "Or with your job?" I nod toward his broken wrist. It's a known fact that Gil would like to be a full-time director, or at least do something that involves theater.

"No . . . I think I'd like to get married."

"You mean, to a *woman*?"

"Well, yes, when you put it that way."

Damn Bernard! He *knew* this and he didn't tell me.

"I see. I mean, I didn't know. Because I just thought . . ." But I don't know what I thought, unless it was that once you declared yourself gay it's illegal to switch sides. All I can think to say is, "Do you . . . do you have someone in mind?"

"As a matter of fact, I ran into an old high school friend at Clifton's funeral. Her name is Doris. She's divorced, no children. We've sort of started dating." Only he says this more as a question than a statement of fact and doesn't smile or look well pleased by this turn of events.

Oh gosh, it suddenly flashes into my mind what Bernard might say if he'd just heard that last line, and as a result I accidentally laugh out loud. But I quickly cough to cover it up.

"What's wrong?" Gil asks, not sure if I'm laughing at him or truly hacking.

Obviously I have only a split second to convince him of the latter. "Coffee went down the wrong way." For additional emphasis I stand and pound my chest while coughing some more.

Gil appears relieved. Only I can't control my laughter at the "What's wrong with this picture?" absurdity of it all—Gil dating a woman! So the scene becomes a bit like the funeral of Bernard's father, when we couldn't stop laughing because Bernard made me check to see if there was really a body in the casket, after Olivia had secretly donated it to science, and the lid slammed down on my head.

Every time I stop laughing I imagine Bernard sitting here while

Gil, with the same incredibly bewildered look on his face, announces that he has a girlfriend. And the second I do, I burst into giggles again and have to immediately fake more coughing. Because there's no doubt in my mind that Bernard would correct him and say that "having a girlfriend" is another one of Gil's management euphemisms, and what he's really trying to describe is a *hostage situation.*

Chapter
Thirteen

♥ ON THE DRIVE BACK FROM CLEVELAND A LIGHT RAIN FALLS, making the night cool and filling the air with the blended sweetness of flowers, trees, and damp earth. Despite the fresh scent of spring rushing in through the car window my mind is stuffy, like an overly warm house in wintertime, and my body is anxious, straining forward in the driver's seat. I try to relax and breathe more slowly but every nerve is quivering with restlessness. Ray and his ultimatum, Louise going berserk, the cash crunch, Bernard stalking Gil, Gil dating a woman—what will happen next? Watch, it will turn out that my father is a cross-dresser. Actually, that's impossible. His knees are so bad from playing football when he was younger that he can barely walk in loafers. High heels would be suicide.

I do the HALT self-therapy that Debbie learned in her group for children of bipolar parents. It supposedly enables you to focus on exactly what's bothering you rather than succumbing to a general nervousness or rage. In H-A-L-T, H stand for hungry, A equals angry, L means lonely, and T is for tired. I race through the list and decide that I qualify for all but hungry. Every time there was an uneasy pause in my conversation with Gil I ate another cookie and now feel as if I should be heading to some sort of Pepperidge Farm detox facility.

In an attempt to take my mind off the letters A, L, and T, I consider the design competition, which is for a dishwashing detergent. If I could just be certain that I'd win the full-year scholarship, there'd be no reason to offer to freelance for Cappy in his bookmaking business. And the guidelines sound simple enough. Contestants need to create a state-of-the-art, computer-generated storyboard for a sixty-second television ad. But in my current state of mindlessness all I can think of are those stupid commercials where a well-meaning neighbor comes to your home for a party, discovers spots on the glasses, and rushes you into the kitchen for a *serious* chat.

When I finally pull into the driveway it's almost midnight and all the downstairs lights are still on. Bernard has obviously been waiting by the window, because the front door swings open the second I turn off the engine.

"Tell me about his appearance," Bernard demands before I've even closed the car door behind me.

"His wrist is broken," I say angrily.

"Oh horrors!" But Bernard appears almost giddy. "I should have sent vichyssoise. Surely he needs someone to come help keep up with the cooking and cleaning."

"I can't believe you set me up like this!" I burst out. "You lied to me!"

"What?" He is a study in wide-eyed innocence.

I storm right past Bernard and on into the house. "Women! He said he wants to date women!" Even if Gil didn't seem altogether convincing on the subject, this appears to be his intention.

"That's absolutely ludicrous!" insists Bernard. "Anyway, I told you he had a crisis after his brother died."

"Bernard, the man wants to get married and have children. You call that a crisis?"

"All right then, it's a phase."

"You'd better tell that to Doris."

"Doris?" His jaw goes slack and he looks stunned, as if he's just taken a blow to the head. *Who is Doris?*

"His *girlfriend.*" I don't say this in a mean way, but more like *Hello!*

Bernard crumples into the chair in the hallway as if he would have fallen directly onto the floor without it.

But by now I'm so exhausted I could cry. Ignoring Bernard's latest scene I head for the kitchen and pour a glass of water to take with me out to the summerhouse.

"Wait! Come back here!" He leaps up and chases after me.

"What?" Now I'm feeling cranky and a little bit mean, too, after being deceived and made to look like a complete idiot in front of Gil. "I'm going to bed!"

"Oh Hallie, this is terrible! What am I going to *do*?" Bernard isn't being melodramatic now. I can see the fear and loss in his eyes.

Only I'm too worn out to be properly sympathetic. Not to mention that I'm currently the *last person on earth* who should be giving relationship advice. "You want my honest opinion? I think you're going to have to get over him and find a new boyfriend."

Bernard props himself up against the kitchen counter, still looking shell-shocked. "Doris?" he hisses, as if the very name is an evil incantation.

"We'll talk about it tomorrow. I promise." But I feel guilty leaving him in such a state. "In fact, we'll do an Internet search on her and find out about any bad debts or if she's done time in jail." My roommate Robin had succeeded in ruining the life of a stepfather she despised by discovering that he was wanted for child support and back taxes in Maryland.

Bernard doesn't rise to the bait, though. He stumbles into a chair at the kitchen table and lets his head fall onto his arms.

"Gil served Pepperidge Farm cookies and instant coffee," I say, trying to cheer him up. "And the tabletop is tangerine-colored Formica."

"Do me a favor and get the aspirin from the bathroom."

Bernard mumbles something about getting a tension headache worse than Bette Davis had in the movie *Dark Victory.*

I retrieve a bottle of Bayer out of the medicine cabinet and hand him the last two capsules. The Stocktons aren't exactly pill poppers, and so a bottle of anything lasts a long time around here, at least since Olivia's husband, who everyone simply called *the Judge,* passed away. I fill a glass with water, leave it in on the table, and then kiss Bernard good night on the cheek. His face resembles a great empty fireplace, where all the warmth and light has died out.

For so long I've wanted to be in love. The kind of love that Olivia's poets write about, involving melodious lutes, sunsets that streak the horizon with red flame, and the watery brilliance of the moon. Only now I'm not so sure it's possible in real life. Though I have certainly become clear on one point. The saddest thing in the world must be to fall out of love.

Chapter
Fourteen

♥ BLARING SIRENS AWAKEN ME IN THE MIDDLE OF THE NIGHT. MY first thought is that there's a fire. I hurry outside and around to the front door of the main house to find Olivia on the porch exchanging hurried talk with paramedics, though there isn't a stretcher being hauled out of the back of their emergency vehicle, and no fire trucks have arrived on the scene.

Inside the house Ottavio is pacing the front hall drinking coffee, and a distressed Rocky is hopping from room to room with his hands covering his ears. Through the archway I can see Bernard sitting at the kitchen table exactly where I left him, arguing with a tired-looking Officer Rich.

Because Officer Rich is one of a few African Americans in an otherwise mostly white town, people might think it's hard for him to command the necessary respect to succeed in law enforcement. The truth is just the opposite, however. Perhaps it's in part because he's so tall and large, though in a pillowy sort of way. But I believe it's mostly due to the fact that Officer Rich's reassuring presence combined with his easygoing manner serves to make a person feel that everything is going to be okay. And also, you want your police to stand out a bit, like an orange cone in the middle of the highway, reminding folks to be careful and not go too fast.

A woman wearing a yellow vest and carrying a walkie-talkie prevents me from entering the kitchen, but when Bernard hears my voice he shouts for me to come through. "Hallie, thank goodness. Now, will you *please* tell Officer Rich exactly how many aspirin I consumed."

I learned a long time ago never to answer any questions without first assessing the lay of the land, so you don't accidentally incriminate anyone, particularly yourself. Thus I take a quick look around before replying. An empty bottle of bourbon that wasn't there when I left sits on the table, along with a cocktail glass.

Officer Rich becomes suspicious when I hesitate. "It's okay, Hallie," he says. "Just tell the truth. Rocky found Bernard passed out here at the table and Olivia believes he may have tried to overdose. She wants us to drive him over to Dalewood for a psychiatric evaluation. Olivia claims that lately he's been . . . well—"

"Stop talking as if I'm not here," interjects Bernard. "Hallie, please tell him that all you gave me was aspirin—*two* aspirin. That's *all* that were left in the bottle." His voice is hoarse and hollow with despair.

When I nod my head in agreement, Officer Rich studies us both to see if there's a conspiracy afoot.

"Okay," confesses Bernard, "I probably shouldn't have had a bottle of Wild Turkey as a chaser, but I did *not* attempt to *kill* myself!"

They both turn toward me as if I'm the tiebreaker on whether Bernard was trying to off himself. "There were only two aspirin left," I say. "He had a headache." I don't think it's necessary to include the fact that as I left I could hear Bernard singing, "Make It

Another Old-Fashioned, Please," the torch song lament Ethel Merman sang after losing the love of her life in the musical *Panama Hattie.*

"Thank you!" barks an irritated Bernard. "Now please tell that to Mother and have her show the bandage brigade to the door."

When I go into the living room Brandt has by this time joined the nocturnal throng, wearing a *Star Trek* T-shirt and boxer shorts. He's sitting on the couch next to Rocky, using his hands to communicate. Rocky is enthusiastically responding and occasionally jumping up and down on the cushions, which I assume is his version of an exclamation point.

I take Olivia aside and tell her about Doris.

"Oh," she says, and then whispers back, "The name *Doris* is from the Greek language and means 'a sacrificial knife.' "

Meanwhile, Ottavio goes around the room offering coffee to everyone. Only I'm sick of coffee and return to the kitchen for a chocolate Yoo-hoo, since I'd noticed that Bernard had put in a good supply as part of my sign-on bonus.

Unfortunately the scene I come across now is exactly like the one with Professor Harris at college. Bernard is giving the unabridged version of the breakup to Officer Rich, who is nodding his head sympathetically. Only, with his large hands and bowling-pin body, Officer Rich appears uncomfortable in the role of confidant for a failed romance, especially one that involves two men.

"Uh, Officer Rich," I say, "Olivia wants to see you in the living room."

Officer Rich knows that I'm lying but he appears relieved. Normally when he has to pay an official visit to the Stockton house it's because Olivia has been causing some sort of public disturbance as a result of her many protests. And on those occasions, Bernard is the one who undertakes the role of the voice of reason, usually employing checkbook diplomacy to keep his mother out of the hoosegow.

"I did *not* attempt to take the swim that needs no towel," a depressed Bernard says with all the indignation he can muster.

"Whether you did or didn't," I say, "you'd better pull yourself together, because Olivia is threatening to rent you a rubber room over at Dalewood so you can write recipes on the walls with a purple marker between your toes!"

"What difference does it make?" he says with enough doom to qualify as one of Shakespeare's tragic heroes in his final scene.

"It makes a *big* difference," I answer. "The yard looks like a hurricane swept through it. When was the last time anyone pulled a weed around here? The flower beds haven't been turned, there are mulch piles of last year's leaves everywhere, and no one has placed an order at the garden center."

"I've been preoccupied," he says.

"Yeah, well I got preoccupied with a few guys at school and yet I somehow managed to pass all my classes."

"*Please,* Hallie." He doesn't mean for his voice to be unkind, I know, but that's how it sounds. "Gil and I were together for twelve years. This wasn't some *little college fling.*"

"What does *that* mean?" I say angrily. "That I don't have a heart or feelings? That I don't fall in love and wonder and worry whether he's the person I want to spend the rest of my life with?"

"I simply meant that you have no idea—"

"Bertie," Olivia calls as she enters the kitchen. She's never been one to eavesdrop on other people's arguments and always gives warning before entering a room of raised voices. "They've gone."

"I don't know why you had to call them in the first place!" he snarls, still fuming at her.

"Because Rocky woke me up and I found you slumped over the kitchen table next to an empty pill bottle!"

"I was *resting,*" insists Bernard. "And it was *aspirin.*"

"Can you blame me for worrying that you've not been drawing a clear distinction between *letting go* and *giving up.*" Olivia turns to me. "Hallie, it's not even five o'clock. Everyone else has gone back to bed. Why don't you do the same and I'll sit up with Bertie." She goes over to the stove and turns on the gas for the teakettle.

I'm surprised Bernard doesn't stop her from touching the stove, because she's always forgetting to fill the kettle with water or else leaving the house without remembering to switch off the gas. But he just slouches in his chair, wearing the ravaged expression of an earthquake survivor. I add some water to the kettle just to be safe.

"I don't *need* anyone to *sit* with me, Mother," says Bernard.

"Well *I* do," replies Olivia with the sweetest of smiles.

Bernard puts on his theatrical declamation voice, lifts his chin, and quotes Bette Davis. "What we had can't be destroyed. That's our victory—our victory over the dark. It is a victory because we're not afraid."

Olivia interrupts him by declaring, "*Dark Victory* goes back to the video store the minute it opens, and I'm canceling the subscription to cable TV! You're self-prescribed *cinematherapy* sessions have officially come to an end, as of this minute."

Chapter
Fifteen

So much for getting an early start on the gardens. When my eyes open, the sun is high above the treetops and it must be close to eleven o'clock. I stumble into the yard wearing the shorts and tank top I slept in. The air looks warm, but isn't yet, though it's hectic with birdsong and the soil is full of sunlight. Thick white clouds laze about in the distance and a scrim of pollen drifts through the air.

It feels good not to wake up to tests and overdue projects. Now I can finally concentrate on my two remaining problems, starting with the one that doesn't involve making money. Only for that I need Olivia.

When I enter the main house the scent of flowers is overwhelming, almost annihilating. Further inspection reveals that great big vases of white calla lilies have been placed all throughout the house.

If it were a frame out of a "Batman & Robin" comic, the bold-faced zigzag letters overhead would shout, *Kabloom*!

From the living room I can see Olivia in her den, quietly checking over something she's written. When at peace she looks like a dove with its wings folded.

The aroma from the flowers is so pungent and perfumy that it makes me start to cough, or more accurately, gag.

"Oh, good morning, Hallie." Olivia's voice is light and confidential. "I know. These flowers have to go. But with Bernard working his last nerve I thought we'd just leave them until tomorrow. Perhaps we can open all the windows, switch on the overhead fan, and provide complimentary fragrance for the entire neighborhood." She goes over to the window and raises it the rest of the way.

"But where did they all *come from*?" I ask. I've never seen so many flowers in one place outside of a florist, not even at a funeral home.

"Bernard must have been standing outside the flower wholesaler in Timpany when they opened this morning and then proceeded to purchase every white calla lily in stock. They were all here when I came down at nine and he was already gone."

"But why are they all the same?"

Olivia sets down her papers and invites me to sit down next to her on the love seat. "Flowers are very symbolic. For instance, orchids tend to be viewed as a symbol of lust. Its botanical name is the Latin *orchis*, from the Greek *orkhis*, meaning "testicle," which is what the slope of its root resembles. It's also said that orchids go to extreme measures to propagate themselves. And then you have zempasuchil, the yellow marigold, which was the flower of death to the Aztecs."

"Oh," I say. "So what do white calla lilies mean?"

"To tell you the truth, I have no idea."

A nearby urn of the enormous snowy flowers catches my eye in addition to my nostrils. Arcs of bright orange pollen practically erupt from their centers like fireworks.

"Though I could take a guess," she says. The soft lines around her eyes crinkle slightly with mischief. "The white calla lily happens to be the flower they put in Mr. Doolittle's hand as he was carried out of the chapel."

"*My Fair Lady?*" I ask. Because there aren't any Mr. Doolittles in town, at least that I know of.

She nods, then shrugs her shoulders and raises her hands, as if to indicate that it's not for us to determine how others should grieve.

It's then that I notice Olivia is wearing a WWJD bracelet on the wrist of her right hand—white beads with black lettering followed by a question mark, connected by bright pink and blue silk thread. Last time I was in a church pew, which, admittedly, was a while ago, these things meant "What would Jesus do?" Yet it seems hard to believe that Olivia, the devout Unitarian, of all people, would be sporting such a message.

"Isn't it sweet?" says Olivia when she sees my interest in her bracelet. "Ottavio bought it for me at a craft fair. He loves to give me little presents." She smiles adoringly at this token of her lover's affection.

"But . . . you *do* know what it means?"

"Oh, I've changed it to *What would Jefferson do?* You know, Thomas Jefferson. He was a Unitarian."

I'd almost forgotten how the Stockton house is like living in Alice's Wonderland. Things oftentimes don't mean what you always thought they were supposed to mean. And absolutely anything can happen at any moment. Usually the last thing you expect.

"I'm sorry you ended up being the bearer of the bad news last night," says Olivia and gently touches my shoulder. "Bernard really should have explained Gil's reasons for breaking up. It was only a matter of time before he found someone."

"Just because he's dating a woman doesn't necessarily mean that he's going to marry her," I say.

"When people deeply desire something they can move very swiftly," she philosophizes. "Almost as swiftly as when they're fleeing from something."

"That's sort of what I wanted to talk to you about." I gather up my courage because I can no longer keep this matter to myself. I'd even recently read the name for my disease in *People* magazine. Rather than look at Olivia I flop down on the love seat and stare up at the bookcases with carved beveled tops and etched glass doors.

I finally blurt out the words as if they're sparks erupting from some banked fire. "I—I'm a sex addict."

Chapter
Sixteen

OLIVIA LOOKS AT ME WITH CONCERN BUT I ALSO THINK SHE APpears slightly amused at this proclamation. And though her eyes are quick to read a human face, she rarely comments unless specifically asked.

"Seriously," I continue, "all I think about is sex. I hardly finished any of my schoolwork on time and almost received incompletes in two classes. Even my dreams are filled with men and, well, you know. . . ."

"Some of the best Presidents and artists have been sex addicts," quips Olivia. But then she turns serious. "Hallie, a sex addiction entails *having* sex with inordinate frequency, not just *thinking* about it. Thinking about sex qualifies merely as *lust*. And I'd be very surprised if most of your peers were not in a similar predicament."

"Well, that's just it. They've pretty much resolved the problem one way or another—by settling down with a steady boyfriend, or going through a few of them. But to me it seems like such an important decision to choose the guy who will be the first one—that I should really love him and he should love me." I roll over on the small sofa and face the wall. "Maybe Bernard and I should go and see a psychiatrist *together*—do they have double rooms over at Dalewood?"

"There's absolutely nothing wrong with you and you don't need a psychiatrist," replies Olivia.

"You wouldn't say that if you knew how insane I've felt the past few months." Such an aching and longing had arisen inside of me that at times I couldn't catch my breath and actually felt as if my heart might explode.

Olivia gently takes my chin in her hand and swivels me around so that I'm facing her. She has a wonderful way of giving her entire attention to a young person. "It's perfectly natural for a woman about to turn eighteen to be contemplating romance."

"*All* the time?"

"Intimacy gives shape to your desires from out of all the scattered images in your mind. Then it becomes a melody that you can remember, thereby repeating the ecstasy. You just said that you managed to finish your assignments, despite your preoccupation."

"Yeah, but I think I could of done a lot better if my brain hadn't been so distracted."

"I'm quite certain that there are more than a handful of college freshmen who feel that additional time spent hitting the books rather than the hay could have transformed C's into A's. If it weren't for the interruptions caused by mating rituals, parties in particular, there'd be a greater number of students on the dean's list all across the country."

"I suppose sex *is* more or less what everyone majors in the first year."

"Except for you," clarifies Olivia.

"It sure feels that way. I hardly thought about it at all last year. And now suddenly I'm possessed."

"Last year you had other things on your mind. And besides, you were a girl then."

"Most of the freshmen guys read Jack Kerouac's *On the Road* and then went around thinking they were really impulsive and cool, and acting as if the girls should fall all over them."

"If you want to study Mr. Kerouac for his development of 'spontaneous prose,' that's one thing; however, I certainly wouldn't use him as a guide to relationships and personal responsibility. In that area he and his friends were sorely lacking, leaving in their wake an untold number of distressed women, minor felonies, and unpaid bills."

"At least the guys felt as if they'd found a book with some answers," I say. "Because what I'm wondering specifically is, how do I know if a guy is the right one?"

"Hallie, you're either having flashbacks to Sunday school or else you've been watching too many romantic comedies. No one automatically knows for sure—an orchestra doesn't play Rachmaninoff, and fireworks don't explode overhead the way they do in Bernard's favorite movie, *To Catch A Thief*. You have to find out over a period of time. Although that doesn't mean you have to sleep with them all to find out. Usually dating is sufficient. But inevitably you'll have to kiss a few toads along the way." She is tender with her words, treating them like pressed flowers that might fall apart if roughly handled.

"What if I make a mistake?"

"How do you mean 'a mistake'? It's perfectly acceptable to have safe sex. That's why there are red-light districts and escort services. In fact, someone has even figured out the number of calories you burn off during intercourse, and so I can only assume that *somewhere* sex is part of a weight loss plan. Furthermore, I'm inclined to agree with Nietzsche when he posited that certainty causes more madness than doubt."

"So I should just go to a bar and pick up the first guy I see and get it over with?"

"Of course not! I didn't mean to sound crass or unromantic. But don't fret so much about being in love. Your stirrings of desire mean that you're ready to make love. You're *not* necessarily ready to choose a partner for life and start a family. The *mistake* would be to convince yourself that you have to be in love with some young man in order to give yourself permission to act upon your feelings. Believe me, you won't end up as damaged goods. Though there are of course certain people in this country who'd like for you to believe that."

"It shouldn't be this complicated. Should it? Maybe I'm just not ready."

"What happened with Craig, if I'm not being too inquisitive?" asks Olivia. "He's a nice young fellow. And he certainly cared for you. In fact, I rather miss having him around, taking soil samples and talking to the trees in the backyard when he thought that no one was watching."

"Sure, I would have liked to stay with Craig. But now we live fifteen hours apart and can't see each other. I wasn't even planning to be here for the summer. And if Craig gets the chance to come back, which he's not even sure that he'll be able to, it will only be for a few weeks in August. So we agreed to see other people. And I have. There's this guy Ray who really wants to be with me and I do, too, but . . ."

"If he's a pleasant fellow and it feels right, then why not?" she asks.

"I don't know if I love him. I mean, Ray's nice and he brings me CDs that he knows I'll like. His clothes are always neat and clean and he takes me to real restaurants instead of college hangouts. I've invited him to come and visit this Friday before he leaves for New York. So it's sort of now or never." I decide not to go into detail about the ultimatum.

"As the great Persian poet Rumi wrote, you must open your hands if you want to be held," she quotes.

One could easily assume it's Olivia's firm belief that some well-placed verse has the capacity to solve most of the world's problems.

"But for the rest of my life he'll always be the first," I say.

"Yes, eventually somebody has to be," she agrees. "Now, do I need to give you The Talk?"

"Yes. I need *all* the talks."

I turn my face back to the wall and this time Olivia doesn't seem to mind speaking to the back of my head.

"Number one, don't make the mistake I made. Be sure to tell him it's your first time. And I certainly wouldn't count on any orgasms in the near future."

Quickly turning my face back around I give her a questioning look.

"You know, climaxes," she says.

"Yes, I mean, I've read . . ."

"Men have them all the time, of course, but it can take years for women to have a single one while actually making love."

"Why?"

"Same old story, like they say about Ginger Rogers—she did everything that Fred Astaire did, except on six inch heels and backward."

"But it doesn't seem fair," I say. "We have the hymen, we have the cramps, we have the babies, and we don't get the orgasms for maybe years! What do we get?"

"A higher threshold for pain." Olivia smiles wryly. "And believe me, it comes in handy when you sew children's Halloween costumes."

"That's it?" I ask. "That's The Talk?"

"Well, there's one other good thing for the girls," she says slyly.

"Please tell me before I have a sex change."

"Multiple orgasms."

"Maybe *that* explains my mother having nine kids."

"Speaking of *children,* be sure to use a condom. Men think they're the only ones who despise them, when they're universally abhorred. If only the Christians understood that free condoms can advance committed relationships and the institution of marriage more than all the abstinence crusades and prayer vigils in the world."

"In health class they taught abstinence," I say.

"That's because the so-called 'educators' hired by parochially minded school board members are afraid that teaching safe sex will encourage promiscuity. Yet they claim to teach English and I don't see anyone running around speaking *it* properly."

"What about afterward?" I ask. "Then will I know whether or not we're truly in love?"

Olivia runs her fingers over my disheveled hair. "Sometimes you don't search for love, exactly, but for what makes you feel alive."

I let out a teenage moan. It's all too complicated. However, I know what's not alive, and that's the gardens. It's time to get to work on both the yard and then the design competition. Love will have to wait.

"I'd better start working on the lawn while I can still use the mower and not a scythe," I say.

Olivia rises and looks out the window. "It's such a shame to cut the grass. Grass is so democratic. Walt Whitman said it was the handkerchief of the Lord and also the beautiful uncut hair of graves."

"Well, Bernard is currently paying me fifteen dollars an hour to give the grass a crew cut," I say. "But definitely call me if Mr. Whitman is offering twenty to leave it alone."

Chapter
Seventeen

THE YARD IS READY TO BE CONDEMNED BY THE DEPARTMENT OF Agriculture. In the way back, just beyond the orchard, where the woods begin, I spy a half-dozen deer plotting a takeover. The buckeye trees are in full bloom and the breeze carries their noxious odor right into the shed.

Another rancid smell awaits me deep within the shed, where a quick inventory illustrates the need for a varmint excavation. Apparently a squirrel decided to take his leave of us inside the leaf blower and has been going to heaven just an ounce at a time since at least the middle of winter.

A further accounting reveals that we're out of everything from mower gas and oil to weed killer and trash bags. Likewise, Bernard hasn't bought *one* plant or started any seedlings in the greenhouse. What have these people been doing all spring? It's already June and everything at the nursery is going to be picked over, if not gone entirely.

Buying the actual plants and flowers will have to wait until the weekend. I make a list of the basics—whatever's necessary to get the mower going and start a general cleanup. Before heading to town I stop in the kitchen to grab a sandwich and check the message pad by the phone. Nothing from Auggie. Maybe he changed his mind. And nothing from Ray, though we have a definite date for next Friday. At least I *think* we do. And no word from Craig, either. We were in the habit of talking on the phone once a week during the school year, usually on Sunday night, and it has been his turn to call for the past three weeks.

And to think I'd actually been considering getting a cell phone. Why bother if no one is going to call me except Bernard? Anytime a good late-night movie was on he called my apartment, told me the channel, and we watched it together over the phone, complete with Bernard doing his favorite parts along with critiquing the costumes. The good thing about this situation was that even though my roommates knew I wasn't having real sex, between the overheard snippets of dialogue and our discussions about what everyone was wearing, they at least thought I was having phone sex.

When I try to start my car the engine groans and then there's a *thud* that sounds as if it dropped onto the driveway. Mr. Shultze, the new neighbor, and owner of Lulu the Great Dane, has been watching this automotive drama unfold from the adjacent front lawn, where he's pruning a tree with one of those poles that have a small saw at the top. He's your typical male Ohio retiree—baseball cap with whatever branch of the service he was in emblazoned on the front, big American flag hanging out front, and tons of tools, parts, and paint cans neatly organized in the garage.

I climb out of the driver's seat, open the hood, and start by checking the oil. Voilà! That's the problem. It's completely dry. Only how did that happen? I'm almost positive the gauge says it's supposed to be full. Is there a leak? I check underneath the car but nothing appears to be dripping and there aren't any stains on the gravel.

There's no oil left in the shed and so I wander over to Mr. Shultze, introduce myself, and ask if I can borrow just enough to get to the gas station. Fortunately he seems thrilled to be able to assist a neighbor in need. When he returns with a brand-new can of motor oil I explain how the gauge says that it's almost full. I don't want him to think I'm an irresponsible car owner.

"Uh-oh," says Mr. Shultze. "Sounds as if your gauge may be broken." He bends down close over the place where the oil goes and studies the engine. Then come noises from the back of his throat indicating that all is not well in Cabrioletland. "This has been dry for a while. I'm no professional mechanic but it's safe to say you're going to need a new engine."

Judging by the number of shiny tools in Mr. Shultze's garage it's safe to say that he probably could have been a professional mechanic and that he's undoubtedly correct.

"A new engine! That's going to cost like $2,000."

He nods in agreement and says, "Maybe $2,500, depending on where you go."

"How could I be so stupid?" I lean my head against the hood of the car as if in agony. "I remember looking down at the gauge one time and thinking that I must have the most oil-efficient car ever manufactured."

"It could happen to anyone." Mr. Shultze says this in a nice-enough way, but it's clear that something so dumb would never have happened on his watch.

"What should have been two dollars and fifty cents' worth of oil is now going to cost me a thousand times as much!"

"I have a buddy who works at a yard in Cleveland who might be able to find a good used engine for you," he offers. "Sometimes people total the back end and the car itself isn't worth repairing but the engine is fine."

"I'm definitely interested, if you don't mind," I say appreciatively.

"It would only save you about five or six hundred—I mean, a good used engine is always saleable."

"That's still five or six hundred I don't have," I say. "Thanks for your help. I'd better go see if I can borrow the Buick." I nod in the direction of Olivia's car and then head back inside the house.

Olivia is busy at her writing desk and Ottavio has a pile of travel guides on his lap. They've been talking about taking a big trip to Italy to meet Ottavio's relatives and then visiting the Greek Islands for some relaxation and classical culture.

I explain that my car conked out, without going into *all* the details. As it happens, Olivia and Ottavio don't have any special plans for the afternoon and she's happy to lend me the *QE2,* so designated by Bernard because it's more like driving a living room set than an automobile.

As soon as I enter the hardware store, Mr. Burke gives me a big smile and shows me some new super-strength lawn and leaf bags that he especially likes. The Stocktons have an account here and my name is listed on it, so technically I can spend as much money as I want. This is a detail obviously not lost on Mr. Burke, particularly since he doesn't appear to be as busy as he was before the big discount variety store opened up a few miles outside of town. And when I'm painting, the tab often runs into the hundreds of dollars. Sometimes it's hard to believe I'd managed to go from local juvenile delinquent to valued customer within the short space of a year.

After finishing my shopping I notice the long yellow line of empty buses lurching toward the high school and realize that it's time for classes to let out. I'm sure that Gwen and Jane, my best friends from high school, are busy with finals and all sorts of end-of-senior-year stuff, but I decide to try and dig them up so we can make plans to get together.

Pulling into the parking lot it doesn't appear as if anything has changed. Kids still come hurtling out the doors in a frantic rush, as if being freed from a long imprisonment. Only I'm astounded by how small the brick building now looks. I remember it as being much larger and more imposing. Though it's just as ugly as ever. Apparently they tried to tart up the front with some hedges, but if you ask me, the dark gray cinder-block tomb still screams out: *Hunker down and pray for daylight!*

A heavily made-up gaggle of girls whip out cigarettes the minute they're on the other side of the metal doors and strut toward the hot-rod section at the back of the parking lot. The reason they're able to light up so easily is because they're not carrying any books or folders. I spot my sister Louise right smack in the center of the group, waving her smoke as if it's a sparkler on the Fourth of July. Not that I have anything big against smoking. But it definitely contributes to her aura of a soon-to-be dropout.

"Hey, Louise," I yell out the car window.

She swivels her head to seek out the owner of the voice, giving her long shiny hair a sexy toss in the process. But as soon as she sees me and my decidedly uncool cherry red Buick Park Avenue she quickly turns away, as if I'm a mother in hair curlers and a fuzzy pink bathrobe arriving with the bag lunch that she purposely left at home.

At that moment Just Call Me Dick saunters past like a farmer checking his sheep pen for wolves, with his old-fashioned trousers hiked so high that his chest is in danger of being swallowed up. All that's missing is a shotgun. I wonder if when other grown-ups call him Richard he still trounces on them with that high-pitched nasal voice that could sharpen pencils, "Just call me Dick!" thereby announcing "I'm an asshole!" barely a split second before people figure it out for themselves. If my life were an animated short feature, then last year Just Call Me Dick would have to be considered the arch-enemy, making it his full-time job to harass me about playing hooky.

As JCMD comes closer to the car my heart skips a beat and I automatically duck down underneath the dashboard. It's only then I realize that I'm not even doing anything wrong. Muscle memory is a powerful force. No wonder eighty-year-olds can still ride bikes. After he passes by I return to an upright position in the driver's seat.

According to my friend Jane, Just Call Me Dick had finally received his coveted promotion and is now assistant vice-principal. Instead of having to scrounge up kids cutting classes in the video arcade and bring them to justice, his new commission is to ensure that justice is indeed served. Or more accurately, in the words of *The Mikado,* to make sure the punishment fits the crime. Jane also reports that JCMD now metes out sentences in his own private bunker next to the janitor's closet. And watching him survey the throng of kids scrambling to catch their buses, I must admit that he indeed possesses the aura of a man rising up within his world, his beaklike nose in the air the way a turkey vulture catches a whiff of an injured muskrat coming from out of the northwest.

Finally I see the back of Gwen's smooth golden hair and honk my horn as she's about to climb onto her bus. She spots the familiar car and hurries over.

Chapter
Eighteen

"HALLIE! WHAT ARE *YOU* DOING HERE?" GWEN SOUNDS AS IF she's worried that I've dropped out of college and reverted back to my wicked ways. No wonder my mother is concerned about Louise—a reputation is a hard thing to shake.

"No more teachers, no more books," I chant. "My exams finished a couple days ago. Can I give you a lift?"

"Thank goodness, yes. Joel is staying after to lift weights."

Joel has been Gwen's boyfriend since January, when Owen was replaced because he hung out with his friends too much at the holiday dance. She climbs into the car and carefully adjusts the pink blouse that barely contains her exuberant femininity, so that the puffy sleeve doesn't get caught in the door. After checking her matching lip gloss in the passenger mirror she turns her porcelain face, which is mounted on a neck that fashion models can only dream about, to examine me. "When are you going to let me pluck your eyebrows, blow-dry your hair, and apply some mascara?"

"Next Thursday," I say. "My boyfriend, Ray, is coming to visit on Friday. And well . . ."

"You're finally going to sleep with him, aren't you?" She leans over excitedly and squeezes my knee.

Suddenly I'm embarrassed and feel my cheeks flush. "Yeah. I mean, probably."

"Oh, Hallie, that's *so* cool. Promise that you'll tell me all about it."

"Didn't you sleep with Joel after the prom last weekend? I thought . . ."

"No. I mean, of course he wanted to. But I'm going to college in San Diego and he was finally accepted at the University of Pennsylvania after being wait-listed."

"So?"

"*So,* I don't want my first time to be with someone I'm never going to see again. He's doing an internship in Des Moines at his aunt's advertising agency all summer. And besides, I'm *Catholic.*"

"You're a Catholic when it's convenient, like for getting out of school early to supposedly attend religion classes," I say with laughter. "What about Jane?"

"What *about* Jane? She's still married to her baseball mitt. Somehow about a week before every dance she manages to dig a hunk of male flesh out of the guys' locker room for a date, basically a brisket in a uniform. And then after the party we never hear about him again, unless his name is read over the announcements for scoring the winning goal." Gwen laughs at Jane's well-known love 'em and leave 'em mode of operation.

"Do you think she's—you know . . ."

"Oh *gosh,* no!" exclaims Gwen. "She has a huge crush on that famous South American soccer player, what's-his-name? And she almost went all the way with Bruno a couple weeks ago when they hooked up at a post-game party."

"*Really?*" I say.

"Yeah, she just doesn't want to be bothered with all the day-to-day relationship stuff," explains Gwen. "Jane organizes make-out sessions like doctors schedule appointments—get them in, get them out, and then leave her alone to watch ESPN. Because you can be sure no guy is ever going to get *that* remote control."

It's true. Jane can watch three games at once and be right about which team is going to win every one.

"I don't know, maybe she's onto something." Gwen gives me that look that says, *Sometimes guys can be such jerks!* "Oh, she finally decided to go to Bucknell University. Coaches from three different schools were still fighting over her until last week."

"That's great, because I know she really wants to play on their soccer team." We're both well aware that it's Jane's dream to eventually play soccer on a European travel team and maybe even try out for the Olympics, so this is definitely good news. Meantime, Gwen certainly has no cause to be jealous of our friend. She wants to become a fashion designer and her father can afford to send her wherever she's accepted. Besides, Gwen's never had any interest in playing sports. She doesn't think uniforms are figure-flattering and is convinced that anything played outdoors causes chapped lips and permanent sun damage to your skin.

"I probably shouldn't tell you this . . . ," says Gwen, her usual challenge for you to try and coax the latest gossip out of her.

"Tell me *what?*" I try to sound as if I'm dying from curiosity. Gwen is a lot like Bernard in that she responds better to an enthusiastic audience. "You did *so* sleep with Jocl! Or *somebody!*"

"No," she whispers, as if the willow tree hanging over the driveway might have a microphone hidden within its branches. "It's about Jane. Her parents are getting divorced."

"Huh?" I'm speechless. Mr. and Mrs. Davenport always seemed like the perfect couple. And Jane's mother is from some small zippity-do-dah town in the South, so she's constantly smiling, baking things, sewing name tags into her kids' clothes, and busy making a nice home. It's not as if Jane's mom has ignored her family for the sake of some big career. She put in the long hours teaching her kids right from wrong—and didn't just leave notes on the fridge. In fact, we were all entertained by, and truly fond of, Mrs. Davenport. She is a Southern version of Miss Manners, peppering her speech with such chestnuts as "Speak only well of people and you never have to whisper," and for the complainers, "Would you like cheese with your whine?" Whenever someone says they were lucky, Mrs. Davenport insists that, no, they were blessed, thereby implying they had better not scrimp on their prayers that night.

"But Jane doesn't want *anyone* to find out," Gwen says, and raises her eyebrows in a way that indicates "anyone" of course doesn't apply to her but means "anyone *else*."

"Why?" I ask.

"Who *knows*." Gwen rolls her eyes. "Apparently her folks have been saying they're not sure if they *ever* loved each other, they're not sure what would make them happy, they're not sure if the earth is round. I get the feeling she's still hoping that they'll be able to work things out."

"Thanks for the tip-off," I say. "I won't mention it unless Jane does first." I guess Jane's parents weren't informed that they're supposed to wait three more months, until she's away at college, and then call her there with the news of the breakup. At least that way she'd have an instant support group of freshmen finding out about their newly broken homes.

"So are you excited?" asks Gwen, quickly returning to the topic of my pending loss of virginity. "Have you decided what to wear?"

"I don't think you wear much of anything," I say.

"Beforehand, silly! I could loan you my green silk T-shirt. That would look good with jeans. And we all know how devoted you are to your jeans."

"So you think that sweatpants are too casual." It's a joke but Gwen takes her fashion so seriously, I know it will get her.

"Hallie!" she practically shouts. "You can't wear sweats for your first time! I mean, what kind of mood does that set? What a terrible memory it would make." She covers her face with her hands as if to expunge the very thought.

"I was kidding!" I laugh like crazy and she punches me in the arm.

"Aren't you nervous?"

"Yeah, I guess. A little bit." Leave it to Gwen to make this into a *Cosmo* quiz. "I—I guess I wish it was already over with. It feels as if there's a big test hanging over my head."

"What do you mean?" Gwen appears stunned. "Aren't you in love with him?"

"I like him a lot, okay." My frustration must show. "I don't know for sure what being in love even feels like."

"I love Joel," Gwen says definitively.

"And what does that mean, exactly?" I ask.

"I don't have eyes for anyone else and whenever I'm away from him I wish that I was with him."

Her answer sounds like a Top 40 ballad. "But what about after he leaves for Des Moines in a week?"

"I'll have to stop loving him and fall in love with someone else," she says matter-of-factly.

"Right. How dumb of me."

"I've been considering Neil," says Gwen with a gleam in her bedroom eyes. "I don't think you know him. He's a friend of my sister's husband's younger brother. I met him at the wedding and he lives near San Diego. We've been E-mailing. He works for a company that books cruises on those big ocean liners and goes on vacation all over the world practically for free. Imagine all the cool clothes I'd get to wear!"

Leave it to Gwen to have a replacement boyfriend waiting in the wings. Not only that, but one who requires a brand-new wardrobe.

We arrive at her farmette a few miles from town. They have a real barn in the back that is home to a couple of horses and a few dozen chickens. There's an owl, too. I hear it all the time, trash-talkin' the mice and baby chicks, but have never actually seen it.

Out here in the country it is impossible not to be conscious of the fact that we are knee-deep in spring and there's no turning back. Everything in nature seems to be stirring. Clouds of tiny pale blue butterflies dive and dart among the bushes while baby rabbits zigzag across the wide front lawn. The air is saturated with earthy smells, including the farmers off to the east fertilizing with fresh manure. Above us the trees are full of rustling noises and swelling buds. Now and then the dazzling wing of a cardinal flashes through the thick leaves.

"You'd better come in and say hi to my mom," Gwen tells me as she gets out of the car.

"I'm running sort of late," I say. "And you *know* how she is with all the questions." The CIA has nothing on Gwen's mom when it comes to performing an interrogation. "Can't I talk to her on Thursday when I come for my makeover?"

"All right. And mark your calendar that on Saturday afternoon I'm throwing a huge graduation party. We're going to decorate the whole barn in school colors and my dad is even going to let us paint a bulldog on the roof. Be sure to bring Ray along so I can check him out."

"Let me see how it goes." Playing volleyball in Gwen's barn isn't quite the afterglow I had in mind. On the other hand, by graduating early and leaving for the summer session at college, I'd missed out on all the end-of-the-year high school festivities except for the prom.

"And I was wondering if you'd mind if I invite Craig," says Gwen.

"He won't be home until the end of July or the beginning of August, if at all. He has to make up a lab," I explain. "Apparently college biology is really hard. And he wouldn't have taken it with calculus *and* Spanish if he'd known how bad it was going to be."

"Do you think that you two will ever get back together?" asks Gwen, the part-time matchmaker.

"I doubt it. I mean, if we really cared about each other then I guess we would have stayed together, right? Besides, everyone I know who did a long-distance relationship ended up miserable and eventually broke it off anyway."

"Yeah, that's what everyone says," agrees Gwen. "Steer clear of LDRs." She says this as if long-distance relationships are a virulent virus.

"Besides, every time we talk on the phone it sounds as if he has a million girlfriends," I say.

Gwen giggles. "So! Every time we talk on the phone you have a different boyfriend."

"Only that's not by choice," I hate to admit.

Chapter
Nineteen

By the time I arrive back in town it's already half past four. I've accomplished nothing today other than stock up on gardening supplies. I guess that's what happens when you don't start work until noon. And having promised my mother to look into the wayward sibling situation, I should really stop and see Officer Rich. From what I saw in the school parking lot this afternoon, I can't exactly accuse Mom of overreacting, for once.

The police station is housed in a fancy government town hall that dates back to the 1920s. It's easy to tell when a building went up in Cosgrove. Either it's really pretty and from 1800 to 1930, or an ugly slab of concrete from the What Were They Thinking school of architecture in the 1960s and '70s. However, this particular structure is from the earlier period, with tall columns out front and big white-robed statues at the top, like galaxy judges peering down to determine if you've been naughty or nice.

At one end of the long marble hallway is the office where titles and zoning information about local real estate are kept on file. Motor Vehicle and the window where you can get birth and death certificates are in the middle. At the opposite end is the courtroom and where Officer Rich runs his small department. Mostly people go to him to file complaints or ask him to give a safety lecture to their school or church group.

A brick building around the back contains the one-cell county jail. If someone is arrested here in Cosgrove, he's usually from out of town, and so the next day the person is moved to Cleveland or wherever it is he or she is wanted. Mostly the jail serves as an apartment for Marty-the-Town-Drunk. It used to be that when he was particularly down and out and in need of a meal and a warm place to sleep it off, he would purposely get himself arrested for vagrancy by passing out in a public place. Finally Officer Rich got tired of being Marty's taxi service and just gave him a key to the jail. There's a hot plate, vending machines, and some cans of hash and beans. The only rule is that Marty has to clean up before leaving.

I haven't been inside the police station for years, not since I delivered to Officer Rich the proof that I didn't take the missing money from the charity golf tournament. However, just walking down the highly waxed cavernous corridor serves to make me slightly jittery, as if there may still be some outstanding violation they haven't yet caught up with me about.

Lining the walls are imposing portraits of pasty-faced town forefathers with beady black eyes frowning down as if they know you haven't said your prayers in months. In addition to jangling my nervous system, they remind me to ask Olivia how she's doing with raising money for the portrait of Unitarian social worker Angela Holst. She's the woman who brought modern sanitation to the town back in the 1940s and single-handedly stopped local kids from contracting typhoid. And thus Olivia wants her honored as a town "foremother." Bernard claims that the only thing scarier than a Unitarian task force with a political petition is the Unitarian Women's Alliance with a health concern.

There's a bank of pay phones across from where Officer Rich

works and I decide to call Ray to make sure that he is indeed coming to visit on Friday. He sounds happy to hear from me but explains he's busy doing something with his father and can't talk right now, other than to say he's still planning to drive to Cosgrove, *unless I've changed my mind.* This of course doesn't refer to having dinner together, but rather to me making good on my promise to sleep with him. After hanging up I justify the plan to myself by recalling what Olivia said about having to start *someplace.*

The front desk where Carol the receptionist usually sits and works on her nail tips is empty. However, I can see Officer Rich in his small office, with his size fourteens perched on the pulled-out bottom drawer of an adjacent filing cabinet. He's leaning back in his chair with his cap over his face, either doing some serious brain work or more likely having a snooze. His belt with the gun holster and parking-ticket book are draped across the desk next to a half-dozen framed pictures of his family.

"Hello, anybody home?" I call out.

Chapter
Twenty

Officer Rich jerks forward and grabs for his gun belt as if he's about to mow down the entire Youngstown Mafia. But upon seeing that it's only me he sets the belt back down on the desk and glances at the clock on the far wall. "Hallie! Hey there. Come on in so I can get a closer look for the sketch artist," he jokes. "I'm not accustomed to seeing you during daylight hours."

Though I don't know how much of anything he can actually see in this cave. The windowless room is poorly lit and the desk calendar hasn't been changed since January second. The wall calendar is also still turned to January, and I've often noticed the one on his car dashboard is the same. Officer Rich seems to live in perpetual January. But that's not uncommon around here. It wasn't so long ago that Cosgrove County was an agrarian community, and thus most older people still measure time by the seasons, not the days or hours, and especially not by sheets of paper tacked to the wall.

"I hope you're not turning yourself in," he continues lightheart-edly, referring to the old days when I was the town perp, "because Carol went home sick and I don't know where any of the forms are kept."

"Don't worry. I shot the only witness, so there'd be no point in a trial anyway."

"Good, good." Officer Rich grins as if it's a relief not to have to act interested while hearing about a fender bender in a parking lot or kids spray-painting the library. He notices that I'm checking out all the family photos on his desk and selects one of an attractive young black couple to show me. "It's my thirtieth wedding anniver-sary today."

"Oh my gosh!" I say while studying the photograph.

Officer Rich chuckles, assuming that I can't believe he's been married so long, but what I'm really thinking is that there's no *way* Officer Rich was ever that skinny. His wife is still just as pretty as ever and has kept her figure, more or less. The only difference is that she has gray hair now. And glasses. It's always been obvious that he's devoted to her. In fact, people like to say that Officer Rich runs the town so well because Felice runs him so well. He's heard the famil-iar line as well. Only he just laughs and nods as if it's essentially the truth.

Officer Rich leans back in his chair the way old people do before they start to reminisce, even though at age forty-nine he's not *that* much older than my parents.

Taking the photo back he smiles at it and then gives the glass a dusting with his shirtsleeve. "Probably got married a little too young. But back then there wasn't all this nonsense about enjoying your life, and regular folk didn't take jobs in far-off cities. You just looked around at a church social, picked a nice girl, met the parents, courted her a bit, and then tied the knot."

Of course this gets me to thinking about my own disastrous love life. So I decide Officer Rich might be a good person to interview in order to gather more data for my romance file. "But how did you *know* that Felice was the right one?" I ask.

"Ha!" He carefully places the now polished-up photo back

down where he can easily see it. "*Everyone* thought Felice was the right one, for *himself*. She was the minister's daughter and the most beautiful girl in the choir. I had to court her hard and run off some fierce competition." He grins at the recollection.

"Then how did she know that *you* were the right one?" I continue my love interrogation.

"You'll have to ask her that. Though when I think back on it, I doubt either one of us really knew much of anything. We were both babies—nineteen, not much older than you are now. Whew. Ha ha." Again he thrusts backward in his chair, only this time for a second it appears that it's going to tip over from the sudden and sizable weight shift. Fortunately Officer Rich uses the nearby metal file cabinet to steady himself just in time. "But the Good Lord provided and everything took care of itself."

Well, I wanted another view and now I have one—leave my love life up to fate, or God, or the Magic 8-ball.

Officer Rich leans forward and thumps a sheaf of papers on his desk as the chair groans from another sudden redistribution of weight, and once again I briefly fear that he's going to drop through the floor. "You know what everyone is complaining about nowadays?" Officer Rich lifts the stack and gives it a wave in my direction. "Potholes! These old farm roads weren't made for all this traffic, especially the trucks. Everyone is losing hubcaps and ruining their suspension and the tractors are run right off into the ditches." He plunks the papers back down. "But surely you didn't come to hear about potholes. What can I do you for? Is it about Bernard? Poor fellow . . . I felt so darn bad for him last night."

"Yeah. I mean, no. It's about my sister." Then I remember that I have four sisters and possibly another one on the way and so I really need to be more specific. "My sister Louise, she's fifteen, dark hair, really pretty—"

"Sure, I know Louise Palmer," he says, though not in a way that indicates it's because she recently received any awards for outstanding citizenship. Even though the town has been growing, most adults in any type of public position make it their business to know all the future voters.

"Well, she's—she's been giving my parents some trouble."

Officer Rich folds his hands behind his neck and appears to be weighing his next sentence. "I shouldn't say anything, because technically she wasn't breaking the law. . . ."

"But . . . ," I say, since he seems to need a little encouragement.

"Last month I picked up a local boy for a DUI and your sister was in the backseat of the car. Best I can figure it, they'd just come from buying cheap beer with fake IDs out at Valueland, that big new variety store a couple miles to the south."

"Was *she* drinking?"

"Police history tells us that when the teenager driving a black Trans Am loaded with kids has been drinking, usually it's true for the rest of 'em," he says. "But that's just conjecture. I didn't ask for a Breathalyzer from the passengers. And of course they poured out all the beer as soon as they saw my squad car coming."

"So what should I do?" I ask. "I mean, my mother is going crazy worrying that Louise is ruining her life. Do you have any sort of scared-straight programs or tours of the jail?"

"Kids don't buy that stuff anymore. If she'll listen to anyone, it would be you, since you're closest in age. Teenagers think people from my generation are out of it, living on another planet. And I guess they're right. Parents and teachers don't cuff the kids anymore. It's not even punishment to send them to their rooms, what with video games and the Internet. Just pray and hope they come through it is about all that's left. Come day, go day, God send Sunday."

"Isn't there *anything* I can do?"

"Sports can be good for girls. Does Louise play something?"

"She's a cheerleader," I say.

"Okay, then. They're nice girls, a little boy crazy sometimes, but it's good exercise and keeps them busy with practice and games."

"Oh, she's busy all right."

Officer Rich laughs, though it quickly becomes apparent that it's not at my lame joke, or even at Louise's expense. More like my own.

"Life was easier last year, back when you knew everything, huh?" he says.

"Yeah, it definitely was."

"And how are *you* getting on, college lady?" he asks, and looks me up and down in that cop way, as if checking for any telltale scratches or bloodstains.

Oh my gosh, someone has finally asked me how *I'm* doing!

"My life is no jeans ad, that's for sure. But I haven't resorted to smash-and-grab robberies, at least not yet. Otherwise, I guess it's okay, especially when compared with some people's problems."

"Good," he says. "I'm a little worried about our friend Herb. The new Valueland discount superstore is putting his drugstore here in town out of business. The Rowland family has been on Main Street since 1910. They started as a dry goods and feed store. Herb's grandfather gave people credit during the Depression and Herb and his father have done the same during a lot of tough times since then. It'd be a shame for the place to close. Not to mention it will take more shoppers away from town and out to the malls and factory outlets. Rents will plummet, buildings will be abandoned, and that's when the trouble starts, especially with the young folks. I'd hate to have to sober up old Marty long enough to deputize him." Officer Rich ends with a little joke, the way he almost always does when talking about serious matters, to make people feel comfortable.

"Oh," I say. "Is there anything we can do to help?" Maybe Officer Rich is able to deny Valueland a parking-lot permit or get them on a zoning technicality.

"Not much, I guess," he replies sadly. "The Kunckle family owns Valueland and Edwin gives lots of money to the church and the hospital, at least he does so long as it's used to attach the family name to a wing, archway, pew, or painting." Then Officer Rich adds in his whisper that is not really a whisper at all, but one notch below his normal booming bass, "However, I'm encouraging people to shop at Herb's store rather than go out to Valueland. It's not as if the Kunckles need another nickel."

"Okay," I say. "I'll be sure to tell the Stocktons and my parents."

Officer Rich gives me a thumbs-up, and I head toward the door.

"So is the poker game on for tomorrow night?" I call back from outside his office.

"Lord willin' and if the creeks don't rise!" comes Officer Rich's reply.

Driving away I pass the neat rows of red and yellow tulips along the well-cared-for median that divides this section of Main Street. Soon the Garden Society will replace them with bright zinnias for summer and then in September pumpkins and gourds will be arranged on the back of an old hay wagon, with scarecrows at either end. I think how terrible it would be if all the familiar stores went out of business and downtown became a drag strip for marauding youth, like Officer Rich had said.

This of course makes me think of Louise and her fast friends driving their fast cars. She's undoubtedly headed for Big Trouble, and it doesn't appear that there's much to be done about it. Meantime, I don't seem to be any further along with my quest to know Mr. Right when I find him. If I really wanted to be with Ray next weekend, then why do I find myself hoping that Auggie will call?

Passing the old haunts is a painful reminder that Craig, my first real boyfriend, is now nothing more than a friend. And this doesn't seem fair, because if we hadn't both gone off to college I very much doubt that we would have broken up.

But most of all, driving back through town makes me feel as if everything I once knew to be true is suddenly on the point of vanishing.

Chapter
Twenty-one

THE FOLLOWING MORNING I FINALLY GET AN EARLY START working in the yard and take only a short break for lunch. By late afternoon I'm aching all over, and except for a turned flower bed, the place looks exactly the same as it did seven hours ago.

Olivia and Ottavio wander into the yard dressed to go out somewhere nice. Olivia moves with the soft delicacy of a reed in the breeze and Ottavio stumbles along by her side because he's so busy gazing up adoringly at her. They're holding hands like teenagers and it's very sweet. I think my parents might actually try and hold hands if they could get close enough to each other, only they're usually balancing a howling baby and a restless toddler between them. However, my parents are sappy in the same way as Olivia and Ottavio and kiss whenever they've been away from each other for even an hour.

Olivia gazes up at the horizon and says, "My goodness, with all those gauzy streaks of light blue, pale rose, and mother-of-pearl, the sky resembles a painting by Giovanni Tiepolo."

"Venezia!" Ottavio says proudly. He likes to ensure we don't forget that so many great artists were his countrymen.

"We're off to a potluck supper at the church," says Olivia. "There's a guest lecturer talking about slavery in the Sudan. Apparently it's very complicated. Community groups and schoolchildren raise money in order to buy these people their freedom, yet this only serves to fuel the continuation of the situation—much like providing guns and ammunition to Latin American rebels."

Ottavio looks around at the garden and shakes his head as if he's gazing on the equivalent of an ancient ruin. "Ottavio will assistance you *domani*," he kindly offers.

"Grazie." I'm not about to turn down any assistance.

Ottavio drops Olivia's hand and goes over to feed the rabbits, Alessandro and Manzoni. It's a good thing, too, because I doubt Olivia ever remembers to do it, and certainly Bernard doesn't, at least not in his current state of bereavement. He can barely remember to feed himself.

"Now, Hallie, I don't mean to impose upon you," says Olivia. "I'm aware that you've just arrived home and surely want to visit with all of your friends. But would you mind keeping an eye on Bernard until we get back? After what happened the other night, I think he's still registering at a half bubble off plumb." She rolls her eyes skyward to convey the internationally recognizable signal for lunatic-at-large.

"Sure, no problem. I haven't made any definite plans." Although this isn't entirely true. The church poker game is tonight and a little walking-around money would be nice, not to mention the start of a tuition stake. Especially since I haven't yet come up with any great ideas for the design competition.

"Wonderful," says an appreciative Olivia. "Ottavio left some spinach tortellini in the refrigerator. There's plenty of greens to make a salad, and fresh bread from the bakery on the table." Bernard's bread machine sits abandoned on the kitchen counter, like a cold metal memorial to glory days gone by.

Olivia casts an eye at the skeleton of a rosebush that I've uprooted and thrown on the pile of dead plants to be bagged up. "Bertie has to come to terms with the fact that nothing stays forever," she says wistfully. "The flower fades to make fruit and the fruit rots to make earth. The roses of memory and the roses of song, they're the only ones that last, like the *Roses of Picardy*. How I miss Gil playing that on the piano. He has such a lovely voice."

After they leave I realize that I'm too exhausted to turn one more spadeful of dirt. If extreme gardening becomes an Olympic sport anytime soon, I'm certain that I'll make the team. Lying back in the cool earth I stare up at the canopy of trees overhead and watch the Easter-colored sky turn deep blue with approaching dusk. It's a perfect velvety spring evening—soft, warm, and serene. Yet my flesh burns with restlessness, as if a flame has been lit somewhere deep inside of me.

Gravel crunches in the driveway and Bernard's silver Alfa Romeo comes rolling up to the garage, a cloud of dust chasing after it. In the old days he would have been carrying armloads of groceries and singing his favorite line from *Funny Girl*, *When a girl's incidentals are no bigger than two lentils, then to me it doesn't spell success* . . .

But tonight he has only his leather account book tucked under one arm and glumly wanders over to where I'm sprawled in the dirt. Glancing around at the devastation Bernard remarks, "It would make a rather good setting for a Franz Kafka short story. I wasn't really aware the situation had become this dire."

"Don't worry," I say cheerfully and rise to a sitting position. "I'll have it back to the way it was in no time. Why don't you come with me to the nursery tomorrow and we'll pick out some plants and flowers." Planning the gardens always puts Bernard in high spirits.

"Oh, you go and buy whatever you think is best," he says offhandedly. "Besides, with this new client transacting everything by computer and phone, I need to straighten up my bookkeeping."

It's a well-known fact around the Stockton house that where

most small retail stores have two sets of books, Bernard has at least six.

"Heaven forbid I show a profit to the government," he adds. But it's a lame joke, and unaccompanied by his usual good cheer.

I stand up and yank off my mud-soaked gardening gloves. "Your mom and Ottavio went off to some Unitarian thing."

"Most likely the Pagan Pride Parade."

"Actually, I think it was a potluck supper followed by a lecture," I correct him.

"What a sight to behold those are," says Bernard. "They serve Heathen Helper and Gorp made by hippies in rural Maine and then hear from some benevolent anarchist wearing a batik jersey with hemp gauchos. Poor Ottavio is actually proud of the fact that Mother is a regular churchgoer, operating under the misconception that the Unitarians are the American version of Roman Catholicism—you know, *United* States, *Uni*tarian. It's doubtful that his English is advanced enough to understand that he's in with a bunch of liberal firebrands, confessional poets, and amateur clog dancers."

"Yeah, just this morning your mom showed me a *Christian Science Monitor* article labeling the Unitarians as a cult. Only she was *thrilled* by it, quoting Oscar Wilde—'There's only one thing in the world worse than being talked about, and that's not being talked about.' "

"She's stealing my lines," mutters Bernard.

"Ottavio left some tortellini in the fridge," I say. "But if it's all the same to you, I'm sick of pasta."

"I suppose we could scramble some eggs." He offers his heart-wrenchingly fatal Greta Garbo in *Camille* sigh.

I momentarily collapse back onto the ground from surprise. Bernard is suggesting *scrambled eggs* for dinner? He's finally convinced me that he really *does* need psychiatric help. "I saw a new Thai takeout place next to the hardware store when I was in town today and picked up a menu. How about something from there?"

"Sounds fine to me," he says and exhales heavily, like a tired horse. Bernard turns and walks toward the house without so much as suggesting *The King and I* for a theme to our dinner and singing a few bars of "Shall We Dance?" His stride is slack and indifferent, so unlike the step he normally uses.

I decide instead to pick up his favorite sweet-and-sour shrimp from the Chinese Palace. Maybe that will cheer him up.

When I return with the cardboard containers of food, the only culinary flourish Bernard suggests is that we use his ceramic chopsticks so as not to get splinters from the cheap wooden ones that come with the meal.

"Do you mind changing the music?" I politely ask. Judy Garland has been singing "The Man That Got Away" so much over the past two days that the first stanza stuck in my head the entire time I was working in the garden. Not even putting on my Discman with a Dido CD could delete it. All the melodies just started to sound like Judy singing: *The wind blows colder, And suddenly you're older, And all because of the man that got away.*

Bernard goes to the stereo and switches to "Stormy Weather," only it's still Judy.

"I meant something *without* Judy Garland," I clarify. "You know, just for a change."

"But I thought you *liked* Judy singing 'Melancholy Baby,' " complains Bernard.

"I do. I *do.* But we've heard it ten times in the past forty-eight hours," I argue. Not only that, but I've watched Judy Garland in the movie *A Star Is Born* with Bernard and happen to know that it ends with James Mason committing suicide by walking into the ocean.

"Then you go and pick something," says Bernard. "It's too depressing for me to see the gaps where Gil's albums and CDs used to be."

If I wanted to be mischievous I could put on the Ethel Merman disco album that Gil and I had given Bernard as a joke for his last birthday. It was recorded in 1979, five years before Merman's death, and it's, well, rather vibrato-laden. Bernard says that Ethel's "disco debacle" will stand up through the ages as the second-best example of why one should always exit while on top and leave your public wanting more. First prize, according to Bernard, goes to the final footage of aging film actress Mary Pickford, where she appears to have turned into a marionette.

Bernard seems neither pleased nor dissatisfied with his sweet-and-sour shrimp and side order of spring rolls. It certainly isn't like the old days when he made a big fuss about food. I playfully toss him a fortune cookie that he opens and silently reads the piece of paper inside.

"Come on, read it out loud," I say.

"Try something new and you will be surprised," he reads.

"You have to add *in bed* at the end," I say.

"What?" he asks.

"That's how we do it at school." I open my fortune cookie and read it aloud. "Others will benefit from your creativity," and then I add, *"in bed."*

Bernard laughs for the first time since I've been back. "I—I want to . . . well, to . . . ," he begins haltingly, "to apologize for being insensitive to your personal life the other night. I was distracted and just . . . out of sorts."

I take this to mean drunk and miserable. "Forget it."

"College guys really put the pressure on, huh?" he says.

"Sure, but it's not really that so much as I wonder how important it is to be in love with the first one, and how, you know . . ."

"What's the rush?" he asks. "Why be bothered with entanglements and the inevitable heartbreak? You're young, you should be having fun."

"Yeah, well some people consider having a boyfriend to be *fun.*"

"For a while. They love you and then they leave you, if they ever loved you at all. It's like embracing the perfect antique Coalport vase—hold it either too loose or too tight and it breaks."

Bernard doesn't seem to be in exactly the right frame of mind for discussing romance tonight. Though I'm impressed by how he's managed to draw a parallel between a shattered love affair and collectibles.

Reaching across the pile of duck sauce and plastic utensils I pull out the last fortune cookie. I pretend to read the little piece of paper but instead make it up. "If Bernard and Hallie leave right now they can get to the poker game on time." Looking up hopefully at Bernard I ask, "In or out?"

"You've gotta be in it to win it," he perks up slightly, parroting one of my old poker expressions. We stuff the empty food cartons in the garbage and head out the door.

"You drive," I say. "My arms are too tired to hold a steering wheel." And it's true. It feels as if they dropped off two days ago and no one bothered to tell me.

"But you hate it when I drive," he says.

"That's only in broad daylight, because you brake in front of every pile of trash, as if there could be a three-thousand-dollar lamp buried inside of it," I say. My only other complaint is that after the garbage has been collected and there's no longer anything roadside to capture his interest, Bernard tends to be an avid consumer of red lights.

Tonight is no exception. Every time we approach a light that's been yellow as long as we've been able to see it, Bernard hits the accelerator, throws his right arm across my chest so I don't crash through the windshield, and shouts, "Pink light ahead!"

Covering my face with my hands and peering out between my fingers I say, "I don't think this is what Kay Thompson had in mind when she sang the song 'Think Pink' in the movie *Funny Face.*"

Chapter
Twenty-two

As we drive over to the church with the car windows down it's possible to hear the almost continuous gasping of sprinklers that make the lawns glitter as if they're encrusted with tiny diamonds. The air is sweet with the breath of blossoming apple trees and in the distance a large tract of farmland slopes away from us into a horizon misted in pink and purple.

A clutch of tall, thin poplar trees stands near the front entrance to the church, their branches just grazing the slate-shingled roof. As we pull into the back parking lot I see three men in suits talking to each other while heading toward their cars. About twenty feet behind them, walking by himself, is a lean man with a long stride. He's tall to begin with, but made even taller by an Elvis-like pompadour of thick silver hair.

"Drive around the back," I instruct Bernard. "It's Edwin Carbuncle the Turd. I can't stand him."

"I believe you mean Edwin Kunckle the Third."

"I *know* that," I say.

"So what's wrong with him?" asks Bernard. "Why are you constantly casting nasturtiums on this pillar of our community?"

"He's a hairdo."

"Despite an affinity for extra lift in his already full-bodied coiffure, I'll have you know that Edwin Kunckle is filthy rich. And his wife, Patricia, happens to have a lovely collection of hand-painted Royal Copenhagen china and Lalique crystal that she's constantly adding to." Bernard says this dreamily, as if just envisioning a beautifully set table raises his spirits. "Patricia is one of my best customers and she also has marvelous taste in silver platters. When I was fourteen and Father still worked downtown he took me to an open house at their place one New Year's Day. I'd never seen such stunning interiors! And an expensive art collection, I might add. Though I think Mrs. Kunckle found it slightly unusual that I inquired about her sunflower clock from the Gold Anchor period and remarked that it was a masterpiece of British Rococo design."

"Please. You should see him at church," I say. "He wears a powder blue silk hanky around his neck."

"That happens to be an *ascot,* silly. He's very stylish. Look, that's a Burberry raincoat and a calfskin briefcase."

"Yeah, and what about the cane? Is that by blueberry, too? Do you use it to hit the bushes so the berries drop into your fancy briefcase?" I point to where Edwin the Turd is about to climb into his navy Lincoln Continental, which is so highly polished you can probably bake a blueberry tart directly on the hood in the summertime. "Or is the cane in case he suddenly has to perform a soft-shoe number like Gene Kelly in *Singin' In the Rain?*"

"It's a *walking stick.* And I'm not sure that *you* should be critiquing anyone's personal style." Bernard widens his eyes in mock horror at my aqua bowling shirt with REGGIE stitched in black thread above the front pocket and CARMODY CAR WASH stenciled on the back.

Bernard stops the car and before I can ask what in the heck he's doing, he rolls down the window and shouts hello at the Turd.

However, I know exactly what he's up to. Bernard is never one to miss a selling opportunity, not even a drive-by.

"Mr. Kunckle, it's so lovely to see you," Bernard calls out the window.

The other men, who'd been walking slightly ahead of Kunckle, quicken their pace and climb into their cars. And who can blame them for not wanting to be seen with the guy? My dad says that if you want to get in on the ground floor of anything that happens in this town, then Kunckle is the one you have to cozy up to. When Dad was on the board at church, Kunckle offered him a chance to own stock in some real estate consortium that bought up local farmland and resold it to developers from Cleveland. And even though Mom wanted to do it, probably with thoughts of a big new clothes dryer spinning in her head, Dad turned him down, saying the price was too high, only he wasn't talking about the cost of the stock. I took it to mean that Dad didn't want to be forced to run for Town Council or get on the zoning board in order to act as another one of Kunckle's flunkies.

With his path-clearing gait, the Turd approaches the car and greets Bernard in a friendly but reserved manner. At least until he spies me in the passenger's seat and scowls. Kunckle was on the school board when I dropped out of high school, and he happened to be the only member *against* allowing me to have a tutor and graduate early. Not only that, I'm positive he was the one who wrote that anonymous editorial published in the newspaper last year about wasting taxpayer money on social problems. The "social problem" in that case just so happened to be *me*.

"Mr. Kunckle, I believe it's your anniversary at the end of the month. There's a silver-gilt tea urn in the eighteenth-century Regency style down at the shop that Patricia has her ever-so-tasteful eye on." Bernard is at his most charming and using what sounds to me like a British accent. "It would be splendid for entertaining, which we all know Patricia does so brilliantly."

As phony as all this comes across to me, Bernard's amiability is quickly rewarded. Kunckle taps his sorcerer's stick twice on the ground and says, "Excellent! Call my secretary and have her take care of it." Then he nods his big poufy head, raises his pointy chin imperiously, and turns away—or rather, dismisses us.

"That's disgusting!" I say as soon as the window is rolled up.

"That's five hundred dollars!" crows Bernard.

"Would it be worth another five hundred dollars to talk in that fake accent at the poker game?" I tease him. "Since when did you become a subject of the British Crown?"

"Since I drank English breakfast tea this morning," says Bernard. "It has that effect on me. Just like watching the Queen open a new session of Parliament every fall puts me in the mood for Welsh rarebit."

We park the car in back and hurry inside the church and down to the basement. Bernard rubs his hands together as if he's about to rake in another easy five hundred dollars.

Chapter
Twenty-three

At the bottom of the dimly lit staircase the usual suspects are gathering around two card tables pushed together. The room is already filled with the aroma of potato chips and will soon reek of cigarette smoke from Al's Marlboros. His wife won't let him smoke at home and since they've banned it from government buildings, including the water authority where he works, Al makes up for lost puffs during the game. Pastor Costello is busy handing out runny deli sandwiches while Herb Rowland, the owner of the local pharmacy, is high-speed-shuffling the cards, anxious to get started.

"Well, look who's here—Hallie Capone!" says Herb. "Did you get an early release for good behavior?"

"Nah," I quickly retort. "Spending the evening with you counts toward my community service."

Bernard and I carefully thread our way around boxes and

rolled-up carpets stacked atop old wooden pews. There'd been a flood in the sanctuary right before Easter.

"Welcome home, Hallie," says the mild-mannered Pastor Costello. "And good evening, Bernard. We haven't had the pleasure of your company in a few weeks. I was going to stop by and make sure that everything is all right." Leave it to Pastor Costello to consider a pastoral visit for missing the poker game. Perhaps he smells a convert.

"Everything's fine and dandy," Bernard assures him, attempting a jaunty air.

I'm relieved, because if he's going to break down again this would be the moment, right when the father is doing his direct eye-contact greeting with the overly long handshake. That's when people are genetically programmed to lose it.

"It's been very busy down at the shop," explains Bernard. "A chain of old-fashioned diners has opened in the southeast and they're purchasing a large variety of décor items. Heaven knows you can't depend on street traffic in this town anymore."

"Tell me about it," grumbles Herb. "My drugstore is out of business if Valueland doesn't put their prices up. There's no way they can continue to sell below cost like this."

"They're probably only planning to take a loss until they drive you under," theorizes Bernard. "That's what the new supermarket did to the mom-and-pop video store. The supermarket rented new releases for ninety-nine cents. But as soon as Couch Potato closed, they suddenly wanted two ninety-nine—a dollar *more* than the video store had been charging."

When Officer Rich's earthquake footsteps are heard coming down the stairs, Bernard tenses, apparently embarrassed by the other night's drama. However, Officer Rich acts as if it's the first time he's seen us in months. You can always count on him not to mix business and a breakdown. And to keep people's private lives as exactly that, private. Officer Rich rarely comments on anything that happens while he's on duty, and when he does, he never mentions names.

Al Santora is the last to arrive and doesn't waste any time in lining up his ashtray, cigarette pack, and lighter. He also doesn't waste any time getting his digs in. "Look who's back from the big city! And were you *gamefully* employed all year? Have your professors taken out second mortgages?"

"I *wish*. I haven't sat in on a game of poker in months. All that I can find anyone playing at college is dumb old hearts."

"And Lord knows you don't have one of those," quips Herb. "Sorry, Father," he automatically apologizes for the out-of-context Lord reference. It isn't really a bad one, but we're all just in the habit, especially on church grounds.

Even though the stakes aren't high, the poker game is notoriously competitive. Herb gives the deck another shuffle, sets it in front of Al for him to cut, and then begins to deal. When I raise on the opening hand Al says, "Trying to clean us out the first fifteen minutes with a Broadway, huh?"

He is referring to the fact that with an ace and a king showing, I'm probably angling for an ace-high straight. And with the jack and ten in my hand, he's exactly right. "You have no idea how much tuition costs," I complain.

"Oh yes I do," Al shoots right back.

I'd forgotten that Al's son just finished his freshman year at Marquette University in Wisconsin.

Bernard has a queen and a four showing and Herb deals him another queen faceup. So much for my straight, since that's the exact card I'm missing.

"Another queen," says Herb. But then he apparently remembers that Bernard is gay. "I mean, a pair of ladies."

However, we all burst out laughing, including Bernard. Everyone looks to make sure that Bernard isn't just being polite, but it seems he's truly amused.

"It's okay to be straight, Herb," Bernard tells him with a twinkle in his eyes. "Just so long as you act gay in public." This cracks everyone up even more and I'm starting to believe that coming to the game was a good idea after all. Finally Bernard seems to be concentrating on something other than the breakup.

When Herb deals Pastor Costello an ace of spades it reminds me of playing hearts at school. It hadn't taken me long to determine that it was best to try and shoot the moon if you had more than a fifty-five percent probability of succeeding. The only exception is if you're playing with someone who's a shoot-the-moon addict. There are people in life who will always swing for the fence, no matter what the odds are. So when it comes to winning at hearts, it's necessary to hold something back in case you need to gum up your opponents' plans later on. And this is best done by insuring your hand with a high heart. In other words, if you decide to pass a couple hearts at the beginning, or play one early, make sure to keep a higher one in reserve, in case you need to cover a heart later on.

Holding back. It's the same strategy I've been using in my love life. Only I'm beginning to wonder if just because it's smart in cards means it's also the best strategy in life, when it's your real heart on the line. And your heart's desire may actually be an as-yet-undealt card. Though the way my luck is going right now, instead of the king of hearts, my next card will probably turn out to be a joker.

"C'mon, Hallie, pay attention!" urges the ever-jittery Al. "It's your bet."

He yanks me out of daydreamland. "Sorry." I toss in a blue chip worth ten bucks.

"Overbidding another low pair," Herb correctly guesses my strategy.

"Up the slope with the antelope," Al raises with one of his poker expressions that makes us all groan.

This raise scares off everyone except Pastor Costello, who stays in the game and manages to beat Al's three tens with an ace-low straight.

"Nice going, Father!" says Herb, who would rather see Pastor Costello win than the rest of us.

"Way to clean up!" adds Officer Rich, even though it's a relatively modest pot, but Pastor Costello never does anything but break even, so we all tend to cheer him on.

"Jolly good show!" says Bernard, and I briefly fear that surrounded by all these kings and queens he's going to slip back into British.

"I see they finally started work on the new entrance hall," Al says to Pastor Costello as he gathers up the cards. "Did the contractor lower the price?" Al works for the town and knows all about construction. Which is one reason his wife believes that he's at a Building and Grounds Committee meeting that's actually a build-a-better-poker-hand gathering.

"You kidding?" asks Herb. "Contractors around here lower their prices? When hell freezes over!" He turns to Pastor Costello and automatically says, "Sorry, Father" before continuing, "That would be the new *Kunckle* entrance hall—excuse me, *vestibule*—you'll be walking through." As a small businessman Herb is in charge of advising the church on finances, which is why his wife thinks he's also at a Building and Grounds Committee meeting tonight.

"Is the plaque going to be bigger than the vestibule?" asks Officer Rich, making reference to the stained-glass rendition of *The Last Supper* donated at Christmastime by the Kunckle family, where the plaque really was as big as the artwork itself, if not slightly larger.

"Attendance isn't what it used to be. I have to accept donations wherever I find them," says a resigned Pastor Costello. Though it's not a very well-kept secret that even he becomes tired of the Turd grandstanding at the opening of so many church functions and Edwin's twenty-one-year-old daughter, Edwinna, always getting solos, even though her voice could make an angel use its wings to cover its ears. "If I were a better poker player perhaps I wouldn't have to go around with my hat in my hand so often," jokes Pastor Costello. It's been two hours and Pastor Costello has the same thirty dollars in front of him that he started with.

"A gay waiter!" announces Bernard as he excitedly lays out his hand.

We all glance toward the stairs to see if one of his friends has just arrived. But the stairwell is empty and so we look back at him with puzzled expressions.

"Queens with trays." He points at the full house of three queens and two threes now displayed faceup on the table.

"I think you've been seeing too much poker slang on the Internet," I say, while the rest of the guys chuckle.

We finish the night with Bernard ahead twenty dollars, though this doesn't seem to thrill him the way it normally would. And I'm down forty-two dollars, which is unusual, but not a surprise, at least to me, since I can't seem to concentrate on anything these days.

"Looks like all that fancy book learning has drained away your natural instincts," Herb is quick to lay into me. "Be sure to come back next week." He happily pockets his sixty-something dollars in winnings, and for a second I don't feel so bad about his store not making any money.

Chapter
Twenty-four

"I REALLY SHOULDN'T TELL YOU THIS," I SAY TO BERNARD ON THE way home, "but you stroke your chin when you're trying to bluff."

"I do not!" However, he thinks back to when he had the two tens showing and scared everyone off with a big raise to make us believe there was a third one hidden in his down cards. And he lucked out because the other two were still hidden in the deck. "Hmm, maybe I do, just a little bit. I've always thought of it as part of my charm. But thanks for the tip."

"It's too bad about Herb's store," I say. "Just when he got back with his wife and the kids stopped collecting stacks of juvenile delinquent cards."

"Really?" says Bernard and perks up a bit. "Whatever happened to the young woman who worked at the pharmacy—*directly under Herb,* I believe it was."

Thank goodness he hasn't lost his ability for double entendres or his taste for gossip, or else I'd really be worried. Gil always used to joke that Bernard's answering machine down at the shop should say: *Hi, I'm out right now, but if you'd like to leave a rumor . . .*

"Her name was Jemma," I remind him. "I heard that she married some guy she met while on vacation in Antigua and then moved to Seattle."

"And so Herb crawled home and begged Mrs. Herb for forgiveness?" suggests Bernard.

"Hell no!" I almost add, "Sorry, Father," before realizing we left Pastor Costello back at the church. "Nina got so tired of him running around that she had an affair with the earth science teacher over at the high school." I recount the story Gwen had told me during winter break, including how she saw the two of them together at a Hyatt in Cleveland while attending her parents' anniversary party. And I mean *together.*

"Nina is such a charming woman," Bernard says about Herb's wife. "She recently stopped by the store to purchase a candy dish for her Waterford collection. I *never* would have thought she had it in her."

"Why is it so easy to accept a guy fooling around?" I jump right in. "But if it's a woman, then suddenly it's scandalous and *unthinkable?*"

"Will you stop it, already," says Bernard. "You sound just like Mother. Next thing you'll be going to that church of hers on Sunday mornings and insisting the money wasted on the space program could buy health coverage for every uninsured child in the country."

"I thought her church didn't have regular services during the summer."

"They don't," he says. "Which is exactly my point. They've apparently decided God trusts them enough to take the summers off."

Chapter
Twenty-five

WHEN I WANDER INTO THE MAIN HOUSE FOR BREAKFAST THE next morning, the bright and cheerful tune "Pick Yourself Up" from the Fred Astaire and Ginger Rogers film *Swing Time* is blasting throughout the downstairs. And though it's too loud, it's a nice change from mournful dirges and the medley of breakup songs from Broadway musicals, particularly "This Nearly Was Mine" from *South Pacific* and "What I Did for Love" from *A Chorus Line*. A person, even a yard person, can only take so much despair.

Despite the assault and battering on my eardrums, I immediately notice that the attack on my nostrils has vanished, and that the fifty or so white calla lilies have mercifully disappeared. Not only that, but the vile aroma has been replaced by the delicious smell of fresh cinnamon bread. The bread machine is back on!

Upon entering the kitchen I'm pleasantly surprised to find that Bernard is a new man, or rather the old man—specifically, his former self, full of vitality and quick with a smile. His trousers are neatly pressed, his button-down shirt is tucked in, and his socks are color coordinated with his loafers. The pink is back in Bernard's cheeks, and his blue eyes sparkle and appear even brighter because they match the blue of the threads in his silk vest. As he sprints from oven to fridge to pantry like a fruit grower after a hurricane, my first thought is that Gil has returned, and I actually glance around for a suitcase or some boxes. Only I don't see any.

Bernard begins singing "Hello Hallie," to the tune of "Hello Dolly," while thrusting a plateful of "Eggs Bernard" in my hands.

Then he announces, "I'm getting on with my life. The grieving period has formally concluded and the healing process has officially commenced. Now please come with *moi.*" Bernard marches me into the dining room, where the table is covered in fabric swatches, wallpaper samples, and paint chips. "I'm redecorating. No more of this maudlin maroon, Tyrian purple, Dubonnet red, and heavy damask." He gestures toward the living room with his right arm. "From here on in I want everything to be light and airy—cotton, linen, and perhaps a teensy bit of moray silk. We'll use carefree colors like ivory, taupe, shell, and maybe a pinch of lemon for accent. The Oriental rugs can stay, but I want Brasilia weave sisals for the front hall and also the summerhouse."

"Sounds good to me." I understand that recovery can be very project-oriented. After Uncle Russ had a stroke Aunt Vi stenciled the entire house, including the basement and the garage.

"And we need to add a new garden! Maybe something all in white like the one Vita Sackville-West had at Sissinghurst." He pauses to envision it. "No, I've got it! A hosta garden—Blue Monday, Curtain Call, Mississippi Delta, and Sunny Delight."

Ottavio and Olivia, still in their bathrobes, enter the room carrying cups of hot tea and plates filled with Bernard's fresh cinnamon bread.

"Buon giorno!" Ottavio gives us both a big smile.

"This bread smells delicious, Bertie," says Olivia, and kisses us both on the forehead. "It's been so long since you've made some, I can't resist it."

Bernard moves aside some of the fabric swatches so they have room to eat their breakfast.

"Are you working on a project for school, Hallie?" inquires Olivia.

"No, Mother," Bernard says gaily. "I'm redecorating!"

"I see," says Olivia, surveying the ocean of swatches. "Just like the Ottoman sultans—refurbishing while in a period of decline."

However, Bernard pointedly ignores this reference to his previous state of mind. "And not only that, but Brandt is installing a computer down at the shop. This way I'll be able to post all the merchandise on eBay. Myself!"

"Galileo!" Ottavio says proudly. Although Brandt may be useless when it comes to gardening and getting doors to stop squeaking, there's no denying he's a whiz with computers. He'd even set up a Webcam so that Ottavio can see his daughter and grandchildren in Italy while chatting with them online.

"Speaking of Galileo," Bernard perks along, "I thought that tonight we'd have a Renaissance repast—roast sparerib of pork arranged on the plate like an arched crown, wild mushroom pie, and almond fancy cake sprinkled with sweet rose water. And of course cider from barrels and wine from the vineyards." Then he practically waltzes into the kitchen for more coffee.

"That poker game certainly seems to have cheered him up," observes a surprised Olivia. "We haven't had a theme dinner since before Gil's brother passed away." She smiles broadly at me as if I'm the one to thank for this sudden turnaround.

And I wish I *could* take credit for Bernard's overnight recovery. But every gambler's instinct left in my body tells me there's something suspicious about the whole thing. Thinking back to the poker game I attempt a review of everything the gang talked about. Only it was the usual stuff—the high cost of hockey equipment, wives wanting expensive new furniture, and kids so overscheduled that they need to be dropped off and picked up every fifteen minutes.

"Yes," I agree. "He certainly appears to be much better." Emphasis on *appears*.

"I'm so relieved," says Olivia. "Because Bernard is in his prime and should be enjoying life. Hallie, you must remember to embrace your thirties. It's a magical decade between your last pimple and your first wrinkle. And yet we tend not to notice it since the majority of us spend those years chasing after toddlers or teenagers, which of course explains the wrinkles."

Bernard, with his seismographic hearing, reappears in the archway. "Speaking of toddlers, I have another announcement," he says, pausing for dramatic suspense before proclaiming, "We're going to have a baby!"

He must be referring to my mother. Did she tell Bernard about the new baby when she came over to talk to me about Louise the other day?

As usual, Olivia is the first to recover. "Won't *that* be something! When are you due?"

"Don't be ludicrous, Mother," scoffs Bernard. "I'm adopting a little girl from China. Everyone there wants a boy and so foreign adoption keeps the females from being thrown down the well. Won't everyone at your church be pleased!"

"I know all about daughters and infanticide," says Olivia. "But I think this is a bit extreme, Bernard. It's not as if you won't find another contemporary with whom you can share a loving relationship. You have a lot to recommend you—you're handsome, you have grace and style, and you're the sole proprietor of a thriving business."

"Oh, Mother, if I wanted unconditional love I'd get another dog. I want a *child*! Hallie and Brandt will go off and get married and have families of their own. And after you and Ottavio are gone I'll be all alone."

Olivia appears thoughtful and takes a sip from her teacup. "As much as you might like me out of the way, I have no plans to expire anytime soon. Otherwise, I think you should give it a few more months just to make sure. And then if you still feel—"

"Mother, when the doctor recently prescribed heart medication for you it was very traumatic for me."

"Oh Bertie!" scolds Olivia. "I don't *take* those pills, they're just supposed to be on hand if I suddenly feel short of breath. You heard what the doctor said—a lot of people have an irregular heartbeat."

"Well, it made me realize that we're not getting any younger, and the importance of family. I've given this matter serious consideration and I've never been more *certainement* of anything in my life. I'm ready to commit to a child."

But it's obvious from Olivia's expression that she's thinking of another definition of *commit,* specifically one that involves a rolling green lawn and visits on Sunday.

"How about planning a nice trip and then giving yourself some time for additional consideration," suggests Olivia. "I realize that you're a reluctant flyer, but there's always the train, or maybe even a cruise."

"I'm *not* afraid to fly," insists Bernard. "It's the reduced air quality on planes that I object to. It's terrible for your skin." He strides purposefully toward the front hall, as if there's a two-for-one sale on cloisonné happening out there. "And now it's *A* for *away*! There's an auction in Ashtabula that I should really pop in at." He waves good-bye, flashes us a big grin, and calls out, "Have a ball, and hugs to all."

Olivia silently butters her toast. I begin to say something but the words die on my lips. Ottavio looks completely confused. I'd venture to guess that in the small Italian town where Ottavio is from there's a good chance that single gay men don't adopt baby girls from China.

"Bambina?" he asks us searchingly.

"Apparently his clock is ticking," explains Olivia.

Which only serves to remind me that my clock is ticking as well. Ray is coming in a few days. Meanwhile, no call from Auggie. Of course, I hardly know him, and so it's not really as if he's a candidate for anything more than a date. But he did seem awfully nice. And still no word from Craig. His fraternity brother claims he's off in some swamp collecting plants to make mold. I suppose I should be happy to know that he probably won't be meeting a lot of women there. I mean, a swamp doesn't exactly provide the same opportunities as sketching nude models in an art class.

After ten minutes of convincing one another that we didn't hallucinate Bernard's announcement, Olivia and Ottavio go upstairs to change and I call Ray at his home in Cleveland Heights to find out what time he's planning to arrive on Friday.

"Howdy, country girl," Ray answers the phone after recognizing the area code on his caller ID.

"Hi, Ray."

"I was just thinking of you—walking out of the barn looking sexy in your coveralls with a piece of straw stuck in that gorgeous hair," jokes the suburban slicker, knowing full well that I live in a *town*.

This probably isn't true, that he was thinking about me, but nonetheless it reminds me of how charming Ray can be when I call and he's not in the middle of doing something.

"Hang on, I'm going to play this terrific new song for you. It's by that Swedish band you like." Ray is obviously in his car because I can hear him fumbling and accidentally honking the horn.

When Ray is interested in you he can be extremely attentive—remembering what you like to eat, your favorite music, and even the names of your friends from back home.

Finally it's possible to hear music, but it's mixed in with traffic noise. "I'm in my dad's convertible and it's hard to hear with the top down," he says. "I'll give it to you when I see you. Am I still invited out to Mayberry on Friday?"

"Well, yeah. I mean, that's why I'm calling," I say.

"And we're going to parallel park together, right?" Ray not so subtly asks *before* confirming that he's willing to make the ninety-minute trip. Apparently he doesn't want to waste any gas.

"I was hoping we could eat something first," I say. In other words, the answer is still yes. For some reason getting past this huge hurdle seems like it will solve my most pressing problems. First and foremost, allowing me to concentrate again, so I can figure out a way to make extra money before fall tuition is due. And let's face it, the front porch isn't exactly groaning from the weight of what Bernard likes to refer to as "gentlemen callers."

After I give Ray directions to the Stocktons', we talk about what

everyone else is doing over the summer and who is rooming together in the fall.

"So then, I guess I'll see you on Friday," Ray finally says. "What
should I bring?"

"Oh, we're all set. You know how Bernard loves to entertain," I
say. "Though he always appreciates a good bottle of red wine."

"That's not what I meant," says Ray. "I was thinking more along
the lines of edible underwear."

"No, that's okay," I reply. "We always have plenty of food here."

Chapter
Twenty-six

THE MINUTE DINNER IS FINISHED ON THURSDAY NIGHT I head to Gwen's house for my makeover. Or perhaps "suburban renewal project" more accurately depicts the enormity of her task. After ringing the bell, I enter the house and attempt to dart up the stairs past Gwen's mom, who is at her usual surveillance spot in the living room, in front of the big picture window.

As always, Gwen's mother stops me before I can reach the second stair. Mrs. Thompson is very much the leopard-print enthusiast and today she's sporting a wraparound leopard-patterned skirt with a matching headband, making her hard to miss against the sage green sofa. This is the part of the evening where Gwen's mom updates her records.

"I was surprised when Gwen said you were at last permitting her to give you a makeover," says Mrs. Thompson. "You're the final holdout. Even her father had to submit to a facial last month. And the dog now has a wardrobe for every season."

"Well, you know, she likes the practice," I lie. But I'm positive Mrs. Thompson knows just from looking at me that I've agreed to the makeover because I'm planning to have sex with my boyfriend. And it's for sure that Gwen didn't tell her. On the other hand, it's obvious where Gwen gets her highly tuned radar.

"Are you still seeing that boy who went to high school with you girls?" asks Mrs. Thompson. "I think his name was Craig Larkin, wasn't it?"

As if she's ever forgotten a name, car model, or license plate. "No, we're just friends. We both thought it'd be best to concentrate on our schoolwork for the first year of college."

She smiles as if I get credit for saying the correct thing but also as if she doesn't believe a word of it.

"Mom!" Gwen hollers from upstairs. "*I heard* the doorbell ring. Stop giving Hallie the third degree. Just ask if you can read her diary."

"I do *not* read your diary!" shouts back Mrs. Thompson.

Once I'm safely upstairs I ask Gwen, "Does she really read your diary?"

"Yeah, but it's a fake. I write stuff about what movie stars I have a crush on and log in good test scores. The *real* diary is hidden inside Grandma's old hatbox down in the basement."

Forget fashion, Gwen and her mom should open a mother-daughter detective agency. "It sounds like Bernard's bookkeeping system for his antiques shop," I say.

Gwen's room is a jumble of patterns, sketches, bolts of fabric, and half-finished outfits. There are three full-sized mannequins in various states of undress, and brightly colored silk scarves dangle from lamps, bedposts, and off the edges of mirrors like flags on a windless day. Gwen instructs me to go and wash my hair in her flowery-smelling bathroom, handing me a gallon jug of conditioner to rub into it that's actually for horses! Following that I'm supposed to run a comb through and let it sit for ten minutes before rinsing. "I'd better not wake up craving hay and oats tomorrow morning," I tease her.

By the time I'm finished with all that nonsense, she's cleared off a chair in the front of her 1,000-watt Hollywood-style vanity mirror. And Jane has arrived in her usual uniform of shorts, the polychromatic jersey of some Ecuadorian soccer team, and a Cleveland Indians baseball cap. She sprawls on top of Gwen's bed, and just barely misses redesigning her sweat socks with a pair of pinking shears tucked into the folds of the comforter. Glancing at Gwen's sketches of a fall clothing collection, which are taped above the headboard, Jane is her usual snide self when it comes to fashion. "I don't know how a person could even bend over wearing any of that stuff."

"They're clothes for going to *work,* silly," says Gwen. "Not playing sports."

"Then remind me not to get a job where I have to prance around in panty hose, over-the-calf boots, and a hat that doesn't have a visor," says Jane.

"Get the glue stick," I chime in. "I'm ready to apply that."

Gwen looks at us both as if it's difficult to comprehend how her two best friends from kindergarten turned out to be such total fashion failures.

I congratulate Jane on being accepted to Bucknell and she says, "Tell me it's true that they don't take attendance in college."

"One professor did in a freshman writing seminar. The rest didn't, but in design and computer classes they move through stuff so fast that if you miss just a few sessions you're sort of screwed," I explain. "Why? Is Just Call Me Dick the Attendance Nazi making your life miserable?"

"Let's just say that life was a lot easier when you kept him busy twenty-four/seven," replies Jane, who is in the habit of skipping first period on a game day in order to enjoy a big breakfast at the diner with some of her teammates.

"It's *Doctor* Dick now," chimes in Gwen. "How about showing a little respect."

"You're kidding!" I roll my eyes up so hard that my head follows them in a single whiplash motion. "He got a Ph.D. in *attendance?*"

As I'm imagining graduate courses on how to create the perfect seating chart and a thesis about advanced alphabetizing, Jane picks at the little tufts on Gwen's chenille comforter and says, "I guess Gwen told you about my parents."

There's no point in trying to pretend that Gwen didn't because we both know she can't keep a secret unless it means not telling grown-ups. "Yeah, I'm sorry about that," I say. "What happened?"

Meantime, Gwen has drawn a pattern for new and improved eyebrows over my old ones and starts plucking as I wince and occasionally yell out like I'm at a revival meeting.

"I don't know." Jane sighs and in a voice tinged with sadness continues, "All they'll say is that *'it's mutual.'* My father can hardly bring himself to speak to any of us and my mother goes around crying all the time. They used to be so in love. Where did the love *go?*"

"To become the title of a Top 40 ballad." I attempt to cheer Jane up. Only she looks as if she's going to cry.

Gwen deftly changes the subject. "Speaking of breakups, Hallie, what happened with Bernard and Gil? My mom says that Gil is living in Cleveland!" At least Gwen comes by her tracking skills honestly. It's apparently in her DNA.

"I'm not sure, exactly," I admit. "Although it would seem that Gil wants to date women. And I can tell you that it definitely *isn't mutual.* Bernard still really loves him."

"How can you still love someone after they tell you they don't love *you* anymore?" asks Jane, still preoccupied with finding the secret hiding place of love after it's been given a pink slip.

"I have no idea," I say. "That's graduate-level romance you're talking about. I'm only a freshman. You'd have to ask Olivia."

"Why would *she* know?" Gwen likes to be aware of any competitors on the information-gathering front, especially when it pertains to matchmaking.

"Olivia's a poet," I say. "She also writes pornography, because it pays a lot more than poems and she likes to have her own income."

"So call and ask her," says Gwen, always eager for dating tips. She tosses me her phone.

I dial the number for the Stockton house. "Hi, Olivia, I'm at Gwen's."

Olivia immediately wants to know if anything is wrong: She can do that—suddenly fall victim to a latent maternal gene. I tell her that everything is okay. "We—I mean my friends and I—we're just wondering, uh, how people fall out of love."

"Put her on speakerphone," says Gwen, and points toward the red button on the base of the phone.

"Wait, is it okay if I put you on speakerphone," I ask. She doesn't mind and so I do.

Then we can all hear Olivia's light, airy voice coming out of the phone on the dresser like an electronic oracle. "Falling *out* of love, you say?"

"We're wondering how couples that love each other suddenly stop, or at least one person does," I more or less repeat the question.

"Hmmm." She takes a moment to collect her thoughts. I doubt she was expecting to be ambushed right before bed by a bunch of teenagers doing their hair and searching for the meaning of life. "I'd say that people expect the passion of love to fulfill every need, whereas nature only intended that it should meet one of many demands."

"Oh," I say. "So it's a good idea to have some other stuff in common."

"I would say so," she heartily concurs.

We all three nod in silent agreement, not unlike the day Gwen's older sister told us where babies come from.

"Anyone have anything else?" I ask before signing off.

Jane moves up to the phone. "Why do people waste so much time on love in the first place if it just ends up making everyone miserable?"

"Good one," Gwen cheers Jane on, as if it's a game show.

"I'm afraid that human relationships are the tragic necessity of life, and yet they can never be entirely satisfactory because at the end of the day we're still just individuals," comes the voice. "Don't ever count on someone else for all your happiness, dear, whether it be a parent, friend, lover, or child."

"Deep," muses Jane.

"I'm going to put that in my diary," proclaims Gwen. "We should light some incense."

"I told you she'd know," I boast a bit. "Thanks, Olivia."

"Drive home safely," she says.

After we hang up the phone Jane says, "I know what we should have asked."

"What?" demands Gwen. "How to catch and keep the man of your dreams?" Gwen is always cutting those kinds of stories out of *Cosmo*.

"No, whether to spit or to swallow," says Jane, and then laughs dementedly.

"Swallowing is disgusting!" Gwen is adamant. "You can get a disease. And why bother when you can just fake it?"

"Because the testosterone might make me a better athlete."

"Where did you hear *that*?" I ask. "It's not the same as taking steroids. But we can look it up on the Internet if you want."

"Hold still so I don't poke your eye out," warns Gwen as she finishes my brows.

"And what about you?" Jane asks me.

"I gag. It isn't pretty." The fact that I'm not destined to be a great lover is quickly becoming obvious. Not only do I lack the patience and tolerance for the pain that beauty requires, but when I'm not chickening out on going all the way with my date, I'm choking to death.

Gwen starts combing through my wet hair, but at least with the conditioner there isn't the usual thicket of tangles.

"Next topic," I announce. "What *is* the story with my sister Louise's friends?"

"Oh," intones Gwen in a way that usually precedes unpleasant news. "That's a *bad* group. They're a lot worse than the burnouts in our class. For one thing, they all have cars. Eddie, the guy with the bronze Camaro, has a real mustache, and looks as if he's about nineteen. I don't know if he was officially held back or just doesn't go often enough to realize when a new school year starts."

"Your sister's definitely not part of the cheerleading mainstream," says Jane, who's knowledgeable about what goes on in the athletics wing of the building. "Most rah-rahs keep up their grades and plan on going to college. I mean, they can definitely be silly about guys and wear too much makeup, and I can't for the life of me understand why you'd spend your time *cheering* for a team as opposed to *playing* on one, but you know, overall they're okay. Only this year there are about four who are outliers, sort of rogue cheerleaders."

"Rogue cheerleaders?" I ask. "Sounds like the title of an educational after-school special, or better yet, a horror film—they make a pyramid at halftime and then release poisonous gas from their pompoms."

"For the most part the cheerleaders stick together—sitting in the same section of the cafeteria, pilgrimages to the mall on weekends," explains Jane. "You know, so they can get discounts on bras that make your breasts look perky." She grabs her boobs and pushes them together and upward to demonstrate. "Sorry Hallie, but I think the squad would be happy to get rid of those four girls, including Louise. In off hours they hang with the rats. And one of them has a brother who's in a fraternity at the U of Akron and they seem to have gotten involved with that crowd."

"Drugs?" I ask.

"Who knows." Jane shrugs her shoulders and picks up a well-thumbed copy of *Vogue* off Gwen's dresser.

"Come on, you can tell me," I say.

"*Honest,* I don't know. The Palmer women must just have some sort of mutinous streak."

Gwen switches on her industrial-strength blow-dryer and we can't talk above the high-powered shriek. After she finishes the hair and forces me at tweezer point to put on mascara, even I have to admit the change in my appearance is of epic proportions.

"I wish you'd bring Ray to the graduation party I'm having here on Saturday," Gwen urges me.

"Yeah," Jane says sarcastically. "I'm sure Hallie would much rather be playing volleyball and drinking grape Hi-C in your barn than getting it on with some hot college guy."

However, come Saturday, drinking Hi-C and playing volleyball is exactly what I end up doing.

Chapter
Twenty-seven

I'M SITTING AT THE KITCHEN TABLE REVIEWING MY FINANCIAL quagmire the next morning when the phone rings. Assuming it's Ray calling to firm up our plans for tonight, I pounce on the receiver.

"Hey, Hallie." Ray has the best phone voice, deep and soft, like running water.

"Hi back," I say. "So, what time are you coming?"

"My dad needs an extra on the golf course early Saturday morning to complete some big deal, so I'm afraid I can't make it," he says matter-of-factly. "And then I leave for New York."

"Oh." Apparently when your dad is paying for your brand-new car, college tuition, vacations in Acapulco, and summer at Parsons School of Design in Manhattan, it's kind of hard to blow him off.

"But you should come to Manhattan the first chance you get," he adds.

"Sure, Ray." I don't bother to mention that not everyone's parents give their kid a credit card and a travel allowance. And he doesn't exactly invite me in a way that indicates we're still a couple, either. I'd say it's safe to assume you're single when conversations end with "See you around, then," as opposed to "I love you" or "I miss you."

I'm devastated. But in a weird way I'm also relieved. When Bernard enters the kitchen I'm still standing next to the phone looking slightly deranged from this sudden simultaneous blast of yin and yang.

"As I live and breathe—conditioned and styled hair, designer eyebrows, and smooth, radiant skin! Let me guess, you've been placed in the Federal Witness Protection Program and altering your appearance was part of a court order," guesses the man with a headwaiter's eye for detail.

"Gwen needed a guinea pig," I lie slightly.

"And it's the night of your big date, if I recall correctly—what a marvelous coincidence!" crows Bernard.

"Ray's not coming," I say, and nod toward the phone.

"Oh, sorry about that." Bernard gives me a sympathetic pat on the shoulder.

"Bernard, how do you tell when a guy is lying about why he breaks a date with you?" It wouldn't be the first time Ray has changed our plans at the last minute, presumably to accept a better offer.

"Simple," replies Bernard. "You follow him around and find out, bringing along a pair of those night-vision goggles and some snacks. I've always liked chicken potpie for a stakeout. It's hearty yet easily transportable and stays warm for hours. But a shish kebab can work nicely if you don't mind eating it at room temperature."

"I'm not going to trail Ray all over Cleveland!" I say.

"Then when life gives you the lemons, take a lesbian to lunch," says a cheerful Bernard.

"*What* is that supposed to mean?" I ask.

"I'm not sure, but I *adore* the alliteration." He places several bags of groceries on the counter. "What about that nice boy from the pool hall you told me about? The one who writes short stories *noir* and counts using his fingers?"

"He never called," I say.

"So, we'll call him!"

"I thought *you* wanted me to get back together with Craig."

"I can't get ahold of him," says Bernard.

"Me neither," I say. "Hey, wait a minute! What are you doing trying to get in touch with Craig?"

"I merely want to ask him a question relating to horticulture, Miss Nosy Parker."

I'm the nosy one? Yeah, that'll be the day. Olivia is always saying that Bernard's autobiography should be called *Too Nosy to Die.* And I don't entirely trust him on the "horticulture question," either. It's certainly possible, but I think it's more likely that Bernard *did* talk to Craig, and found out that he's seeing someone else.

Bernard hands me the phone and begins singing, *"What good is sitting alone in your room? Come hear the music play. Life is a Cabaret, old chum, come to the Cabaret!"*

"It looks too desperate. I mean, *he's* the one who asked if he could call *me,*" I say. "And the number one rule in poker is never to chase the pot."

"Poker shmoker!" declares Bernard. "This is where my extensive knowledge of the theatrical arts comes into play. Now dial up this wagering parlor and trust Auntie Bernard to take care of the rest."

Why not? Nothing I do seems to be working out these days. I call Cappy's betting hotline at the back of Bob's place and when I hear Auggie's voice on the other end I quickly hand the phone over to Bernard.

"Hello," Bernard says into the receiver. "Yes, this is Bernard Stockton and I'd like to place a thirty-dollar wager on an athletic competition." After a pause he says, "An account? Well, I'm sure Hallie does and so I'll put her on the line."

I back away and wave my arms at him.

Bernard shoves the phone into my ear.

"Hey, Auggie, it's me, Hallie Palmer."

Auggie sounds thrilled to hear from me and I have to wonder if maybe he did attempt to phone but in his excitement got confused by all the numbers. A few of them were awfully high—the nines, for instance.

"I was just about to call and see if you wanted to go out tonight!" he says. "Isn't this incredible karma?"

I cover the mouthpiece and whisper to Bernard, "He was just going to call me."

"Tonight is fine," I reply to Auggie. "What did you have in mind?" I figure it's the usual teenage date—miniature golf or a movie. The league bowlers basically take over the lanes on the weekends.

"There's a poetry slam at a café over in Timpany," he says. "I went once before and it's lots of fun."

I agree to go and am about to hang up when he asks what Bernard wants to bet on. Whoops, I'd forgotten about that.

Turning back to Bernard, I ask, "What did you want to bet on?"

He looks at me as if I've lost my mind and shrugs his shoulders, body language for, *You think of something!*

"Okay," I say to Auggie, "he wants the number one horse in the first race at Belmont tomorrow." I figure I'll keep the numbers low and simple for him. "Thirty dollars to place."

"Place it on the one horse," confirms Auggie.

"Yes. I mean, no. *Place* is how you say to finish second. You know—*win, place,* and *show* are the names for first place, second place, and third place." Oh boy, Cappy would have had a stroke if he'd overheard this goof. And the local racetrack opens tomorrow!

Auggie reads it back and I say, "Right—thirty on the first horse to come in second."

"Who's on first?" chimes in Bernard, implying that we're on the brink of reviving Abbott and Costello's famous routine.

Finally Auggie asks for my address so he can pick me up and I promise to give him the money to cover Bernard's bet when he arrives.

When I hang up the phone Bernard looks pleased with himself and in his martyr voice says, "I seem to be one of those rare individuals destined to assist others in finding romance, but unable to help myself."

"Wow, I can't believe I have an actual date for tonight!"

"Now," says Bernard, "I've changed my mind about not accompanying you to the nursery. It's time to get these gardens going. And the birdfeeders haven't been filled since the Ashcan School painters organized their first group exhibition."

Before we head over to the nursery Bernard and I spend an hour deciding on the number of flowers and plants we need for the yard.

"I'm thinking Chu Hing-wah," says Bernard.

"I'm thinking *Bless you,*" I say as if he just sneezed.

"Very funny," comments Bernard. "Chu Hing-wah is a Chinese watercolorist who mixes modern and traditional techniques. He illustrates the Chinese preference for displaying plants in pots, instead of mixing them in a flower bed. So in addition to the regular gardens, I thought we could place long lines of planters of varying heights down the walkways."

"Lots of pots," I say, and make a note on my growing list of things to purchase at the nursery.

"For the plants I'm envisioning Odilon Redon, godfather of the surrealists." Bernard gestures toward the mesh rack that holds the kitchen implements as if it's been transformed into a painting. "A phantasmagoria of color, shape, size, and texture—flowers burning with an inner fire that makes them seem like an emanation of the life force itself."

"An inner fire like the emanation of the life force itself." I pretend to add this to our list.

Bernard sails onward like Auntie Mame planning one of her outrageous parties, heading out to the car while still calling out names for me to jot down. "Dinner Plate dahlias, tiny tot gladiolus mix, Japanese toad lily, and lots of vine, vine, vine—particularly Serotina honeysuckle and blue wisteria."

The workers at the nursery always jockey with one another to assist Bernard, not just because he's so knowledgeable, but he's always funny and enthusiastic. Joanne, the manager, insists that he must be in show business.

Bernard gives her his "Who me? Oh, don't be ridiculous." And then he proceeds to imitate Bea Lillie trilling her signature song:

"There are fairies at the bottom of our garden, not, not so very very far away. You pass the garden shed and you just keep straight ahead. Oh, I do so hope they've really come to stay!"

As usual, this impromptu performance sends everyone, including innocent bystanders, into fits of laughter. All except for the greenhouse bulldog, Wilbur, who starts whining and trots out the door as fast as his slow-moving legs can carry him.

Bernard also receives plenty of attention because he pays in cash and doesn't skimp on anything. By the time we've finished our shopping the order is so big that it has to be delivered. As the flats of plants, pots, and bags of soil are being loaded onto a large dolly, Bernard says with an air of satisfaction, "Yes, I believe this will turn their heads."

Their? It's at this instant I realize Bernard has a dual agenda with regard to his sudden interest in the garden. While we're waiting to pay he confesses that an employee from the adoption agency in Cleveland could show up at the house at any moment for a spot inspection. Apparently they don't make appointments because they're afraid people will spruce things up, hide undesirable relations, and create a false picture of how the home operates on a "normal day." I can't help but wonder how long it will take the agency to discover that *normal* is one of the few words that will never be used in association with the Stockton household.

After finishing at the nursery we decide to head over to Sears for a new hedge trimmer and a patio umbrella.

"Olivia seems pretty open-minded about the adoption," I say as I climb behind the wheel.

"Mother is so open-minded that it's a miracle all of her brains haven't fallen out," says Bernard.

Chapter
Twenty-eight

Auggie arrives at exactly eight o'clock and, rather than allow him to be inspected by the troops, I hurry outside the minute I hear a car churning up the gravel driveway. Only Bernard, ever the opportunist, comes flying out the front door before we can escape, and claims that he just wants to make sure that I have the thirty dollars for his bet. He knows darn well I have the money in my back pocket, because he gave it to me not even five minutes ago.

Bernard goes around the driver's side of the beat-up tan Chevy Cavalier so he can get a good look at my "gentleman caller." Auggie is dressed pretty much the same as he was that day at Cappy's, with his beaded necklace and worn black leather sandals, only now he has on a pair of black jeans with lots of bleach marks on them and a bright purple T-shirt with a green palm tree on the front pocket. His shoulder-length hair is tied back in a neat ponytail. It's a little strange to go out with a guy wearing a ponytail, since I have one, too.

Maybe we should have called each other first so that one of us could have done a braid.

Once we escape Bernard and the polite chitchat is out of the way, Auggie hands me a thin book with a red cardboard cover that has HARBINGER printed on it in black script. "One of my stories won a prize," he says, and then looks away as if he's suddenly embarrassed.

"That's great!" I say. And I mean it, since he's the only published author I know aside from Olivia.

As I open the book to find Auggie's entry, he says, "You don't have to read it."

"Of course I want to read it."

"Okay, then, but don't read it now. You can keep that copy."

"Are you sure?"

"Yeah, they sent me some extras."

In the table of contents I find an entry for "Thanatopsis Spoken Here" next to Auggie's name. "This is really cool. What is *thanatopsis?*" I ask. "Is that like a made-up language?"

"*Thantos* is Greek for *death,* so it's a sort of meditation on death."

"Oh. I guess death is really big in literature. I mean, Olivia knows lots of poems about death." Could I have said *anything* dumber? It's just that my nerves get all jangled up around Auggie, and as a result everything that comes out of my mouth seems to arrive with a side order of stupidity. Wanting to change the subject quickly I ask about the aluminum band on Auggie's wrist, which upon closer inspection appears to be stamped with a long series of numbers. "Is that so you don't forget your Social Security number?" I joke, and nod toward the bracelet. Though as soon as this gem escapes from my lips I'm suddenly worried he's going to think I'm making fun of him for having trouble with numbers at the office the other day.

"It's to protest the fact that our government is holding political prisoners without access to legal counsel and no set trial dates," explains Auggie while holding up his wrist so I can get a better view. "That's a prisoner's ID number, see?"

Actually, what I see looks more like an identification band that the National Park Service tagged him with. "Yeah, that's really cool. I get it now." I try to sound enthusiastic, though what I'm actually thinking is that this certainly solves the problem of what to get Olivia for her next birthday.

We can't find a parking spot in front of the café and so Auggie drives around the side streets until we finally locate a space. I had no idea that poetry was sweeping the nation. The inside is filled mostly with people our age, but some are in their forties and fifties, and a few appear to be really old, with white hair and a distinct lack of cosmetic surgery. There's so much body jewelry in the place, particularly nose, navel, and eyebrow rings, that you could easily clear out the room with a gigantic magnet. From strictly an investment standpoint, I would say that it's a good time to start loading up on scrap metal.

The walls are painted dark red and the ceiling isn't finished, so big silver pipes run overhead with lots of little black stars painted onto them. Otherwise the design motif is decidedly Spencer Gifts— lava lamps on the small tables, fuzzy neon black-light posters taped along the perimeter, and long strings of beads dividing the restrooms and the juice bar from the "performance space."

Auggie pays our cover charge and orders some kind of herbal nectar from a woman with short pinkish-blond hair who is wearing a T-shirt that says: BOMBING FOR PEACE IS LIKE FUCKING FOR VIRGINITY.

An overweight man in a *Sesame Street* sweatshirt and black beret takes the stage and begins shouting out a poem called "Stop the Jargon," with the title repeated after every line. Fortunately Auggie has judged a few of these competitions and is able to explain to me the system of Olympic-style scoring for each three-minute performance. He describes the first four pieces as neo-*Waste Land* thrilling, Hallmark drivel, anti-imperialistic, and drug-induced, which is apparently a shade different from drug-inspired. And I can't help but wonder what Olivia would make of the woman resembling a tall stalklike bird of the wading variety who finished her poem entitled "Self-Rape" by ripping her shirt open and exposing her breasts, which just happen to have a vulture with an undetermined wingspan tattooed across them.

After the winner is announced we stay on and have a cup of chai, talk with a few of the poets, and listen to a trio that combines zither, xylophone, and chimes. The resulting sound is soothing but also slightly eerie, like it would be good for background music in a biology lab if you were dissecting a fetal pig.

As we head back to Cosgrove around midnight Auggie asks me, "So what did you think?"

"It was different." I'd seen signs for these kinds of things around my own college campus but was always too busy to check them out. "It's nice that the people stayed fairly quiet and sober. I'm a little tired of everyone getting drunk at parties in dorm rooms and frat houses, with the stereo ramped up so that it blows out your eardrums."

Auggie pulls off the main road and drives down a dirt strip for a mile or so until we're overlooking an old rock quarry. There's a chain-link fence surrounding the drop-off, and at least twenty signs threatening to prosecute anyone who climbs over it, but the view is nice. The navy sky is embroidered with stars and moonlight spills through the windows and across our laps, turning everything silver and blue. Auggie slides a CD of Macy Gray's *The Id* into the stereo and places his hand on my hand. His smooth face, half-covered in shadow, looks as if it belongs on the statue of an ancient hero, and I surreptitiously tuck my lips inside my mouth so I can lightly wet them with my tongue in preparation for a kiss. My heart beats too fast for a moment, and then suddenly downshifts so that it's too slow.

I turn slightly in my seat to face him but Auggie continues to stare straight ahead as if listening to something far away.

"This is a pretty spot," I say in an effort to bring him back.

"Hmmm," he agrees. "It reminds me of Russia. If you come here at dusk you can watch the moon rise above the forest like a glorious memory. See, in Russia everything is much more about the past. It's not like America, where people are constantly looking to make money off the future, so that's all anyone cares about."

Whether one favors the past or the future, I decide that I'd really like to kiss Auggie in *the present*. However, just as I'm contemplating whether we'll end up at second or third base and Macy Gray starts singing *Hold me close cause I'm the most and make a toast to you and me, see that's the way love's supposed to be* . . . Auggie turns the key in the ignition.

"It's getting late," he says. "Grandpa has me starting early tomorrow. It's opening day at the racetrack."

So much for even making it to first. Total strikeout. On the other hand, it's a pleasant change to be with a guy who doesn't try to rip your clothes off on a first date.

"Listen, Auggie," I say, "it's none of my business really, but you shouldn't be in the bookmaking business. You love writing, and you're obviously good at it. So why don't you do something with that."

He concentrates on navigating the dirt road while I worry that I've made him angry. Finally he says, "Yeah, I know, I thought it'd be sort of fun to try it for a while. I imagined meeting interesting characters, the kind you read about in stories by Damon Runyon and O. Henry. Only it turns out that Cappy's customers are all just a bunch of bankers, doctors, and lawyers who can't go to the games or the track because they have to work or else attend their kids' baseball games and birthday parties on weekends. Plus I really suck at math."

"But you know lots of cool words," I say. "Like *thanatopsis*. And how you described the moon was really pretty."

Auggie nods as if to say that I'm right *but* . . . and I wonder if there may be a little more to the story than he's telling me. Is it possible he landed in some sort of trouble and Cappy is making him work it off? It's obvious from his car and clothes that he doesn't have much money.

"So what about you?" he asks.

"What about me?" I say. "The only way it would really make sense for me to work for Cappy is if I'm going to do it full-time. But after visiting you over in that cramped cave the other day I think I've decided to stick with yard work, at least for this summer. I guess it's no secret that Cappy isn't exactly known for his comfortable working conditions. Plus there's this contest where design students can win a scholarship by—"

"That's not what I meant," says Auggie. "Are you in love with anybody?"

"Oh! Not that I know of." Love? Who talks about love on a first date? However, my heart suddenly skips a beat at the prospect of the fabled "love at first sight." I don't count the time we met years ago at the racetrack since we both had braces. Yet I do think back to how I kept losing my train of thought in Cappy's office while I was with Auggie and the way I felt warm all over when it wasn't even that hot. "What about you?" While waiting for his reply I experience a strange combination of trepidation and hopefulness that makes me catch my breath.

"I don't know," he mutters more to himself than to me. But as he turns onto the main road he quietly adds, "Maybe."

Inside my head I suddenly start to hear Shirley Jones and Robert Preston singing the love duet "Till There Was You" from *The Music Man.* Though whether it's the tingle of excitement upon finally finding "him," or else a direct result of having lived with Bernard for too long, is impossible to tell.

Chapter
Twenty-nine

♥ PARTIES OUT IN THE BARN AT GWEN'S PLACE ARE ALWAYS TONS OF fun in an intramural sports sort of way, and this one is no exception. In fact, attendees have brought along their own soccer balls, baseball mitts, and especially kneepads for volleyball. It's common knowledge that a social gathering at the Thompsons' will *not* involve lying around a dimly lit basement and ingesting large quantities of vampire punch, which consists of whatever kids can steal out of their parents' liquor cabinets and serves as quite an eye-opener. Oftentimes a leg-opener as well.

Practically the entire senior class has turned out, dressed in shorts and class T-shirts with everyone's name printed on the back in tiny block letters. And all the players on the boys' lacrosse team have dyed their hair half red and half black to celebrate winning the state championship for the first time in the school's history. A few kids who formed a garage band back when we were freshmen crank out some rock songs at the far end, next to big rusty rain barrels and bags of oats. I have to admit that they've gotten pretty good since that first homecoming appearance, when the amplifier kept screeching and the bass player had to be home by eleven.

Seeing the old gang takes my mind off this latest series of romantic crises. And not having attended any graduation celebrations last spring, I feel as if it's my party, too.

At the center of the indoor ring Gwen's parents barbecue chicken and shrimp on their enormous grill while her aunt Sharon serves up the punch with mountains of red and blue sherbet floating in it. There's really no reason to have a server other than to make sure the punch doesn't get spiked. Gwen's folks obviously kept careful notes back in high school. Every twenty minutes her uncle Vernon heads out to the section of the lawn where the cars are parked to make sure that no one is drinking or becoming too intimate in a backseat. The rest of the time he's serving up the nutty buddy ice creams, and to get one you have to try to answer an incredibly stupid riddle.

Today my incredibly stupid riddle is: What's the only ship that doesn't sink? We all know enough not to give up right away, because Vernon is an elementary school gym teacher and if you quit he'll mark you for life as a person who "doesn't try." And more important, you will *not* get your ice cream.

"Oh, that's a good one," I say. "How about a submarine?" Usually two guesses makes you into a "tryer" in his eyes and then you can escape.

"Nice try!" he chortles. "Guess again."

"Yeah, c'mon, guess again," says Seth, who is waiting behind me for his ice cream and bad riddle.

"A hydroplane." It's the only thing that comes to mind.

"A *friendship*!" Uncle Vernon passes me the ice cream as if I've just won a hundred-dollar bill.

"I don't know where you get all these jokes," I say as if it's a compliment.

Seth leans forward and whispers in my ear, "From the first-graders he plays Simon Says with all day long."

However, Uncle Vernon has already started in on him, "What's the only dog with no tail?"

As I move away Gwen rushes over to get the full report on what happened with Ray. "Oh my gosh." She claps her hands to the sides of her face and looks into my eyes. "You're in love!"

"A *hot dog!*" Uncle Vernon gleefully shouts out from behind us.

"Whatever do you mean?" I glance down at my shirt and shorts for any telltale signs, though I don't know what they'd be other than some loose buttons or a broken zipper.

"I can tell by the glow in your cheeks," she insists and then looks over my shoulder and around the barn for the perpetrator. "Where is he?"

"Not here," I say through a mouthful of ice cream.

Gwen appears completely puzzled. Her radar for new couples is rarely wrong. "Then how—"

"He canceled at the last minute," I explain.

She sighs with disappointment but it's obvious that something is still troubling her about my appearance.

"There's another guy," I fill in the missing piece. Then the excitement pours out. "His name is Auggie, he's really cute and nice, and he's a writer. Just a year older than us, but from Dayton and so I doubt you know him."

"Wow, you work fast," Gwen says with admiration. "And did you two, you know . . . ," she says, and gives me a mischievous smile.

"Nope," I say proudly. "At least not yet. We're dating like normal people and then whatever happens happens. He's asked me out again—a picnic dinner in the park. Isn't that romantic?"

"You should have brought him to the party!" Gwen is wide-eyed with how stupid I can sometimes be.

"Oh, he has to work today," I say. "It's, uh, a family business."

Fortunately Gwen's mother pulls her daughter away to say hello to some cousins who've come by with a gift and I'm rescued from further interrogation. I mean, it's true that Auggie had to work, since it's opening day at the track and also the start of baseball season. But I don't exactly want to tell Gwen that I'm in love with a bookie-in-training. Especially after last year, when my penchant for gambling compounded all of my other troubles. It seems that as soon as any money goes missing, everyone automatically assumes that the person with a copy of *The Daily Racing Form* under her arm has something to do with it.

In the far corner of the barn, underneath the hayloft, Jane is talking to Mary-Ella and a few other people I haven't seen since last year's prom, so I walk over and join them while attempting to keep the ice cream from melting down my hand. The hayloft has always been the designated make-out area and the grown-ups have agreed not to go up there. I guess they figure the hay is so scratchy that no one will want to remove their clothes. And though some kids manage to sneak up a bottle of vodka, you need to be pretty careful about hiding it in transit because Gwen's mom makes sure to always have a good view of kids climbing up and down the ladder. For us it's a party. For Mrs. Thompson it's a fact-finding mission. And thus it's safe to say that if a couple does somehow manage to go all the way, there won't be any paternity mysteries.

I spot Brandt kicking a Hacky Sack around with a group of guys I vaguely recognize from the science lab, chess club, and Mathletes. Apparently Brandt's no longer a loner, but firmly established in the high-tech clique—kids off to colonize Mars, clone their pet hermit crabs, and write the next *Star Wars*. Their crack is to crack the genetic code.

Brandt jogs over to where I'm standing. "I thought you said you weren't coming to the party," he says.

Not surprisingly, Brandt had gone directly to his job at the community college lab after graduation on Friday. Then he left the house again before anyone was up this morning. Brandt is almost always busy with science projects, computer programs, and Trekkie conventions.

"My friend from Cleveland couldn't come to visit after all," I explain.

"So is he your boyfriend?" Brandt has a habit of asking personal questions as if he's taking a government survey.

Preoccupied with thoughts of Auggie, rather than my past history of dodging Brandt's advances, I say, "No, apparently not."

Brandt appears uplifted. "Maybe you want to go up to the hay-loft?" he suggests.

I must look horrified because he immediately says, "Just to talk. You know, to catch up. Back at the house I never get a chance to be alone with you."

Yeah, there's a reason for that, I think. And besides, no one goes up to the hayloft to talk. But Brandt is sort of sweet, with his watch that tells time on all seven continents and probably in at least three galaxies, and so I don't want to hurt his feelings. "It's probably better if we talk down here," I say. "There are a lot of people I haven't seen in a long time."

Brandt nods in understanding but his face looks more like I'd just told him there would be no more reruns of *Star Trek*—and not just for *The Next Generation,* but *all* generations. Then a pile of loose hay gets kicked over the side of the hayloft and lands on our heads, followed by a girl's sandal and a cascade of giggles from above. It seems safe to assume that *someone* is getting lucky.

Chapter Thirty

THE NEXT MORNING I AWAKE TO THE SOUND OF A LARGE THUD against the door to the summerhouse, as if someone has hurled a basketball or a dead woodchuck at it. The good news is that even though the sun says it's only about 7 A.M., I don't have a hangover, like after keg parties at school. About the most damage you can do at one of Gwen's heavily chaperoned soirees is a sherbet-stained tongue or else a sprained wrist from too much tetherball.

When I first open the door I don't see anything but grass and gardens. However, a loud sniffle directs my attention to the area next to the steps. Squeezed between the small cement porch and a forsythia bush is what appears to be the top of my sister Louise, hunched over and with shoulders shaking as if she's crying.

"Louise?"

She stumbles inside and curls up into a ball on the couch. It's obvious I'm the first stop after one heck of an all-night party, since her makeup is smeared, her hair is a mess and reeks of beer and smoke, and she's decked out in a skimpy top and Lycra hip-hugger pants. Though I suppose there's no need to be jealous, since my T-shirt still smells of horse manure and burnt marshmallows and I have a hunk of peanut stuck in one of my molars.

"Louise, *what* is going on?" I sit down on the couch next to the bed. "Are you drunk?"

But Louise only curls up tighter around herself and continues to weep.

"Are you hurt?" I walk over and gently pull at her limbs, checking for broken bones and other signs of an accident. Everything appears to be working, though she's definitely way too thin. Maybe she *is* into drugs.

Still no reply.

"If you don't stop crying and tell me what's wrong I'm going to have to call Mom and Dad."

"No!" She appears to panic.

I start to feel panicked as well. Where is the despicable wiseass sister who I know and love to hate? What could have possibly happened? I stand over her and go for the worst-case scenario. "Louise, were you raped?"

"No . . ." She turns her head away. "I mean, I don't think so."

Oh boy. Maybe I should call the police. No, she'd just take off. "Okay, you got drunk and something happened."

She nods her head yes.

"Something bad?"

"I don't know." She wipes her nose on her sleeve and I retrieve the tissue box from the end table and hand it to her. She blows her nose and then says, "I think I had sex with Tim."

"What do you mean, you *think*? Did he drug you or something?"

"Jell-O shots," she says, as if that explains everything. And if you've ever had the sweet-tasting vodka-loaded cubes, it does. Downing a dozen is like eating dessert. And throwing them up leaves a cool smooth aftertaste like gargling with shaving gel.

"We were fooling around and then it gets all blurry and I woke up feeling really sick. And kind of sore."

"Well, you were a virgin, right?" I say this hopefully. And thankfully she nods her head yes. "Was there any blood? Does it feel as if you had sex?" As if I would know how it felt. Because now it's clear I'm destined to become the spinster aunt, sewing dowries for all my younger and more desirable female siblings.

"I don't know." Louise resumes sobbing. "It happened in his dorm room. And the next thing I knew, Karen was dragging me out to the car because her brother needed it to go to work in the morning."

Louise goes into extra-strength distress. "*Hallie,* what if I'm *pregnant?*"

Oh shit, I hadn't even thought of that.

"Mom and Dad will *kill* me!"

Putting my arm around her, I say, "No they won't." However, I know that of course they will kill her. Actually, Dad will be torn between which to do first, murder the guy who did it or murder Louise for underage drinking and dressing like a tramp. But only if they find out.

"They *won't* find out," I say. "We'll figure something out. I'll help you, I promise."

"I don't want to get an abortion!" she howls through a cascade of tears.

"Louise, stop getting ahead of yourself. We don't know for sure whether or not you even had sex."

Then I suddenly make a connection—Olivia and her morning-after pills. This is exactly what they're for! "Louise, this happened late last night, right?"

"Yes." The waterworks are slowing to a trickle.

"Have you ever heard of the morning-after pill?"

Louise shakes her head to indicate that she hasn't. It's no wonder Olivia is always complaining about the lack of information given to young women.

"It's a pill that you take after you've had sex and it works the same as a contraceptive," I explain. "We have them here. I mean, Olivia does." It doesn't seem the right moment to go into details about Olivia's back-door pharmacy—how she imports the pills from Europe and makes them available locally because doctors around here won't prescribe them. Only it's not illegal because she gives the pills away to anyone who asks and doesn't sell them.

"But I can't tell *her* what happened." It's apparent from the way Louise's words are crumbling that she's about to start wailing again.

"Sure you can," I try to assure her. "She's very understanding."

"Hallie, she's the same age as our grandmother! Besides . . ." Louise looks down at the carpet. "It's embarrassing. And she'll yell at me."

I know from experience that Olivia isn't in the habit of berating her customers. If anything, it's just the opposite. She says it's a waste of time telling people things they aren't ready to hear, because "knowledge is of little use without wisdom."

"Okay, okay, I'll get it," I finally say. "Wait here."

Chapter
Thirty-one

Outside the sparrows are complaining in high-pitched voices and a blue enamel sky blazes overhead. The trees are thick with new leaves that throw complicated patterns onto the ground. Nature appears to have reached a simultaneous peak of beauty and chaos right alongside my sister.

I find Olivia and Ottavio finishing their tea in the dining room while Bernard is preparing to head off to the shop.

"Good morning, Hallie!" Bernard practically sings. "Was that Louise I saw going into the summerhouse earlier?"

Heaven help the person who tries to sneak something past Special Agent Bernard Stockton.

"I made a Spanish omelet that's big enough for the both of you. I'm keeping it warm on the top rack. Just be sure to turn off the oven." He nods toward Olivia as if she'll never remember, which she probably won't.

"Okay, thanks."

"There's freshly squeezed pineapple-orange juice and my own special sunflower-seed bread."

"Okay, thanks."

"Hallie, you appear to be a bit out of sorts," observes Bernard, who possesses the only known copy of the map of my nerves. "Rather like our old dog, Buster, after he ate an entire devil's food cake that I'd set out to cool. Is something the matter?"

"No, no. I mean, I think I need to talk to Olivia for a minute."

"Oh," Bernard's eyes widen with magnified understanding, as if it's a feminine situation in which he and Ottavio are *most* grateful not to be included.

"Why don't we go into my den?" Olivia gracefully rises and smoothes the folds of her skirts. With its accordion privacy doors, her den happens to be the only room on the first floor where you can't be overheard. At least unless Bernard is pressing his ear to the door, which isn't an unknown occurrence. He claims to be "naturally curious" the way others are natural athletes, thereby implying that the condition is an attribute or even a birthright.

Olivia sits down at the mahogany writing desk and smiles, as if I ask to have a private word with her every day. Meantime I stand near the door, like an anxious kindergartener down at the principal's office for the first time.

I'd planned on saying the pill was for a friend, but since Bernard has already spotted Louise, that would be pretty dumb. "I was wondering . . . I mean, if I could borrow some of those pills . . . because I think my sister . . ." Why did I say "borrow"? What is Louise supposed to do, swallow one and puke it back up so I can return it?

"Yes, I see," says Olivia, and the pleasant expression on her face remains unchanged. She opens the bottom desk drawer and hands me a little plastic packet with Italian lettering on the outside.

"She was afraid you'd give her a speech," I continue, without firm direction, "and . . . she's already feeling sort of bad. . . ."

"I don't traffic in lectures, just remedies that *should* be available locally. Besides, it's safe to say that when the old preach to the young we meet with the same amount of success as when the dead talk to the living." She hands me the typed piece of paper I'd seen her pass out with the pills so many times, but that I'd never before bothered to read. "The most important thing is that just like any other contraceptive, this is not a hundred percent," she says. "So please remind Louise to follow up with a pregnancy test."

"We're not completely certain that she even . . . you know . . ."

Olivia appears momentarily perplexed, but if she's curious she doesn't ask. And I'm sure Louise isn't the first girl to get drunk, have sex, and not remember it.

"Thanks for understanding," I say. "Louise is, uh, pretty embarrassed, and she'll be relieved that you don't want to tell her she was stupid and all that."

"Isn't that what big sisters are for?" There's a twinkle in her celestial blue eyes.

In the kitchen I pour two big glasses of juice to take back with me. It's a long walk to the summerhouse. I hate to sound like my parents but Louise truly does have to straighten out or she really *is* going to end up in a home for unwed mothers. And what is she doing hanging out with college guys? They're sex fiends. I think I would know.

Louise is lying on the daybed in the fetal position, quietly weeping. Unsure if I can pull this off, I take a deep breath and ignore her crying.

"Okay, I've got it." My voice is stern and I'm acting slightly plucky, like a British heroine, stiff upper lip and all that. "This should take care of everything. However, these are my conditions."

When Louise turns to look at me I'm amazed at how she resembles a little girl again, with her tearstained face, and her doelike eyes wide with fear. But I refuse to melt. "Every day after summer school you come over *here* and do your homework. If you don't want to baby-sit for Mom then you can make some money weeding the gardens." I sound just like all the grown-ups I hated so much in high school. "I need to spend some time finishing a design project for a contest that could get me a scholarship I *desperately* need." Honestly, I think, my sister has *no* idea how good she has it with Mom and Dad still paying for everything.

Louise appears relieved. Only she doesn't realize that I haven't finished with her yet.

"And I'm sick of these so-called *friends* of yours. For the rest of the summer if you want to hang out with people then I meet them first."

Louise rallies at this final injustice, which I take as a good sign. "Like hell you do! You're not my mother!"

"No, I'm not. But if you'd rather, we can call her right now and ask her what she thinks about all this."

"Oh, all right." She furiously pounds a fist into the pillow. And I'm relieved to see a glimpse of the petulant old Louise who once crazy-glued all my drawers shut.

I hand her a pill and she quickly swallows it, followed by a big gulp of juice. When she removes the glass from her lips the sun hits her full in the face. Now she appears totally wrecked, with dark circles under her eyes and her normally lustrous dark hair a stringy mess.

"Why don't you sleep here for a while," I offer. "I won't mow the grass until this afternoon."

She puts her head in her hands. "Okay, but would anyone mind if I take a shower first?"

"Not at all. Go ahead." And I truly wish that washing away this entire experience were only as simple as standing under a hot shower. She looks as if a chapter of girlhood has been closed by an unseen hand.

Suddenly Louise doubles over and clutches her stomach. "I think I have morning sickness."

"I think you have a hangover," I say. "Don't you dare barf on my bed. Those are Egyptian cotton sheets with a *very* high thread count!"

Chapter
Thirty-two

THE FOURTH OF JULY DAWNS CLOUDY AND GRAY WITH RAINDROPS spinning on the sidewalk like shiny silver coins. However, when you are truly in love for the first time in your life, the weather no longer matters. Nor does food or a broken lawn mower seem very important. All that I can think about is that Auggie called to confirm our date—a picnic dinner *al fresco* on Saturday night.

When I take Olivia's car to the filling station to put air in the tires it's obvious that the morning rain hasn't diminished the level of holiday excitement in town, which also happens to be celebrating it's bicentennial. A bandstand has been erected in front of the courthouse and festooned with red, white, and blue bunting, along with four enormous American flags, just in case any visitors from the Far East are confused about what country they're in.

Later this afternoon the lantern-jawed Edwin Kunckle will dress up as Uncle Sam, like he does every year, and on this occasion he'll be wearing a top hat. Though it probably has fishing weights sewn inside for ballast atop that Marie Antoinette hair situation. Kunckle will also make certain that he's standing right next to the mayor when she gives her usual speech about how a strong community equals prosperity. Not only that, he'll leap from his seat and clap obnoxiously when his daughter, Edwinna, finishes singing "The Star-Spangled Banner."

Everyone else claps, too, but because it's over. Edwinna chases some of those notes far and wide, and still only comes about as near to them as I've gotten to winning the Miss Universe Pageant. Meantime, at the back of the crowd a few of the boys will imitate the struggling (and monumentally busty) soloist to one another's great amusement, until a parent gives them an angry glance accompanied by a swift kick.

Following that the veterans stand and fire off their rifle salute. A rush of birds comes crashing out of the surrounding trees and usually a woman screams after one of them craps on her head.

Barring a torrential downpour, there will be a modest fireworks display over at the town park after sunset. My parents always stake out a picnic table and barbecue pit by noon, or as soon as they've finished watching the parade go down Main Street. My ultraconservative dad whistles along to "America the Beautiful," completely unaware that the lyrics were written by Katharine Lee Bates, who, at least according to Bernard, was a lesbian.

Meantime, singles and couples wander over to the bandstand to hear music, visit the beer tent, and maybe take a turn on the small wooden dance floor. Adolescents escape from parental surveillance at the park and sneak down to the bandstand as well. The girls do it to prove that they're too old for three-legged races and tug-of-wars. And the teenage boys go to cadge beer and light firecrackers.

It's the day of the year that Officer Rich says he dreads the most. Because no matter how many safety lectures he gives, there's always going to be a kid who blows his fingers off with an M-80 and another one who lands a rocket on a roof and almost burns down a house or garage.

By evening the sky has cleared and so I dig my old bike out of the garage and ride over to the town park to join my family. Olivia and Ottavio may want to take a drive later so I don't want to ask to borrow their car.

My brother Teddy has run out of sparklers and smoke bombs so he's pinching and poking the twins while anxiously awaiting the fireworks. The medium-sized siblings are cranky and tired from overeating and running around, playing endless games of tag with no discernible rules. And the little ones are asleep in or near Mom's lap, fingers still sticky and crusty dribbles of ketchup clinging to their shirtfronts. Mom is also exhausted, a result of making sure the potato salad and other perishables didn't get left out in the sun all day and from being pregnant. Dad gathers up all the bats and balls. To him the words *national holiday* are synonymous with "sports camp."

However, when the fireworks finally begin, everyone settles down, either lying back on the grass or leaning up against a tree, oohing and ahhing as the rockets explode in the sky overhead and bright showers of green, blue, red, white, and pink gently cascade back down to earth. Bernard claims that if there is such a thing as reincarnation, then Olivia is going to come back as a firework. (And that he'll return as Regency furniture.)

My mind briefly drifts to Auggie, as it's been doing a lot the past four days, and I wonder what he's doing at this very moment—perhaps working in Cappy's office, struggling to crunch a pile of numbers, or better yet, maybe writing one of his stories about death.

Eventually the grand finale lights up the sky, accompanied by lots of whistles, booms, and bangs. Afterward there's a big round of applause, followed by a rush to the parking lot in order to avoid being caught in the town's one traffic jam a year.

Chapter
Thirty-three

THIS TIME IT'S THE MIDDLE OF THE NIGHT WHEN THE SOUND OF crashing and banging awakens me. And now the noise seems to be coming from the shed. My first thought is that the lawn mower I repaired yesterday afternoon has started itself up like in a Stephen King novel and is headed directly for the summerhouse. My second and more rational theory is that a burglar is searching for some of Bernard's antiques. But then I decide it's more likely one of Olivia's late-night contraceptive customers who has taken a wrong turn. Though at the Stocktons' it could be almost anything. In fact, it was fast becoming impossible to get any sleep around here during the day or night.

I yank on my jeans and search for the flashlight I used to keep hidden in the drawer of one of the end tables. When I finally open the door I see a figure clad all in black and waving a shovel above his head while rushing toward me.

Back to the Stephen King train of thought. I scream and slam the door to the summerhouse. Then I glance around the room for a piece of furniture to use as a blockade, since the door only has a latch to keep it closed.

However, I already feel someone pushing his way in, quickly followed by Bernard's voice. "Oh, Hallie, I'm glad you're still awake!" He doesn't even take a second to apologize for scaring me half to death. "I can't find the cutters."

Breathing a huge sigh of relief I inform him, "That's because they're wherever you left them inside the house after making that huge arrangement of proteas."

"Oh yes, of course," he says.

Bernard has been doing at least one fabulous floral arrangement every other day in the hopes that the person from the adoption agency will unexpectedly arrive and see it.

"Why are you wearing a black turtleneck?" I ask. "And what are you *doing* out here? I thought you were a *murderer*! It must be three o'clock in the morning."

"Three-thirty," he corrects me, as if this is a perfectly normal time to be gardening. "I'm going to rescue a lily from the evil clutches of my horticultural nemesis, Mrs. Hortense Graham."

I'm aware that Bernard occasionally pulls a late-night "lily liberation," but I usually only find out after the fact, when I see the illicit booty in the yard the next morning. Gil was always his wheelman.

"I've pleaded with Hortense for years to sell me one of her Devil Star lilies," Bernard attempts to justify his foray into floral crime. "They're twelve feet high with white shooting stars and pointed crimson seedpods surrounding emerald green centers. And they bloom right into November! I've even offered to trade for one of my stupendous Casablanca lilies, or else give her an item from the shop." He becomes annoyed all over again just recounting his frustration over the matter. "It's not as if I'm going to enter them into a show or try to sell them—it's only for the glorification of our own private inspirational *jardin,* like Katharine Hepburn's jungle garden in *Suddenly Last Summer.*" Bernard could justify raiding an Egyptian tomb by convincing people how much better off the mummies would be with some fresh air and sunshine.

I follow Bernard into the house in order to locate the cutters for him. Olivia appears at the top of the stairwell in a satiny purple kimono-style robe, with her hair hanging loosely over her shoulders.

"On the way in or out?" she casually inquires.

"Out," whispers Bernard.

"Off to pilfer petunias?"

"Devil Star lilies," says Bernard.

"We've always depended on the bulbs of strangers," says Olivia.

"Can I go with you to steal flowers?" I ask, by now fully awake.

"*May* I go with you to steal flowers," Olivia corrects me.

"No, you mayn't," says Bernard. "And I much prefer the term *previously owned* flowers, if it's all the same to the both of you."

"But why not?" I ask.

"You're the one who insisted that you were going straight this summer," Bernard reminds me. "What if we're apprehended?"

"I won't be eighteen for another eight weeks, so I can't be tried as an adult."

Bernard capitulates. "All right, then you may be the driver."

"The wheelwoman," I correct him.

Olivia promises to send us lots of blues albums and Berlitz language tapes in prison before heading back to bed.

After fishing a black face-mask out from underneath the scarves and gloves in the front hall closet Bernard pretends to be Gloria Swanson in the movie *Sunset Boulevard* and barks, "Max! Get the car!"

As soon as I pull Olivia's Buick up to the door he jumps in and places a heavy-duty flashlight and two cell phones on the front seat, along with a trowel and several plastic bags. Bernard continues to impersonate Gloria Swanson and in his best stage voice announces, "This is my life. It always will be. There's nothing else. Just us and the cameras and those wonderful people out there in the dark."

"Are you ready for your close-up?" I ask.

"Almost." He takes the ski mask out of his pocket and pulls it on over his head. "Drop me at the corner of Sparrow and Thrush. If I don't need the stepladder from the trunk I'll flash the light twice and you'll drive back to the main road and wait for me to ring you on the cell phone for a pickup."

"How do you know where the lilies are?" I ask.

"I cased the place last week," explains Bernard. "I pretended to be soliciting for a theater donation at the house directly behind the Grahams' and persuaded the owner to show me her garden. The two yards are back to back."

"But you'll be the prime suspect when she realizes the lily is gone," I say. "Mrs. Graham is well aware that you want it."

"No one will know it's gone," insists Bernard. "There are almost a dozen Devil Stars back there and the selfish old biddy can't even see well enough to get her wig on straight anymore."

With the headlights turned off I watch the Lily Pirate hastily make his way across the Graham yard. Bernard disappears over the top of the fence, a smudge against the darkness, and then the light flashes twice.

I drive slowly back to the main road, park on the shoulder, and check to make sure my cell phone is turned on. A car coming from the opposite direction passes me and I say a silent prayer that it won't stop because the driver is concerned I have a flat tire or ran out of gas. This is one of the drawbacks of living in the heartland and having neighbors who view helpfulness as their full-time job. Whenever you're doing something you shouldn't be doing, especially at four-thirty in the morning, there's an excellent chance that a Good Samaritan will assume you're in distress and pull over to offer assistance.

Finally the phone rings.

"Hurry up!" Bernard pants into the phone. "Part of the fence caved in and the alarm went off. I'm heading for the corner."

Sure enough, a loud bell jangles crazily from the direction of the Graham house.

I speed back to the corner as the lights inside the house are going on one by one. Bernard dives into the car and pulls the door closed behind him. My heart is racing and I'm not sure I remember to breathe until we're safely around the corner. Though my life hasn't been all that long, I nonetheless experience a detailed review of it.

"Just turn the headlights back on, not the brights, and drive normally," Bernard instructs me between gasps, chest still heaving after his mad dash. The puffed-up plastic bag in his hand indicates he met with success. The alarm must have been tripped on the way out. "If we're stopped I'll simply say that we're getting an early start for an antiques show in Pittsburgh."

"We're driving away from Pittsburgh," I point out.

"Oh, yes, you're right. Then Philadelphia. I should have brought a normal shirt to change into. This black turtleneck is a dead giveaway. Gil always joked that we looked like the Bowery Boys."

Despite the tense situation, I can't help but register that it's the first time Bernard has made a reference to Gil without some sort of drama. In the distance a squad car with gumballs flashing and sirens blaring races directly toward us. "Should I pull over?" I ask.

"No," says Bernard. "They're probably heading for the house."

Even so, we're the only other car on the road in the middle of the night, and so I imagine we'll automatically attract suspicion. Just then a huge delivery truck comes around the bend on the main road at breakneck speed and rumbles past us. I hurriedly turn and get directly behind it. Miraculously, another Mack truck appears right in back of me. They must be traveling in a convoy.

"Perfect cover," I say. "We're in the rocking chair."

"What rocking chair?" Bernard quickly scans the side of the road for a discarded antique rocker that he might be able to resell.

"It means we're between these two trucks. We'll just go wherever they're going for ten minutes or so, and no one will see us."

Like a proud magician pulling a rabbit out of a hat, Bernard holds up a perfect red-and-green Devil Star lily, complete with bulb attached to the bottom. He turns on the map light so we can have a better look and I must admit that it's truly gorgeous and exotic-looking.

"*Wonder of wonders,*" sings Bernard, quoting from *Fiddler on the Roof.*

"Miracle of miracles," I supply him with the next line.

Bernard continues to sing in a robust though not entirely tuneful voice. And he changes the words, as he often does, to fit the situation at hand: *"Bernard took a lily once again, snuck it out of Mrs. Graham's private garden. I was afraid that God would frown, but like he did so long ago in Jericho, God just made a fence fall down!"*

After about ten miles of traveling seventy on the unlit narrow road on which you're only supposed to do forty-five in the daylight, the truck in front signals a turn into the acre-wide parking lot of Valueland. I continue on and in my mirror watch the other truck follow it into the lot. Floodlights are on alongside the massive store and a team of workers waits by the loading dock.

Another mile down the road I pull into an empty church parking lot and turn around. Before getting back on the main road, I look carefully in both directions to make sure no cop cars are around. Though I wish we had a police scanner to be sure.

"Looks as if we're in the clear," I say, and start in the direction of home. The predawn darkness gives way to a quick flush of pink in the east and the waking of the breeze in the tops of the trees.

"I can just see the staff at the adoption agency reading the newspaper headline," I joke. "Future father foiled filching flowers."

"This isn't just a *flower.*" He pats the bag as if it holds a diamond necklace. "It's a Devil Star lily!"

"I needed the alliteration," I say the way Bernard always does. "How about *bulb bust*? Having one of those grainy black-and-white lineup photos could save me money when it comes to submitting a picture for the yearbook."

"You're well on your way to tremendous riches," Bernard says confidently.

"Oh, really? And why is that?"

"Balzac said that every great fortune starts with a great crime." He nods at the bag and winks.

The evaporating dew makes a fine white mist that blurs the edges of houses and turns the landscape into an enchanted dream. The rolling lawns appear to be freshly laid green carpets and chirping birds rise above us into the pearl-colored air.

"So if Balzac is right, then where is *your* great fortune?" I ask. Bernard has been in the previously-owned-flower business for quite some time.

Bernard picks up his song from *Fiddler on the Roof*. "*But of all God's miracles, large and small, the most miraculous one of all, is that one I thought could never be. God has given you to me.*"

And I understand what he means—the boyfriends might continue to come and go, for us both, but we'd always have each other. Right then and there I decide that if miracles really do exist and they're only one per customer then ours is definitely a keeper.

Chapter
Thirty-four

FRIDAY EVENING BERNARD ARRIVES HOME FROM WORK IN HIGH
spirits after having made another big sale to his diner chain. While
singing "Doin' What Comes Natur'lly" from *Annie Get Your Gun,*
he hands me ten crisp new hundred-dollar bills.

"What's this for?" I interrupt just before the bridge.

"Seven hundred for services rendered." He wags his head approvingly toward the backyard. "And a little bonus for coordinating
transportation the other night."

Still short about twelve thousand for continuing education, I'm
in no position to decline his generosity. "Thanks."

Bernard picks up his song again as he heads toward the stairs.
*"Folks like us could never fuss, with schools and books and learnin', still
we've gone from A to Z, doin' what comes natur'lly."*

The words, along with the sudden influx of cash, serve to nur-
ture an idea I've only been toying with up until now. I have a little

over two thousand dollars saved from working in the yard, enough to buy the new engine for my car, which Mr. Shultze's friend has offered to sell me for two grand even. *Or* enough to stake myself at Cappy's poker game tonight. With its unlimited upside potential, the second option is infinitely more attractive. And if I blow my entire stake, which is how it often goes in Texas Hold 'Em, I won't need the car anymore because I'll be too broke to go back to school in the fall.

When I arrive at the pool hall there are mostly beater cars and rusty pickup trucks parked out front. However, around the back of the building I spot a brand-new gold Lexus SUV and a black Mercedes—not your typical choice of conveyance for local pool players.

Unlike the quiet afternoon I stopped by and talked with Auggie, tonight the room is filled with cigarette smoke and the smashing of solid breaks followed by the *clackety-clack* of billiard balls smacking and kissing and then skidding across the green felt and thumping into hard rubber. The players' jeans are smudged with blue chalk, and a cloud of dust hangs in the air under every long rectangular light fixture. Emmylou Harris singing "One of These Days" drifts out of an old-fashioned jukebox against the far wall.

A few women shoot pool but most are in attendance to cheer on their boyfriends, have a few drinks, and collect ideas for their next tattoo. I quickly thread my way through the dozen heavy wooden tables and head toward Cappy's storeroom at the back. As much as I'd love to run into Auggie, I decide that I'd rather not have him see me squinting over a pile of cards all night as our second date. Besides, the picnic is tomorrow.

Cappy must have been in his office, because we almost collide in the narrow corridor leading to the storeroom. He looks exactly the same, wearing his trademark boating cap, checked pants, and white patent-leather shoes, a cigar in his left hand and a stubby pencil in his right hand.

"Well, if it isn't the Calculator Kid! I haven't seen you since we fixed last year's Super Bowl," he jokes and gives me a friendly pat on the shoulder with his pencil hand. "Though I hear you ran into my grandson." There isn't much Cappy doesn't hear about, one way or another.

"Yeah, we, uh—"

"So how's life on the straight and narrow? Or is the joker back to being wild?" Unlike parents, just because Cappy knows about things doesn't mean he's angling for any confessions.

"The straight and narrow puts a person straight into debt is what it does," I say.

"I thought you would have given me a call by now." He pretends to look hurt.

"I'm calling now if you've got a game going on."

"Right this way." Cappy leads me into the renovated storeroom.

Sure enough, a game is starting up. Rod Green, the deputy mayor, is standing in the corner of Cappy's storeroom-turned-casino; already sitting at the table is some guy in a suit I don't recognize; and about to take a seat next to him is the dreaded Edwin Kunckle the Turd, his pompadour resembling a big swirl of silver mousse. The only apparent purpose this particular style serves is to soften the prominence of his ample nose and detract attention from tea-colored teeth.

"Hey, what's *she* doing here?" asks the deputy mayor. I assume because my dad works for the State of Ohio that Deputy Mayor Green is afraid I'll mention his little poker pastime to my folks.

"I guess she's here to play some cards," says Cappy with his bookie coolness.

"Well, she doesn't look any twenty-one to me," counters Green.

The Turd watches the conversation with interest. It's obvious that he agrees with Green. However, he's also a man accustomed to having others do his bidding for him.

"This isn't the Indian casino," says Cappy, which translates to *This is an* illegal *game.* "It's just a friendly game," Cappy continues, which means, *It's* my *game.* Cappy has the ability to effortlessly put people in slots like dropping coins into a candy machine.

I notice that Cappy uses one of the dealers from the Indian

casino, rather than let the players manage the deck and risk ruining a hand. As proprietor he would never dream of dealing, since it'd be like the owner of a restaurant filling the water glasses. And I haven't seen any sign of Auggie, so he's either off duty or Cappy has decided that running the poker game isn't part of his job description.

When I hand Cappy my fifty-dollar entrance fee he slides it back to me so that no one notices. I don't complain because at the racetrack I'd often run to the betting window for Cappy while he was busy calculating odds and taking last-minute phone calls. And back when I was in high school I'd helped him out in the office during a couple of busy playoff weekends. He'd paid me for my efforts, but he'd also made a nice chunk of change. So the free admission is more like an employee discount.

Along with the others I exchange a thousand dollars for poker chips. Then we all pull our chairs up to the table, which is outdoor patio furniture with a brown vinyl cloth covering the plastic surface, including the hole for the umbrella. Just before the dealer asks Green to cut, Al Santora charges into the room, breathing heavily, as if he ran the entire way over. Compared with the smoothly shaven and freshly pressed businessmen, Al, with windbreaker, baseball cap, and five o'clock shadow you could use to sand a floor, looks like an advertisement for a blue-collar guy.

I'm probably more surprised to see Al here than he is to see me. For one thing, his wife would kill him if she knew he was at a high-stakes poker game, for religious *and* financial reasons. Furthermore, with his modest salary from the Water Authority needed to support four kids, including one in college, I know he doesn't have any money to lose. Even a forty-dollar hit at our church game leaves him gloomy and faced with the prospect of some serious deficit financing. But Al pays his fee, changes five hundred dollars for chips, and an extra chair is brought to the table. Al and I nod to each other, as if to say, *Good luck*. Because we're both aware that no matter how experienced a player you are, winning at poker requires as much luck as it does skill, the same way that successful pool is a mystical combination of physics and geometry. Finally the game begins.

No one is more aware than Cappy that Texas Hold 'Em has

been around for years but only recently became popular as the featured game at big-money poker tournaments in Las Vegas, and then around the globe. When they started to televise the World Series championship with its prize money of over a million dollars, the number of entrants went up tenfold, and some journalist even wrote a best-selling book about it. So now everyone wants to play Texas Hold 'Em. It's quick and exciting and the money can change hands faster than gossip races through a small town. This is because any player can at any time put his entire stake into the pot.

The basic principle is that each player gets two cards that only he can see. The winner is the player who can put together the best five-card poker hand as a combination of his two pocket cards and the five open cards, so-called "community cards," on the table. However, rounds of betting are interspersed between the cards being dealt. And after each bet the players can either raise the bet, fold up, or call, which means matching the bet of the previous players.

The unknown player at our table turns out to be a businessman from Australia who goes by the name of Seymour. It eventually becomes apparent that Seymour seems incapable of bluffing and so his money leaks away slowly, like a tire pierced by a small nail. Meantime, it transpires that Kunckle isn't a fool when it comes to poker and knows his way around reading the rest of us. I have to be careful not to give anything away by scratching or squinting or checking my cards too many times. Al, on the other hand, is constantly fussing with his cigarettes, shifting in his chair, and rearranging his hand so often that it's impossible to determine what all the frantic activity actually means.

Cappy occasionally circles the room, even peering over shoulders to look at a person's hand. Normally that wouldn't be allowed if he were just a bystander. Players would be afraid he might give away their cards by an expression, or maybe even throw a signal to tip off an operator in the crowd. But since it's Cappy and he has a reputation for clean games, no one minds that he periodically checks on things. In fact, it's reassuring. Because Cappy knows every possible way to cheat, from switching decks in the middle of a deal, marking cards while the game is in play, to working the room with a partner. As a teenager he had a job as a busboy in a restaurant where magicians did table tricks, and Cappy managed to pick up more than a few of them. He can move an ace from his left sock to the eighth card from the top without you seeing him so much as twitch. So his patrols are a way of making sure everyone has the cards they were dealt and that nobody is playing footsies under the table.

For the first two hours the money moves back and forth mostly between Green and Kunckle. I keep folding, with the worst hands in the history of the world, and this eats away at my bankroll. Al goes up and down, not initiating any large bets of his own, but answering most bets with a call and sometimes a raise. Most of us have had to cash in another five hundred or so for chips by now.

Just when I'm convinced it's not my night, the dealer sends a double belly-buster my way—a string of five cards showing, 2-3-5-7-8, with two gaps, the 4 and 6, which happen to be my hole cards. I bet a little too aggressively, which scares off the wily Rod Green. But Kunckle and the others don't think I could possibly fill the straight and so they play right up until the last round of betting, when Kunckle, confident that his hand will prevail, calls for a two-thousand-dollar raise. This frightens off Al and Seymour, and I'm the only one who matches. With a little over five thousand now in the pot, Cappy watches intently from the doorway with a hint of a smile on his face. He loves action, especially when it's carving holes in everyone else's stomach while simultaneously filling his bank account. With games like this, they'll all be back next week. And maybe with a flush friend or two.

The Turd arrogantly flips his hole cards, displaying the pair of aces that, when combined with the one in the middle of the table, gives him three of a kind. I slowly turn over my four and six and he's flabbergasted to see the unlikely straight take shape when joined with the community cards. Yes, it's official. I'm the big winner tonight! Kunckle gives me a look with those piercing dark eyes that basically says, *I'll get you, and your little dog, too!* Obviously, it's not the money that matters, since, as Cappy likes to describe Kunckle's balance sheet, the man farts against silk. Edwin the Turd is simply a guy who isn't accustomed to losing. And from the narrowed eyes and clenched fists it's apparent that this upsets his digestion more than it should.

Al and I talk for a few minutes in the corner before departing. He's down about a grand and I feel a little guilty knowing that I took almost five hundred off him with my straight. But he just jokes about it, and doesn't act all grumpy the way he does when he loses at our church games. Who can tell, maybe he got a raise or inherited some money that his wife doesn't know about.

On the way home I perform a few quick calculations in my head. With the two thousand dollars from my folks, seven grand in financial aid, and now this five thousand, I would really only need another ten thousand dollars not to have to take out more student loans for the upcoming year. I'll make about four thousand working on the yard over the rest of the summer, and so that leaves me down six thousand. Whoops—forgot about the new car engine, which I'll tell Mr. Shultze to go ahead with in the morning. So I'm back to needing about eight grand. But if I win that contest, I'll be free and clear with regard to rent and tuition. Furthermore, if I could win *another* four or five grand playing poker, I'll be able to buy one of the good computers that can run state-of-the-art graphic design programs, and have a little cushion for real food and some desperately needed new front tires for my car.

Chapter
Thirty-five

♥ ON SATURDAY AFTERNOON I BIKE OVER TO BERNARD'S SHOP TO help him take digital photos of all his lamps and mirrors and post them on Internet auction sites. He must be indeed doing okay because there are lots of new items on display since I'd last been in the shop during my Christmas break.

Bernard dusts the white marble Parian busts and then arranges them for photographing on a purple velvet cloth. "No young people ever come in here," he complains. "What if I were to change the name of the shop from *The Sweet Buy and Buy* to *The Den of Antiquity?*"

"It sounds pornographic," I say.

"Exactly!" says Bernard. "People will be so embarrassed to have come in looking for smut that they'll feel obligated to buy something in order to remove the stain on their conscience as well as the perceived public perception of disgrace."

"Try again," I say.

Bernard removes the price tag from a dainty statuette of the Venus de Milo. "How about *Venus Envy?*"

"I think you'd be better off filling the Trojan horse in the window with free condoms." I plug in the battery charger for the digital camera, probably the main reason Bernard couldn't get it to work.

"You've been awfully smiley this past week," observes Bernard.

I hesitate to tell him that I've finally surrendered to love—because I feel the need to make absolutely sure first. My date with Auggie is tonight. And also, in view of his recent breakup, it's not the sort of thing I want to throw in his face, even though he seems to be well on the road to recovery.

"I won some money playing poker last night," I say to explain my newfound happiness. Normally I don't tell Bernard too much about my finances, since whenever I complain about going into debt he simply offers to give me some money, which I can't accept as long as I'm able to earn it. As it is, he usually rounds my hours up and finds reasons to add in little bonuses.

Bernard doesn't look entirely satisfied by my explanation.

"And I took most of it off Edwin the Turd."

"I see," says Bernard, as if he thinks there may be more to this story.

A long scarf with a brightly covered bird on a red-and-blue background catches my eye. "This is a pretty scarf!" I offer as a way to change the subject.

Bernard comes over, begins to artfully wrap it around my shoulders, and says, "It's a shawl, actually, from the Mauve Decade."

"The *Mauve* Decade?" It's a well-known fact that Bernard enjoys giving his own names to things. For instance, when he refers to *The Basement Years,* we all know he means the period in his life from age nine to eleven when Olivia home-schooled him to protest segregation in the local district. They worked during the mornings, and then when Olivia went out to protest, Bernard devoted his afternoons to performing Broadway musicals in the basement. It was sort of like Picasso's Rose Period, at least that's how he explains it.

"Honestly, *what* are they teaching you in art school for $30,000 a year? The Mauve Decade was the 1890s. A young chemistry student named William Perkin came up with an attractive purplish dye that he called by the French *mauveine*. His colleagues, scientists—what did *they* know—ridiculed it as 'purple sludge.' But then Queen Victoria wore mauve to her daughter's wedding and the wife of Napoleon III, Eugenia, Empress of France, also took a shine to the new hue."

By now Bernard has me all togaed up like I'm part of a Greek chorus. He turns me toward the mirror and smoothes out the fringe and then stands back to examine the overall effect. If Gwen could only see me now!

"Shawls became a necessity with the advent of the late eighteenth-century neoclassical sleeveless shift," continues Bernard. "The dresses were only wearable in Northern Europe if accompanied by a warm wrap. However, the truly priceless shawls were handmade in Kashmir in the fifteenth century." Bernard opens one of the many books about antiques on his countertop and points to a picture of a colorful wrap. Then he turns a few more pages and says, "These are copies that were later mass-produced in Paisley, Scotland; Norwich, England; and Lyons, France."

I raise and lower my arms like a bird getting ready to take flight and watch how the fabric catches and holds the light. There must be gold and silk threads in the material, because it practically glows. "Are they all this colorful?"

"Unfortunately not. I just picked up this one because it reminded me of Isadora Duncan, and, well, I thought maybe we could use it in one of Gil's theatricals. He'd talked about directing *Sweet Bird of Youth* next year." A tear forms in the corner of Bernard's eye at the mention of Gil and their old life together.

"Who's Isadora Duncan?" I ask, once again attempting to change the subject.

"Who is Isadora Duncan?!" Bernard clutches at his chest and pretends to fall backward into a Hepplewhite chair.

"Only the *inventor* of modern dance!" He rises and strikes a dramatic pose in the form of a swan. "I must insist that you drop out of that college at once! Isadora thrived between the Mauve Decade and the Roaring Twenties and was greatly influenced by the natural world. However, she died when her long shawl with trailing fringes caught in the wheel of a sports car."

"Oh, c'mon!" I say with disbelief. "She was strangled by a *shawl?*"

"You bet your sweet aster," he replies.

Bernard dashes over to his old-fashioned record player and puts on a 45. "This is 'Bye Bye Blackbird.' Isadora was famous for doing a dance inspired by the red poppies of her native California to this song. She was fond of saying that life is the root and art is the flower."

He begins to lead me in a bizarre series of movements not at all like the cha-cha or the Lindy, while gaily singing along, "*Make my bed and light the light, I'll arrive late tonight, Blackbird bye bye.*"

When the music ends I ask, "So is *that* who you're talking about when you say that something is Isadorable?"

"Exactly—a combination of garish but wonderful. Isadora insisted that no flower of art ever fully blooms unless it's nourished by tears of agony."

Bernard goes and puts on another record. "Just before she died Isadora danced and sang to this—'I'm In Love Again.' Then as the driver pulled away from the curb she cried, '*Adieu, mes amis, je vais à la gloire!*—Good-bye, my friends, I go to glory!' "

"I don't believe a word of that." *Honestly, where does he get these stories?*

"Google it!" Bernard is smug about having finally learned how to use a computer. "Or better yet, ask Mother."

Just then the squeal of brakes makes us both look up and rush to the front of the store. Through the big display window I see Officer Rich's squad car parked so close to the shop that the front corner of the passenger side is actually a foot up on the sidewalk. My first reaction when I see a police car is still to run in the opposite direction, and so I quickly scour my brain for anything I may have done wrong. *The stolen flower!*

Chapter
Thirty-six

DESPITE OUR RECENT BULB EXCAVATION, BERNARD APPAR-
ently has a clear conscience, and immediately goes to meet our
friend at the door. Although the stocky Officer Rich has only run
around the front of his car and a few feet across the sidewalk, he's
winded when he reaches the threshold.

"Olivia!" wheezes Officer Rich. "Just heard over the radio—
woman down. Your address."

"Down? Down where?" Bernard is clearly puzzled. It's obvious
that he doesn't watch crime shows.

"Unconscious!" I translate the radio slang for him.

"Ambulance to the hospital," continues Officer Rich.

"Oh my God!" Bernard digs into his pockets. "Where are my
keys?"

"Hop in my car," says Officer Rich as he heads back around to the driver's side in the determined jog trot that acts as a substitute for running among tub-shaped men.

Bernard flies toward the car while I lock the door of the shop and then jump into the back of the squad car. Officer Rich throws the switch on his gumball and hits the gas so hard that the car jerks forward and within seconds we're going seventy.

"What happened?" asks Bernard, his voice edged with panic. "Is she . . . did she have a heart attack?"

Officer Rich turns up the volume on his police scanner. "Don't know. I was a few blocks from the shop when I heard the call." He's still catching his breath and gulping air. "Thought I'd see if you were there."

The squad car squeals to a stop in front of the admission area of the new hospital and we rush into the building. Standing at the desk arguing with a stern-faced woman in a crisp light blue uniform is Ottavio. His face is beyond deep red and quickly approaching purple. Not only that, he's gone into full-blown Italian. Ottavio's hands are flailing around to accentuate his words and a fist suddenly slams onto her desk to serve as what must be intended as a punctuation mark.

"What happened?" Bernard shouts at Ottavio as we hurry toward him.

But Ottavio continues to rail in Italian and we can only make out the frequently occurring words *Olivia* and *marito*.

However, the woman at the desk keeps repeating what must be her standard instruction, "Please take a seat in the lounge area and we'll inform you of any news." She calmly slides a ballpoint pen behind her ear.

"Olivia Stockton!" Bernard says to the woman. "She just came in!"

The woman appears to be *very* familiar with the situation. "She's just asked for a priest."

"A *priest*!" Bernard's eyes grow so wide you'd think the woman had announced that Olivia is dead. "Where *is* she?" It's obvious from the way Bernard is poised to run that he doesn't think there's much time left.

And quite frankly, neither do I. Over Christmas vacation, when Gil was still home, we'd all watched the *Brideshead Revisited* episode that included Lord Marchmain's deathbed conversion. I'd always heard that the greatest sinners made the greatest converts. Just like reformed smokers.

"Are you a relative?" the woman demands to know.

The word *relative* throws Ottavio into another round of wild gesticulation and shouting in Italian.

"Of course I'm a relative," says Bernard. "I'm her son!"

"Intensive Care is down the hall, make a left, and go through the double doors." She removes the pen from behind her ear and begins to prepare a visitor's pass, but Bernard isn't about to waste the last moments of his mother's life waiting for a name tag.

He grabs my arm. "C'mon."

"Is she a relation?" the woman shouts after us.

"Granddaughter!" He yells this lie over his shoulder. We're already too far down the corridor for her to catch us. And it's now apparent that Ottavio is being denied admittance because he's not a family member. However there's no easy way to lie about him. With his darker complexion, thinning hair, and lack of height, Ottavio doesn't exactly bear a family resemblance. And this isn't even taking into account that he seems to have lost any and all command of the English language.

Before we're allowed to enter the Intensive Care Unit, a nurse hands us green paper masks to wear along with slippers in exchange for our shoes.

"Olivia Stockton." Bernard pleads for information as his nervous fingers fumble with the elastic on the paper slippers.

"She took a fall," the nurse calmly replies. This particular hospital employee appears to be much more compassionate than the woman at the reception desk. "She was unconscious for a few minutes, so we want to make sure there's no concussion. And also that the fall wasn't precipitated by a mild stroke or heart palpitation."

All I really manage to infer from these words is that Olivia is alive and will not be a vegetable for the rest of her life.

"First bed on the left," says the nurse.

We hurry through the double doors. It's easy to find Olivia for several reasons. There's only one other patient, and he's in an oxygen tent at the opposite end of the room. Then there's an honest-to-God priest sitting in a straight-back wooden chair next to Olivia's bed. And she's *arguing* with him.

The priest can be heard saying, "But the Bible clearly states that—"

Olivia cuts him off. "And the Bible also says to kill trespassers. So let's just put literal interpretations aside for a moment." She waves to us as if we've just arrived at our designated meeting place near the mall fountain. "Now, how is a woman supposed to educate herself if she's having babies all the time? I'm not suggesting we use abortion as a form of birth control, but—"

"Mother!" shouts Bernard. "I thought you were *dying!*" Tears flash in his eyes and he collapses onto the empty bed next to her. The nurse runs over, believing that he's fainted. The priest also rises, probably thinking the entire family is experiencing fits.

"I'm perfectly fine," says Olivia. "I was daydreaming and tripped over that little step on the way into the living room. You've arrived just in time to take me home." She pulls back the covers and begins to climb out of bed.

"Not so fast, Mrs. Stockton." The nurse places her hands on Olivia's shoulders and urges her to lie back down. "We need to keep you overnight for observation."

"That's ridiculous," says Olivia.

The priest takes me aside and whispers, "She's really quite addled. You should make sure they run some tests." He points to his head, the way we did in third grade to indicate that someone is crazy.

But Olivia is already up and searching for her shoes.

"Honestly, Mother, I thought you were a goner," Bernard says plaintively. "And that I was an orphan—all alone in the world."

The doors burst open and it's Ottavio—no mask, no slippers, and with the reception storm trooper in full pursuit. Like a good Catholic, he runs to the priest for sanctuary, grabs on to the man's shirtsleeve, and starts explaining himself. Only he's still yammering away in the mother tongue. Ottavio must automatically assume that all priests know Italian.

"What does *marito* mean?" I throw the question out to anyone, since it's the word most often heard.

"Husband," Olivia states matter-of-factly. "Ottavio is saying that if he were my husband he wouldn't be kept out like the milkman." She's located her shoes and purse and begins neatly pulling up the blanket on the bed.

That explains the repetition of the word *latte,* too. I kept wondering if he was trying to order a coffee.

"Mother, I really think we should cooperate with these people," says Bernard. "What if you have a spell during the night? Then what will I do?"

Ottavio momentarily reverts back to English. "How can she treat me like zis? Attsa no good!" He angrily raises and drops his arms with palms facing up, as if summoning the heavens. "*Non famiglia!* Hmph!"

"Excuse me," Olivia says tersely, "but *I'm* the one who had the accident." She waves the plastic hospital bracelet in their faces. "Now, would someone like to give me a ride home, or shall I call for a taxi?"

The nurse turns to me with her clipboard and says, "We couldn't quite get your grandmother's age."

"She's approaching sixty-five," Bernard interjects. "We're just not sure from which direction."

Chapter
Thirty-seven

OTTAVIO DROPS BERNARD AND ME BACK AT THE SHOP, AND BY THE time we finish up and drive home, it's almost six o'clock. Auggie is running around the front yard playing Frisbee with a large schnauzer.

"Oh darn," I say as we pull into the driveway. "I totally lost track of the time."

"You didn't tell me you have another date with him tonight!" exclaims Bernard.

"It just so happens that I do. And why do you sound so surprised?"

"No reason," says Bernard, though he becomes fidgety and I can tell he's up to something. Had he finally been in touch with Craig? Did Ray call? Is there something he knows that I don't?

Looking out the passenger window I see Auggie climbing the elm tree in order to get the Frisbee unstuck from between some branches. *"What?"* I ask Bernard. "You don't like it that he's, well, sort of earthy?" Gil was more L.L. Bean and Brooks Brothers, while for his own wardrobe Bernard favors Italian silk jackets, suede vests, and pleated pants with cuffs. And from the photo albums I've seen, neither Gil nor Bernard had ever been the long hair, goatee, and tie-dyed T-shirt type.

Bernard opens his mouth as if to say something, and then closes it again before any words have had a chance to escape. Then he starts again. "It's just that I think he's, well . . ."

"Well *what*?" I'm already late enough as it is.

"Well . . . gay."

"He is *not*! Why would Auggie ask me out if he's *gay*?"

"Maybe he doesn't know it yet," suggests Bernard. "It takes some people longer than others to discover their true selves."

"It just so happens that Auggie loves to read and write and think about things, and so I'm sure he would have found out by now!" I say defensively.

"How did it feel when he kissed you?" asks Bernard.

"He hasn't kissed me," I say, and stare down at the floor mats that are miniature antique carpets.

Bernard gives me an I-told-you-so harrumph and opens his door.

"But it's only because this is the *real* thing," I call after him. "And you'd better get your gaydar checked ASAP because it's seriously on the fritz!"

Having retrieved his Frisbee from the tree, Auggie comes jogging over to the car and introduces his adorable dog, Ivan, who is maniacally friendly. How could I not love a guy who has such a sweet dog? Auggie and Bernard shake hands pleasantly enough, though I know Bernard is on the lookout for "signs."

"Sorry I didn't call you," I say. "We had to go to the hospital and I wasn't thinking straight."

Bernard's head pops up like a prairie dog's at the word *straight*.

"I mean, I lost track of time," I say to Auggie, and then flash Bernard my best glare.

"Don't worry," says Auggie. "Your friends told me all about it."

He nods toward the house, indicating that he'd spoken with Olivia and Ottavio. "Glad everyone is okay. Do you still want to go on the picnic?"

"A picnic!" Bernard can't help himself. "How divine. And creative." He gives me a meaningful stare. "You two get a move on and I'll hold down the fort."

However, Ivan catches sight of Lulu, the Great Dane next door, and goes bounding toward the fence to greet her. Their meeting doesn't last long before Rocky comes racing out of the front door and angrily breaks up the sniffathon. With Rocky hooting and spitting at him, poor Ivan runs back to us for protection, his tail down and his exuberance temporarily demolished.

"He's protective of Lulu," I say, making excuses for Rocky.

"I think Ivan is the one who needs protection." Auggie kneels down and comforts the whimpering dog.

Bernard waves good-bye from the front porch while Ivan beats a retreat onto a blanket in the back of the car, safe from marauding primates. Auggie drives us over to the park at the edge of town. Most of the grassy area is used for Little League games, but a narrow creek runs along the back, bordering a stand of ash and maple trees. Beyond those are the old railroad tracks from when Cleveland was an industrial hub and shipped grain and steel all across the country. Nowadays, since the commuters have a separate train line to go from the city to the suburbs, the tracks are overgrown with grass, weeds, and wildflowers.

"Ivan is an interesting name for a dog," I say.

Thinking that he's being summoned, Ivan excitedly pokes his head up front and gives me a big lick on the cheek.

"After high school I spent a year in Russia," says Auggie. "It's been sort of hard to adjust to being home and so I thought a dog would be good company."

"Russia sounds like fun. What were you doing over there?" At the risk of being completely boring, I'm trying hard not to say anything stupid.

"I was in Moscow mostly, practicing my Russian and studying some of the great writers, like Tolstoy and Dostoyevsky."

"I'd love to see that famous museum—the Hermitage." Bernard has a book about it down at his shop.

"I went there!" enthuses Auggie. "It's in St. Petersburg. The museum is in a reconstructed palace, which is stunning, but it isn't air-conditioned, and so in the summertime they just open the windows and the breeze and the bugs blow past these million-dollar paintings." He laughs wholeheartedly at the memory.

So far, so good, I think. *We're talking, he's smiling, I'm having fun. Bernard is so off base on this one. Auggie's not gay.*

In the park we find a spot far enough away from the kids playing ball that we won't get hit, and close enough to the creek that we can enjoy the water but not have to share grass space with the hundred or so ducks. Auggie spreads a blanket on the ground and takes out some sandwiches and soda and opens a collapsible water bowl for Ivan.

As much as I'm sure that Bernard is wrong, what he said keeps popping back into my head. And though I know it's terrible, I try to come up with a few "gay tests" while we eat.

"Bernard and I were watching *The Music Man* on television last week, the old one with Robert Preston and Shirley Jones. Have you ever seen it?"

"Nope. Musicals are okay, but I prefer dramas—Eugene O'Neill's *Long Day's Journey Into Night* and Arthur Miller's *Death of a Salesman.*"

I'm not sure how to score that one, so I try again. "These sandwiches are delicious! Did you make them?"

"I bought them at that new organic food store on Orchard Street. I had one for lunch last week and it was really good. The barbecued vegetable protein tastes just like real bacon, don't you think?"

So there! He doesn't like musicals and he didn't make the sandwiches. Bernard is wrong, wrong, wrong.

"But I made us some peanut butter fudge for dessert." Auggie digs into his backpack and pulls out a tinfoil pack that immediately attracts Ivan, who runs over for a closer sniff. "It's really good."

Uh-oh, that's bad. "Great! I love fudge."

"My aunt and uncle have a candy store in Cape Cod and I've always spent my summers working up there. At least until this year."

That's fine, then. It's okay to know how to bake if you work in a business. It also explains why Auggie never visited Cappy when school was out. I mean, it's not as if he was off trying out for summer stock theater.

After we finish eating, Auggie says, "C'mon, let's take Ivan for a walk." We wander along the trail on the other side of the creek, where the trees haven't been thinned out. Ivan dashes ahead to chase squirrels and barks excitedly every time something moves through the undergrowth.

As we're walking, Auggie eventually takes my hand. Upon reaching the rusty old railroad tracks we stand and stare at the thousands of shiny buttercups that make it look as if a bright yellow ribbon runs straight across the countryside and then drops off the edge of the earth. Off to our right the sun is sinking behind the trees and filling the sky with bands of pink and violet light.

Finally Auggie turns and faces me and we look at each other for what feels like a long time. Leaning in close he whispers, "So is it okay if I kiss you?"

He's waited so long that I actually feel a thrumming sensation in my chest over the prospect of a simple kiss. And I can't remember the last time a guy *asked* if he could kiss me.

"Kiss away," I say.

Our lips meet for a second and then part just as quickly. I haven't kissed that fast since playing Spin the Bottle in seventh grade.

Auggie takes my hand and we begin walking again. "I'm sorry, Hallie, but there's someone in Russia who I'm trying to forget. And . . . it's not going all that well."

"Sure," I say. "I understand." But my heart plummets like a kite in a storm.

"I keep telling myself that I'm not in love, that we can't be together," he says, now sounding completely agonized. "I mean, what am I going to do? Move there permanently? It's crazy. And yet I can't focus on my life back here for two seconds. Actually, it's worse than that. I just don't seem to be able to care about anything else!"

"Wow," I say. "Sounds as if you *are* in love." I must sound dejected, because Auggie puts his arm around my waist.

"I'm sorry I asked you out," he says. "I just thought . . . well, I *do* like you."

"No. I'm glad you did. I like you too." I suddenly start to laugh thinking how *completely* wrong Bernard had been.

"What's so funny?" asks Auggie.

"Nothing."

But he looks injured, as if I'm laughing about him being in love or having tried to date me.

"Bernard thought you were gay is all," I blurt out and then laugh even more. "He can be such an idiot sometimes. According to him, if a guy so much as bakes his own bread then he's gay."

"I've baked bread," volunteers Auggie.

"That's what I mean." I throw up my hands. "And see, you're not gay." But suddenly I realize he hasn't exactly denied it. Nor did he give a name to this "someone" in Russia. I simply assumed that he meant someone of the opposite sex, like when Marion the Librarian sings "Goodnight, My Someone" in *The Music Man* and her *someone* is clearly a man. "I mean, you're not gay . . . are you?"

"No," says Auggie.

"Well that's what I *told* him." I shake my head and decide that this is the *last time* I'll ever take advice about guys from Bernard.

"Though I've been with some guys," says Auggie.

"*Huh?*"

"I've had boyfriends," he clarifies. "And girlfriends."

"Oh," I say as it slowly dawns on me. "You're . . . you're . . . bi."

"I guess," he says. "But I hate labels and just prefer to think of myself as a people person."

"Sure," I say.

"Does that bother you?" he asks.

"No. No, of course not," I say. "Why would it bother me? I mean, it would be great to have so many people to date, right?"

"That's one way of looking at it, I suppose," he says.

"Then, um, this *person* in Russia?" I ask.

"Svetlana," he says.

"That's a woman?" I confirm.

"Yes, most definitely," he says.

Only now I'm sorry I asked. I don't think it would have felt so bad to get beat out by a Sergei so much as a Svetlana. "It's wonderful that you're in love, honestly," I say, and try to make my voice sound as if I'd never really been interested in Auggie *like that* in the first place. It's not an easy bluff for me, after having thought that he's really and truly The One, but I think I manage to be convincing. I quickly start asking him questions about Cape Cod, since I've always wanted to go there.

Only it's hard to concentrate. Once again the elusive pursuit known as love resembles a game of chance. Any poker player worth his salted pretzels knows the good hands come along so rarely that you have to be prepared to bluff here and there if you're ever going to have a shot at eventually winning big.

Chapter
Thirty-eight

It's the second week of July and summer has officially settled upon the heartland. By nine o'clock in the morning plants begin to droop, birds cancel all but emergency flights, and not a single bee rises above the flowers. The pungent aroma of fresh mint fills the stagnant air around the summerhouse.

It's also the tenth time Louise is supposed to help me weed the garden and she tries to wriggle out of it by saying that if she *is* pregnant, it could be dangerous for the baby. Following the Auggie drama, I'm cranky and frustrated and in no mood for her crap. So after asking Olivia exactly how soon you can use one of these pregnancy tests, I hightail it over to Herb's drugstore on Main Street.

In the store windows are big, red-lettered discount signs that I've never seen before. Yet inside it's empty and quiet, except for some Muzak playing softly in the background. In fact, it would appear that Herb never replaced Jemma and now works by himself as both pharmacist and cashier.

"Hey, Hellraiser," he greets me. But it's with none of his usual sarcasm, more just out of habit.

"Hey, yourself. Business still bad?"

"I found this cooperative on the Internet—a hundred or so mom-and-pop drugstores buy in bulk so that we get the deepest discount possible, like the big guys." He unhappily scans the vacant aisles. "But that Valueland, I'm telling you, they're selling below cost and taking a loss. I don't know how long they can keep it up. In the meantime, they're definitely getting all the traffic. I'm just hanging on through customer loyalty. Only the kids coming up don't care about that. Same with people on a tight budget."

I head toward the aisle with all the women's stuff. Most of the boxes and bottles feature cover art with birds, wings, and big white swooshes. It's obvious that men were the first to get their hands on designing the packages for feminine hygiene products. Who else would have equated a menstrual cycle with the Age of Flight? Wouldn't featuring an armchair or a meatloaf dinner on the box be more of a come-on than a flock of seagulls?

There are at least five different kinds of pregnancy tests. I can't imagine how one is different from another. And they're all around the same price. So I finally choose the package *without* the smiling woman on the front of the box. And then I retrieve a bottle of chocolate Yoo-hoo out of the cooler in back.

The one neat thing about Herb is that he never comments on your prescriptions or purchases. He rings up tampons, hair dye, and hernia trusses as if they're shampoo and toothpaste. Same with itch cream and antibiotics. If I stop and consider it, he probably knows more about people in town based on what they buy than any lawyer, minister, psychiatrist, or even medical doctor.

And though it's none of his business, for some reason I don't want Herb to think the pregnancy test is mine. "It's not for me," I say as he puts the box in a brown paper bag.

"Right," he says. "It's for a friend."

He knows that I live with the Stocktons and I suppose it's pretty obvious that it's not for Olivia, Ottavio, or Bernard.

"Hope everything works out," says Herb. Then he takes a box of condoms from the display next to the counter and drops it into the bag. "Free gift."

Chapter
Thirty-nine

THE FOLLOWING MORNING LOUISE IS IN THE DOWNSTAIRS BATH-
room taking *forever* with the pregnancy test. I've been waiting outside the door so long that I'm getting nervous and begin to hop from
one foot to the other. Finally I order her to open the door before I
kick the damned thing down.

Louise undoes the lock and lets me into the cramped powder
room. She sits down on the toilet seat lid and proceeds to stare at this
small vial on the countertop while holding the crumpled page of directions in her hand. "It had better turn blue," she says with conviction.

But the tube is standing in front of the cabbage rose wallpaper
and appears to take on a pinkish cast, so we start shouting, "No pink,
no pink!"

Bernard appears in the doorway and asks, "Which team are we
rooting for?"

"Blue," I say.

"Blue! Blue! Blue!" Louise and I chant as if we're cheering the University of Michigan in the Rose Bowl, and Bernard enthusiastically joins us.

Olivia and Ottavio come downstairs to see what all the commotion in the small powder room is about. "Is there a flood?" she asks.

However, something starts to happen with the test and Louise's eyes grow wide and she raises her hand to indicate silence. Bernard whispers something to his mother and she in turn whispers to Ottavio.

Louise puts her hands together and quietly chants, "Yes, yes, yes." In a voice that's barely audible she says to me, "I think it's turning blue."

From his position just outside the tiny bathroom, Bernard grabs my shoulder. "*What?* What's happening?"

"She thinks it's turning blue," I whisper to him.

He turns to Olivia to pass on the news and then she tells Ottavio, as if we're all playing a game of Telephone.

"Yes!" Ever the cheerleader, Louise jumps up and down in victory.

"Let me see!" I push her aside. The indicator is indeed bright blue. "It's blue!" I yell. We hug each other and hop around like when we were little kids discovering new bikes on Christmas morning.

"Such a relief," exhales Olivia. "And isn't it wonderful that we no longer need to kill a rabbit like they did in the old days!"

"What's going on?" A sleepy Brandt staggers into the hallway. He probably didn't arrive home from the lab until his usual three in the morning.

"Nothing," we all say in unison. But the vial is sitting right on the counter for anyone to see.

"An experiment," I say. "Louise is taking science in summer school. Only we must have done something wrong because it didn't work properly." I quickly toss the test into the garbage before Brandt can manage a closer look.

"Oh. Well, maybe I can help," offers Brandt.

Louise looks at me with sudden panic in her eyes that practically shouts, *What if this* geek *finds out what happened?*

"Actually, that would be great, Brandt." I ignore her frantic eye signals *and* her foot stepping down on my toes. "Louise failed science and history. Olivia is already helping her with the history."

"No problem. I get an hour for lunch, so I can come back here between one and two every afternoon," suggests Brandt.

"That'd be terrific," I say.

"Thanks a lot," says Louise.

I'm the only person who knows her well enough to pick up on the fact that she means her reply to be sarcastic.

The other good news is of course that now Louise has run out of excuses to avoid weeding and watering the garden. And this is perfect timing, because the storyboard for the scholarship has to be in the mail by midnight tonight.

After hustling my sister out to the yard with a trowel and some gardening gloves, I sit down at the computer and work out a concept based on an idea Bernard planted with his story of how Isadora Duncan was inspired by the red poppies of her native California. Only I use pictures of buckeyes and other flowers indigenous to Ohio and get the computer to make them dance to Bernard's favorite version of the song "No One Ever Tells You" by Diane Schuur and B. B. King. At the end, when the flowers all take their bows, the camera cuts to the detergent bottle standing in the orchestra pit waving a little conductor's wand as if coordinating the production number. The metaphor is supposed to be the perfect dinner party—with food, wine, good company, and of course glasses without spots, so your neighbor doesn't have to pull you into the kitchen for a tête-à-tête. The last few frames show the detergent/conductor turn to the audience, wink, and say in B. B. King's canyon-deep voice, "Because no one ever tells you!"

Pleased with the format for the commercial, I spend the rest of the afternoon tweaking the graphics and synching up the sound. It's actually a relief when The Veal Fight breaks out, because I desperately need a break.

The Veal Fight used to occur so regularly that Gil had eventually abbreviated it to TVF. TVF happens when Bernard is preparing his favorite meal of lemon veal piccata with tomato bisque soup and garlic mashed potatoes. I can tell that it's starting when I hear Olivia's opening salvo, which is the recitation of statistics. And I've got to give her credit for research, because she uses new ones every time.

"A male calf born to a dairy cow is locked up in a stall and chained by his neck to prevent him from turning around for his entire life," Olivia lectures Bernard in the next room. "They inject him with antibiotics and hormones to keep him alive and make him grow. He's kept in darkness except during feeding time and then finally slaughtered."

"That's not what they said at my PETA meeting," counters Bernard, and I can hear him begin pounding the veal cutlets with his wooden mallet.

"Since when have you been going to meetings of People for Ethical Treatment of Animals?" demands Olivia, and I can visualize her hands on her hips. It's a good question, too, because certainly she would have seen him there.

"My group is different from yours," Bernard teases his mother. "Our PETA stands for People Enjoying Tasty Animals. We serve Beef Wellington made with lots of veal pâté or a tasty Butterfield leg of lamb topped with herbed mayonnaise."

Olivia storms out of the kitchen and into the den, where I'm using her computer. She throws up her arms and starts haranguing me. "Did you know that our modern dairy cow lives with an unnaturally swelled and sensitive udder, is likely never to be allowed out of her stall, is milked up to three times a day, and is kept pregnant nearly all of her abbreviated life?"

Looking up from the computer screen I say, "Uh, actually I didn't."

"Her young are usually taken from her immediately after birth," continues an agitated Olivia.

Bernard pokes his head into the den. "Vegetables are alive, too. They're just easier to catch." He disappears back into the kitchen.

"Do you want to see my detergent ad?" I ask in an effort to calm her down.

"Of course." Fortunately it's easy to distract her with anything creative. Olivia pulls up the other chair.

"All the frames haven't been run together yet, but here's what it will look like, more or less." I click through them in time to the music so it resembles a slow-motion cartoon book.

"That's wonderful, Hallie!" Olivia claps her hands with obvious delight. "I adore the way you used a delphinium as the bass player."

I explain how you're supposed to get the feeling of a perfectly coordinated event, like one of Bernard's dinner parties.

"One without veal or lamb," she quickly adds.

"Of course," I say. "All vegetarian."

"A meatless diet yields forty percent lower risk of cancer," she says. "Maybe you can work *that* into your commercial."

Chapter
Forty

TRUE TO THEIR WORD, THE ADOPTION AGENCY DOESN'T GIVE YOU an opportunity to flush your drugs down the toilet or hide your chimpanzee in the neighbor's garage. On a Friday five weeks after Bernard's announcement about adopting a baby, a woman with a briefcase full of paperwork unexpectedly shows up for a spot inspection.

Her name is Mrs. Farley. She's shaped like a Bartlett pear but is efficient-looking, with a dark brown helmet of hair and crepe-soled shoes that I imagine are good for examining those hard-to-reach places, the ones where babies inevitably ferret out the poisons and peeling lead paint.

She peers hard at me and then glances down at her clipboard. "Hallie Palmer?" Mrs. Farley inquires as if she's taking attendance.

"Present and accounted for," I say.

"According to my records, Bernard Stockton is your legal

guardian. He's applying to adopt a baby and therefore I need to ask you a few questions."

"Sure," I reply. "Fire away." I can't help but take pride in how I've risen up in the world—going from local juvenile delinquent to official reference in the short space of twelve months.

The legal paperwork signed to make Bernard the guardian for me and also Brandt was really only completed in case we ever need emergency appendectomies, but apparently the adoption people award points for this and classify him as a foster parent.

"Has Mr. Stockton provided a nurturing home environment for you?"

"Yes, very nurturing, and nutritional, too. He taught me to cook and I can make orange roughy, tarragon chicken salad, and Pompey's head—a roll of ground meat in a tomato and green pepper sauce, named for the Roman general Pompey the Great, who was known for having an exceptionally broad head. Bernard demonstrated that recipe last year when Olivia and I were reading *Julius Caesar* together."

"Oh really?" asks Mrs. Farley, as if she's not quite sure whether this is some sort of put-on.

"Yes, and I almost forgot, *schiacciata con l'uva.*"

She appears puzzled.

"Tuscan grape bread."

"Of course." Mrs. Farley appears slightly stunned by my recitation, but now smiles approvingly. However, when she looks down at my mud-streaked legs it's obvious there is some concern over whether we have indoor plumbing.

"And I work in the garden."

"I see." She makes a note on her clipboard and I'm pretty sure it's a positive one, as if this wholesome outdoor exposure has contributed to making me a responsible and productive member of society.

It's a good thing she didn't see the yard six weeks earlier, because it was the kind of jungle where a toddler could have been lost for good. But now most of the perennials have found their way up through the soil, including a border of pretty pink and white tulips,

and along the fence shy red and purple petunias have begun to unfold. The rose garden also looks presentable after being dug out
from under two tons of leaves and dead weeds like a lost continent.
And I take it as a direct compliment that the bumblebees have returned to carefully work over the unfolding petals.

It's pretty much a one-way conversation, with Mrs. Farley asking the type of sensible questions that perfectly match her outfit.
There doesn't seem to be any point in inquiring about *her* childhood,
since it's pretty obvious that she was born a middle-aged woman.
And I'm careful not to mention that I've recently become a sex maniac.

When we're finished she tells me that she also needs to interview
Brandt. By a fortunate coincidence the lab where Brandt works is
being painted and it's the one time he's actually at home all day. We
head from the living room into the kitchen. When Mrs. Farley
walks, her stiff denim dress moves in the opposite direction of her
hips, and oval-shaped perspiration stains are visible under her arms.

The fact that Louise and Brandt happen to be sitting at the
kitchen table doing science homework when Mrs. Farley enters is
obviously a major coup. Not only that, but it's easy to tell that Brandt
actually enjoys science. He's using a bowl of ice cubes and a pitcher
of water to demonstrate the weight of a liquid versus a solid. And
when Louise eventually gets a right answer, an observer would assume they'd just won the lottery from all the cheering and clapping.
Wow, I think to myself, *we couldn't have scripted this scene any better
for one of Gil's plays.*

Mrs. Farley is also pleased by the fact that Olivia is a certified
teacher. Though she definitely doesn't get a chance to see Olivia in
action. Because on that score Bernard *did* prepare in advance. He has
repeatedly warned his mother to act normal and not initiate any discussions on subjects such as how Lord Byron's sleeping with his
nanny at the tender age of nine and then later having an affair with
his sister may have influenced his poetry. Olivia's also not supposed
to ask anyone from the agency to sign her latest petition to save the
small-scale Latin American coffee and cocoa farmers from being
squeezed out of the global marketplace by multinational companies.

Likewise, in his attempt to refashion her into a potential doting grandmother, he doesn't mention anything about Olivia not being allowed to cook. Bernard once confided to me that when he was young and she made dinner for the family, he and his father prayed *after* the meal instead of before it.

When Mrs. Farley is finished going through the house and questioning us, Bernard takes her on a stroll through the yard, and for a few minutes they stand near the spot where I've just begun weeding a flower bed. He's definitely behaving like his old self now, spreading warmth and optimism as he passes, just like the sun. Bernard proudly points to the bright flares of asters as if he's planted and watered them himself. Mrs. Farley nods appreciatively and draws closer to him.

"So, have you considered how you're going to work full-time *and* care for a child?" she inquires, pen and notepad poised to record his response.

"The great actress Ethel Barrymore made movies during the day, worked on stage at night, and raised three children all by herself," says Bernard. "Similarly, I am my own boss. Thus the child can come to work with me when she's not in school, and I can stay at home if she's ill. Mother has said that she'll be happy to baby-sit here at home, and should circumstances warrant it, I'll hire a professional nanny."

If Bernard is the first potential adoptive parent to compare himself to screen legend Ethel Barrymore, Mrs. Farley doesn't let on, or seem to hold it against him. The only moment that doesn't appear to go swimmingly is when Mrs. Farley meets Ottavio and asks if he's Olivia's husband. Ottavio throws a fit in Italian and once again starts insisting they must get married at once so that the grandchild isn't a *bastardo*. Bernard calls for Olivia and deftly steers Mrs. Farley away from Ottavio and back into the house.

However, the good news is that overall Mrs. Farley and Bernard appear to get on exceptionally well and they talk for almost another hour in the dining room. When I go inside for some chocolate Yoo-hoo, I hear her complimenting Bernard on his taste in furnishings. And old fox that he is, Bernard casually asks if *she* collects anything.

Indeed she does—Rommel figurines, which I happen to know that he secretly despises. But lots of people in town collect them or give them as gifts, so he keeps a substantial supply in a glass case down at the shop.

Sure enough, after further softening Mrs. Farley up with some of his homemade iced oatmeal cookies, Bernard whisks her off to the shop, *just to have a look*. However, there's no doubt in my mind that she'll be going home with a few of her favorites, and anything else that catches her fancy. Certainly Bernard won't ask her to move his name up on the adoption list. On the other hand, I won't be surprised if a *special circumstance* should arise, where he might just be the only applicant qualified to accept a child that unexpectedly pops up ahead of schedule.

Chapter
Forty-one

Now that the gardens are all planted and weeded I can finally do some more work on the lawn itself. I start with ripping out some of the worst patches of crabgrass by the roots and then reseed those areas, along with all the places where the healthy grass has rotted from being buried under wet leaves for too long. The border of overgrown grass surrounding the house, shed, shrubs, and trees will also have to be dealt with by hand or the electric trimmer after I see how close I can get with the mower.

Two hours and three lawn and leaf bags later, Olivia comes out back and lights up a cigarette. I find this odd, being that she never has a cigarette during the day. And also because since the Judge died, she rarely smokes at all.

"Ottavio asked me to marry him," Olivia announces, and gazes off into the distance.

"Congratulations!" I say, and drop my spade.

"Again," she adds.

"Oh." I pick up my spade. "What did you tell him?"

"What I always tell him. That I don't see the need to marry. Our children are grown and we're certainly not having any more. So what's the point?" Though she sounds more like she's trying to convince herself rather than me. "If we continue to love each other then we'll stay together. And if not . . . well, there's no mess to clean up."

That makes sense. On the other hand, I've noticed that most people enjoy the idea of belonging exclusively to another person, and making it official in one way or another. "Maybe he just wants to make some sort of statement to the world about how much he cares for you."

"That's it *exactly,*" she says. "We're planning a trip to Italy in the fall to meet his family and Ottavio insists that his generation doesn't approve of living together."

"So you're not positive that you'll always love him?" I ask, not wanting to miss an opportunity to collect more information for my growing love file.

"Oh, it's not that. I *do* believe I'll love Ottavio forever. I simply don't feel the need to sign a contract." Then she momentarily turns her attention toward me. "Just when Bernard is starting to look better, you now look . . . well, exhausted."

She's being kind by not just saying "exhumed," which is also exactly how I feel.

As I'm about to tell her about my short-lived romance with Auggie, Ottavio comes dashing out in the yard looking frantic, as if he's been searching all over for Olivia.

While he rushes down the path toward us, she whispers in my ear, "You see, even solitary love can be a torment, though hopefully a sweet one."

"Olee-ve-ah," he implores her, and clasps his hands together as if actively praying, then begins babbling away in Italian. Olivia turns and walks toward the orchard, where the pink and white blossoms have been replaced with tiny green apples that cling to the boughs of the trees. Ottavio follows her, talking and gesticulating like a preacher at a revival meeting.

Funny thing is, I never would have guessed that people in their sixties fretted about love the same way that we teenagers do. I'd actually been looking forward to reaching thirty and having all that romance nonsense settled and out of the way.

As I'm working near the fence on the far side of the yard, I hear a tremendous crashing in the bushes and suddenly a bear is breathing in my face. Only bears don't bark. And most of them probably don't lick you, either.

Fortunately I've become somewhat accustomed to Lulu the Great Dane charging up to the fence when I least expect it. She's actually very friendly, a regular 120-pound, four-legged welcome wagon. And tall, too. When she puts both front paws on top of the fence she's taller than I am, and able to lick my forehead. I can only hope the Shultzes didn't get her as a guard dog, because I think they'd have been better served by a Yorkshire terrier.

Upon hearing Lulu's joyful barks, Rocky bolts out of the house, swings up into the tree branches, and manages to dangle above her, just out of reach. Lulu goes berserk, leaping in the air in an effort to catch him, and for a moment the humongous dog becomes so frantic that I worry she's going to attack him.

It turns out that Rocky has a piece of bologna in his hand. And after Lulu practically does a summersault in midair, he finally gives it to her, then drops down onto the lawn so they can play a game of high-speed chase. Whenever Lulu's about to catch Rocky, he quickly climbs a nearby elm tree so that she just barely misses him. Then Lulu proceeds to bark and jump around the base as if she's treed a squirrel. However, Rocky scampers high up into the branches, swings to another tree, and then sneaks back down behind her.

Just when I start to think how much Rocky is like a human, because of the way he seems to understand so much, or looks at you with those expressive and comprehending brown eyes, he does something totally chimplike. For instance, he'll steal my trowel and then whiz around the yard on his knuckles, showing off his pink gums by hooting and grinning.

Olivia and Ottavio eventually return from their walk. Since they don't mention anything about an engagement I assume Olivia has held her ground for the time being. They're strolling hand in hand and smiling at each other, so it's safe to say that no unpleasant ultimatums have been issued. It makes me think how nice it must be to have someone to care about.

Apparently Olivia has been doing some thinking as well. "Perhaps we should start growing medicinal marijuana," she says to me. "One of my church friends has the worst case of glaucoma and there's no way for her to get pot now that her son has moved to Seattle." She scans the yard as if searching for a good plot for reefer growing. "What do you think, Hallie?"

"I think you'd have to get some gro-lights and expand the greenhouse," I say. "But you haven't been arrested in a while, so it'd probably help to get your name back out there."

"It's tempting, but I suppose I'm a little oversubscribed right now. Maybe that's one for you and Craig to work on." Olivia and Ottavio continue on their walk. However, she turns before disappearing around the side of the house and calls back to me, "You're never too young to start planning what sort of revolution you'll lead. Thomas Jefferson said that every generation needs a new revolution."

I'm afraid that right now my dire financial position necessitates that I work only as a paid revolutionary, and there are definitely no extra funds lying around for start-ups. But it's still nice to know that when it comes to championing the greater good, Olivia's neighborliness extends so far as to invite the party faithful to break local, state, and federal laws on her property.

Chapter
Forty-two

WHILE LENDING BERNARD A HAND IN PREPARING DINNER, I DE-
cide that the house finally seems back to its old self. The new sofa
and chair that he ordered for the living room arrived the other day
and look nice with their clean, white fabric, and certainly more
modern than the big old wooden pieces that had carved animal
hooves for feet. Olivia's occupied with her writing and protesting
and Ottavio is busy planning their trip to Italy and Greece.

All is well except for my own crappy mood and of course the absence of Gil. It's hard not to think of Gil whenever something happens that I know he'd laugh at, like Bernard overbasting the coq au
vin the other night so that the oven caught fire and the door blew
open. And I miss hearing Gil's Buffalo Springfield albums on Saturday mornings.

Meantime Bernard has this CD of greatest opera arias playing *loud.* He puts down the cutting board and asks me to carve the chicken cutlets into strips.

"You're making *chicken fingers?*" I'm stunned that Bernard would stoop to such double-wide-trailer cuisine.

"Oh my Lord and Taylor, absolutely not. We're having a night at the opera," he proclaims with an air of mystery.

"What *are* you talking about?" When Bernard is preparing to tell one of his stories, a certain amount of cajoling and disbelief is always rewarded in the end. "Are we going to shape the chicken strips into music notes?"

"Not at all. We are preparing Chicken Tetrazzini."

"Sounds like a disease."

"Chicken Tetrazzini was named after the coloratura soprano Luisa Tetrazzini, who enjoyed great popularity in this country at the turn of the nineteenth century. Cooked spaghetti and strips of chicken are combined with a sherry Parmesan cheese cream sauce. Then we sprinkle breadcrumbs over the top and bake until bubbly and golden brown."

"Sounds a bit rich," I say.

"It's probably not a coincidence that Luisa was a POW," allows Bernard.

"She was a prisoner of war?"

"No," he says, "a Person of Weight."

Next he sets me to halving peaches and shaving almonds while *La Donna e Mobile* competes with the high-pitched whir of the blender and the bubbling of beans cooking on the stove.

Bernard continues to expand on his opera motif. "The Australian soprano Nellie Melba gave her name to Peach Melba. In fact, the famous French chef Auguste Escoffier created the dessert expressly for her. It's made with two peach halves poached in syrup. Each half is placed hollow-side down on top of a scoop of vanilla ice cream and then covered with raspberry sauce, whipped cream, and sliced almonds."

"What did Ms. Melba do to earn her own dessert?" I ask. "Was she a POW, too?"

"I believe her measurements were rather typical for an opera singer of that time, at least during her performing years. Nellie Melba was born Helen Porter Mitchell and chose her stage name as a way of honoring her hometown of Melbourne, Australia. When Nellie's health was failing in later years, Escoffier devised for her the crisp and easily digestible Melba Toast."

"So if I change my name to Hallie Cosgrove after our town, then maybe some famous chef will name a dessert after me," I suggest.

"I'm sure you'll be the inspiration for much great cuisine. In fact, perhaps that could be the key to your fortune. You see, Nellie was so incensed at not receiving royalties on her eponymous food items that she trademarked her name and became even wealthier by investing the proceeds. And in time her face came to adorn Australia's hundred-dollar bill."

"They can just *give* me the hundred-dollar bills," I say. "Hmmm. Those chocolate and banana sandwiches I make are pretty good. Maybe I can start selling those and get rich like Nellie."

"You don't want to be *exactly* like her," cautions Bernard. "She died from an infection after having a face-lift."

"Get out!" I say. "You're definitely making that up."

"Google it," he confidently replies.

Rolling my eyes, I seriously wonder why we ever thought it was a good idea to encourage him to learn how to use a computer.

"You haven't said a word about Auggie," Bernard says coyly. "Would you like to invite him over for dinner tonight?"

"Thanks, but it's over."

With eyebrows raised, Bernard looks up from slicing a hard-boiled egg.

"He's *not* gay!" I insist. "At least not a hundred percent." There's no point in mentioning Svetlana. It's embarrassing, and worse, he probably wouldn't believe it anyway.

"Whatever you say." Bernard goes back to his egg but not without giving a distinct sniff that practically shouts: *I told you so!* Gil always used to say that Bernard is in possession of the world's most finely developed sense of rumor.

Time for a change of subject. "So you look really nice." Bernard has had a haircut, appears freshly shaved, and the new blue shirt he's wearing looks perfect with his coloring.

"Shall I compare me to a summer's day?" asks Bernard.

"It must be a constant struggle to remain so modest," I say.

"As one in possession of such enormous talents, yes, I suppose it is," Bernard replies with a false sense of world-weariness.

As usual, Brandt calls from the lab at six to say that he won't be able to make it home for dinner. Apparently something went wrong with Louise's science project and they're going to try and fix it. For a few days Brandt stopped back at the house in the afternoon for an hour to help Louise with her homework, but they quickly decided it was easier for her to meet him over at the lab where he works. It's less running around for Brandt, and Louise claims that the air-conditioning helps her allergies.

I should really buy Brandt a present or invite him to a movie. He's been so kind and absolutely devoted to helping Louise do well in summer school. My only fear is that she might be using Brandt, knowing full well that none of her friends will see her with him over at the lab.

I start removing the extra place-setting, but Bernard says to leave it because it's not for Brandt.

"Well, there are six places set and it's just you, me, Olivia, Ottavio, and Rocky." Rocky sits at the dinner table just like a person, only he's allowed to put his feet up on the chair. However, if he doesn't like what we're having, there's always a big bowl of fruit salad on the bottom shelf of the refrigerator.

"I've invited a guest," he says.

I should have known. Bernard rarely puts out the individual porcelain salt dishes with the tiny matching spoons when it's just us. Same with the monogrammed silver napkin rings. And there are new pale pink candles in the polished silver holders.

"Mrs. Farley?" I wouldn't put it past Bernard to wine and dine her in order to help move his name up on the list. He'd been approved for the adoption, but was told that he may have to wait as long as two years. Though this hasn't stopped him from diving in and drawing sketches to transform Brandt's room into a nursery after he leaves for college in August.

"A male friend." Bernard flashes a mischievous grin.

"A *boyfriend?*" I ask.

Chapter
Forty-three

As if in answer to my question, the doorbell rings. Bernard frantically pulls off his apron, checks his appearance in the hall mirror, and dims the lights in the dining room.

Our mystery guest is in his mid-twenties, as best I can tell, which makes him roughly ten years younger than Bernard. He's extremely handsome, with jet-black hair neatly combed back behind his ears, tan skin that glows with good health, and soft brown eyes with dark copper-colored parentheses around the irises. Bernard introduces him as Melik, a rug dealer from Columbus whom he recently met when appraising some acquisitions from Kurdistan.

I'm polite to Melik, but promise myself that I won't *really* like him. No one can ever replace Gil. However, I realize that it's not going to help Bernard get over Gil if I start acting like the teenager of divorced parents who hates all of her mother's new boyfriends. Also, Melik is very nice and tries hard to make a good impression by saying how lovely the house is and asking us all what we do.

The only thing I find slightly odd is that Melik doesn't seem very sophisticated. For instance, he doesn't take an interest in the wine on the table the way Gil always did. And he wears plain old jeans with a T-shirt, which is fine with me, but it's more like an outfit one of *my* boyfriends would wear on a date.

Over dinner Melik tells us all how he was raised in a village about four hours east of Istanbul in Turkey. And when he finds out that I played soccer in high school his entire face lights up. He says that his cousin is a forward on the best team in Turkey and proudly relates their recent victory against Greece, play by play. I'm tempted to call Jane and ask her to come over since I get the feeling the two of them could talk international soccer for hours.

Olivia, always the gracious hostess, is very attentive to our guest. If she's bothered by the fact that her son's new boyfriend is ten years his junior, and outfitted in jeans and sneakers, she certainly doesn't show it. "So tell us more about you and your business," Olivia encourages him.

Melik appears a bit hesitant and glances at Bernard. I can't help but wonder if they're involved in some sort of dodge such as marking up the purchase price of rugs and then reselling them. That's one of Bernard's favorite tricks, to show a customer an auction catalogue listing a similar item that's being sold for much more, and then insist how he isn't turning a profit, but making the sale because the person is such a good customer and Bernard wants to keep him coming back. Though I must admit, people underestimate the trouble Bernard goes to in order to find all the great stuff displayed in his shop. Not to mention his taste—being able to spot that one terrific item in piles and piles of junk at an estate sale. And no matter what the price, even if it's fair or a good deal, they always think they should negotiate. Yet the same customers would never try that in a supermarket, or even a regular home-furnishings store.

Not surprisingly, Bernard Stockton, *raconteur par excellence,* rescues Melik and takes up the story of their acquaintance. "The best rugs in the world are coming out of Kurdistan nowadays. And with the current political situation in the Middle East, the money is *most* welcome there. It allows people to buy food, health care, and clean water." Bernard has a gift for locating the humanitarian aspect in all of his dealings.

"Ha!" says Olivia. "I can imagine how much of that money actually reaches the women and children who do most of the labor."

Bernard ignores her. "So Melik generously shares his Kurdistan connections to help facilitate some global commerce."

"I'm sure you'll both be asked to share a Nobel Peace Prize," says Olivia.

I can't help but think how this is coming from a woman who has no problem with smuggling morning-after pills into the country.

Melik smiles and nods in agreement the entire time Bernard is talking, and when we all look to him for a response he simply says, "The Kurds make the best carpeting."

"I'm not going to argue with that," says Olivia. "But you must admit that the Turkish government has been rather undiplomatic by not acknowledging the Kurds' desire for autonomy."

This appears to be a subject that is of much more interest to Melik than rugs. He sits bolt upright in the chair as he practically shouts, "Not diplomatic?" A look of genuine astonishment crosses Melik's face and he becomes very animated. "My brother is in the Turkish army. Do you have any idea the amount of money that our government spends *protecting* the Kurds?"

As the discussion continues to heat up, Bernard appears to grow concerned and strokes his chin the way he does when he's trying to bluff in poker.

"Protecting *them?*" Olivia confronts him. "Protecting their *oil* is more like it. Ever since the Ottoman Empire collapsed—"

"Speaking of ottomans," Bernard rapidly interjects, "I was thinking of having the footstool re-covered or maybe buying a black leather Eames lounge chair with a walnut back and aluminum trim."

"Turkish cities offer the Kurds jobs!" insists Melik. "They want assimilation!"

"How can you be sure, when under Turkish law people can be

sent to jail for teaching Kurdish in schools, running a political campaign on the basis of ethnicity, or broadcasting in Kurdish?" counters Olivia.

"Speaking of the media," Bernard once again interrupts the escalating quarrel, "Melik is very interested in film, particularly Federico Fellini. Perhaps Ottavio would like to talk about that."

A look of bliss appears on Ottavio's face at the very mention of the word *Fellini*. "*La Dolce Vita,* yes? But *The Bicycle Thief* by De Sica, this is better, *non?*"

"Yes, I couldn't agree more," says Melik, gracefully acquiescing to the change in subject. "And what about Fellini's *Amarcord*—the countryside is like a character."

It transpires that Melik is extremely knowledgeable about foreign films and directors and I have to revise my opinion of him not appearing sophisticated. It turns out that he's even working on a script for a film he's planning to shoot back in Turkey. Only, I'm still having difficulty imagining Melik as Bernard's new boyfriend. Or else I just won't allow myself to imagine it. Instead I find myself wishing that I had agreed to help Bernard try and figure out a scheme to win Gil back.

Chapter
Forty-four

♥ When I enter the main house Wednesday morning, Olivia and Ottavio, dressed in nice clothes that suggest they're going to church, are rushing around searching for the car keys.

"*Forty* miles per hour!" Bernard is shouting after Ottavio. "*Quaranta!* It's the law! *Non polizia!*" Bernard theatrically places the back of his hand on his forehead. "I don't understand it. The Italians can take four hours to eat a single meal and then they have to drive home from the restaurant at eighty miles an hour. Ottavio's stack of speeding tickets is almost as high as Mother's pile of citations for disturbing the peace."

I would have to agree with Bernard on this, since a cherry red Buick Park Avenue the size of a modest cabin cruiser is bound to draw attention at any speed. Especially with Olivia's collection of bumper stickers, which include GIVE PEAS A CHANCE! A CLOSED MIND

IS A WONDERFUL THING TO LOSE, and UNITARIAN—HONK IF YOU'RE NOT SURE!

"Why are they attending church on a Wednesday morning in the middle of summer?" I ask Bernard.

"They're going court-watching in Cleveland. It's Mother's latest—she's convinced that the legal system prosecutes the prostitutes and not the customers. And those who *take* bribes rather than those who *offer* them. Apparently she's reworking the disincentive part of the penal code, or something along those lines. Honestly, who can keep track?"

"And what does Ottavio think of her extracurricular legal activities?"

"Given his limited knowledge of English, and the volume of her correspondence with the government, he probably thinks she's employed as a public defender," speculates Bernard. "Which he'll soon need in traffic court if he wants to continue driving in this country."

Olivia must hear Bernard complaining and calls through to the kitchen, "Clarence Darrow, the famous lawyer who argued the Scopes Monkey Trial, was a Unitarian!"

"Here we go again," Bernard says to me. "Famous Unitarians for five hundred." He pokes his head around the corner and calls back to her, "Clarence Darrow lost! Not only that, P. T. Barnum, the greatest charlatan of them all, was one of *your people.* And let us not forget the captain *and* the architect of the *Titanic,* while we're on the subject."

Olivia appears in the archway and gaily adds, "You forgot the woman who wrote *"Nearer My God to Thee,"* the hymn they played as the *Titanic* went down. Sarah F. Adams. The *F* was for *flower.*"

"Of course," says Bernard. "What else? Obviously it wasn't for *float!*"

Olivia and Ottavio say good-bye and hurry out the front door.

"Craig's coming home today," I say. I'd finally gotten around to checking my E-mails.

"I know," says Bernard, looking smug. "He's building my pond."

"What?" How could he ask Craig without first asking me? *I'm*

in charge of the yard! Not only that, we already have four gardens, over a dozen birdhouses, and a gazebo! And that's just in the *back*. The front still features the merry-go-round that came with one of Bernard's auction lots.

"I wanted to go down as the first person in history to surprise you," says Bernard.

"Well, what if I'm mad at Craig and don't want him hanging around here?"

"Are you?" asks Bernard.

"No . . ."

"So, then what's the problem? Besides, I thought you two agreed to see other people, that going your separate ways was mutual."

"We did," I say. "I'm just used to working in the yard by myself, that's all." This is a stupid thing to say, because Louise helped me for a while. And before that, Ottavio. Even Rocky runs around gathering up dead branches when he's not busy teasing Lulu or making cocktails for Olivia and Ottavio. Rocky never lost his flair for bartending and Ottavio has recently taught him how to use the blender to make frozen daiquiris.

"As a matter of fact," Bernard casually tosses off, "I've invited Craig over for dinner tonight so that we can discuss the plans. I thought perhaps we'd employ an all-American theme of burgers and fries and a big honeymoon salad."

"A *what*?" Now it's confirmed that Bernard is attempting to get us back together.

He grins at me. "You know, just *let us* alone."

Chapter
Forty-five

In addition to having no intention of letting us alone, Bernard has no intention of cooking burgers and fries. He comes home with the ingredients for another meal entirely, saying that he arrived at his shop to find a big purchase order in his computer from a hotel in New Orleans. They've offered him top dollar for all the Americana merchandise in the photos he sent—some William-and-Mary-style tables, nests of baskets, Chippendale chests of drawers, and even four decoy ducks. Thus Bernard insists that it's a gesture of thanks to the voodoo gods to employ a Mardi Gras theme.

The new menu includes crab cakes with remoulade to start, shrimp Creole on a bed of rice as the entree, Caesar salad with big homemade croutons, and for dessert, bread pudding with bourbon sauce. I should have realized there was no way in bell peppers that Bernard was going to serve plain old hamburgers and fries.

I head out to do a late-afternoon watering since it hasn't rained in over a week and the plants are starting to wilt, especially in front of the house where there's not as much shade. When Mrs. Farley pulls up in her brown Volvo wagon I peer into the back half expecting to see a baby, despite the fact that I know there's a long waiting list. She appears troubled when she asks if Bernard is at home. And even though he's already been approved for the adoption and sent in all the paperwork, it's obvious that whatever news she has isn't good.

Bernard and Mrs. Farley talk for a long time in the backyard. Now I'm sorry that I decided to work out front, because it would look suspicious if I suddenly began a project in their vicinity. Whenever I go around the side of the house to adjust the water pressure, I see Mrs. Farley's mouth doing most of the moving and Bernard staring off into the distance, occasionally nodding his head.

Mrs. Farley is very nice to me on her way out and pats my arm as if she has an inside track on knowing that I'm going to amount to something in life, despite any past tragedies. If only she was aware that I'd gone from sex maniac to spinster in only four weeks. I'm tempted to ask where she buys her Bass Weejuns and corduroy jumpers, in order to fully prepare for a life of chastity and good works.

As soon as she's turned out of the driveway I dash into the house to see what's happened. Bernard is leaning in front of the sink and carefully slicing onions.

"I'll explain over dinner." It's hard to tell whether it's the onions or something Mrs. Farley said causing his eyes to water. Perhaps there's been a delay. However, he soldiers on, meticulously finishing the preparations. Cooking a wonderful meal is Bernard's cure for most of life's downward turns. He possesses the rare ability to transform out-and-out tragedy into the most amazing lobster thermidor.

As I set the table, Bernard starts playing Louis Armstrong's *When the Saints Go Marching In* on the stereo.

It's a quarter to seven by the time we've finished getting everything ready. Bernard casts a disapproving glance at my cutoff jeans and Mr. Bubble T-shirt and announces, "You still have fifteen minutes to change."

"I'm not going to change. I like myself the way I am, thanks."

"I meant your ensemble, of course. With your sunburn and strong shoulders, those clothes just look a little, well . . ."

"What?"

"Well, Home Depot, that's all. I suppose a flowered sundress and a pink cotton summer sweater with eyelet lace is out of the question?"

"You suppose right," I say.

"I guess I should look at the bright side—that you'll never expire like Madame de Bussy, the fashion adviser to Marie Antoinette."

"Do I dare ask?"

"She tripped over her hoop skirt and died."

"Why do I feel as if you're trying to get Craig and me back together?"

"*Moi?*" Bernard asks, as if he's been falsely accused. "I'd never deign to interfere in your love life."

"Actually, it's impossible to interfere, since I don't *have* a love life. And besides, I *hate* guys!" I still refuse to admit to Bernard that not only was he right about Auggie—well, *half* right—but that I lost out to another woman, one in another country, on another continent, and one whom Auggie will probably never see again! Not only that, between Auggie's rejection, two thousand dollars paid out for the car engine, and the first installment of fall tuition due next week, it's all the more clear that my destiny is to become a female kissing bandit, carving big *H*s into pillowcases and Plexiglas bank teller windows with my gardening shears. Life goes on but love continues to be as mysterious as electricity or death.

Bernard comes over to where I'm standing and lifts my hair as if it's a bunch of carrots. "If you refuse to change clothes then at least take your hair out of that ponytail, put on some lip gloss, and dash through a spritz of Chantilly. Honestly, when you meet someone new, do they ask what you're studying or what position you play?"

But I stubbornly refuse. Kissing bandits don't take orders from anyone, and they certainly don't try to impress old boyfriends. Especially an old boyfriend who has stopped calling and most certainly has a new girlfriend.

When Olivia and Ottavio return from their adventures they stop in the kitchen to find out what time we're eating. Bernard asks, "Mother, don't you think Hallie looks pretty when she takes her hair down and styles it?"

"It was Gwen who did that," I say. "And the process was not only incredibly time-consuming, but downright *painful.*"

"I think her hair is just fine the way it is," says Olivia. "The cosmetics industrial complex profits by making us psychologically dependent upon their overpriced products and treatments. We've become a nation enslaved to plastic surgeons and beauticians, while developing countries don't have enough to eat."

"I suppose the good news is that Hallie certainly needn't worry about people trying to steal her *exterior decorator,*" says Bernard.

Olivia gives her son a scornful look. "If it were up to you, we'd all be at the beauty parlor for a wash and set twice a week and sleeping on bridal satin pillowcases with toilet paper wrapped around our heads."

"May I remind you that the earliest form of art was body adornment, followed by primitive pieces of jewelry and clothing," retorts Bernard. "In the good old days a lady took pride in her appearance."

"Yes, the good old days when children worked in factories and sweatshops, and blacks and women couldn't vote? And even after women fought the patriarchy to finally win the vote they still made fifty cents to a man's dollar," says Olivia. "*Those* good old days?"

"We're all anxiously awaiting your memoir of growing up in Boston, the cradle of feminization, during the dawning of the Women's Movement," says Bernard.

The timer and the doorbell go off simultaneously. Bernard hurries to the oven while pulling off his apron, and I head for the front hall to let in our guest.

Chapter
Forty-six

CRAIG ARRIVES LOOKING BUSINESSLIKE IN A BLUE BUTTON-DOWN shirt tucked into neatly pressed khaki pants and carrying a leather satchel under his arm. He gives me a smile instead of a kiss, as if there was never anything special between us. And I guess maybe there wasn't.

It's only been six months since I've last seen Craig, and yet he looks somehow different. At first I can't figure out what exactly has changed, but it soon becomes apparent that he's managed to grow another inch and shed some of his football muscle, especially around the neck and shoulders. However, the rest of Craig seems exactly the same. His eyes are the color of sea mist and it's easy to see why his yellowy hair reminds people of sunlight. Bernard of course doesn't miss noticing how handsome Craig looks and gives me a glance that clearly states, *Now, aren't you sorry you didn't change and put on lipstick?*

"So, Craig, tell us all about school," says Olivia.

Craig discusses his roommate who snores, favorite classes, a few professors, and how a student named Charlotte told him about a program where you work as an assistant Forest Ranger for a semester, which he thinks sounds interesting. I listen carefully to try and determine if this Charlotte woman might be the thing he's particularly interested in. But like most college students being quizzed by grown-ups, Craig sticks to the party line about academics and sports, careful not to allude to sex and parties. Adults paying thirty thousand dollars a year in tuition aren't interested in hearing about the Halloween bash where everyone got drunk and installed a giant pumpkin on the spire of the bell tower, even though a substantial amount of engineering knowledge was required to accomplish the task.

Everyone exclaims over the lovely presentation of the meal. Bernard has reused the crab shells to hold individual servings of tartar sauce, and the entrée is garnished with paprika and green onions. Only he doesn't seem to take pleasure from the compliments the way he normally does. Instead Bernard clears his throat and finally announces, "I have something to tell you. My adoption application has been rejected."

We all appear stunned, while Bernard stares down at his plate, reflexively picks up his fork, and then puts it back down again.

"Oh, Bertie darling, what a shame!" Olivia is the first to respond.

"Attsa no good!" says Ottavio, who tends to catalogue all life's twists and turns as either "attsa good" or "attsa no good."

"But you were already approved!" I complain.

I've been watching Craig, who is seated next to Bernard and directly across from me. It's unlikely he even knew about the adoption plans to begin with, but his expression changes from shock to extreme sympathy in less than a minute. At the Stocktons', such surprises are around every corner. If Rocky isn't carefully mixing a Singapore sling in the living room then Olivia is out front being carted off by the police. Besides, Craig always told me that the thing he loves best about being here is that you never know *what* is going to happen next.

"Apparently they have a problem with that fact that I'm gay," Bernard finally lays it on the line.

"I'm sorry, but adoption by same-sex singles *and* couples is perfectly legal within the state of Ohio!" Olivia slams down her fork as if it's a gavel and tosses her napkin onto the table as if she's going to sue somebody right then and there. "We'll simply go down to the agency and straighten them out!" And the way she rises up from her chair, I get the feeling that I should bring the car around right this minute.

"Sit down, Mother," says Bernard. "It's not that simple."

"But she's right," chimes in Craig. "This is a classic case of discrimination."

Craig's an only child and his father is a lawyer, so he's had to listen to adults talk his entire life and as a result knows all sorts of legal ins and outs, such as how to take someone to small claims court or fight a parking ticket.

Sensing that a grave injustice has been done, Ottavio immediately jumps to conclusions. *"La Cosa Nostra!"*

"There's no Mafia around here, Ottavio," Bernard corrects him. "You have to go to Youngstown or Cleveland for that."

Craig gives me a look that indicates he's heard otherwise from his father's dealings down at the courthouse, but remains silent on the matter.

"It's probably why we don't have any good Italian restaurants," says Bernard. Only it's obvious from the pained expression on his face that this joke is meant to hide his disappointment.

"We'll organize a protest," declares Olivia. She seems almost pleased to have a mission and continues with increasing gusto, "I'll make up petitions and placards and go to their main office and—"

Bernard takes such a deep breath that I sense the chandelier may have briefly swayed in his direction. "Mother, of course it's *illegal,* but that's not what they're going to say in the official letter. It will simply state something to the effect that we failed the home inspection or didn't meet all the financial guidelines. That's why Mrs. Farley came in person. Apparently . . . apparently a very large contributor to the adoption agency lives right here in town—Edwin Kunckle. And he put the kibosh on it."

As Bernard utters my least favorite name he looks over at me, fully expecting the look that says: *I told you he's a jerk*. Only I'm too distracted wondering if this happens to be revenge for my beating Kunckle at poker.

"Oh dear," cries Olivia and her hands fly up to her face.

"I believe he's a member of your church, Hallie," says Bernard.

"Not *my* church," I fire back. "It just happens to be where the poker game is held. And it's not my fault that my parents belong there."

"Anyway, it's easy to make the connection," continues Bernard. "If gays adopt babies, then *he* stops making donations to the agency."

"You really could sue for this!" A furious Craig lands a fist on the table and the silverware and crystal clank and jump.

Craig's indignation is sweet, but in my estimation he's a bit too optimistic about the way businesses and agencies really operate. My dad works for the state and is always telling stories about insider dealings and mutual back-scratching. Furthermore, it seems to me that Bernard, with all his experience buying and selling antiques, has the most heightened sense of awareness with regard to human nature and how the world actually works, much like my bookie pal, Cappy. And according to both of them, favorable transactions are more often the result of kickbacks and pulling strings rather than anything written in law books.

"I'll pen a scathing editorial that will rally sympathizers to our cause," declares Olivia.

"I appreciate your good intentions, Mother," Bernard says graciously, "but I don't want a spectacle to be made of the way I live, with protests and stories in the newspaper and on television. Heaven knows, we've had enough of that around here." He's obviously referring to Olivia's continuous stream of activism, which ranges from buying all the toads from the pet store to marching in support of the gay Boy Scout troop leader who was dismissed a year ago.

"But the best test of truth for any idea is to have a public debate on the matter," argues Olivia. "That's one of the main tenets that the English poet and scholar John Milton championed in his pamphlet 'Areopagitica.' "

"Yes. And after the restoration of Charles II your beloved Milton was arrested, if I recall correctly. So let's just drop the matter," Bernard says with an air of finality and lifts his head high. He has an appetite for good food and fine wine as much as he does for martyrdom.

"We'll drown our collective sorrow in the world premiere of Bernard's Bona Fide Bread Pudding in Bourbon Sauce."

With great ceremony Bernard places a large chafing dish in the middle of the dining room table and majestically removes the vaulted silver lid so that a delicious cinnamon smell explodes into the air and causes us all to exclaim and lean forward with anticipation.

By the time we finish dessert Bernard is conversing and joking around as if the adoption rejection had never occurred. He once told me that he's able to channel Ethel Merman performing "There's No Business Like Show Business" in order to make it through almost any difficult three-hour period without succumbing to his emotional distress.

Chapter
Forty-seven

When the table is finally cleared Bernard spreads out his sketches for the new pond and enthusiastically reviews them with Craig. "But of course I want you to be happy with the plan as well, so feel free to make changes and suggestions. Though I do believe the first thing Edith would ask is, 'What are we trying to evoke?'"

"Who?" asks Craig.

"Edith Wharton," I fill in the blank.

Bernard has been poring over her books for days. He removes a well-worn copy of *Italian Gardens* off the highboy and passes it to Craig.

"It should bring to mind the concept of liberty," says Olivia.

Bernard rolls his eyes. "We have flags for that, Mother, thank you."

"*La famiglia,*" offers the ever-helpful Ottavio.

"Actually," says Craig, "I've been thinking of what's known as a wild pond."

"Wonderful!" Olivia claps her hands together approvingly.

"That sounds perfect," says Bernard. "I've never cared for anything that smacks of being overly staged, thereby giving the impression that we're trying too hard. Therein lies the key to aesthetics—making the results appear natural and of course effortless."

From his leather satchel Craig removes a notebook and several catalogues with a variety of colored Post-it notes marking several of the pages. "Then let's start with the greenery, because it's essential for maintaining the ecological balance—you know, algae levels, filtration, and things like that. And plants provide fish with places to hide, which reduces their stress level."

"*Pesce!*" says Ottavio excitedly. Though he's obviously picturing something prepared in a white wine sauce with a side of linguini.

"No, it's not a pond for fishing," explains Olivia. "A place of beauty—*posto pittoresco.*"

Craig places some photographs on the table and begins to describe them one by one. "First we'll choose the floating plants. There's lotus, floating heart, parrot's feather—this isn't a good picture, but it has feathery light green leaves that drift on the surface. Then there's pennywort—that's the one with the emerald-green cupped leaves that creep across the border or float on the water, and tiny white flowers rise above it."

Bernard studies each image carefully.

"I adore the sound of *lotus* and *floating heart,*" Olivia says dreamily.

"Mother, you can't just choose these things based on whether or not you like the name."

"They'd all work in this environment." Craig passes around three more photos. "We might try one of these as well—there's water four-leaf clover, water hawthorn, and water hyacinth."

Without even glancing at the photos, Olivia says, "Definitely hyacinth. In Greek mythology Hyacinthus was a beautiful youth with whom Apollo, the god of prophecy, medicine, music, and poetry, fell in love. However, Zephyrus, the West Wind, also fell in love with the boy and became very jealous of Apollo. One day as Apollo was instructing the boy in discus throwing, Zephyrus seized the missile in midair and hurled it against Hyacinthus's head. The boy was killed, but where his blood fell there sprang up the hyacinth flower."

Bernard snorts.

However, before they can start arguing Craig moves on. "Fish are a good idea since they help reduce pond waste. And of course they're attractive and interesting. Most people stock with goldfish."

"Well, we certainly don't want what *most* people have," says Bernard.

Olivia nods in agreement. Although mother and son constantly bicker with each other, they almost always present a united front against ordinariness.

"Personally I like Japanese koi," says Craig. He flips to a page showing a gorgeous fish that's a kaleidoscope of bright orange, gold, black, and pearl gray. "Then there are two breeds of goldfish that are European imports and not as common, Green Thech and Golden Orfe." Craig points to the opposite page.

"Not too much gold," cautions Olivia. "That's my only complaint about Willa Cather, she tended to overuse gold."

"Willa Cather didn't have a famous garden," Bernard states with authority.

"I meant in her descriptive writing—golden sunsets, golden fields, golden leaves, golden steeples."

"Hmm," says Bernard, studying the pictures and ignoring his mother. "Edith doesn't say anything about fish." He places his hand on the cover of Wharton's book as if trying to channel her opinion on the matter.

"We don't have to decide about the fish right now," says Craig. "Actually, they come last. First we need marginal plants, border plants, and most important, oxygenating plants—possibly some duckweed, eel grass, Sagittaria or Anacharis."

"Definitely get that last one for Mother," insists Bernard. "It sounds like *anarchy*."

Chapter
Forty-eight

AFTER EVERYONE AGREES ON THE PLANS FOR THE NEW POND, Craig and I head out to the yard so he can get a better idea of the space he has to work with. There's not a star to be seen, but the blackness above us is velvety and soft. Alongside the stone pathway azaleas bloom with undimmed ferocity, their bright red and orange flowers practically glowing in the darkness. And though we can't see the roses in Olivia's garden, they manage to exhale their sweet perfume.

"It's really great to see you," says Craig. "You look terrific."

Despite the fact that it's dark out, I'm suddenly self-conscious about my appearance and try to fix all the wispy strands spiraling out of my ponytail. "Oh gosh, Bernard had me helping in the kitchen until the last minute and there wasn't time to change or even brush my hair."

He lifts his hand as if he's going to take my arm but instead shoves it deep into his pocket. "So how do you like college life? Gonna stick it out for three more years?"

"Yeah, if I can afford to. It's a lot better than high school, don't you think?"

"I guess so," he says in a manner that isn't overly convincing. "I had more fun in high school."

"Are *you* going to stick with it?" I ask.

"My parents would kill me if I quit. When you're an only child there's no room for a black sheep. You're lucky."

"What's *that* supposed to mean?"

"All of your parents' expectations aren't dumped solely onto the shoulders of one child. My mom sent me that story about Eric in the local newspaper—how he started his first football game and has a full scholarship. And even if you and Eric do mess up, they still have Louise and Teddy and so on down the line."

"If the next one of us written up in the newspaper is Louise, it might not be such a great story," I say. "Rather than Most Likely to Succeed, she's currently distinguishing herself as Most Likely to Repeat Tenth Grade." I don't add that I'm currently vying for "Most Likely to Die Alone."

But Craig doesn't ask what's going on with Louise and instead catches me off guard with, "So, do you have a boyfriend?"

Good question. And how differently I might have answered a week ago. But now I don't know. Is Ray to be considered a boyfriend? He's phoned exactly once since bagging his visit. And yet if he is still in the boyfriend category, for some reason I'm not sure I want to tell Craig. Likewise, as much as I'd like to know if *he* has a girlfriend, I'm not really interested in picturing him kissing some girl.

The wind suddenly picks up and dime-sized raindrops splatter against our skin. A clap of thunder like the rattle of sheet metal comes from beyond the orchard and lightning appears in great zigzags across the heavens, making everything stand out and appear close to us for a moment.

We dash to the safety of the nearby gazebo. However, when an entire curtain of water starts attacking sideways and forks of lightning move in on us following every crash of thunder, Craig says we'd better make a run for the house. He grabs my hand and we race around the garage to the front door.

Bernard is standing in the vestibule with big fluffy towels. "I saw you both running to the gazebo and thought of Leisl and Rolf singing 'I Am Sixteen Going On Seventeen' in *The Sound of Music.*"

Obviously Bernard is not going to stop trying to get us back together anytime soon.

"Well, I'm seventeen going on eighteen," I inform him, "And Craig is nineteen going on twenty."

"That's true. But don't you think I'm perfect to play the Baroness Von Schrader?" He quotes his favorite line after she's sent Julie Andrews packing: "Good-bye, Maria. I'm sure you'll make a very fine nun."

Craig accepts an umbrella from Bernard and then gives me a chaste kiss good night, the kind you confer upon a geeky cousin at a wedding. And then with a wave to Bernard he heads out into the night.

Bernard is leaning against the balustrade as if he no longer has the energy needed to stand unsupported, and it's apparent from the dullness in his normally bright blue eyes that the adoption rejection is more of a disappointment than he's been willing to acknowledge.

"I'm off to bed," says Bernard. "All alone, just like Garbo."

"Me too," I say. "I mean, it's doubtful I'll ever get married. You know, we could just live here and . . . and . . ."

"That's very sweet." He gives me a chaste kiss on the other cheek.

This seems to be my evening for chaste kisses. Saturday nights at the bingo parlor is probably just around the corner.

"And I appreciate the consideration," says Bernard as he starts up the stairs. "But perhaps it's better if I live in your heart, where the world can't see me," he quotes Greta Garbo just before she dies in *Camille*.

Oh great. Here we go again.

Chapter
Forty-nine

I STOP IN THE KITCHEN TO GRAB A CHOCOLATE YOO-HOO WHILE debating whether or not to wake Olivia and tell her that we may be back on suicide watch, and Bernard might be upstairs this very minute drafting a note. Until this past month it was simply a source of amusement that Bernard has memorized the last words of so many famous artists, such as the Russian ballerina Anna Pavlova's "Get my swan costume ready and play the last measure softly."

"Hallie," a delicate whisper comes from Olivia's den, which is dark except for the flame of a single candle.

"Olivia?" It isn't surprising for her to be up late working on a poem or a letter to the editor of the local newspaper. Or else on a pornographic story for *Milky Way* magazine. As she's fond of reminding us, "erotic narratives" earn considerably more money than poems and provide readers a harmless outlet for their fantasies. The latter she claims helps to cut down on domestic violence and sex abuse.

"Why are you working in the dark?" I ask.

Olivia leans against the wall in front of the open window, wearing a burgundy silk negligee with a kimono-style robe draped over her shoulders while smoking a cigarette and gazing up at the night sky. "The horns of Isis," she says, and nods toward the vast darkness.

I search the sky for a constellation but it's drizzling outside and no stars are visible, just a crescent moon with its points turned upward.

"The cow was sacred to her, and so when the tips of the moon face heavenward it evokes Isis, the great Egyptian Mother Goddess. Lucius of Patrae, the Greek author of a lost *Metamorphoses,* addressed Isis in a hymn, saying, 'Thou dispellest the storms of life and stretchest forth thy right hand of salvation, by which Thou unravellest even the inextricably tangled web of Fate.' "

I assume that Olivia is attempting to summon ideas for solving Bernard's adoption problem, in her own poetic way. "It's kind of you to want to help, but I get the feeling he won't appreciate us interfering in this one," I gently suggest to her.

The dampness from the rain enters the room as she attempts to fan the smoke out through the open window with a cardboard folder.

"Oh Hallie, I'm afraid that the adoption trouble is all *my* fault!" Olivia's mouth tightens as if it pains her just to think about it. "A few months ago I wrote an editorial exposing the fact that Valueland was breaking the labor laws. They hire people to bag groceries and help customers to their cars, then reduce compensation based on the estimated amounts of tips received by employees. And in the editorial I included his name."

"Who? Edwin the Turd?"

Olivia looks at me quizzically as she crushes out her cigarette.

"I mean, Ed Kunckle, Mr. Church Deacon and Town Spirit."

"Yes, he's the owner or the majority shareholder or something like that," she says with an anxious inflection in her normally warm and delicate voice. "It was difficult to find the exact details on how the ownership is structured based on the papers filed down at the courthouse."

"So Kunckle is doing this to get back at you?" I'm stunned that anyone could be so ruthless in their cruelty.

"Exactly!"

"I thought that maybe it was because I beat him in poker." There's relief in my voice.

"I'm afraid he's settling a much bigger score than that," says Olivia.

"My gosh, that guy would stab a person in the back and then have him arrested for possession of an illegal weapon!" I say this in my best crime-show-detective voice.

"Well, I won't allow it!" insists Olivia. "This is too important to Bernard. And he'd make a wonderful father. So that's why I've decided to work from *inside* the system! Though just this once."

"Shouldn't we ask Bernard about your plan?"

"Absolutely not!" Olivia dismisses the very suggestion with a wave of her hand. "Bernard abhors the idea of becoming embroiled in gay rights issues. He claims that doing so in such a small town objectifies him. Only I disagree. I think he simply refuses to acknowledge the fact that discrimination is much more prevalent than people would like to believe."

"But what can you do?" I ask. The situation appears to be a prime example of what Cappy describes as "The Golden Rule"—he who has the gold rules.

"Hallie, you didn't know my husband back when he was an influential barrister in this town. I still have a few connections with people in high places, and tomorrow I'm going to start making some calls."

"Let me know if I can help," I offer.

Olivia closes the window, and ties up her robe as if she's suddenly become chilled. "You just keep an eye on Bernard so as to make sure we don't have any more late-night *dramas*."

Chapter
Fifty

CRAIG COMES OVER ON SUNDAY MORNING SO WE CAN DRIVE TO the town of Warren, where there's a building supply center that sells most of what he needs to make the pond. Olivia and Ottavio are coming along because the store also stocks a large selection of lawn statuary and Olivia has decided that we need some Roman gods and goddesses to honor Ottavio's homeland, and maybe a miniature Coliseum or the Leaning Tower of Pisa.

"Sorry I'm late," Craig calls out as he does a loose-limbed jog over to the front porch, where we're all standing around waiting. "My parents made me go to church." He rolls his eyes as if he only went along with it to make them happy.

"I worshipped privately this morning," says Olivia. "Fortunately attendance isn't mandatory in my religion."

"Your *religion*?" scoffs Bernard, as if to suggest that being Unitarian is more akin to being a supporter of the Cleveland Zoo. "First off, your church doesn't have services in the summer, because everyone is too busy organic gardening. And second, had you been born two hundred years earlier, it's most certain that you'd have been burned at the stake by now."

"That may be so," trills Olivia, "but I have faith. Faith is to be found in the head and the heart, not a sanctuary or a temple. Furthermore, I'll take this opportunity to remind you that Unitarianism *is* a recognized religion."

"Tax-exempt social club is more like it," retorts Bernard.

"Well at least I *have* a religious home," says Olivia. "Remember the month you were a Buddhist and used the word *mums* as your mantra?"

Craig and I giggle as we imagine Bernard in the lotus position, chanting the name of his favorite flower.

"I suppose I'm a sinner nowadays," jokes Bernard, and for a moment I think he's referring to the thwarted adoption and glance toward Olivia to gauge her reaction.

But she only offers us her placid *each to his own* smile.

"Hallie taught me some tricks to improve my odds at blackjack this morning," continues Bernard.

"That counts as religion," I say. "There are twenty-one epistles in the Bible and that makes blackjack. Only these days I'm more spiritual than religious. For instance, this fall there's a good chance I'll be having an out-of-money experience."

"Funny, you seem too large to be a medium," quips Bernard as he hustles us all into the car.

After last night's rainstorm it's turned out to be a shiny July morning with a clear arc of blue painted in the east, over the farms, and buttery sunlight filtering down through the treetops. With Craig at the wheel of the big cherry-red Buick we get a chance to test the new tires and brake pads that I had installed for Olivia last week. I tend to think that for once Bernard might not be exaggerating in that Ottavio really is racing around at ninety miles an hour in order to go through tires and brakes so quickly.

It's probably a good thing Craig is driving, because neither Bernard nor I could sleep last night. He was distraught about the adoption being canceled and I was worried about him having another late-night party for one where he's the designated drinker. I suggested that he call Melik to commiserate, but Bernard insisted he didn't want to be a downer so close to the start of a new relationship. And so we were up until five in the morning playing cards and watching Tallulah Bankhead in *Die! Die! My Darling.*

In fact, Bernard is still speaking in Tallulah's whisky-and-cigarette voice when he tells us the story of how she was once in a restroom in New York and knocked on the wall of the next stall to ask for toilet paper. Supposedly the woman on the other side immediately recognized the distinctive smoke-cured voice and said, "I'm sorry, Ms. Bankhead, but there's no toilet paper in here, either." After which a husky Tallulah replied, "Then, dahling, do you have two fives for a ten?"

I haven't the slightest idea of where Bernard gets these stories and I don't know if they're the least bit true, but they sure are hilarious, at least the way he tells them.

On the way home Bernard makes us stop at not one, but *three* yard sales. Olivia is happy to find some inexpensive and fairly large porcelain statuettes of The Muses and also a Cupid, since her search for Roman gods and goddesses at the garden center had been a failure. Their inventory was more along the lines of gnomes and grazing animals rather than Venus and the wonders of the Middle Ages.

By this time we're starving, so Bernard instructs Craig to drive us over to The Garden of Eatin' for lunch. Whenever life gets Bernard down, he loves to order blueberry blintzes with sour cream and play Barry Manilow's "Mandy" on the wall-mounted jukebox.

When we finally arrive back at the house it's apparent from the minute we pull into the driveway that something is amiss. The front door is ajar and the curtain rod on the picture window is hanging down by about three feet on one side.

"Uh-oh!" Craig says ominously. "It looks like you've been robbed."

Chapter
Fifty-one

It's terrible, but the first thing that enters my mind is that at least I can't be blamed in *any* way for whatever has happened, because this time I am in possession of a solid alibi.

We all charge toward the front door, but with his long legs Craig arrives there a half hour before the rest of us. Chairs are knocked over, rugs are pushed back, and lamps are lying sideways on the floor. It appears more like the house was ransacked by a person searching for something specific, rather than just vandalized. Above the fireplace the large Palladian-style mirror with the mask of a Roman god at the top is dangling from a single wire, as if the burglar checked behind it for a safe.

"Whew!" says Craig and then lets out a long low whistle as he surveys the mess.

"Do you think someone might still be here?" I ask. "Maybe we should call the police."

"I'm sure they would have run out through the back after hearing a car pull into the driveway," says Craig.

"But what about upstairs?" I ask. Bernard has valuable antiques stuffed into every corner of every drawer and closet all the way up to the attic.

"I'll go up and check," says Craig. He grabs the gold-plated shovel from off the floor next to the sofa that must have fallen out when the rack holding the fireplace tools toppled over.

"It appears that the thief knew what he or she was after," suggests Olivia.

"I should say so," agrees Bernard as he unhappily surveys the destruction and then carefully picks up a small bronze statue of a naked woman with long flowing hair reclining atop a butterfly. "This little piece is easily worth five thousand dollars—any art thief worth his salt would have grabbed it." A puzzled look crosses Bernard's face as he quickly discovers other valuable items disturbed but not stolen.

"Same with these." From off the floor Olivia gathers up a half-dozen cameos, some encrusted with real jewels, which are usually displayed on a marble pedestal in the corner of the living room. "Bertie, you'd better check on that Rembrandt etching."

Bernard hurries into Olivia's study and opens the drawer in the file cabinet where she keeps the household records. Leave it to the Stocktons to have a Rembrandt etching stuck between the telephone bills in an unlocked file cabinet. "It's here!" he calls out with relief.

"En maron!" Ottavio shouts from the kitchen. "Olee-vee-ah! Rocky es hurt."

We converge in the kitchen to find Rocky crumpled up in the corner with a crushed lamp shade stuck on one foot.

"Oh no!" Olivia quickly gets down on her knees to check for signs of life. But when she lifts Rocky's arm and then his head, they both go limp. "Oh no, oh no," repeats Olivia as she puts her face up close to his in order to feel for his breath.

"Oh no is right," says Bernard, though not with the same note of concern. He picks up an empty bottle of Gordon's gin from off the

floor. And then a bottle of Jose Cuervo tequila from underneath the step stool.

Rocky slowly comes to and Bernard starts yelling at him about being a drunkard.

But Olivia keeps her calm. "Hallie," she says, "call Brandt at the lab and tell him to come home right away. The number is taped next to the phone."

"What's Brandt supposed to do?" asks an angry Bernard.

"He can talk to Rocky and find out what happened," says Olivia.

"It's obvious what happened!" shouts Bernard. "That stupid monkey went on a spree and ruined how many thousands of dollars' worth of antiques!"

"Attsa no good," concurs Ottavio.

"Perhaps he fought off the burglar," proposes Olivia, though doubtfully. Her voice is filled with worry. It's obvious that Rocky will have to go if he's capable of this kind of destruction. And we all know from when he first arrived that there's nowhere else to go except to sleep, for good. The zoos had made it quite clear that they don't run AA programs for chimpanzees.

"Mother, he's clearly intoxicated!" Bernard is fuming. "I can't believe the mess that he's made!" He looks down with disdain at the chimp, whose eyes are now half open. "Rocky! I thought you'd reformed."

Bernard storms out of the kitchen and continues moving through the house in an effort to assess the damage. Though several lamps and vases have been knocked over and silver boxes and statuettes are on the floor, aside from the ruined lamp shade on Rocky's foot, only a Delft dry-drug jar and a gilded Bohemian goblet are smashed beyond repair. However, it's certainly going to take a while to put things back in order. There are chips of firewood everywhere and a lightbulb has been smashed, leaving small shards of glass across the rugs and in the sofa cushions. The Dirk Van Erp table lamp has a crack in the base, but Bernard says it can probably be repaired so that it's not noticeable.

Otherwise, the liquor cabinet is wide-open, the mesh screen is dented, and bottles are strewn across the floor in front of it. I'm surprised that Rocky didn't at least use a glass. Whenever he tends bar he almost always makes mixed drinks.

Craig comes back downstairs and reports, "All clear. In fact, it doesn't appear that the burglar even made it upstairs. Everything is in order. Maybe he did get scared off when the car pulled up, and escaped through the woods."

I nod toward the kitchen, indicating that Craig should look in there if he wants an answer to the purported break-in. Then I take out a broom and begin sweeping up the glass and broken pottery.

After a few minutes Craig calls out, "Hey, Hallie, come look at this."

I return to the kitchen, where Olivia is still tending to Rocky, who is now sitting up slightly, his face in his hands.

"It looks as if someone tore chunks out of his fur." Craig points to the back of Rocky's neck, which we couldn't see before when he was lying down.

"Sure enough, either Rocky had a run-in with my weed whacker or else he's developed one heck of a case of mange."

"Maybe there *was* an intruder and Rocky fended him off," suggests Craig.

But Olivia doesn't appear encouraged and tears well up in her eyes. She sits with Rocky while he comes out of his daze and gently strokes his head.

The noisy engine of Brandt's rust-bucket Dodge can be heard in the driveway and I run out to meet him.

"Brandt, you've got to find out exactly what happened, because I'm afraid they're going to put Rocky to sleep," I hastily explain as we head toward the kitchen.

Brandt immediately starts signing at Rocky. But Rocky just stares back at him with glazed eyes. Rocky's expression appears so humanlike that one would almost think he's too humiliated to answer. Only it's more likely that in his current state, Rocky doesn't understand what Brandt is trying to say.

Bernard stands behind us holding an orange-and-blue Imari plate broken neatly in two that he's just discovered under the dining room table. "It's just as I told you," says an angry Bernard. "He went on a spree!"

It turns out that Rocky understands Brandt perfectly. After a few minutes he begins to slowly sign back.

Brandt nods understandingly and motions some more at Rocky. The chimp becomes excited and starts gesturing frantically and then hopping up and down and making hooting noises, followed by what sounds like a dog barking.

"*Oh!*" says Olivia. "I think I'm beginning to understand."

"*What?*" asks an increasingly frustrated Bernard. "What is he prattling on about?"

"Lulu," says Olivia.

Rocky suddenly looks over to her with hurt in his eyes.

"He had a fight with that damn dog?" asks Bernard. "In the *house?*"

"He's in love with Lulu," says Brandt. "Rocky wants more than she does from the relationship. And so he got upset."

"It's summertime," Olivia says wistfully. "Thoughts turn to love."

"And love turns to disaster," I can't help but add. It's tempting to ask Brandt to tell Rocky that I'm actually doing considerably worse when it comes to the dating game. The only difference being that I haven't ripped apart a house yet. But that doesn't mean the thought hasn't crossed my mind.

"Well, tell him that *she's a Great Dane* and *he's a chimpanzee,*" says an irate Bernard. "And I'd be happy to show him the difference in a mirror, except that all of mine appear to be broken!"

Chapter
Fifty-two

EARLY THE NEXT MORNING A DELIVERY TRUCK PULLS UP WITH everything that Craig ordered for the pond. He's already at the site and directs the two men in unloading the flagstone, pond liner, bags of concrete, imitation stone bridge, filtration system, water testing kits, and heaven knows what else. It's the biggest mess I've ever seen, and fortunately Craig is expecting some guys he used to play football with to help him get started. In the meantime, it looks as if it's going to rain any minute, and so I search the garage for some tarps to cover the boxes and especially the concrete. If Bernard didn't use the area to store all the furniture he's someday planning on refinishing, we could just put everything in there.

On one of the shelves in the back of the garage I come across Gil's baseball glove. It's not as if I need an excuse to call him, but I know he'll want his beloved mitt for the annual company picnic, where he always plays first base. Besides, it's been weeks since we've spoken and it's easy to see how kids of divorced parents can lose touch with the one they don't live with, no matter how much they may like or miss that person.

After finding Craig some big sheets of plastic that were used to cover the floors when I painted last year, I go inside and phone Gil. He sounds thrilled that I've called and invites me to Cleveland for dinner that very night. He also asks if I'd like to meet his girlfriend, and even though it's not exactly at the top of my to-do list, I say okay. However, I don't tell Bernard that she's on the menu.

It ends up raining most of the day, and so after shopping for some new tomato cages over at the hardware store, I sit down with my school course catalogue and try to figure out what classes to take in the fall. It's hard to believe you can actually earn three credits for studying "The Societal Implications of Television." My dad would have a fit if he thought his money was going toward something like that. Dad has made it clear on numerous occasions that he believes television, which he did not have growing up, turns people into unemployable idiots. Though he seems happy to make an exception when it comes to watching televised sporting events.

Finally at four o'clock I shower, dress, and head out the door to make the one-hour drive to Cleveland. "Have fun," Bernard calls after me from the front porch. "Melik and I are off to a Danish film tonight." And then as if it's an afterthought he adds, "I don't mind if you tell Gil that I'm seeing someone. In fact, I'm sure he'll be relieved to know that he has no more home-cooked meals to fear from me!"

Gil and Doris have arranged to meet me at an Indian restaurant just down the street from his new place, which I guess is not so new anymore, even though it will never really seem like his home to me. A young woman wearing a brightly colored sari escorts me to their table.

Gil rises and gives me a full-sized hug. His wrist is out of the cast and he looks okay, though perhaps a bit somber and slightly thinner. However, a big smile crosses his face when I surprise him by pulling his baseball glove out of my backpack.

Doris is in her mid-thirties, maybe a year or two younger than

Gil, wearing a flowered dress with two strands of pearls, looking very proper and midwestern. She has short brown hair, hazel eyes, and seagull-shaped eyebrows that appear to have been penciled in about an inch above and to the right of the originals.

"Sweetheart," Gil says, turning to Doris, "this is Hallie."

"It's wonderful to finally meet you, Hallie. Gilbert has told me so much about you that I feel as if we already know each other." She speaks in a cheerful Kentucky drawl that sounds slightly fake, at least the cheerful part does. Her smile could power all of downtown Cleveland, and perhaps one or two suburbs, depending on whether or not air conditioners are in use.

I go to shake her hand but she uses the contact as an opportunity to reel me in for a big hug like I'm her partner at a square dance. There's nothing to do but hug back and try not to burp.

Despite the fact that Doris has a shapely figure and only a few discernible lines (though they appear to be more a result of cracks in her pancake makeup than the onset of old age), she seems the older of the two. I don't know if it's the way she calls him "dear" like in those 1950s movies that Bernard is always watching, or because she wipes down everyone's silverware with her napkin.

Obviously they've been dating a lot, because Doris points to all of Gil's favorite dishes on the menu, as if her happiness depends on him having the perfect meal. Then she asks me about school and if I like to ride horses.

"I've bet on a lot more horses than I've ridden," I tell her truthfully.

"Oh, what an interesting hobby. Did you know that Gilbert's family once ran the best horse-breeding farm in all of Kentucky?" She affectionately squeezes his arm. "Isn't that right, dear?"

"Maybe it was one of the top ten," Gil says modestly.

Of course I knew that! I only lived with him for almost a year— longer than she's been dating him! "Actually, I did," I say, trying to sound polite and yet at the same time inform Doris that she doesn't know more about *Gilbert* than everyone else in the world.

"Maybe after we're married we'll have some horses and you can come over and ride," suggests Doris.

"Married?" I look at her hand, and sure enough, there's the diamond ring.

"I didn't want to tell you over the phone," Gil says apologetically. In other words, he probably didn't want to tell me while Bernard was listening in.

Gil and Doris, Bernard and Melik—it's all so *wrong*. I want my adopted parents back! But I try to appear happy for them. Raising my Coke to toast their engagement, I say, "Oh, well, then congratulations!" But I do it too fast and some cola spills onto the tablecloth and down my arm. "Excuse me, but I have to go to the ladies' room."

I rush to the back of the restaurant and grab the receiver off the pay phone. But who am I going to call? Bernard might stick his head into the bread machine. No, I'd tell him in person, with trained professionals standing by. Craig? What is *he* supposed to do. Olivia? She'll just say, "*Que sera, sera.*" I'll just have to deal with this one on my own. And suddenly I have an idea of how to do exactly that.

When I return to the table Doris charges ahead with her sunny conversation. "And what about you, Hallie? Do you have a boyfriend?"

"Oh sure," I say as if my phone rings so much that I've worn out two answering machines just in the past week. "Tons of them. Why be tied down to one person?"

"I suppose not, at your age," agrees Doris. "But in a few years you may find yourself thinking about settling down and starting a family." She automatically scrunches closer to Gil in the booth and I'm scared to look down for fear that she may be initiating a game of kneesies under the table.

"Maybe," I say. "But I feel as if I have two perfectly good families already—my own and the Stocktons. Hey Gil, remember the time Bernard put the earrings on while we were having breakfast and the coffee sprayed out of your nose and all over the tablecloth?"

But Gil is shaking his head from side to side indicating that this would *not* be a good thing to recollect right now. He moves his eyes toward Doris and I think I get his drift. However, I'm suddenly curious as to exactly how much of Gil's old life Doris knows about. If I really wanted to be evil I could call her up at home and tell her. Or else anonymously send her the picture of Bernard and Gil dressed up as Antony and Cleopatra.

After dinner we drop Doris off at her town house. At first I think it's rather odd that she doesn't stay over; however, Gil explains that Doris leaves for her job as a bookkeeper early in the morning. He invites me back to his place and I'm surprised to find that he still hasn't unpacked. But I suppose that soon enough he and Doris will be buying a house together, and so why bother.

"How is everyone back in Cosgrove?" Gil finally asks. "Is Craig home for the summer?"

"Just for a few weeks, but he's working on building a pond over at the house, and so I guess I'll see him a lot." I feel a sudden rush of excitement talking about Craig. "It's a wild pond—there are going to be lily pads and fish and even lights for at night!"

"So Bernard finally went ahead with the pond." Gil says this a bit regretfully, I think, as if he's fondly recalling the many nest-building projects that were constantly under way.

"He has a new boyfriend." I say this casually and pretend to look over at the pole lamp but keep a careful eye out for any reaction from Gil. "He's a rug dealer, and so of course they have a lot in common."

"I see," Gil appears interested, but not necessarily in a happy sort of way, more like he's listening to bad test results from a doctor's office.

"He loves Bernard's cooking, but then who wouldn't?" I begin to lay it on thick. "And they go to lots of movies together. Melik, that's his name, he's very knowledgeable about foreign films." I'm careful not to mention the recent adoption trauma.

"Oh, Melik, is it? No wonder I haven't heard from Bernard in a while. Does this *Melik*—I mean, is he . . . what does he look like?"

"He's Turkish, with dark shiny hair and these really gorgeous eyes. I figure he's in his late twenties, and in nice shape, too. I guess you get pretty good muscles from lifting all those rugs." I laugh as if this is a joke. But Gil looks really depressed. So I take this as my cue to continue.

"Gosh, he missed you like crazy at first. I was *really* worried about him. Same with Olivia. But now he's back to his usual happy self. Brandt installed a computer down at the shop so, believe it or not, he actually sells merchandise online. And he finally bought one of those grills that you set up on top of the kitchen stove. It has cast-iron construction for superior heat retention and distribution," I quote directly from the manual.

It's hard to tell whether it's the strain of the engagement or the new grill that does the trick, but it's at this moment that I know Gil is going to fall right into line with my plan.

Chapter
Fifty-three

WHEN I ARRIVE BACK FROM CLEVELAND, THE DOWNSTAIRS lights are still on and so I assume that Bernard is waiting in the living room to ambush me. The wreckage from Rocky's rampage has been more or less tidied up, aside from a few pieces that were thrown away or sent out for restoration. But Bernard certainly hasn't forgiven him. Not only does he have the chimp on probation, he's been giving Rocky the silent treatment as well.

It turns out to be Olivia, who's reading a book in the living room while awaiting my arrival, and that Bernard went upstairs to bed after returning from the movies. And Olivia's not there because she's interested in being the first to get the latest gossip on Gil, either.

"I'm afraid the Kunckle situation is going to be more difficult to resolve than I initially thought," she confides in me. "Most of the lawyers with whom the Judge used to work have since retired. And the only one remaining whose legal expertise I respect attempted to get me in a clinch this afternoon, the crazy old fool."

"Sorry to hear that." However, I don't know if I agree that he's crazy, since Olivia is attractive, fun, and sexy. After her husband died, a lot of men in town tried to date her. In fact, if I didn't like Olivia so much, I'd be jealous that she has so many admirers *and* a steady boyfriend, while I've been spending most nights playing hearts against the computer.

"Oh, if only the Judge were still down at the courthouse," says Olivia. "He would have known exactly how to fix this mess!"

"What are you two witches whispering about down there?" Bernard's voice can be heard from the top of the stairwell. He comes down wrapped in his bathrobe and sits in a chair opposite us.

Olivia gives me an exasperated look meant to convey how impossible it is to have a discussion in this house without Bernard either eavesdropping or inserting himself. She's constantly accusing him of being too nosy for his own good. Bernard insists he's been imbued with insatiable curiosity the same way that virtuosity is in the genetic code of all great musicians.

"Mother, you've been entirely too chummy with Hallie over the past few days," says a not-to-be-left-out Bernard. "Whatever are the two of you cooking up? And it had better not be a surprise party for me! Or if it is, I at least need to have some say regarding the menu. And the theme should involve sequins—they're all the rage right now. Maybe Las Vegas or Motown or—"

"Would you be devastated if I said that we weren't discussing *you*?" Olivia cuts him off.

Only I'm secretly guessing that Bernard is actually giving this little performance as a way of demonstrating to us both just how *over* Gil he really is.

"Yes, I *would* find that difficult to believe," Bernard says with mock astonishment. "But if it's the truth, then may I take the liberty of proposing myself as an endlessly fascinating topic of conversation?"

Just then Rocky sneaks up behind Bernard and places his hands over Bernard's eyes the way you do when you want the other person to guess who it is. However, Bernard refuses to play along. "Rocky, stop being a pain in the neck!" he says while removing the chimp's hands from his face. "You've done enough damage for one week. And besides, I'm pretending you don't exist."

When Rocky is no longer directly behind Bernard, I can see that he's wearing a blue-and-white gingham dress complete with white lace gloves, blue hat with white plastic peonies sewn onto the brim, and has a matching blue pocketbook slung over his arm. I recognize the getup from the costume rack in the garage as an outfit worn by Laura Wingfield in Gil's production of *The Glass Menagerie*. This isn't the first time that Rocky has made use of the clothing. He always gets to pick something for bartending at Bernard's theme parties. And once Rocky, Gil, and Bernard dressed up as the Three Gay Caballeros, complete with vests, chaps, and six-shooters, for a benefit to raise money for Gil's theater group.

Now that Rocky has our full attention, he strikes a pose with one hand above his head, the way he's seen Bernard do when showing off a new item of vintage clothing that he's found for the shop.

Olivia laughs so hard that her eyes water. Bernard turns around to see what his mother finds so humorous, and despite the gaily dressed and posed Rocky, he remains in character as the disgruntled homeowner.

"Take that off right now!" orders Bernard.

But Rocky flashes him a wide grin and by this time the overall effect of the ensemble has also struck Bernard and he's beginning to chuckle, silently at first, as if he's still determined to remain angry and is only having a slight body spasm. However, when Rocky opens his pocketbook and offers Bernard a lace-trimmed hankie, Bernard completely loses it, suffers an attack of laughter that sounds not entirely unlike whooping cough, and has to lean on the arm of his chair to keep from toppling over.

Olivia comes over and pats Rocky approvingly and says, "I think you're very convincing as Laura Wingfield."

Bernard looks down at the floor as he attempts to catch his

breath, but every time he glances up and sees Rocky he starts snorting with laughter again. Finally he manages to gasp, "We can tell the audience that Rocky's fur-covered body is *just a slight imperfection!*" Bernard quotes the famous line from the play and then leans backward in another gale of giggles.

Chapter
Fifty-four

BERNARD STILL HAS YET TO ASK ME ABOUT MY DINNER WITH GIL. When I enter the kitchen the next morning he's singing "Mad About the Boy." *I know it's stupid to be mad about the boy, I'm so ashamed of it, But must admit, The sleepless nights I've had about the boy. On the Silver Screen, He melts my foolish heart in every single scene.*

Bernard stops his off-key crooning to deliver a message. "Ray phoned while you were in the shower and wants you to call him back."

"Thanks," I say, and head for the refrigerator.

"He wants you to visit him in Manhattan this weekend," continues Bernard. "Of course, it's much too dangerous to fly these days, not to mention the city itself, and so I implied that I didn't think you should go." Bernard proceeds to tell me about the drafting class Ray is taking at Parsons School of Design. Not only that, but he's pressed Ray into service by asking him to stop at a nearby antiques store and check the price tag on a Hans Holbein rug decorated with stylized Kufic script that Bernard has placed there on consignment. Apparently Bernard is convinced that the owner is lying to him over the phone, insisting he can't sell the rugs that Bernard sends him for nearly as much money as he really does.

"What did you *do*?" I ask. "Interview Ray for the newspaper?" But everyone knows that if Bernard happens to pick up the phone when he's the least bit bored or anxious, he'll talk for an hour, even to someone he doesn't know. Same with customers who wander into the shop. Olivia says she has to at least give Bernard credit for being an "equal opportunity gossip."

"I suppose he sounds like a nice-enough young man," Bernard says and sighs.

It's obvious he had his hopes up that Craig and I would reconnect, especially after throwing the two of us together in the yard. But as anyone can plainly see, Craig arrives in the morning, does his work, and heads off again before dinner, despite Bernard's invitation to join us. Though unbeknownst to Bernard, yesterday when everyone else was gone, Craig and I did have a fun lunch together. We sat in the shed eating Fluffernutter sandwiches and drinking big glasses of chocolate Yoo-hoo with scoops of vanilla ice cream in them. I keep the peanut butter and marshmallow Fluff hidden behind the lawn mower because Bernard insists that it's for "philistines" and will throw it away if he finds it in the kitchen.

Upon finishing the rundown on Ray and the Manhattan rug swindler, Bernard chatters away about the movie that he and Melik went to see as part of a test audience. Afterward they were asked to fill out questionnaires and then participate in a discussion with the famous Danish director Gorm Eghoff.

"The movie takes place in the 1920s and I felt it was my duty to point out that the Zephyr clock on the night table of the wealthy landowner was designed by Kim Weber, inspired by the German Bauhaus style of the period, but not in fact on the market until 1934."

"You told the director that there's a mistake in his movie?" I ask.

"Of course," says Bernard. "I also took the liberty of explaining that Art Deco wasn't meant as a negation of the hard lines and harsh materials of the Industrial Age, as he implied in the film, so much as the design world's answer to jazz—a series of riffs and improvisations on the moods and themes of the early twentieth century."

"And what did Mr. Eghoff say to *that*?" I ask.

"He took my card and expressed an interest in having me consult on the set design for his next film. It's about an impoverished Scandinavian fisherman who moves to Ohio in the 1890s and becomes a hugely successful wheat farmer."

"And let me guess, you may just happen to have some items down at the shop that would be perfect for it."

"Indeed, I might. Mother would have adored the film we saw last night," he continues. "The migrant workers revolted in the end."

"Gil is engaged to Doris," I find myself blurting out.

"Good for him." Bernard is the essence of cool, but I can tell by the way he clenches his jaw that he wasn't prepared for *this*. "I hope she registers at a place where I can buy them some driftwood sculptures, ceramic salt-and-pepper shakers shaped like windmills, and a macramé plant hanger with a big philodendron in it."

"It's time to bury the spatula," I say firmly. "We're going to have dinner with them on Friday night."

"Absolutely not! I will not be seen at a restaurant with those pseudo-heterosexuals. Besides, I've moved on. I've washed that man right out of my hair. And I have no intention of going to his place and making a fool of myself like Freddie, singing 'Here on the Street Where You Live' in front of a periodontist's office."

"You *won't* make a fool of yourself. We'll have dinner here. And you can invite Melik. Don't you want Gil to see what a handsome new boyfriend you have?"

Bernard immediately brightens. "Oh, well, that's different. I suppose that would be okay. But *not* the trollop, just Gil."

"It's too late. I already asked them. And *the trollop* happens to be his fiancée."

Bernard looks horrified upon hearing the *F* word, but appears to pull himself together in short order. "Very well, then. I'll have to plan a special dinner."

In fact, Bernard appears to take the engagement in stride much better than I thought he would, especially since it's coming practically on top of the bad news about the adoption. And whether Bernard is really fine, or simply wants to appear so, he announces that it's the perfect morning to try out his new family-sized frittata pan. It has a latch that releases the bottom of the pan so your creation emerges perfectly intact every time.

When I return from taking out the garbage and turning on the sprinklers, Bernard is just finishing a frittata made of ham, onion, red and green pepper, and mushroom that has golden-brown edges and fills the kitchen with a delicious aroma. He carefully removes the pan from the stove and carries it toward the table, where the china plate is ready to go, warm from being in the oven and now garnished with a bed of purple kale. Only the latch slips and the entire frittata slides onto the floor, splattering into dozens of tiny red, yellow, and green chunks.

"Dammit!" he curses at the pan without a bottom that's in his right hand. He puts his other hand up to his face as if this is the last straw and he's going to burst into tears.

"Don't worry about it," I say. "I'll clean it up. The latch probably just needs tightening."

Bernard recovers himself and studies the side of the pan. "I don't think I locked it the way the directions said to."

"I was in the mood for cereal anyway." Grabbing a wad of paper towels, I start to wipe up the floor.

He lets out a weak laugh. "I guess it's like what Brandt is always telling me about the computer—a frittata pan is only as good as its operator."

Chapter
Fifty-five

Once the frittata fiasco is under control and we're all gathered at the table with toast and cereal, Bernard announces, "I've invited Gil and his girlfriend, Doris, to dinner Friday evening." Only he says this as if it's all *his* idea. And he appears careful not to use the *F* word.

"Well, I think it's wonderful that the two of you have decided to try and be friends," Olivia replies with a smile.

"Since discovering my womb is barren, I'm turning over a new leaf as a more forgiving human being," says Bernard.

"Ah, Gilberto, he is like a zon," Ottavio says with regret in his normally cheerful voice. It's obvious that he misses playing chess with Gil in the evenings while Olivia would work on her poetry, pornography, and blistering editorials.

"Now Hallie," says Olivia, "Bernard told me about your invitation from Ray, and I read in the paper that a new discount airline flying out of Cleveland is offering a fifty-nine-dollar fare to New York this weekend. So if it's simply a matter of the money—"

"Mother, what on earth are you thinking?" asks an indignant Bernard. "Trying to send Hallie off to Manhattan unchaperoned, right into the arms of . . . of . . . a . . . well—"

"Bertie, *what* are you talking about? I was a year *younger* than Hallie when I went to New York on my own for the first time," interrupts Olivia. "How is one to learn about life without living it? The German philosopher Hegel said that the owl of Minerva spreads its wings only with the setting of dusk, meaning that we don't really understand anything until it's done."

Ottavio gets the drift, too. And he sides with Bernard. "Oh Hallonia, why do you want to be with zis boy if he iz not going to marry you?"

"Yes, it's so much more romantic to save yourself!" Bernard is pleased to finally have an ally. He passes me a dish of fresh blueberries. As it turns out, he couldn't bring himself to let the cereal go unembellished.

Fortunately I don't have to defend myself, because Olivia lays into them both, and good. "Stop promoting the idea that women should deprive themselves while men run about pollinating the world like so many bumblebees. As much as we can thank the ancient Athenians for our democracy, they also started this nonsense of finding a woman and then locking her up. Poor Penelope waited faithfully while Odysseus fooled around all over the place."

Not to be deterred, Ottavio places his hands together in front of his face as if cupping something very precious. "Ze woman should be on ze pedestal."

"Pedestal?" harrumphs Olivia. "*Double standard* is more like it! If a woman strays, she's penalized as damaged goods or accused of being an unfit mother. Meantime, men are practically *celebrated* for their conquests. Even today a politician's ratings can go up when he's caught with his pants down. But of course the wife is still criticized—whether she stands by him *or* leaves him. Don't even get me started on countries where men get off scot-free for adultery while the women are stoned to death."

"But Mother, once a young lady throws away her virginity, that's it," says Bernard. "She can never get it back again."

"You should read John Neihardt's poem 'If This Be Sin,' " says Olivia. However, she saves us the trouble, as she often does, by reciting it, and giving special emphasis to the lines: *Can this be sin? This ecstasy of arms and eyes and lips, This thrilling of caressing fingertips.*

Ottavio proudly beams at Olivia as if she's the light of his life. But then he turns to Bernard and says, "Virgin woman is better, I think. Like virgin olive oil."

"And don't forget virgin wool," says Bernard.

Olivia takes a deep breath as if about to continue arguing and then apparently changes her mind. "Oh, what do you know about women anyway?" She directs this comment to her son.

Bernard gives us a mischievous smile. "It so happens that I dated a woman in college."

"This is certainly news!" exclaims Olivia.

"The event in question was similar to visiting an amusement park," says Bernard. "It was someone else's idea, I felt sick afterward, and I never want to go again. No offense, ladies."

"None taken," says Olivia.

"Whereas dating a man is like reading a good mystery novel and I'm always looking forward to the next chapter," continues Bernard. "But I'll have you know that the young lady did continue to consult with me about her wardrobe."

"I'll tell you what the problem is, Hallie," says Olivia, as if Bernard and Ottavio have ceased to exist. "Men are threatened by our sexuality. They can never really be entirely sure who fathered the baby. That's why in Judaism the religion is transferred through the mother. It's rather difficult to fake childbirth."

"Mother, why must you politicize everything?" demands Bernard and then turns his attention back to me. "It's just taking me a little time to accept the fact our little girl is growing up. I miss the frilly pink organdy dresses and matching hair ribbons."

"I *never* wore dresses and hair ribbons!" I strenuously object to this accusation.

"But you would have looked darling in them," Bernard teases me. "Especially with white tights and Mary Janes."

"I'm merely attempting to simplify the matter for Hallie by filtering out some of society's more outmoded views on the subject," says Olivia. "As Georgia O'Keeffe's paintings became more simplified, they became more sensuous."

"Yes, and Georgia O'Keeffe also posed nude for the photographer Alfred Stieglitz," says Bernard, a distinct edge of disapproval in his voice.

Olivia smiles and narrows her eyes at him. "Stieglitz was a world-renowned photographer, and not that it should matter, but he became her husband. Besides, what if I told you that *I'd* posed nude while I was living in Paris."

"I'd say that you were part of a scoliosis screening run by the French Surgeon General's Office." Bernard squeezes his eyes shut, covers his ears with his palms, and makes a humming noise like a ten-year-old who doesn't want to hear one more word of the conversation.

Suddenly Craig comes bounding into the dining room, and when Bernard opens his eyes and removes his hands from his ears, Craig is standing directly in front of him.

"Hello, Daddy!" he addresses Bernard, and envelops him in a bear hug.

Being the caring person that he is, Bernard returns the hug, but says, "Son, I met your mother briefly at the Judge's funeral, and she seems like a very nice woman, but I think we're getting into sort of a gay area here, because I can *assure* you that—"

"Not me!" shouts an excited Craig. "You! You're back on the adoption list! My dad just told me."

I immediately turn to Olivia and blurt out, "But I thought you said the lawyer wanted to sleep with you in order to fix it?" What an *idiot* I am for opening my big mouth! And what if Olivia *had* agreed and decided not to tell me. Fortunately the verb *sleep* drifts over Ottavio's head and he probably assumes that someone was tired, since he remains calm and looks at Bernard for some reaction to this stunning news.

Only Bernard doesn't appear to be at *all* happy with this sudden turn of events. In fact, he looks as if he might take a swing at Craig.

"I thought I made it quite clear that I did *not* want to become the centerpiece of any gay rights campaign," Bernard says in a stern but controlled tone. "And what kind of fresh start is it for some poor little girl to end up on television and in all the newspapers, especially one who is already struggling with a cultural adjustment?"

Olivia pops up like a startled bird and darts to her son's side. "Oh Bertie, calm down. It was *me* who Kunckle wanted to exact his revenge upon."

"Yeah." A stunned and well-meaning Craig finally recovers his speech. "My father said exactly the same thing—that Kunckle is pissed at Olivia for starting an investigation by the labor department. My dad does a lot of work for Kunckle's accounting firm, and when they realized he could end up with even *more* bad publicity if this latest scheme is revealed, Kunckle stopped threatening to pull funding if the adoption wasn't blocked."

For a moment Bernard seems unsure whether to believe that Olivia didn't organize some sort of hunger strike or chain herself to an orphanage in the Far East. But like the rest of us, he knows that his mother never lies about such things. It's simply that her undertakings always sound so wacky, any slightly sane person couldn't possibly believe them to be true. Finally Bernard relaxes and shakes Craig's hand.

Olivia gives Craig a hug, mostly around the chest because he's so much taller than she is. However, she leaves one arm on his waist, steers him from the dining room, and in a somewhat conspiratorial tone asks, "Being as you're studying botany, have you ever considered becoming an activist in support of the environment, formerly known as *nature*?"

Chapter
Fifty-six

On Friday I skip working in the yard in order to help Bernard prepare our dinner party for Gil and Doris. Only I'm not good for much aside from chopping and scrubbing, because Bernard is cooking stuff I've never heard of before—pasta puttanesca, *pollo al diavola,* and tansy pudding.

However, it's a quiet morning, which is a nice change from all the recent drama. Bernard is back on the adoption list, Louise is getting good grades, and Rocky is on the wagon.

The other commotion that has finally come to an end was from the various installers implementing Bernard's redecoration scheme, which Olivia refers to as "Madame Bernard's retail therapy," after Flaubert's Emma Bovary and her propensity for shopping. The workers have finally finished, leaving the rooms feeling fresh and clean and airy, just like spring. Though I wonder if the new pillows with the needlepoint designs of naked people frolicking by a river aren't a bit too eye-catching. But it doesn't really matter, since we have to keep them flipped over in case Mrs. Farley, my mother, or one of Bernard and Olivia's relatives on the Judge's side unexpectedly drops by.

It's still hard to believe that Bernard has entirely given up chintz. Gil had once seriously proposed an intervention when Bernard arrived home with a chintz-covered notepad and matching penholder.

The special fare to New York comes and goes without my doing anything about it. As much as I'm still certain that I want to lose my virginity, there's no way I can miss this dinner with Melik, Doris, and Gil. After all, I organized it. And Bernard is quick to inform me that he's invited Craig. Only he claims Craig won't be here in the capacity of my date, but strictly as "the extra man."

I'm also puzzled by how Bernard keeps insisting that there's not going to be a theme to the evening. Whenever there's a special dinner, Bernard *always* has a theme, even if it's just a color, or a letter of the alphabet. For instance, there was the night everything started with *C*—cauliflower bisque, chicken, couscous, collard greens, and cherry tarts. And of course we drank cider.

While I slice an avocado for the salad, Bernard goes into the living room and begins blasting "I'm Still Here" on the stereo. So much for a quiet morning.

He grabs a ladle to use as a microphone in order to perform the last chorus as a duet with Polly Bergen. *Three cheers, and dammit, C'est la vie! I got through all of last year and I'm here! Lord knows at least I was there, And I'm here! Look who's here! I'm still here!*

It's obvious that he's in a good mood. As soon as Bernard finishes singing, he announces it's time for some new Unitarian haikus.

"I'll begin," says Bernard.

"Seasons of our lives
Naming, wedding, funeral
Must choose Birkenstocks."

"Worthy of a Pulitzer prize," I say, and laugh out loud. However, I've been saving one that I worked on while bored out of my mind in a poli-sci class, just for the occasion.

"What do you mean that
You didn't vote yesterday?
End of a friendship."

Bernard puts down the pepper grinder and claps enthusiastically. "Bravo! Bravo!"

Ottavio enters the kitchen and after peering into a pot he delightedly says, "Puttanesca!" Ottavio places a spoonful of sauce to his lips and appears more than satisfied. "Attsa good!" he says and exits toward the living room.

I'd helped Bernard make the sauce with a spicy concoction of tomatoes, onion, capers, black olives, anchovies, oregano, and garlic, all cooked together in olive oil.

"What does puttanesca mean?" I ask.

"It's derived from *puttana,* which in Italian translates to 'whore,' " explains Bernard. "The name purportedly comes from the fact that the intense fragrance of this sauce was like a siren's call to the men who visited such ladies of pleasure. Also, the pepper flakes make it as hot as an Italian lover."

I can't help but sense there is indeed a theme emerging, or it might be more accurate to say "buried."

"Now, with regard to the actual pasta, *vermicelli* means 'little worms.' " Bernard continues with a diabolical gleam in his eye. "Vermilion is a red dye that in the old days was made from the dried, wormy-looking bodies of insect larvae."

"And is there anything I should know about the grilled chicken, while we're on the subject?" I ask.

"Well," Bernard says coyly, "*pollo al diavola* does mean 'the way the devil likes it,' but I'm sure that's merely because it's spicy."

Right then and there I decide to be sure and put out the *large* water glasses. This is starting to sound like a spell or some sort of witches' brew rather than a nice convivial dinner.

"What about the coconut cookies and the dessert?" I ask. Though I'm not sure I really want to know the answer.

"Coconut comes from the Portuguese word for 'goblin,'" he says with a devilish grin. "And tansy pudding is made with the tart juice of the tansy plant, which takes its name from the Greek word *athanasia,* a cousin of the word *euthanasia* or 'good death.'"

Well, it certainly isn't as if Bernard hasn't put any thought into the evening. As it stands now, we're about one blast of organ music away from a *Scooby-Doo* episode.

Fortunately I can rest assured knowing that our guests won't be able to tell what's on his mind. There's always a courtesy in the way Bernard treats any and all visitors—taking their things, holding a door, and pulling out their chairs. Especially when it comes to women. I honestly believe that's why my mother likes stopping by, just to get her fill of good manners for the week. Though I also think that lately she enjoys seeing Louise actually doing her homework, for a change.

Craig appears at the kitchen window and shouts, "Can Hallie come out and lend me a hand with the fish?"

"Of course, of course," says Bernard and merrily sends me on my way.

I'll never admit it to Bernard, but it's been fun to have Craig working on the pond while I take care of the yard. Sometimes he even stands behind me on the mower and we try to carve zodiac patterns into the grass or else make big spirals and pretend that they're crop circles.

Once I'm outside Craig asks me to help him "introduce" the fish, which are in a wading pool near the shed, into "the environment," which is his newly finished pond.

"Be *very* careful," warns Craig. "The koi aren't mean-spirited or grudge-bearing, but they have extremely sharp, pointy teeth and will easily mistake your fingers for bite-sized snacks."

We stand across the pond from each other and slowly lower the buckets holding the fish and wait until they swim out on their own. Suddenly Craig yells and quickly yanks his hand out of the pond. The top of his first finger is missing. I scream like a girl and run to call an ambulance, while he falls onto the ground laughing. Of course it was that old trick you do to fool little kids by bending the top of your finger down toward your hand. Only under the circumstances I fell for it hook, line, and finger.

After successfully scaring me half to death Craig leaves to buy a new pump for one of his filters and I set to work hacking off a rogue tree branch that has been threatening to poke Bernard in the eye every time he opens the kitchen window. From up on the ladder I can see him taking great pains over the sauce for the chicken and wonder if I should worry about this hex he's trying to cast. I'm already jinxed enough when it comes to love. Maybe I'd better whip up a peanut butter and marshmallow Fluff sandwich for my dinner just to be on the safe side.

Chapter
Fifty-seven

THE DOORBELL RINGS AND BERNARD ANNOUNCES, "FASTEN YOUR seat belts, it's going to be a bumpy night." He adopts the same sniping tone used by Bette Davis when she originally made the pronouncement about a cocktail party heading for disaster in the movie *All About Eve.*

Gil and Doris are the first to arrive and I can't help but wonder if it feels strange for Gil to have to ring the doorbell at a house where he lived for so long and came and went as he pleased. Bernard pumps Gil's hand as if he's genuinely glad to see him, and I believe that he is from the way they both grin at each other. Gil is neatly dressed in a Rugby shirt and chinos, while Doris is in one of her bright floral-print numbers, and is apparently a member in good standing of what Bernard calls The Cluster Bomb School of Accessorizing. I've never seen so many big white plastic beads in one place, at least not since that surprise hailstorm last summer. And then there's a saucer-sized pink porcelain flower brooch perched above her left breast that matches the flowers on her dress. When she walks toward me she *smells* more floral than she looks, if that's possible.

However, Bernard crows over Doris's appearance. "What a *lovely* dress! Did you make that yourself?" Only he's so gushing with his charm that she seemingly interprets this as a huge compliment.

"Heavens, no, Aunt Sally was the seamstress in the family," replies Doris.

Bernard glances again at the ensemble. "Well, it's best to be comfortable, I always say."

"But I do belong to a quilting group," enthuses Doris, once again apparently unaware of Bernard's backhanded put-down.

"Quilting!" Bernard is practically manic now. "Well, you must tell us *all* about it. Mother in particular is fascinated by handiwork." He graciously steers Doris through to Olivia, who when it comes to fabric is probably best known for her remark *If you can't dry it, then don't buy it.*

Bernard turns back to Gil. "I'm so glad that you could come." They stand and stare at each other somewhat awkwardly. "You . . . you've lost some weight."

"Yes . . . well, thanks for inviting us," replies Gil. He glances into the living room and then the dining room. "You've redone the place. It's looks terrific."

"Do you think so?" Bernard pretends that he's not convinced it turned out at all well. "I don't feel that it's quite come together. For instance, the ivory satin trim on the taupe curtains, and also the placement of the new sofa."

But of course Bernard secretly knows that everything looks splendid, and he special-ordered that trim all the way from France. In fact, an interior design magazine is scheduled to come and photograph the downstairs for a story on Victorian houses in the Midwest. And the rooms look particularly lovely this evening, with the tall floating candles and floral arrangements Bernard has tastefully placed throughout. So he's essentially fishing for compliments, as usual.

"No, I really like the lighter colors," exclaims Gil. "It makes the rooms look so much larger."

"I suppose it was time for a change," says Bernard, and it's impossible to tell if he means boyfriends or else sofas and window treatments.

"And that magnificent finish on the piano really stands out now," says Gil.

I tend to think this is more because Bernard has placed a fabulous arrangement of red gladiolas atop the piano, knowing that Gil would be sure to look there—perhaps longingly? I must give Bernard credit, since he did tell Gil to take the piano, being the only one who plays, and it had originally been intended as a gift from Bernard anyway. In fact, Bernard told me that the first few weeks after Gil left, he couldn't even bear to look at the Chickering upright and almost sold it.

Gil continues to glance around as if he's searching for clues to a crime and then exclaims as if he's suddenly been hit with the solution, "There's—there's no more chintz!"

"That's right," Bernard says as if he's kicked a two-hundred-dollar-a-day cocaine habit. "I've gone cold turkey. Chintz is chintzy!"

Just then Rocky darts into the living room and leaps into the arms of his old friend, which makes everybody laugh.

"You wouldn't *believe* what he's been up to," says Bernard.

Melik enters next and it's obvious that Bernard gave him some instructions about dressing. He's drop-dead gorgeous in a blue jersey shirt with a gray silk sport jacket and black jeans. Actually, I wouldn't be the least bit surprised if Bernard hadn't put together the outfit himself, just to be on the safe side.

Once the group is assembled in the living room with drinks in hand, Olivia acts as naturally as if Gil comes to the house with his fiancée every night of the year, and the three chat easily, as if he never left. Ottavio bubbles over with enthusiasm as he does at all social occasions, and runs around smiling and filling glasses with wine and champagne.

Craig arrives last, since after making sure the fish were thriving and the lights around the pond finally worked, he'd gone home to shower and change. Gil shakes Craig's hand and then introduces him to Doris, who is starting to lose track of how everyone is related. This isn't hard to do, since none of us are related aside from Olivia and Bernard.

We finally enter the dining room and sit down at the table, where the flickering glow of lilac-colored candles and a stunning centerpiece of pale purple hydrangeas the size of pompoms make everything appear dramatic yet elegant.

"This is absolute perfection," exclaims Gil.

Bernard waves his hands as if it's completely effortless, practically an accident, and doesn't mention that he went to three different florists before finding exactly the right color flowers to match the napkins and place mats.

Dinner is delicious and so it's impossible to tell that Bernard had concocted it as more of a hex than a meal. Everyone raves about the food, and the chef finds fault, as he always does, by saying that one dish isn't hot enough and the vegetables didn't turn out as planned. But of course Bernard doesn't really mean any of it. His complaints are intended to set off another round of more forceful compliments.

"I was afraid the Bordeaux would be too woody." Bernard directs this comment to Gil, the resident wine connoisseur, at least when he was in residence.

"Just right," exclaims Gil. He holds up his glass and examines it thoughtfully. "Intense color with elegant layering. Powerful concentration, nice integrity, and a good grip."

"Absolutely divine," Doris agrees with him.

"*Excellenza!*" says Ottavio, and raises his glass at Bernard before taking another sip.

"Very nice," says Craig. "It tastes delicious with this wonderfully spicy pasta."

I don't tell him that we're eating *whore pasta*.

Melik just smiles and nods. It's obvious he doesn't know anything about wine and I admire him for not pretending.

"And Gil, thank you for that lovely bottle of wine you brought," says Olivia, always the polite hostess. "It's so sweet of you to remember how Ottavio loves wine from northern Italy."

"Veneto!" adds Ottavio. "Besta wine."

"It's a 1998 Valpolicella from Dal Forno," says Gil. "I think you'll enjoy how dense and satiny it is, yet at the same time well defined and penetrating. When it comes to Ottavio, the more complex the wine, the better, right?" He chuckles and then takes another large swallow of wine.

One glass of wine usually lasts Gil for the evening, yet I notice he's already on his third, not that I'm counting.

"The wine I brought is in the kitchen," Gil continues enthusiastically. "And if you really enjoy it, then you can order more direct from the vineyard by using the Web site."

"And how's your chocolate Yoo-hoo, Hallie?" asks Bernard, not wanting to leave me out.

"It has a lovely bouquet," I say with the air of a critic. "And a pleasant finish—lengthy yet delicate."

As soon as we finish the main course, Bernard finally drops the bomb and announces that he's adopting a baby girl from China. "It could happen any day now."

"Really?" says Gil. And after only a beat he continues, "Congratulations to the father-to-be!" Gil raises his wine goblet to toast the occasion and we all clink glasses.

I'd filled Gil in on this piece of information beforehand; however he makes a good job of acting surprised, just as I'd coached him to do. And once again Craig can't help but look well pleased that his efforts with his father paid off. Though we most certainly avoid going into *that* drama in front of the guests. It only upsets Bernard to be reminded that the adoption had been canceled and then reinstated.

Taking out a picture of a baby who appears to be about nine months old, Bernard passes it around the table. I look at him quizzically and wonder just how many Rommel figurines have gone out the shop door and into the private collection of Mrs. Farley to secure such a photo.

"Little Hermione," Bernard coos lovingly at the picture.

"Hermione?" about four of us exclaim at once. And not in a good way, like we had about the chicken.

"Absolutely not!" pronounces Olivia.

"But it's after Hermione Gingold, in *Gigi*," says Bernard. "Mother, I've always been under the impression that you *adored* Hermione."

"I admired her as an actress," replies Olivia. "And for saying that she'd tried everything in life except incest and folk dancing. But I've never been particularly enamored of the *name* Hermione, at least not for an American."

"If it's a famous name you're after, then why not go with War Emblem or Seabiscuit?" jokes Gil.

Only Melik believes him to be serious. "Take it from me, high school in the United States is bad enough without having a weird name."

Bernard looks to me for support. But I tell him, "I'm with Melik. A kid named Hermione will die a lonely death on the playground after being hung upside down from the monkey bars until all her lunch money drops out of her pockets."

"Any other suggestions?" Bernard challenges us.

"Maria," suggests Ottavio. Leave it to Ottavio to propose that a single gay man raise an adopted Chinese daughter named after the Virgin Mother.

Suddenly Gil puts his napkin to his face and begins to choke rather dramatically. "Bernard, I can't stand it anymore," he sputters. "I can't live without you!"

Chapter
Fifty-eight

ALL EYES TURN TO DORIS, WHO ODDLY ENOUGH APPEARS COMpletely composed and takes a sip of water as if she's accustomed to her fiancé having a few glasses of wine and declaring his love for a man.

Then our communal glance moves to Melik, who also seems totally comfortable with this development.

Gil rushes around to Bernard's side of the table and falls down on bended knee. "I've made a terrible mistake. Please say that you'll take me back!"

Bernard's eyes well up and his right hand goes to his heart, while with the other he pulls Gil up so that they're both standing. "Of course I will, Gil." Passion flows through his voice like electricity through a ground wire.

Both men hug and I feel as if I should applaud.

"I smell something fishy," says Olivia. "Which usually means that Hallie knows about it." She looks to me for an explanation.

Melik and Doris and Craig and I all burst out laughing.

"That's Gil's sister, Kathleen," I say, and point to "Doris." "We just never met her because Gil wasn't talking to anyone in his family until his brother recently died." Then I nod toward Melik. "And *he* is no more Bernard's boyfriend than I am. In fact, Melik has a girlfriend."

Bernard appears stunned. "Then, why all the—"

"Hallie and I thought I'd have a better chance if we made it all very theatrical, you being the Queen of the High Scenes," confesses Gil.

"Mendacity, mendacity," scolds Bernard as if he's the essence of innocence.

"Well, I for one am very pleased that you're coming home, Gil," Olivia states matter-of-factly. "Life hasn't been the same here since you left."

"Oh, Kathleen!" exclaims Bernard. "With those mothball pearls and that floral-print dress, you really had me going!"

"What do you mean?" Kathleen asks innocently, and glances down at her attire as if she's been insulted.

"Oh, nothing," Bernard hastily covers. "They're just so real-looking that I—I . . ."

But Kathleen laughs to let him know he's off the hook. "Gil put this outfit together," she confesses, and shakes a wristful of the gaudy baubles at her brother. "Isn't it just horrendous?"

However, instead of being overcome with relief, Bernard suddenly turns a steely eye toward me. "Wait just a second, Hallie Palmer! How did you find out about Melik?" asks the prizefighter of deception.

"First off, he referred to rugs as *carpeting*," I say.

Bernard performs one of his most dramatic double takes.

"The plot thins!" interjects Gil.

"And then Louise and I saw him at the movies in Timpany," I continue. "Either he had his arm around his *girlfriend,* or else he was sitting next to an attractive young woman who needed comforting through a romantic comedy."

"All right," Bernard confesses. "Melik *was* . . . shall we say, a decoy. He works at the auction house in Youngstown. But it was just a little fibula." He downplays the charges against him. And he takes care not to mention whatever was in it for Melik—most likely some nice commissions or else *deeply* discounted goods.

"God love you for a liar!" Gil quotes Blanche DuBois in *A Streetcar Named Desire.*

"You'll never be any good at bluffing," I say.

Bernard finally comes clean. "When you told me about Herb's wife making him jealous by finding someone else, well, I became inspired to at least try it."

Olivia just shakes her head at Bernard as if she can't believe anyone would go to such lengths to revive a relationship. "You had *me* fooled," she admits. "Since when did you get a master's degree in reverse psychology?" Then Olivia turns her attention back to Gil. "But what about you? I thought this life had become too confining or existential or something to that effect."

"What was I thinking?" he says.

We all laugh because whenever Gil used to come home from a training program exasperated by some of the idiots he worked with, he would insist that he was going to develop a TV game show called "What Were You Thinking!" A person who had just done something incredibly stupid would have to sit in front of a studio audience and retell the story and at the end the audience would all scream out, "*What* were you thinking!" And then they'd push voting buttons, which would either drop the person through a trapdoor in the floor, meaning they were too stupid to live in society, or else a hundred thousand dollars would pour down from the ceiling and the contestant would have a chance to try to rectify his or her own idiocy.

"Hallie noticed that I hadn't unpacked and didn't go out of my way to have Doris sleep over, so she posed the question 'What if Bernard would have you back?' " explains Gil. "When I first reunited with my family I immediately fell back into the trap of trying to be who I thought they wanted me to be. Doris called after the funeral, we had lunch, and . . . I don't know, it just seemed like . . . no one had told her that I was gay . . . she was clearly *very* interested . . . at least in getting married and having children. Only *I* was the one who was making it into an either-or choice, because my family was finally willing to accept me as I am. And when Hallie told me that Bernard might still be open to reconciling, and about the adoption, I knew that it would be so right for us to be together and start a family."

Bernard still seems slightly miffed that his scheme was uncovered. "*I* of course heard Melik say 'carpeting'; however, I didn't think that *you* noticed. But then I suppose you can't con a con."

"Former con, if you don't mind," I correct him.

"*Who taught her everything she knows?*" Gil sings from one of Bernard's favorite songs in the musical *Funny Girl*. "*You taught her everything she knows.*" He has a beautiful voice and I realize how long it's been since we've enjoyed Gil's singing and piano playing.

And I guess Olivia does too. "The *Roses of Picardy*!" Olivia gaily clasps her hands together. "Gil, won't you please sing it?"

We all take our coffee into the living room and I pass the coconut "goblin" cookies. Gil arranges himself at the piano and touches the keys lightly as if to make sure they're in the same spots where he left them. He tries a few chords and then begins a song that sounds old-fashioned, at least in so much as a person can actually understand all the words.

When Gil approaches the last verse, he nods to his sister, Kathleen, and she goes over to the piano and sits next to him. And with the flowers and candles, it looks exactly like one of those English costume dramas where the ladies are required to entertain after dinner. As they sing the last verse together Olivia takes Ottavio's hand in hers and wipes away a tear.

And the roses will die with the summertime,
And our hearts may be far apart,
But there's one rose that dies not in Picardy!
'Tis the rose that I keep in my heart!

I feel an arm go around my waist and assume it's Bernard, or more likely Rocky wanting to dance, but it turns out to be Craig. My heart is suddenly in my throat and when I look down, his beautifully modeled hand is so full of humanity that I'm tempted to take it in mine. However, when I look up he's beaming at Gil and Kathleen and starting to slowly sway to their lovely song. One glance at the moist eyes around the room makes it clear that everyone is feeling warm, friendly, and sentimental, the way they do on Christmas Eve while singing "Silent Night." Thus it's safe to say that Craig would have put his arm around *whoever* was standing next to him at this moment, including Rocky. It just *happens* to be me.

Chapter
Fifty-nine

It's a joyous occasion when Gil moves back home the following day and Bernard and I help him unpack. We're all making jokes and in terrific spirits, except for Rocky, who follows his old pal around as if he's been assigned to prevent Gil from attempting another escape.

"Why is Olivia wearing a WWJD bracelet?" inquires Gil as we break down the last of the boxes. "Has she gone religious on us?"

"It means 'Who Wants Jelly Donuts?'" jokes Bernard.

Gil laughs like crazy and I'm so thrilled that they're together again and that life is back to how it was.

As Bernard returns Gil's baseball glove to its place on the closet shelf in their room, Bernard says to me, "Hallie, why don't you play something like volleyball or soccer at college?"

"Are you kidding? They travel to schools in three other states, *on a bus.* As it is, I barely have time to do my homework. And if I can work my schedule so that I don't have any evening classes, the first thing on my agenda is to find a part-time job."

"Well, they must have sports *on* campus—you could play club badminton or perhaps learn how to fence." Bernard will not give up.

"Frisbee?" suggests Gil.

"Why do you suddenly want me to play sports?" I demand to know. There's no way that Bernard could be worried about my weight. If anything, I've lost a few pounds, between weeding the gardens and not eating pizza or pasta every night. And I wasn't overweight to begin with. "I get a ton of exercise at school and if I build any more muscle from working in the yard I'm going to have to start wearing a poncho so the women's field hockey team doesn't try to draft me."

"It's just that I read an article saying that playing sports helps young women increase their self-esteem."

"And because I want to lose my virginity that means I have low self-esteem?" I guess.

"Oh!" says a surprised Gil. "I wasn't aware that there's a campaign afoot."

"Playing a sport just sounded like fun," Bernard says defensively.

"And exactly what sport did *you* play when you were my age?" I ask.

"I was involved with organized swimming in high school," Bernard cautiously volunteers.

"Then how come whenever I look at your old yearbooks I can't find you in any of the photos for the swim team?" asks Gil.

"I was probably off at another meeting," explains a defensive Bernard. "There were a number of activities in which I participated."

Olivia comes into the room to see how we're getting along with the unpacking. As always, she moves quickly and gracefully, gliding past objects without actually touching them. It's easy to see from the broad smile on Olivia's face how pleased she is that Gil has returned.

"Perfect timing, Livvy," says a mischievous Gil, clapping Bernard on the shoulder. "How come old Bernard here isn't in any of the yearbook photos for the high school swim team?"

Olivia laughs her mellow easy laugh and in a voice that sounds like an enchanted flute she replies, "Because he was in charge of the costumes and scenery for the water show. Bertie was wonderfully innovative—creating floating bouquets out of Styrofoam and melted wax that safely held candles in the center." Olivia smiles proudly at the memory. "When they turned off the lights in the natatorium it was truly spectacular. In fact, I think we may even still have the videotape somewhere."

But Gil and I are laughing like crazy.

"I said *organized swimming*," Bernard defends himself, "not *swim team.*"

"I should have known," roars Gil and collapses onto the bed. "Synchronized swimming!"

Bernard pretends that nothing is wrong or the least bit humorous. "Now let's be serious for a moment, please. I've finally come up with the perfect name for the baby!"

"What?" I ask, still laughing. "Isadora?"

"No." Bernard shakes his head regretfully. "It was one of the first that came to mind, but I fear the children would shorten it to *Izzy.*"

"Dizzy Izzy!" I take it one step further, but Bernard has already gone on to greater names.

"Esther Williams," jokes Gil. When Bernard can't find an old musical to watch, his second choice is always one of those 1940s and '50s swimtaculars that have elaborate water ballet sequences like the one in *Bathing Beauty.*

"Close!" Bernard declares with enthusiasm. "Ethel! To honor Ethel Merman."

"Or Ethel Mertz." Gil is dubious.

I nix that one by telling Bernard, "Keep trying."

"How about Isis?" suggests Olivia.

Thinking back to the elementary school playground, I say, "Kids might turn it into Sissy or Prissy."

"Bernard is from the High German name *Berinhard,*" says Olivia, "which translates into 'being bold like a bear.' "

"One who wears a beret is more like it," jokes Gil.

"I believe *Gilbert* is also from the German," says Olivia. "*Willibehrt* means 'the desire to be bright.' "

"That would be a welcome change," Bernard jabs him back.

"Sorry, Olivia," says Gil. "But I was named after my uncle's winning racehorse, Gilbert's Gold."

"Oh dear." Bernard places his hand to his forehead with a dramatic flourish. "This is the first we've heard about you being christened after a *quadruped.*"

"I consider myself lucky," says Gil. "My uncle was named Stillman because it was the profits from his moonshine that paid for the first horse."

"Kentucky is only two hours by car," says Bernard, "but for some reason it always feels more like time travel."

Gil does have a slight southern accent, but his speaking voice is lovely and people who phone are always saying how charming he sounds. However, Bernard never misses an opportunity to get his digs in about Gil being raised on a farm.

Olivia has apparently had enough of their reunion silliness. "I'll leave you to play the name game while I help Louise with her history paper."

"I'll go with you." I follow her to the door. "Isn't anyone else hungry? Why don't I make us all some sandwiches?"

"Oh, my spirits is rising like a corncob in a cistern," says Gil in an exaggerated southern accent. "Big Mama, be a dear and throw a brace of possum on the spit for me."

Bernard pretends to ignore Gil's hick routine. "We'll be down in half an hour."

Gil reverts to his normal voice and says, "Yes, with all this help from you and Hallie, unpacking has gone just *swimmingly.*" Then he raises his arms, brings one hand back down to plug his nose, and pretends to go underwater.

Chapter
Sixty

My sister Louise is sitting in the dining room nervously chewing a pencil and looking as if she believes there's a chance that her final paper describing the best and worst President will drop out of the nearby Tiffany lamp. Her natural beauty has returned after the upset of early summer. Without all the dark eye makeup, white powder, and brown lipstick, her hazel eyes and red lips have their own lovely brightness, like the gardens during the first few hours after sunrise.

Louise welcomes the arrival of the knowledgeable Olivia and immediately asks if she should write about James Buchanan as the worst President.

"No, he was only the second worst. That political puppet Franklin Pierce was undoubtedly the *most* dreadful. He was responsible for the Kansas-Nebraska Act, which failed to bar slavery from the new territories. Not to mention he spent most of the time intoxicated, eventually earning himself the title Hero of Many a Well-Fought Bottle."

The front door can be heard opening and closing and a moment later Brandt pops his head into the kitchen, where I'm making peanut butter and jelly sandwiches—definitely not a Bernard menu. Though at least it's not peanut butter and marshmallow Fluff.

"Oh boy, sandwiches!" Brandt shouts as if I'm serving filet mignon.

"I thought you were a bat that only feeds at night." The last time I saw Brandt in the daytime was when I called him home after Rocky's "bender," as Bernard now refers to it.

"It's kind of hectic over at the lab today since some mice escaped last night, so I thought it would be better if Louise and I had a quiet place to study for her science exam."

"I'm sure you're right. Only you'll have to get in line, because Olivia's helping her on the final history paper." I nod toward the dining room, where they're still debating candidates.

"The *best* President," Olivia mulls the question aloud. "Hmmm, that's a difficult choice."

"My teacher suggested Thomas Jefferson," offers Louise.

"Much as I admire Mr. Jefferson, he did his best work beforehand," says Olivia.

"And didn't he own slaves while declaring that all men are equal?"

"Inconsistency isn't the same as hypocrisy," declares Olivia.

"I guess that leaves Abraham Lincoln or Franklin Delano Roosevelt," says Louise.

"Neither were Unitarians." Olivia utters this statement as if it's a black mark against them both. "Though a total of five Presidents were—in addition to Jefferson, there's John Adams, his son John Quincy Adams, Millard Fillmore, and William Howard Taft—not bad, considering we're less than one percent of the population in this country."

Olivia never misses an opportunity to showcase accomplished

Unitarians. You can't put on a Band-Aid without hearing the name
Florence Nightingale or listen to a train whistle without her mentioning George Pullman, designer of the sleeper car.

"There was even one Unitarian King," adds Olivia. "John Sigismund, in sixteenth-century Transylvania."

Bernard trots down the stairs. "Really, Mother, I can't imagine
that Unitarian vampires are a part of Louise's homework." He grabs
a roll of paper towels off the kitchen counter and heads back to the
landing.

"I'll have you know that John Sigismund was an excellent
king," counters Olivia. "He allowed for religious tolerance among
the Roman Catholics, Greek Orthodox, Calvinists, and Lutherans.
Not only that, he was a superior linguist and highly artistic."

"Louise, I'll bet you didn't know that Mother is working on a
petition to have the term *Founding Fathers* changed to *Founding Parents,*" jokes Bernard.

"I'm sorry that in your mind winning the right for women to
vote and earn equal pay isn't as important as Jackie Kennedy redecorating the White House." Olivia frowns at her son.

Bernard is too pleased by Gil's moving home to bicker. Going
back up the stairs he trills his favorite line from *Gypsy*, "*Sing out,
Louise!*"

Olivia and I are used to Bernard's musical interludes and we
usually ignore him. He'd somehow bribed my sister to sit with him
through his favorite musical the other day, probably with one of his
delicious quiches, and so now Louise shouts back another line from
the show, "*My name is Gypsy, what's yours?*"

Olivia shakes her head as if it's no wonder that thirty percent of
the American public doesn't know who the Vice-President is. "Best
President." Olivia directs my sister's attention back to the project at
hand by tapping her finger on the cover of Louise's history book. "Of
course, after the whole Vietnam fiasco, no one ever remembers that
Lyndon Johnson started his career as a teacher to poverty-stricken
children, and later as President he signed the Voting Rights Law.
Not only that, he asked Congress to pass legislation requiring the
registration of guns and the licensing of owners, though the gun

lobby fought and killed the effort. Perhaps we can award LBJ an honorable mention."

"Ummm, I think I'll do Abraham Lincoln," says Louise.

"Because he freed the slaves?" asks Olivia.

"No. It's who they chose on *Star Trek*."

At the mention of his favorite show Brandt practically falls into the dining room, where they're working at the table.

"I beg your pardon?" says Olivia. "Rod Serling was a Unitarian but I believe he was known for creating *The Twilight Zone*."

This is too good to miss. I stand in the archway taking in the scene from the sidelines while peeling oranges for a fruit salad.

"On this one episode of *Star Trek,* the Excalbians have no concept of good and evil and want it demonstrated." Louise stuns us all with her unexpected knowledge of Trekkie lore. "So they design a competition between four of history's best and worst people, and one of the best was Abraham Lincoln."

"You like *Star Trek*?" Brandt is barely able to hide his excitement.

"Yeah, sure." I observe that Louise no longer talks to him as if he's intergalactic pond scum. Obviously she truly appreciates the homework help.

"Do you remember who was the father of all the Vulcans?" Brandt is now bouncing up and down on his toes as if anticipating the release of a new batch of pictures taken by the Hubble telescope.

"Mmm, I think it was Surak."

"Yes!" Brandt practically does a jig. "Spock raises his eyebrows *three* times in that episode," he continues eagerly. "And he says the word *fascinating* twice."

"Well, I didn't watch it *that* carefully," says Louise.

Olivia apparently has little idea of what they're talking about, and like a teacher whose students have been distracted by the first snowfall, she attempts to bring Louise back to the task at hand. "So you've decided on Lincoln for the best President? And now that I consider it, I have to agree with you."

"Because he was on *Star Trek*?" I can't help but ask, knowing full well that Olivia rarely watches television. And when she does, it's PBS, not sci-fi.

"No, because he failed miserably before he succeeded," she informs me. "Lincoln failed as a businessman, as a farmer, and in his first attempt at political office. He lost when he sought to be Speaker of the Legislature, was beaten in his first attempt to go to Congress, failed when he tried to be appointed to the US Land Office, lost when he ran for the Senate, and also the Vice-Presidency nomination in 1856."

"You're kidding!" Louise quickly jots down some notes for her paper.

"Not only that, his sweetheart died and he had a nervous breakdown," adds Olivia. "Oh, if Lincoln hadn't been assassinated he could have gone on to write the first self-help book since Benjamin Franklin's autobiography."

"Then I'm *definitely* writing about Lincoln," says Louise.

"Speaking of Benjamin Franklin," says Olivia, "they probably should have asked *him* to write the Declaration of Independence, rather than Thomas Jefferson, who was indeed a slaveholder as you said earlier."

"So why didn't they?" asks Louise.

"I imagine they were too afraid that he'd put jokes in it," says Olivia.

"Hallie, can I talk to you for a minute?" Brandt asks me in a confidential whisper.

"*May I,*" corrects Olivia. Bad grammar has a way of finding her ear no matter how quietly you think you're speaking.

"Sure." I signal him to join me in the kitchen while I finish making lunch.

"Um, in private," he says.

And since there's no such thing as privacy in this house, we head out the front door and around to the backyard. All the while I'm praying, *Please don't let Brandt start up with the dating thing again. At least not before I've at least had a peanut butter and jelly sandwich in order to fortify myself.*

Chapter
Sixty-one

BRANDT AND I WANDER OUTSIDE INTO THE FULLNESS OF SUM-
mer. Under an enormous dome of blue sky and bright yellow sunlight mingle the scents and colors of wisteria, honeysuckle, clematis,
and trumpet vine. The thick leaves of a twisted oak tree provide
shade, while the trunk offers us something to lean against. Eventually we turn toward each other, and from the look on Brandt's face
I'm suddenly worried that we're embarking on a *Scotty, beam me up*
moment. In other words, that he's going to propose.

"Hallie, you know I've always felt that our relationship is special. . . ."

"Sure, me too, Brandt," I say. "But more in the special-friendship
sort of way. You know, like Frodo and Sam." I attempt to explain it
in *Lord of the Rings* terminology so there's a better chance he'll fully
comprehend.

"Exactly," agrees Brandt, to my great relief. "So, Hallie, I was wondering . . . do you believe in true love?"

Uh-oh. Maybe he misunderstood me and I should have tried for a Carl Sagan reference instead.

"No." At least not for Brandt and me I don't. "Well, yeah, sure . . . for *some* people."

"I believe in true love." He has the same glassy-eyed look as Frodo when the power of the ring starts getting to him. "And also that because human beings are capable of complex thought and emotion, they should mate for life."

"Yeah, that's good," I say. "Like my parents." But all I can think of is what a *total slut* I am, spending the better part of my summer scheming to lose my virginity.

"Anyway, I hope you won't be hurt or anything, but I'm in love with Louise."

"Oh. *Oh!*" I'm halfway between shock and cardiac arrest. "Wow, isn't that *something*."

Brandt starts to explain, "You see, I've been looking for some sort of signal from the universe, and when Louise said that about Abe Lincoln and the Vulcan leader . . . I honestly think it's a sign that we were meant to be together."

"Meaning you and Louise?" I just want to be completely clear on this.

"Yeah," he acknowledges with absolute conviction. "Me and Louise."

Knowing that Brandt is one of these wacky scientists who believe in the lost island of Atlantis and life in different galaxies makes it easier to understand his obsession with "signs." Like Olivia says, when people are searching hard enough for something, they tend to find it. Although from the perplexed expression on my face Brandt apparently senses my concern with using a TV character to facilitate a love connection.

"You know, Hallie, in real life Mr. Spock has published some very insightful love poems."

I'm encouraged that Brandt is now delineating between Real Life and Spock World. "Uh, Brandt, does Louise know anything about this? I mean, have you said anything to her?" Or is this like my two-week romance with Josh, the one Josh never knew about?

"We held hands," says Brandt. "Down at the lab."

Oh my gosh! How did I miss this one? A good gambler is supposed to observe the behavior of all the players, and to be on guard for any changes, no matter how small. Is it possible that I was so wrapped up in Ray and Auggie and then getting Bernard and Gil back together that Louise and Brandt had managed to slip under my radar screen? And is he actually a secret dude? Or has my sister been scientifically transformed into a Trekkie down at the laboratory?

"Holding hands counts," I hear myself saying. "I guess you're well on your way. But, um, Brandt, there's something you should know . . . I mean, you need to be careful, because . . . I don't know if I should be the one to say anything, but Louise had a bad experience. . . ."

"Yeah, don't worry. She told me all about it." Brandt exudes a self-confidence that I have to admit does make him seem rather attractive.

"Okay, then, I was just sort of worried that if anyone pressured her, you know, she might have a flashback and go berserk, or something."

"Actually, I, uh, I don't believe in premarital sex."

He *what?*

"Sure," I say, as if maybe I don't, either. Meantime, I'm wracking my brains to remember his family's religion. Or possibly he took some sort of abstinence pledge after his sister got knocked up senior year of high school.

But it's as if Brandt reads my mind.

"I'm not just looking for a mate. I'm searching for a *soul* mate. The soul is what divides us from the animal kingdom. Species in the wild are only following the laws of nature that are necessary for their survival. They're not even cognizant of their own mortality."

Now the proof is in, I'm obviously a species destined to live in the wild, incapable of ever finding a soul mate. Maybe working as a yard person for so long has put me *too* in touch with nature.

"My behavioral sciences studies also lead me to conclude that you produce better offspring from monogamy," Brandt continues to explain his theory. "Take birds, for example. Some of the most famously faithful are penguins, cranes, pigeons, and parrots. In fact, geese, swans, and doves, and albatrosses are generally believed to remain with one partner throughout their entire lives. You see, one bird is needed to incubate the eggs in the nest, keeping them warm and safe from predators, while the mate gathers food to bring back to the nest, a task that may require flying a great distance out to sea to catch fish. In contrast, mammal mothers have the required milk and so the father is free. What contribution to the family is made by an animal constantly in search of a new mate? Though a female preying mantis eats the male after mating, and so she of course needs a fresh partner every time."

"Of course." It sounds as if maybe *I* should start researching the lifestyles of creatures that need a new partner for every date, since that appears to be my future. "Well then, I'm sure you two will have a terrific time together."

"Hallie, I'm so glad there are no hard feelings about, you know, us not ending up together."

"Oh, sure, life has lots of disappointments," I say. "But I guess you really do have to be like Abraham Lincoln, and never give up. I'm sure Mr. Right is out there somewhere. Maybe even on Jupiter, and it's only a matter of getting there."

Brandt appears doubtful about finding life on Jupiter. I probably should have said Mars. But then he suddenly looks happy again. "Actually, this is even better because, who knows, you could be my sister-in-law, and you could be the aunt to my children! Isn't the universe amazing?"

Holy Hobbits! Brother-in-law Brandt? The next forty Thanksgivings together! I think my contribution to science will be changing the longest day of the year from the Summer Solstice to the third Thursday in November.

Actually, starting *immediately,* I have to forget about middle-school Brandt. Brandt is okay now. He's more than okay. He's tall, cute, sweet, smart, and he has a brilliant future ahead of him.

"Yeah, the universe works in mysterious ways," I agree.

Yet deep down I realize that I might miss the Brandt infatuation. Or, alternatively, if I'm suddenly categorizing his defection as a lost opportunity, this could serve to prove that I've indeed turned into a sex maniac. But there's no denying that Brandt had been a constant in my life. I mean, The Crush has been going on since fourth grade, when he'd sent me a whole box of cut-out valentines, the kind meant for the entire class. We were fast approaching our tenth anniversary of unrequited love. I wonder what the suggested gift is for that—night-vision goggles? No matter, it feels as if a cold autumn wind has just blown another page off the calendar of childhood. My frog had suddenly turned into a prince. Only I'm not his princess.

Chapter
Sixty-two

"Hallie!" Gil calls out to the backyard. "There's a FedEx for you."

Nobody has ever sent me a FedEx in my life. It must be the signed copy of my apartment lease for fall. Then I remember the detergent contest and go racing inside.

Sure enough, on the outside of the big envelope is clearly printed:

THE MARKUM CORPORATION.

Gil and Bernard and Brandt surround me as I tear it open. "You must have won the competition!" enthuses Bernard. "We'll cook a celebratory dinner—I have a new recipe for pork tenderloin that would be perfect with a three-bean salad, and sautéed root vegetables in contrasting colors. I'm thinking turnips, purple potatoes, kohlrabi, parsnips, sweet potatoes—"

"Bernard, how about she reads the letter before you start flambéing kohlrabi?" Gil chides him as I unfold the letter and start to scan the contents for anything about a scholarship.

"Look who's talking—Mr. How to Lose Fifteen Pounds by Living on Your Own in Cleveland," retorts Bernard.

"I was exercising more then," Gil defends himself.

"I won second place," I say rather excitedly, because even though it's not first, it's thrilling to win *something*.

"Congratulations!" Gil and Bernard both hug me.

"Mother, Ottavio, Louise—Hallie won second place in the contest!" shouts Bernard.

They all rush into the kitchen to congratulate me.

"What did you win?" asks Louise.

While I flip through the attached pages, Brandt the Brain deduces, "If first place is a scholarship for an entire year, then maybe second prize is half of that—a free semester."

I finally locate the paragraph on the back about my prize. "A pen," I say gloomily. "They're mailing me a calligraphy pen."

"That's all?" asks Louise.

I read aloud from the letter: "Your prize of a Stephens calligraphy pen will be mailed to your home address following receipt of the attached waiver. . . ." My voice trails off in disappointment.

Bernard persists in being upbeat. "I can sell it for you down at the shop if you'd like. I'm sure it's worth fifty dollars or so."

I feel like crying and hurry back outside to drown my sorrows in weed whacking. What rotten luck. I should have taken that job running Cappy's sports betting operation when I had the chance, worked for a year, and then gone to college with plenty of money in my pockets. Where am I going to find six thousand dollars by the end of November, when tuition is due for second semester? And I'll have no way to pay for housing starting in January, either. On top of that, the day after my car was finally fixed, my secondhand computer began exhibiting psychotic tendencies.

While refilling the birdfeeders I lecture the impatient sparrows on how easy they have it, flying around all day and then rocking up at the birdfeeders for free meals. Eventually Bernard calls me inside for dinner. He's had a recent fascination with Belgian cooking and tonight there's a salad of Belgian endive, meatballs baked in beer, fries (which he informs us all did not originate in France, but Belgium), and for dessert he's planning Gaugres Bruxelloises—crisp waffles topped with sweetened whipped cream and strawberries.

Olivia's favorite lyric pieces by Edvard Grieg play softly on the stereo while Bernard lights the candles on the table as well as the ones in the gold sconces on the wall, giving the room a warm glow.

Louise stays for dinner and Brandt actually joins us instead of returning to the lab. The conversation flows as easily as the music and everyone laughs and enjoys their food and seems to be in love. Except for me, that is.

When dinner is over and the dishes are cleaned and put away I head back to the summerhouse. There was a thunderstorm while we were eating so I tramp through puddles and under showery trees while breathing deeply of the air that's now gentle and cool. Above me the sky is a deep crystalline blue and the stars are few and faint. It's the time of day when most creatures head home, and as the shadows deepen and converge, the yard seems very still. Meantime, everything inside me feels so very wide-awake.

I stretch out on the bed and rethink my entry for the competition. Maybe I should have used hip-hop music, or created a dishwasher rap number with all the pots, dishes, and silverware taking different parts and dressing like they're from The Hood. But it feels as if everybody has already done that in one way or another. However, I can't help but wonder what sort of idea took first prize and how the storyboard looked.

My thoughts eventually turn to Ray, and all the other guys I briefly dated during the school year. And then to Auggie, whose heart yearns for Svetlana. And finally to Brandt, who is so certain that Louise is his soul mate. Why haven't I ever felt that way about anyone? Is it like Olivia said, that I'm just not reaching out enough?

Finally I give up and lie back on the bed and stare into the darkness. Drifting through the windows comes the scent of apple and cherry trees after the rain, a sort of bitter sweetness.

Closing my eyes I touch myself in secret places and in that foggy courtyard between dreams and consciousness I imagine my hand is his hand and the pillow I kiss is his face. And even though I don't know who *he* is, my shipwrecked heart pounds with impatience and longing like African drums.

Chapter
Sixty-three

♥ MAYBE BRANDT IS RIGHT AND THERE REALLY IS A COSMIC FORCE at work in the universe. The next morning when I check my E-mails, there's one from Ray saying that he's coming to Cleveland next weekend and asking if I want to get together. Apparently Ray's mother is having a show of her watercolors that he's supposed to attend. She paints vegetables. I'd seen one, an eggplant, specifically, and though I'm no art critic, it's probably a good thing that Ray's father is the primary donor to the small museum where they've offered to display her work.

Anyway, the Auggie disaster did serve at least one purpose, and that was to make me realize that maybe Ray has more potential than I thought. He's nice, a good conversationalist, and unlike Auggie, he's focused on becoming successful. Eventually he wants to have his own construction company and build entire communities and office parks from the ground up. Ray is the kind of guy who will provide for his family and not waste his life chasing after pipe dreams. Sure, a boyfriend who enjoys poetry and wants to be a professional writer is all very romantic, but it doesn't pay the bills. And if I learned one thing growing up in a household with seven kids, there's nothing like a pile of unpaid bills to take the fun out of life. Oh my gosh, I sound *exactly* like my father!

"Is it okay if Ray stays over Saturday night?" I ask at the breakfast table. "He's going to be in Cleveland for the weekend."

"That's a wonderful idea," says Olivia.

"We promise not to show any naked baby pictures," says Gil. "But only because we don't have any."

"Certainly it's all right," Bernard assures me. "Though I was starting to wonder if this attachment wasn't merely a mirage."

"Don't joke," I warn him. "Imaginary boyfriends *are* the next step for me."

"We'll make up the sunroom," says Bernard. "I've put in some new blackout shades, so it can be made nice and dark for sleeping."

But Olivia shoots him a look. "I'm sure that whatever sleeping arrangements Hallie works out with Ray will be perfectly suitable."

After everyone else has left the table except Olivia, I say, "The strangest thing happened. Yesterday Joanne from the garden center called and asked me out."

"What's so unusual about that?" asks Olivia. "Obviously you both have a lot in common, working with flora and fertilizer."

"No, I mean *out,* out on a date."

"Oh!" says Olivia. "Well, as they say, it never hurts to ask."

"But do you think it's possible that she sensed something? I mean, maybe I can't manage to hold on to a boyfriend because I'm . . . gay?" I think back to Auggie just casually dropping how he'd "been with guys," and how Gil tried unsuccessfully to date a few women in college. And then again with Doris.

"During ancient times homosexuality wasn't the opposite of heterosexuality," says Olivia. "In ancient Greece older men went into battle alongside their younger lovers. The idea was that they'd fight more courageously. Plato once said the greatest army is made up of lovers. Though that doesn't mean the Greeks were right about everything. Their poetry about women is very misogynistic."

"But what about in peacetime?" I try not to sound as bewildered as I feel. "And right *now,* in modern-day America?"

"As nice and economical as it would be to have a partner with whom you could share clothes, shoes, and cosmetics, I don't believe that you're gay," concludes Olivia. Though I notice she takes another look at my shitkicker boots over white sweat socks with cutoff shorts and a sleeveless T-shirt that says LEN'S TRACTOR PARTS on the front.

"No, I suppose not," I say. I've never thought about a woman in that way before. And certainly none of those X-rated movies that Debbie's boyfriend liked her to watch with him did anything for me.

"Just remember what I told you about safe sex. Some women say condoms aren't so bad if they put them on, thereby incorporating the ritual into the mood."

"Thanks." I rise to go and water the gardens and the grass before the sun gets too hot.

As I'm leaving, Olivia calls after me. "Hallie."

I stick my head back into the dining room.

"Do think carefully about this." She pauses for a second as if she's been debating whether or not to say this next part, but there's a soft confiding expression in her eyes and she apparently decides to continue. "Something is gained, but something is also lost, and there's no going back. It's like building a beautiful temple—you can't reclaim the grass, trees, and wildflowers that used to be there. It leaves a little indentation on the heart and soul, like a watermark on a good piece of stationery."

But I don't really feel as if there *is* a choice. It's more like I'm already on a galloping horse that's rushing headlong into the wind, and despite my anxiety, there's no turning back.

Chapter
Sixty-four

Today turns out to be one of those rare instances where everybody has someplace to go, and so by lunchtime I actually have the house to myself. Louise had aced her exams, although she continues to take Brandt his lunch down at the lab every day and often hangs out there while he works. Apparently she's developed an interest in genetics and maintains charts on a professor's rabbit experiment—crossing rabbits with different eye colors and then recording how the offspring turn out.

Even though it's only Monday I'm a nervous wreck about the weekend. I mean, how much of what you read in books and see in movies is actually the way sex happens? Is there some sort of schedule where you go from A to B, and after fifteen minutes from B to C, and so forth? And what about Olivia's suggestion about putting on the condom myself? How am I supposed to know how to put on a condom? I've never even looked at one before.

From underneath the bed in the summerhouse I retrieve the

box of condoms that Herb gave me when I bought Louise's pregnancy test. Carefully tearing open a purple foil package, I take out what appears to be a large rubber bottle cap. I try to unroll it but can't figure out which way it's supposed to open. Searching the back of the box for directions, all I find are a bunch of warnings. Apparently a condom is like shampoo and the makers assume that everyone automatically knows how to use it.

I've seen kids using condoms as balloons at school. So I decide to blow into it as a way of finding the right side. Only there's some kind of slimy stuff covering the top that I didn't see and my lips start to go numb, as if I've just had a shot of Novocain. Not only that, but it tastes terrible!

I go back to the house and rinse my mouth out with warm water. My lips feel as if they're getting puffy. I dig through the crisper in the refrigerator until I find a zucchini. Pretending that it's Ray, I attempt to unfurl the condom and get it onto the zucchini.

"Hallie, is that you?" Bernard rushes into the kitchen. "I forgot my checkbook and there's an estate sale. . . ."

Shit. I must have been in the summerhouse when he came back. I drop the half-covered zucchini into the sink while I feel my cheeks catching fire.

Bernard digs his checkbook out from between several packages of nuts piled next to the bread machine. "They have a case of Staffordshire plates and platters. You know how August is, between the weddings and the garden parties, everyone's thinking serve, serve, serve!"

I finally exhale, feeling safe that Bernard didn't see what I was doing. "Right. I'm uh . . ."

The places on my lips and tongue where the gooey stuff hit has partially numbed them and I suddenly sound like my little sister Darlene. "I'm juhtt about to edgthe the front walk."

"Right," says Bernard. "Then I'll see you at dinner." He moves toward the archway that exits through the dining room.

"Thee you later," I say.

He pokes his head back in. "It's very responsible of you to make sure that the squash aren't propagating in the crisper. Vegetable control is so important these days."

Chapter
Sixty-five

WE'RE JUST SITTING DOWN TO DINNER THAT EVENING WHEN THE phone rings. Great, I think. After I've completely embarrassed myself, Ray is calling to say that he's not going to make it *again*. I leap up from the table and bolt into the kitchen.

However, it's only Mrs. Farley looking for Bernard, which is not unusual. If those two aren't talking about the adoption then they're yammering away about decorating or gardening.

"Please tell him it's urgent," she says. From the sound of her voice it's obvious that she's nervous. All I can think is that Edwin the Turd has changed his mind and the adoption is off again. I call into the dining room, where Bernard is serving the salad and Olivia is explaining to Ottavio how Alexander Graham Bell, the inventor of the telephone, was a Unitarian.

Bernard takes the phone from me. "Mrs. Farley, how lovely to hear from you!" he says in his most charming manner. "And what perfect timing! I've discovered one of your lovely figurines in a lot I purchased at an estate sale this afternoon, the one with the little boy riding the blue dolphin." Bernard turns and makes a face at me to indicate he's never seen anything so *gauche* in his entire life.

There's a long pause while Bernard listens. It's not apparent from his expression whether Mrs. Farley is opining about her new statuette or if she's relating more bad news.

"Special circumstances?" I hear Bernard ask with concern. "Yes, I see."

Gil comes in and stands next to him, sensing that something is amiss.

There's another long pause while Bernard listens. Olivia drifts in, to find the three of us all anxiously gathered around the phone.

"Of course, that's fine. Tomorrow at three. Yes, we'll be at the airport by two o'clock sharp."

Did he just say *airport*?

After hanging up the phone Bernard crumples into a nearby chair without uttering a word.

"Is it the baby?" Gil the executive trainer is clearly mentally prepared for spontaneous parenthood.

Bernard appears to be in shock and doesn't answer him.

"Is there something the matter with the child?" Olivia demands to know.

"*Sisters,*" Bernard manages to gasp. "One is ten months and the other is two and a half. Both have a slight case of rickets that can easily be cured."

Gil, Olivia, and I all hug each other with excitement.

"But I thought there's a two-year waiting list for the first baby, and then you have to get on it again for the second one?" I ask.

"A couple from Columbus was picking them up in Beijing yesterday, when the husband was indicted for white-collar crime back in the States." Bernard sounds like an automaton.

Ottavio enters the kitchen and Olivia explains to him in Italian since that's faster.

"*Due bambine!*" he says, clapping his hands together. One thing you can say for those Italians is they love anything that has to do with church or children. They must go absolutely wild at christenings since it's a double-header.

However, Bernard does not appear to be at all excited.

Gil suddenly looks panic-stricken. "Oh my gosh!" he says. "There's so much to *do*!"

"Yes," agrees Olivia. She jumps into action. "Brandt leaves for school in a few days. He'll have to relocate to the sunporch until then."

Gil is right behind her. "I'll call my office and take a personal day."

Bernard is still sitting at the table, dumbstruck. "You know, I'm not sure this is such a good idea after all." He reaches for the phone. "I think I should call and—"

Grabbing the receiver away from him, Gil shouts, "Oh, no you don't! Those little girls just happen to be our *daughters*!"

"Hallie, make some tea and put a nice shot of scotch into Bertie's," says Olivia. She takes the notepad we use for shopping lists off the counter and places it in front of Bernard, along with a pen. "Now, take a memo—two car seats, sleepers, blankets, bedding, diapers, formula, diaper-rash cream . . ."

Bernard simply stares at the blank page.

"*Now,* Bernard!" says Olivia, "We have exactly twenty-four hours to construct a nursery for two children. Hop to it!"

Gil pulls the notepad away from him. "I've got it, keep going."

I'm almost to the front door when I call out, "I have to tell Craig!" After all, if he hadn't asked his father for help, then Bernard might never have been put back on the adoption list. I dash outside to where he was fixing the filter for the pond, but he's already left. Rushing back inside I phone his house. "Craig's out with some friends," his mother tells me. Ouch. I wasn't invited "out" anywhere tonight. I can't help but wonder if he's with friends in general or one specific friend, as in a date. But I have a date coming up as well and so I can't exactly complain.

That evening as we all race through the department store in

Timpany, Bernard still acts as if he's in a trance, incapable of choosing between the circus mobile and the one with the Looney Tunes characters.

Fortunately Olivia has taken charge, and of course incorporated her own agenda. "Go for the cartoons. I don't trust circuses to treat the animals properly."

Chapter
Sixty-six

BEFORE WE LEAVE FOR THE AIRPORT BERNARD INSPECTS THE house and grounds as if foreign dignitaries from a dozen countries will arrive soon. It's a soft gray day with heavy clouds working their way across the sky. In the hedges the silvery spiderwebs tremble with dewdrops. The gardens are bursting with flowers of all different heights and sizes. The bright blooms and the green grass have a gemlike intensity that will last for about another week before it all starts to fade. The only failure has been the inexplicable verbena blight. Last week the tall spiky plants with the different-colored flowers developed white spots and then keeled over as if they'd organized a mass suicide.

Bernard has calmed down slightly since yesterday, or more likely, the enchanting serenity of the lush backyard, which seems to be taking on the very color of hope itself, is having a temporary relaxing effect on him. He even stops to pull a few half-wilted blooms off here and there, and rinse out the birdbath before refilling it.

Together we stroll over to the pond, which Craig had finally finished the day before, and admire the tranquil preserve with colorful fish gliding through the water as dragonflies pirouette above and whirligig beetles skim the surface. Raindrops hang from the pampas grass around the edges like tears clinging to eyelashes. Bernard had given Craig free rein on the shape of the pond and Olivia had secretly convinced him to make it into a replica of Cuba, in order to protest US government sanctions that prevent the common citizens from raising their standard of living. A lion-head fountain pours a slipstream of water out of its mouth, making a constant ripple to mark the capital, Havana. Near the banks Craig had installed plants that thrive on water—hostas, ferns, Himalayan poppies, candelabra primulas, rhododendrons, irises, bamboo, and dozens of Asian lilies.

When Olivia came inside early this morning she said that with the mist rising off the pond and the lily pads appearing a bit blurry around the edges, it reminded her of a painting that Monet did of his water garden in Giverny.

Bernard clutches his chest and says, "It takes my breasts away." This is the highest compliment he gives to anything.

A faint rainbow starts to spread across the sky in the east. We both look at it appreciatively and then Bernard turns to me and gives the impression that he's scrutinizing my acid-washed jeans and T-shirt with JOE'S CAR WASH emblazoned on the front. Nodding back toward the rainbow, he uses the moment as an opportunity for a fashion lesson. "You see, even God accessorizes with colorful little touches here and there for special occasions."

I return to the previous subject. "Craig did a terrific job on the pond. I'll sort of miss having him around."

Bernard gives me an *I told you so* glance and then innocently states, "Of course, I didn't mean to *throw* the two of you together. I merely thought that as long as you were so determined to do this . . . this *thing* . . . that he's such a nice young fellow. And no matter what happened, you'd never be sorry about it."

"You still want me to wait."

"Yes, of course. But I'd have you waiting until you were forty, so you can't listen to me. It's just that men can be such . . . well, it's not as important to them, that's all. Make sure it's what you want and that you're not trying to please somebody else."

From the kitchen window Gil signals us that we have to leave for the airport *now*. Once again a look of dread crosses Bernard's face, and by the time we're in the car I'm pretty sure he's developed a nervous tic on the left side of his face.

Mrs. Farley meets us at the airport with mounds of paperwork that Gil ends up having to take care of since Bernard is too rattled to cope. However, she assures everyone that "preadoption jitters" are perfectly normal. Then she proceeds to terrify us by explaining that the girls are going to be slightly malnourished, small for their ages, and developmentally behind. But she says this is typical for children who have been in these orphanages and that with the proper care they'll catch up in no time at all. Mrs. Farley passes Gil an index card containing the names and numbers of two pediatricians in Cleveland who specialize in this sort of thing, since Bernard is now pacing in front of the snack bar and muttering to himself at a volume that is arousing the interest of a nearby security guard.

The rest of us stare at the jetway, which has finally begun disgorging tired-looking passengers. I'd thought the babies would be sent off first, but we end up waiting until all the regular travelers have disembarked, and then there's ten long minutes where nothing happens. Eventually we turn to Mrs. Farley, wondering aloud if there's a chance they could have missed the flight.

Meantime, the airport security guard has approached Bernard as a possible terrorist suspect. Olivia is called upon to explain why he's behaving so erratically, and that it's not his intention to plant a bomb. Though Olivia can't help herself when a metaphor is within range, and proceeds to tell the guard how the writer Nora Ephron once equated having a baby to a bomb going off in a marriage. Between Olivia's free-associations, Bernard's muttering, Gil's hand-wringing, and my jumping up and down on my toes to see above the crowd, the guard begins backing away. It's apparent from his expression that he's decided we're not armed and dangerous, just slightly crazy.

When we're about to give up hope, and even Mrs. Farley is biting her lower lip while checking the notes on her clipboard and shifting her weight from one Bass Weejun to the other, two nuns in light brown habits carrying baby-shaped bundles in yellow blankets seem to magically appear in front of the gate.

As the children finally come within reach, Bernard suddenly snaps to. While Olivia, Gil, and I are still exclaiming and cooing over the sleeping little girls, he begins barking orders about bibs and bottles. However, the nuns calmly assure him that the babies have been fed and are ready to go home.

When we get in the car, I notice the little tags around their ankles that say "Ling" and "Ming." "Oh my gosh, we forgot about the names."

"Those names are kind of cute," says Gil. "We could keep them."

"Heavens, no!" Bernard bristles at the very idea. "They sound like *pandas* at the *zoo*."

"Just tell me you're not still considering Hermione and Ethel," pleads Olivia.

"Close," replies Bernard. "I've chosen Gigi and Rose. Hermione Gingold starred in *Gigi,* and Ethel Merman played the part of Mama Rose in *Gypsy.*"

"Gigi and Rose," repeats Gil, testing out the names.

"Or else Cosette and Fantine," says Bernard, "From *Les Misérables.*"

"Gigi and Rose are perfect!" exclaims Gil.

Chapter
Sixty-seven

THE GIRLS ARE ADORABLE, WITH THEIR MOON-SHAPED FACES, cheeks the color of pink impatiens, and dark almond-shaped eyes. The older one, Rose, has thick black hair and red, red lips that make her look like a porcelain doll. She babbles away and we don't know if it's Chinese or baby talk, or more likely, Chinese baby talk. Little Gigi looks like a tiny version of her older sister, but with chubbier cheeks and short spiky hair that Gil claims makes her look like a punk rocker. He sings Pat Benatar's "We Belong" while rocking her in his arms.

The first night goes smoothly enough. We feed them baby food and bottles and they're sweet and all gurgles and smiles. Gigi is the happiest infant I've ever seen and has a sweet little laugh that could probably summon the sparrows right out of the trees. Bernard's most pressing concern turns out to be what music he should play in order to foster their development—Mozart or a Chinese opera called *The Lute Song.*

The next day I have to drive to Cleveland and attempt to dig up a new roommate, since one of ours fell through and we can't afford the apartment without a fourth person. When I arrive home at a quarter past five, Bernard is quick to tell me that having children is the easiest thing in the world. In fact, he is actually criticizing the way Olivia picks up Gigi and Gil's handling of bottle-warming, and generally putting on airs suggesting that after twenty-four full hours on the job he's the new nationally recognized authority on the subject of parenting.

However, after dinner baby Gigi starts crying and *will not stop.* Not even Olivia's gentle rocking and soothing voice can calm her down. And Bernard's rendition of Ethel Merman singing "The Lullaby of Broadway" seems to only make matters worse. Rocky is the first to defect. He heads outside, grinding his teeth and covering his ears with his hands. Though whether he's fleeing because of Gigi's wailing or Bernard's high notes is difficult to determine.

"Maybe she has colic," suggests Gil. "My dad used to have to drive me around in the car for an hour every night in order to put me to sleep."

Gigi continues her howling. Bernard tears through all the baby books. "Look it up on the Internet!" he pleads with me. But all my search reveals is that "Crybaby" is a rap song featuring Snoop Dogg.

After a solid hour of Gigi's nonstop wailing, Bernard is one baby step away from The Nervous Hospital, and announces that he's going to call a pediatrician. And if the doctor can't be reached, they're checking in at the Emergency Room, both of them. That's when I get a truly brilliant idea.

"My mom!" I practically shout, though more to be heard over Gigi than out of sheer excitement. "What an idiot! Why didn't I think of this sooner? She could have written a dozen books on babies, only she's been too busy *having* them! I'll call her right now and ask her to come over."

Relief spreads across Bernard's face and he quickly wraps a

blanket around the sobbing child. "We deliver. It's only half past seven. Do you think she's at home?"

"Are you kidding?" I ask. "You don't *go anywhere* when you're pregnant and raising six kids on a budget."

Gil stays behind to put Rose to bed while Bernard and I bring Gigi to my old house. By the time we arrive, the baby is bright red all over from wailing and I'm surprised she has any energy left at all. Sometimes she'll stop for a few seconds to catch her breath and you think it's going to quiet down but then she gets going again, louder than ever.

We don't even have a chance to knock before the door flies open, as if Mom is St. Peter working the gates and our names are next on the list. She doesn't have to ask why we're there, either.

My mother smiles down at little Gigi and takes the suffering child into her arms. We follow her inside the house. Fortunately, Bernard is too distracted by the baby to be frightened by the decoupage situation. Simply put, between rainy-day projects and Mom's final few weeks of every pregnancy, the house has been hit hard.

Mom sits on the couch, positions Gigi facedown in her lap, and gently rolls her back and forth. "Gas," she diagnoses with quiet authority. Soon some loud sounds emerge from the baby's snuggly and she stops crying. "It has to come out one of two places," Mom instructs us. "Either the basement or the attic."

When Mom lifts Gigi up again, the infant's complexion has reverted to its normal pink-cheeked ivory. The baby glances over at us with eyelids drooping and promptly falls asleep.

Darlene screeches through the room carrying a handheld video game, with her twin brother, Davy, in hot pursuit, only he's slightly hampered by having his foot in a cast and trying to run on crutches.

Mom shushes them and warns, "Give him back his game right now, Darlene, or you're both heading off to bed this second." Darlene relents and they scamper out of the room. Or rather, Darlene scampers off and Davy hobbles after her while attempting to trip her with his crutches. They've only been out of sight for a second when it's obvious from Davy's penetrating scream that Darlene has snatched the game right back.

"What happened to his foot?" asks Bernard, his voice filled with concern.

"Your guess is as good as mine," my mother says offhandedly. "They'll never tell you the truth when it involves the other children. Probably wrestling." It isn't that my mother doesn't worry about us, but with a total of eight kids, there's always one in a cast, one getting flu, one with flu, and one just getting over flu. Teeth are knocked out or pulled out almost daily. It's hard to believe that Mom was actually overprotective when Eric and I were toddlers. But a dozen broken bones and forty trips to the emergency room have turned her into something of a fatalist with regard to health and safety.

Dad enters the room, carefully stepping over a large ant farm and a Lego robot, and then around a blanket fort, which ends up tripping him because a chair leg is sticking out.

"Teddy!" my mom calls toward the back of the house. "Clean up this fort right now or you're not playing baseball tomorrow!"

"So how's fatherhood?" Dad claps Bernard on the back in comradely fashion. Granted, it's taken Dad a year to warm up to the Stocktons, but the fact that I miraculously ended up going to college after living in their house for nine months has had the effect of casting them in an extremely favorable light.

"There are a few things that aren't in the books," Bernard says, and shoots an appreciative glance toward my mother. "I had no idea that parenting is more of an art than a science."

"You learn as you go," Dad says with encouragement. Teddy reports for fort-removal duty and Dad gives him a pat on the head.

"Who dinged the car?" I ask Dad. I'd noticed it in the driveway. There isn't much chance it was my father. Then again, he rarely lends his car to us kids.

"Louise. On the last day of summer school she missed the bus. Your mother says that's what insurance is for." He shrugs and gives a wry smile. "I'm just relieved your sister isn't staying out until all hours and hanging out with those *people* anymore."

"Yeah." I say. "She did really well in her classes."

"And this new boyfriend, Brandt, he doesn't play sports but he's going places. Very academic."

Dad loves a young person who's sensible and "going places." Especially if the places happen to be high school, church, the library, and then college. And the fact that Louise is still hanging around with Brandt now that exams are out of the way and her science project is finished, not to mention *introducing him to our parents,* must mean that she truly does like him. Because I don't think it'd be worth marrying him just for his *Star Trek* DVD collection.

Mom hands the sleeping Gigi back to Bernard. "She's still a tiny thing. After every meal you have to keep bouncing her until you get that burp."

"I can't thank you enough." Bernard is practically tearful with gratitude. I'm sure the day Mom first came to lunch at the Stocktons he never dreamed he'd be asking *her* for advice.

"Give us a call anytime," says Mom. "The door's always open. And fortunately babies aren't as fragile as they look."

"You think this is bad," jokes Dad, "wait until the girls get to be teenagers." He places his hand on my shoulder and gives it a squeeze.

"Ha ha. Very funny," I say. "Let's keep in mind who will be choosing your nursing home."

A fight breaks out at the top of the stairs and Mom looks over at Dad to indicate that he's in charge of fights, the same way he looks at her when one of the kids pukes. My parents have been doing this so long that they don't even need to exchange words anymore.

"Excuse me, but the troops are restless." Dad hitches up his pants and heads toward the stairs. However, he steers me under the archway in front of him. In a quiet voice he says, "Al Santora was laid off six weeks ago."

"Oh no," I say. *Oh no,* I think. That's why he was at Cappy's poker game, probably trying to win money for the mortgage. His wife stays at home with the kids and doesn't have any sort of income.

"It's terrible." Dad shakes his head. "The government is cutting money to the states left and right. This fall the school may only have a four-day week. And it's a tough job market out there."

"What's he going to do?" I ask.

"He'll get unemployment for a while and if worse comes to

worst the church will help. I've spoken with Pastor Costello." Then he brightens slightly. "But if things pick up and the state passes a new budget, he could eventually get his old job back, with all the benefits."

The yelling upstairs suddenly becomes louder and there's a crash followed by accusations. "Ten, nine, eight, seven . . ." Dad heads up the stairs while counting as a way of announcing his arrival, so hopefully they'll break it up on their own and he can save his energy for stopping the pillow fights after lights-out.

I reenter the living room just as the ruckus upstairs stops, and Bernard observes, "Oh, I like the way he does the counting thing, very clever."

As we head out the door, Mom advises, "Forget all the books. Threats and bribery are your two basic child-rearing tools. Remember that and you'll be just fine."

Threats and bribery? I can't believe these words came out of the mouth of my Christian mother. People really aren't kidding when they say that motherhood changes a person. Though I suppose by the time your ninth child is on the way you have to operate with an eye toward efficiency. And this doesn't always incorporate taking into account the views of the child.

Chapter
Sixty-eight

BERNARD STUMBLES INTO THE KITCHEN LATER THAN USUAL THE
following morning, still wearing a bathrobe. With his face all blotchy
and hair uncombed, he appears exhausted.

"The kids slept fine after we got home, didn't they?" I inquire.

"I was up all night—worrying about them at age six and ten and
fourteen and nineteen. They're not allowed to wrestle, date, or
drive. That's all there is to it."

Brandt is making trips back and forth to load his car with chemistry apparatus, notebooks, and a few T-shirts, while Louise slouches
around behind him with a dejected look on her face. Yes, Brandt
had turned out to be more than just a way to pass science, he'd become a way of life and she even admitted to me that she's in love
with him. I didn't venture to ask how she finally came to terms with
his fading but nonetheless ingrained geekiness, only she'd read my
mind and declared, "Hallie, just look at Bill Gates!"

The whole crew gathers out front to wave Brandt off, and Bernard provides a hamper full of food for the drive to Massachusetts that should easily hold him through Thanksgiving. It's hard to believe that only fourteen months ago this now confident young man pulled up in Officer Rich's pickup truck hunched over and anxious. Brandt offers to drop Louise at home on the way out of town and so we end up seeing the couple off as if they're newlyweds, shouting our version of science farewells, such as "Don't break the sound barrier on the interstate." Brandt honks the horn and Louise waves as they turn out of the driveway.

After they've gone we gather around the table for breakfast, and with a twinkle in her bright blue eyes, Olivia announces that she has some news. Meantime, Ottavio appears ecstatic, practically waltzing through the dining room, offering to pour tea or coffee for everyone. If they were thirty years younger I'd lay odds ten to one that she's pregnant.

"Let me guess," says Bernard. "You've single-handedly managed to finally pass the Equal Rights Amendment for women."

"Unfortunately, no," replies his mother.

"Just tell us if we should be taking out more homeowner's insurance," jokes Gil, referring to the protesters and journalists who often mob the front lawn after one of Olivia's famous editorials.

Olivia holds out her left hand. On her ring finger is an oval sapphire that perfectly matches her sparkling eyes, set in white gold and surrounded by ten small diamonds.

Ottavio is by now half-demented with joy and can no longer contain his excitement. He loudly proclaims, *"Essere fidanzato!"*

"We're engaged," Olivia translates for those of us who haven't been keeping up with our Italian.

Bernard and I are actually *more* surprised than if she had single-handedly pushed the Equal Rights Amendment through Congress.

"Congratulations!" we all shout merrily.

Romance suddenly seems to be blossoming everywhere. It actually gives me hope that with Ray coming tomorrow, I might be next!

"Ottavio has even called the hospital to ensure that he's allowed into the emergency room now that he's my fiancé," says Olivia.

Ottavio takes the hand with the ring and repeats, *"Fidanzato,"* as if to make sure everyone is clear about his elevated status. "Attsa good!"

Olivia gives Ottavio a passionate but not indecent kiss, which obviously pleases him even more. I'm always impressed by the way she manages her sexuality with such mature grace.

"And have you set a date?" There's mischief in Bernard's voice.

"Oh, no rush," Olivia says hastily, and waves the hand with the ring through the empty air. "Perhaps winter."

"Or maybe the spring," suggests Bernard, and gives her a knowing smile, indicating that he understands this might be an extraordinarily *long* engagement.

But questions about scheduling fail to dim Ottavio's rapture. He's clearly thrilled by the fact that when they arrive in Italy next month to visit his family, he'll be able to introduce Olivia as his intended.

There's a knock at the front door and I open it to find my friend Jane standing on the porch. "Hallie, my dad is moving out, and it's so awful I just can't stand to be there to watch." Her eyes shine with tears. "Do you mind if I come in?"

"Of course not," I say, and usher her inside. "It's just the usual chaos around here—Gil moved back in, we have two Chinese babies, Brandt left for college, and he and my sister have agreed to try a long-distance relationship, I'm planning to lose my virginity over the weekend, and right now we're having an engagement party."

Her eyes widen with surprise. "Gil and Bernard?"

"Nope. Olivia and Ottavio."

"Wow," says Jane. "How old is Olivia?"

"I guess sixty-something. Bernard says that age is a number and hers is unlisted. I'm not sure that even *he* knows."

"Gosh, maybe there's hope my mom will meet someone else one of these days," says Jane. "She hates being alone."

As we head toward the dining room, I whisper, "And don't ask about the wedding date, either, because I'm not sure there's ever going to be one."

Chapter
Sixty-nine

TOMORROW IS THE BIG NIGHT. THE PAST FORTY-EIGHT HOURS have felt longer than the seventeen years preceding them. We've all been running around like crazy trying to get the children set up with doctors, potty seats, and feeding schedules. I keep glancing toward the clock and there's now only twenty-nine hours and forty-one minutes to go.

As soon as the girls are put down for their naps after lunch, Bernard collapses onto the sofa in the living room. In fact, I'm surprised he has the energy to pick up his menu-planning pad and pencil. Because if there's going to be a dinner theme it should be "cream"—creamed corn, cream of wheat, and diaper-rash cream.

"Now, Hallie," says Bernard, "Mother, Ottavio, Gil, and I have arranged to take the girls to eat out tomorrow night. So what were you planning to prepare for Ray? Perhaps I can offer some culinary advice." And the way his pen is poised, it's obvious he's ready with more than just advice.

"I'm not making him anything for dinner. We'll go to the pizza parlor. Or maybe over to that new Thai takeout place."

It's hard to say whether it's the word *pizza* or *takeout* that provokes the expression of horror on Bernard's face. Or else he's having a stroke.

"Oh my! No, no, no, Hallie. *The dining room is a theater . . . the table is a stage!*" Bernard allows his pad and pencil to drop to the floor. "That was said by Chatillon-Plessis, a nineteenth-century French journalist who knew whereof he spoke. *Mother,* please tell her!"

"I'm afraid he's correct, dear," agrees Olivia, seating herself next to Bernard on the sofa. "Virgina Woolf famously said that one cannot think well, love well, and sleep well if one has not dined well." Olivia has a Virginia Woolf quote for every occasion the same way that Hallmark has a greeting card.

"But I thought that Virginia Woolf filled her pockets with stones and then drowned herself in a river," I say.

"She was a poet. They always have to take these things a step too far." Bernard says this to me but he nods toward Olivia, as if she should take a lesson from that.

However, I still get the feeling that Bernard wishes Olivia would intervene further by suggesting that my amorous evening end on third base rather than home plate. If he's not recommending sports to build my self-esteem then he's leaving articles on my bed about how yoga can "nourish the body and soul." Olivia claims it's because Bernard romanticizes the past, particularly the outwardly chaste Victorians, partly as a result of dealing in the furniture from that period.

"If you've made up your mind to be a modern woman, then you must create a milieu that sets the stage for seduction, not a game of Nerf basketball," insists Bernard. "You need to cook Ray dinner and eat by candlelight with Debussy's *Suite Bergamasque* playing softly in the background." He lifts his pencil and starts by writing "tapered ivory candles" at the top of the page.

I'm suddenly having a flashback to my high school prom, when Bernard more or less took over. Though I must admit that the results were excellent. The dress he chose for me was a dream and the post-prom breakfast back at the house was lots of fun, too. Kids are still talking about Rocky wearing the sombrero and matador's cape to serve the gazpacho.

"You should start with a basil eggplant soup." Bernard continues to write items on his list.

Meanwhile, Olivia takes over the commentary. "Basil was considered the royal herb by the Greeks. And in Haitian lore it comes from Erzulie, their goddess of love."

"For the entrée you'll make a honey-glazed ham," says Bernard.

Gil looks up from playing chess with Ottavio. "Put pineapple chunks on it."

"That's soooo *bourgeois!*" says Bernard.

"What's wrong with pineapple chunks?" I ask.

"Fine. If we're becoming white trash then you may as well go all the way and stick canned pineapple circles on the outside using toothpicks topped with maraschino cherries. And why don't we use pork rinds as garnish while we're at it?"

"Sounds good to me." Gil grins, always proud of his country roots.

"One eight-pound ham," Bernard says as he writes it down.

"What's romantic about *ham?*" I ask.

"Nothing if he's Jewish," observes Olivia.

"Whoops, I forgot about that," says Bernard. "Is he Jewish?"

"Ray Vincent Bolliteri? I don't think so."

"*Italiano!*" Ottavio shouts with obvious delight.

Good, I think. *Maybe this will keep Ottavio from shooting him when he goes back to the summerhouse with me.*

"The honey is what makes it a passion food," explains Olivia. "Honey has been connected with sensuality going back to the *Kama Sutra* and even the Bible. In the fifth century B.C. Hippocrates prescribed it for sexual vigor. And in India a bridegroom is often given honey on his wedding day."

"Attila the Hun drank himself to death with honey on his honeymoon," adds Gil. One of Gil's hobbies is collecting stories about weird deaths, like the motorcycle gang that met at the top of a hill by arriving from different directions, collided, and all died. And the man who was hit with a department-store angel that blew off the roof in a high wind.

"King Solomon said, '*Your lips drop sweetness as the honeycomb, my bride; milk and honey are under your tongue,*'" recites Olivia. "And also, '*I have eaten my honeycomb and my honey; I have drunk my wine and my milk.*'"

"We need a vegetable," Bernard speaks directly to Olivia, as if I'm no longer in the room. "Artichokes or asparagus?"

"Definitely asparagus," says Olivia. "The great French lovers of yesteryear dined on three courses of it the night before a wedding."

"Why asparagus?" I ask.

"The Law of Similarities," Olivia continues. "The theory says that if one thing is reminiscent of another, then it will improve or aid that which it looks like." And to think people are always saying that she doesn't know anything about science.

"Roasted white asparagus." Bernard jots several more ingredients down on his fast-growing list. "And a chocolate torte for dessert."

"Absolutely," agrees Olivia.

"The Aztecs and Mayans were the first to recognize the potency of chocolate, celebrating the harvest of the cacao bean with festivals of wild orgies," explains Bernard. "The Aztec ruler, Montezuma, reportedly drank fifty cups of chocolate each day to better serve his harem of six hundred women. And in the Mayan empire payment for a night at a brothel cost one handful of cacao beans."

"During the seventeenth century, chocolate was considered to be such a sexual stimulant that church officials deemed it sinful to partake of it." Olivia always seems in favor of doing anything the church has prohibited, no matter what the century.

"Grapes," suggests Gil from across the room.

"Goes without saying." Bernard taps his pen to indicate that they're already on the list.

"The ultimate aphrodisiac," says Olivia. "Thank goodness the boycott was eventually settled."

"I wasn't allowed to have a grape until I was ten," explains Bernard. "Mother and her Unitarian cohorts were protesting the insufficient wages earned by the grape and lettuce pickers."

"Bertie, what about those grapes you make with a thin layer of cream cheese rolled in almonds and crystallized ginger?" asks Olivia.

"Oh yes, I'd forgotten about those. They take forever to prepare but are certainly delicious."

I may as well be out watering the gardens the way these two have taken over the planning of *my* date.

"How about caviar?" asks Olivia.

"Too advanced," says Bernard. "Like oysters."

"Yuck," I say right back.

"See, I told you," Bernard tells Olivia. "Same with strawberries."

"But I *like* strawberries," I say.

"Stop being so contrary," says Bernard. "If we'd said you couldn't have the grapes then you would have wanted those."

"But how can eating strawberries be *too advanced?*"

"For the same reason they don't teach Milton in grammar school," says Olivia. "It would be wasted on the young. Besides, we all need something to aspire to."

"But how will I *know* when I'm ready for caviar and strawberries?"

Bernard laughs. "Don't worry. I'm sure that Mother will tell you."

He passes me a clean copy of the final menu. "But I don't know how to make any of this stuff," I protest.

"I'll assist you," offers Bernard. "And then magically disappear right before your beau arrives."

"If you're going to go to all this trouble then why don't you just stay for dinner?"

"We don't want to intrude," says Olivia. "Or intimidate the young man by suggesting that we're evaluating him in any way."

"Okay," I agree.

"But if you *insist.*" Bernard snatches back the list and increases all the portions so there will be enough for six instead of just two.

Gil is chuckling over at the chess table. I guess he saw this one coming about five moves ago.

"What about flowers?" asks Bernard. "Will he bring an arrangement?"

"Doubtful," I say. Though Ray could usually be counted on for a six-pack and a bucket of wings.

"Then I'm thinking agapanthus, asters, or maybe red tea roses with baby's breath," says Bernard.

"I've always preferred a bouquet of Four Roses, myself," says Olivia. It's no secret that she and Ottavio enjoy their five o'clock cocktail.

Bernard shoots her a look as if to say this is *no* time to be fooling around. "Now what about the music?" He walks over to inspect the CD collection.

"I hadn't thought about it," I say. "Ray likes Supreme Beings of Leisure, Soulstice, and Blue 6."

"No, no, and no." Bernard waves his pencil like a laser pointer.

"They sound like cults," adds Olivia. "If music be the food of love, play on." She uses her quotable quote voice.

"Virginia Woolf?" I ask.

"No, Mr. William Shakespeare, author of the greatest love sonnets ever written."

"And the greatest *tragedies*," adds Bernard.

"Ray likes rap music," I volunteer.

"It's a calamity that the listening public doesn't appreciate the fact that rap music was pioneered by Rex Harrison in *My Fair Lady* and Bea Arthur in *Mame* speaking their lines because they couldn't sing." Bernard says this as he flips through his collection of albums and tapes. Then he pulls out a CD as if it's the winning number in a lottery. "Chopin's nocturnes!"

"That's a little too sober, don't you think?" asks Olivia, as if it's perfectly natural that she and her son should discuss the correct music for losing my virginity. "How about the Brazilian jazz album I found at that little boutique in New York."

"Mother, Eve's Playground is not a *little boutique*. It's a *sex shop*."

"Andrea Bocelli," Ottavio casts his vote. "*Romanza.*"

"How about Tom Waits?" suggests Gil, our resident rock-and-roll aficionado. "Heartattack and Vine."

"If you play that *philistine* music for one moment, I'll be the one having the heart attack," threatens Bernard.

Rocky gambols over to the stereo as if he has a suggestion to add to the playlist. He puts on the CD of jungle noises that Brandt gave him and we all laugh when the sounds of birds chirping and monkeys screeching begins to come from the speakers.

Fortunately Rocky has stayed on the straight and narrow since his spree and the Dirk Van Erp lamp was successfully repaired, so Bernard has completely forgiven him. And Bernard even admitted that since he'd also gone on a bender over a broken love affair, he supposed that Rocky was entitled to one, too.

"There is a certain primitive quality to it, rather like that of early-American pottery," says Bernard. "I think you've made an excellent choice." He solemnly shakes hands with Rocky.

Chapter
Seventy

When I next look up at the clock, it's a few minutes after nine. Only now I'm no longer counting down the hours to Ray's arrival tomorrow night so much as calculating that if I leave right now I can sit in for one more game of Texas Hold 'Em. Not winning the prize money has left almost a six-thousand-dollar gap in my tuition payment plan that I wouldn't mind filling by bluffing, rather than buffing floors in the school cafeteria and adding to my loan portfolio. Or worse, have to leave school after the fall semester and work full-time for a year.

Just as I'm about to back out of the driveway, Bernard comes dashing out the front door. I roll down the window.

"You're going to that poker game where you won all the money a few weeks ago?" he asks excitedly.

"Yeah. I wouldn't mind one more win before school starts."

"Do you think, um . . ." He rubs his hands on the front of his pantlegs. "You said yourself I'm getting pretty good. . . ."

"Ooooh noooo," I say. "That would *not* be a good idea."

"Why not?" he practically pleads with me. "Gil is here in case the girls wake up."

There's no point in talking about how rich the game is since Bernard always has a ton of cash lying around because of his business dealings. Or arguing that he doesn't know how to play. I've taught him the basics of Texas Hold 'Em, though not nearly enough strategy. "Listen, sometimes you still bite your lip and hold your breath waiting for a card you really need. And . . . and . . ."

"What?" he says.

"Instead of cursing, you say '*good gravy.*' "

"I promise not to do any of those things!" he says hopefully.

I take a minute to decide exactly how to put this, but unfortunately Bernard thinks I'm on the brink of giving in and begins to smile with expectation.

"If you were out sick, would you want me to negotiate for one of those silver tea services you buy at estate sales and then resell to that guy Conrad in Toronto for almost double the price?" I ask.

"No, I suppose not," he finally agrees, and wishes me good luck before heading back inside.

For some reason it's a commonly held misperception that high-stakes gambling is a lot of laughs. Quite the contrary. Cappy will be the first to tell you that real gambling, if done correctly by measuring all the probabilities and studying your opponents, isn't fun, but a job you should get paid for. And if you really do it right it can eventually become darn boring.

At the intersection I wait impatiently while an old man crosses against the light. What is a person with a walker doing starting to cross when his signal is already yellow, about to turn red? Then I feel bad for having such thoughts. The guy is obviously in some amount of pain as he slowly pulls himself along. Probably arthritis. It's good to be young and healthy, I think while I wait. But don't let anyone tell you that just because your body works well and you still have all your hair that being young can't be painful, too.

I arrive at Bob's just in time to get in before the first hand is dealt. The patio furniture has been replaced by some comfortable chairs and a large round table newly covered in burgundy felt so the cards won't slip off the edges. There's another lamp in the corner, and a haze of gray tobacco smoke lingers above the table like a rain cloud.

"I thought you took the money from last month and ran," Cappy jokes as he quickly exchanges my five hundred-dollar bills for chips.

It appears that Cappy's new venture has caught on, since tonight there are seven players seated around the table, all with large stacks of chips nearby. Four are from the last game I was at—Rod Green, Ed Kunckle, Seymour the Aussie guy, and good old Al. I don't let on about his being laid off, but it certainly goes a long way in explaining why he looks so worn-out and cheerless. Meantime, Kunckle gives me a scowl as if *I* were the one who foiled his scheme to block Bernard's adoption.

There are two additional cigar chompers, one wearing a frayed suit and the other in men's sportswear from the early 1990s, both looking as if they're on parole from an OTB parlor. And finally there's a real-live woman, one wearing enough face paint to suggest that somewhere there's a kindergarten class without a mural. She's poured into a low-cut filmy blouse and tight jeans topped off with a big bright gold belt buckle spelling *Texas* that matches her big bright gold hair. "Hey, gal," she says. "Come on over and sit next to me and we'll show these cowboys a thing or two!" She flutters her heavily mascaraed lashes and tosses her mane in the direction of the open space, like a horse shaking off flies.

There's no doubt in my mind that Cappy is going to keep a close eye on Texas, since a good way to cheat if you're a woman is to take out a lipliner or other cosmetic and secretly mark a couple of cards.

Kunckle and I nod warily at each other like two basketball players right before the tip-off. Seymour the Aussie offers a friendly wave and points to the empty seat on his left. Rod Green gives me a look of mild disgust, and the stogie smokers hardly glance up, probably marking me down as nothing more than extra money in their pockets. Meantime, Texas seems thrilled to have another "gal" in the game. Only it doesn't take 20/20 vision to determine that I'm no competition for her, at least when it comes to our racks, and I don't mean chips. She has organized her bosom so that the fuchsia silk blouse assigned the task of housing it ends up as more of a suggestion than an actual functioning garment. However, this distraction serves to keep all the men busy trying to steal glances, during which time Texas easily takes the first few hands. And I'm left wondering if that might have been her intention in the first place, as in showing the men a thing or *two* means exactly that—or rather, *those*.

Cappy is doing his usual job of policing the perimeter, making himself available to answer questions, settle any disputes, and otherwise ensuring that all his high-rollers are feeling safe and satisfied. He's even throwing a few bucks to Bob's waitress Janine, for bringing drinks back to us every so often.

It's a serious game with thousands of dollars in chips moving swiftly back and forth across the table. Everyone is deep in concentration and the only person who keeps any sort of patter going is Texas. "Don't that rip the rag right off your bush," she hoots while taking a round with a low pair and a king high. Though once again I can't help but wonder if this stream of chatter isn't also a ploy to keep the rest of us a little off balance.

By mid-game it's pretty obvious that Kunckle is out to get me, either for beating him on the final hand last time I played or for living with the Stocktons, or, more likely, on both counts. He smirks every time I lose a hand. When I have the goods he tries to raise me to where he knows I can't afford to stay in. And if I run a bluff and scare everyone else off, he'll hang in there and be what's known as a "telephone booth," constantly calling me just because he can afford to. It's not as if I'm getting any terrific hands to begin with, but I certainly feel as if his deliberate sabotage is what grinds me down almost two grand after four long hours.

By three o'clock in the morning it's just Kunckle, Texas, Al, and me. I'm only out about eight hundred now, thanks to some lucky cards. However, we're all starting to look pale and bleary-eyed except for Texas, who's drinking her fourth Rob Roy and says she's feeling "more wide-awake than a calf in a thunderstorm."

Finally there's a hand that looks to be The One, at least for me.

Chapter
Seventy-one

When the last community card comes up as the five of hearts I have a "steel wheel"—a straight flush when the ace and three of hearts that are my hole cards are combined with the two and four of hearts that are included in the community cards. It's unbeatable, unless someone were to have a higher straight flush; but with the other cards showing—a two of diamonds and a three of spades, that would be impossible.

Kunckle initiates the final round of betting and pushes in two stacks of chips—a thousand dollars. What the heck is he doing? I study the cards and decide he must have a full house, a pair in his hand that combines with the community cards to make fives over twos, or vice versa.

Meantime, Al is concentrating on the row of five cards in the middle of the table so hard that it looks as if he's deciding whether to snip the red or black wire of a ticking bomb. Finally he counts his remaining chips, then goes over to Cappy and borrows a fresh stack. Not only does Al see Kunckle's thousand, but he raises two thousand! Is it possible that Al has four of a kind? Texas pushes a mound of chips toward the center and gleefully booms, "I'm going to pay my money and see the rodeo!" Perhaps another full house—fours over twos? Or maybe she has four twos? It's absolutely the craziest round I've ever seen! Cappy, who doesn't even get excited when he lights his pants on fire with his cigar, is standing behind us wide-eyed and practically slack-jawed.

I'm the only one left to bet. If I play this one out as it is, with my straight flush I'm sure to win the seven grand that's now in the pot! And if I were to raise, I could probably string Al along if indeed he has four of a kind. He'll think I only have a full house and go back to Cappy and borrow another thousand or so, and end up losing that plus the two thousand he already borrowed, along with the two grand he's already down for the night. Yet it suddenly occurs to me that if I don't meet the call and the raise, I'm only out a grand while Al beats Kunckle and Texas. But *does* he have the pair of fours in his hand that will give him four of a kind when put with the pair of fours in the middle of the table? After studying him for a moment I decide that indeed he can make the four fours and if it weren't for my hand, this enormous pot would be Al's.

The air in the room is palpably tense with every nerve strung like tension wire, tightly connecting hope on one end to dread at the other.

"You guys are too rich for me," I finally say, and fold up my cards.

The Turd cannot hide the pleasure he takes in this defeat and sends an arctic smile in my direction. I return the favor by glowering at him as if I'm imagining how he'd look with daylight streaming through a few well-placed holes in his body.

Kunckle is the first to turn over his cards while cockily proclaiming, "A flock of ducks," meaning that he has four twos when his pair is combined with the community cards.

"That's about as welcome as a skunk at a garden party!" hoots Texas as she unveils her full house of fives over twos, which in any other game would surely have been the big winner. "Apparently this barn ain't big enough for tonight," she says, employing the slang name for a full house.

However, Al silently reveals his winning hand of four fours, leaving both Texas *and* Kunckle slack-jawed with amazement, as the huge mountain of chips shifts ownership for the final time. They're all incredible hands! Even more so when you consider the one I folded. It's just too bad for the losers that they had to happen simultaneously.

Al appears more relieved than anything else and wipes his brow with his sleeve. Kunckle nods and massages his undertaker's jaw with his fingers. I assume he's happy enough to have been bested by Al instead of me or Texas. One gets the feeling that Edwin Carbunkle the Turd thinks that women should be decorating houses, not trying to make full houses.

After Al settles up with Cappy, he's expanded his bankroll by about four thousand dollars. And Texas still has all the money she took off the deputy mayor, Kunckle, Seymour, and the other guys.

"C'mon, all y'all, let's belly up to the bar," bellows Texas as if we've just finished bringing in the cattle after a long hard ride. "My treat. We'll drown some bourbon!"

"You bet, Texas!" says Al.

"Sounds good to me," adds Kunckle, and actually cracks a crooked grin.

Jeez, maybe I should start thinking more along the lines of breast implants and peekaboo blouses rather than a new computer.

Cappy places his hand on my elbow as I'm leaving "Hang on a second," he says. "I looked in the muck pile."

"You're not supposed to do that!" I say. It's a well-respected rule in any poker game that if a player folds, then *no one,* not even the dealer, is supposed to find out what cards they did or did not have. And there's a good reason for this. People take note of whether you bluff or not and it's an integral part of the game, *especially* when you're talking about Texas Hold 'Em.

"Well, I did," says Cappy. "I'm not a player and it's my game."

Only now his tone of voice is actually scaring me because it's the way I've heard him talk to deadbeat debtors on the phone. "I can only think of one reason you'd throw a straight flush, the highest hand there is, out the window." I look down at the floor. "All the sudden you and this Al Santora show up at two games, you take a big hand last time, he takes it this time. What kind of fool do you play me for, kiddo? I admit that Kunckle is a pompous ass and that the deputy mayor can be a pain as well, but I run a clean game and they bring their friends."

"Al and I aren't in cahoots, Cappy, I swear!" I'm suddenly so nervous that my voice is quaking. Cappy is not a guy whose bad side you want to be on.

"Well, you happen to be in luck, because I'm still not able to figure out what kind of scam you two were running. I didn't see any signals and neither of you touched any cards but your own. No mirrors, no tapping, no peering next door, nothing. Don't tell me you have one of those electronic gizmos in your shoes. Do you?"

I quickly kick off my shoes. "Cappy, Al . . . Al lost his job. He . . . he goes to my church—well, my parents' church anyway."

"So what? You're telling me you *threw a seven-thousand-dollar pot* to some guy who lost his job?" Cappy seems to consider this for a moment and then he laughs, but not in an aren't-we-all-having-fun way so much as a menacing way. "You know, you almost had me there, but how could you have known that he had the four fours and not the full house or the deuces? What if Kunckle or Texas had them? They sure were betting as if they did."

Oh gosh, this is going from bad to worse. I shove my feet back in my shoes so they're ready to catch the pee that's going to be running down my legs in another minute. Every time Olivia gets arrested she likes to say that no good deed goes unpunished. I can hear the shakiness in my own voice as I attempt to explain. "I've played poker with Al for years. . . . He . . . He's always twitching and lighting up and rushing everyone."

"Okay, I've noticed he's acts a lot like a Mexican jumping bean." Cappy's eyes narrow. "So you're saying this is some sort of a tell."

"Yeah, in a way. Because he got quiet. He wasn't fidgeting with his lighter and cigarettes. He wasn't fiddling with a chip. He was almost motionless. I . . . I just knew he had 'em."

Cappy suddenly smiles as if I've actually managed to pull one over on him and then shakes his head from side to side. "So you handed him the pot. And he'll never know it."

"I wasn't going to mention it," I say.

"Obviously Kunckle hates your guts for some reason I don't need to be told," says Cappy. "You could have run that pot up another three or four grand—you know I would have backed you—and then you could have split the money with your buddy Al."

In principle, Cappy is right, and that would have been the more profitable way to play it.

"But Al would never take money that way," I say. "He didn't even want to accept a donation from the church's relief fund, one that he's contributed to for the past twenty years."

Cappy nods in agreement. "Yeah, you're probably right."

Despite all the fuss, Cappy finally appears satisfied with the outcome of the game and actually pleased by the night's excitement. After all, seeing a round like that last one is a once-in-a-lifetime occurrence, even if you're in the business. And though it's a well-known fact that Cappy thinks it's okay for "broads" to play the ponies and bet on sports, at the end of the day he believes they're "too emotional" to ever really make good poker players. Sure, he was wrong about me trying to cheat, but he's been proved correct on his theory that something was going down, which to him is equally satisfying.

"I guess you're right about girls not really having what it takes to play serious poker," I say now that the storm seems to have passed me by.

"Yeah, no girls at the poker table," he says. Then he pats me on the shoulder and says, "But women are okay. Just don't start getting yourself all tarted up like Texas. In only five hours that perfume of hers ruined the air quality in here. It took me six weeks of burritos and stale cigars to get the atmosphere just right."

I say good night and once again start to leave.

"Hey, you still want a job with me?" he asks.

"Not yet, thanks. But I might be calling in January."

"Good," says Cappy. "You can crunch numbers and do the books and *I'll* take care of the play. I may be an equal-opportunity bookie, but this ain't no charity I'm operating here."

"I know." I also know that Cappy's idea of himself as a defender of minorities refers to his willingness to take money off of any citizen who is in possession of enough cash to waste on making stupid bets.

Cappy switches off the overhead light and walks me out through the poolroom so none of the local guys hassle me. Kunckle and Al are long gone but Texas is sitting at the bar leading a chorus of "Home on the Range," accompanied by a half-dozen guys in cowboy boots.

Chapter
Seventy-two

THE FOLLOWING AFTERNOON I HELP BERNARD IN THE KITCHEN until he shoos me off to prepare myself for Ray's arrival. When I return fifteen minutes later he's busy blanching asparagus for the frittata.

"Is *that* what you're wearing tonight?" Bernard looks at my jeans and orange Chester Cheetah T-shirt with abject horror, and momentarily allows the water to boil over the edge of the pot.

"Of course," I say. "What did you *think* I was going to wear? It's not as if I own a dress or a skirt."

"I suppose the smoke-blue chiffon tea gown trimmed with chinchilla that Edith Head designed for Olivia de Havilland in *To Each His Own* is out of the question?"

Digging back into my past I give him the teenage eye roll combined with one hand placed on jutting hip.

"Don't you ever wear sandals?" he says while glaring down at my grass-stained sneakers.

"And get all my toes chopped off by the lawn mower?" I ask. "No thanks."

"Do the words *casual sportswear* mean nothing to young ladies these days? How is a gentleman caller supposed to compliment your appearance if you don't put any effort into dressing and applying your *maquillage*?" Pointing toward the stairs with the asparagus tongs like he's a drill sergeant at West Point, Bernard orders, "Go upstairs and get a short-sleeved blended cotton-silk sweater from Mother's wardrobe right now! And put some concealer over that clown nose."

Do I cave in to the fashion police? Bernard has managed to get his boyfriend back. And Olivia has Ottavio madly in love with her. Probability theory tells me that they might know more than I do about this sort of thing. I capitulate and bound up the stairs.

"You'd think I was forcing you to wear a corset!" he calls after me.

Exactly three minutes after five o'clock Ray's car pulls into the driveway. I hurry out front and hop into the passenger seat, wearing a pale yellow ribbed sweater with a scoop neck. My white knight has finally arrived, driving a brand-new white Thunderbird.

Ray gives me a sexy kiss on the mouth and as it starts getting good he taps the gas pedal to rev the engine. I've promised Gwen that we'll meet her down at the pizza parlor, though I'm not really feeling completely ready to go public with Ray. Everyone will gossip and ask a hundred questions, the way people do about strangers when you live in a small town. However, Gwen insists that not only does she want to check out Ray, but there's something deathly urgent that she has to ask me in person, which most likely involves what style of shoes most freshmen wear to college orientation.

"We have to stop in the pizza parlor for a few minutes," I say. "It's only a mile from here."

"Sounds fine with me. I could go for an iced tea." Ray places his right hand on my thigh and drives with his left hand. The inside of his car is immaculate, except for the ashtray, which is overflowing with cigarette butts. "That's a nice top," he says while parking the car.

We enter the pizza parlor together and Ray looks cool in his black cotton shirt with shiny black buttons, black leather blazer, and gray slacks. At school one of the things I thought was really nice about Ray was that every night he'd iron his shirt for the following day and ask everyone else if they had anything that needed ironing.

However the first person I see isn't Gwen, but Cappy, which is sort of odd since the pizza parlor, with its cheap eats and video games, is more of a hangout for teenagers.

"Hey, Hallie!" calls Cappy.

"Cappy! What are *you* doing here?" I ask.

"A working man has to eat," he says, and nods down toward an empty paper plate with the telltale tinfoil triangle on top. "It's not as if I keep a plate of steak tartare in the glove compartment, ya know." Despite Cappy always having at least one girlfriend around, between the long fingernails and spiky high heels they never appear to be the types who are much interested in cooking.

"How's tricks?" asks Cappy. As always, he doesn't ask where a person has been or what they've been up to, since this is the kind of information that can land a guy in the witness box when you do business with the characters like the ones in Cappy's Rolodex.

"Same old, same old," I say, and pat my front jeans pocket with my left hand. "Still guarding the launch codes."

"Well, if it isn't Ray Ray!" says Cappy, looking over my shoulder. "I didn't recognize you at first with your hair cut short. What are you doing way out here in The Sticks?"

Only I can tell that Cappy is *really surprised* to run into Ray. Like any good gambler, Cappy isn't known for tipping his hand with facial expressions, but after being around him for so many years I can tell when his eyes narrow slightly, as if strong sunlight has flashed upon his face, that he's been caught off guard. As Cappy approaches Ray he appears to be calculating his next move, like a blackjack player who should really double down but just ran out of chips.

"Hey, Walter," says Ray and gives Cappy a firm and friendly handshake.

Walter? Oh my gosh, Cappy's real name is *Walter*! I have to bite my lip hard to prevent myself from laughing.

"How's your old man?" asks Cappy.

"Great. You should stop by sometime. I know he'd love to see you."

"I'll do that," says Cappy. "I'm keeping busy following the nags these days—Florida in winter, Michigan in the spring, and then Ohio in the summertime." Cappy backs away as he speaks, as if he's suddenly remembered that a ball game is about to begin, which is also odd, since Cappy doesn't back away from anything. In fact, he's often told me that the only time he ever turned the other cheek was when he was in the process of delivering a left hook. But those were in the old days, at least according to Cappy, back when he was in the debt collection end of some other guy's bookmaking business.

The counterman has come over to see if we want anything. Ray asks Cappy, "How about a beer?"

Cappy looks at his watch and says, "Sorry, but I gotta make tracks. You know what they say—it's always post time somewhere."

While Ray orders two iced teas, Cappy leans in close so that we can't be overheard. "Listen, I need to talk to you. Can you stop by my office tomorrow?"

"What if we meet here?" I'd rather not run into Auggie.

"I really need to be at the pool hall. That idiot granola grandson of mine ran off to Russia after some piece of tail."

"He did?"

Cappy gives a dismissive wave. "It's just as well since he couldn't add any higher than his shoe size. And no concentration whatsoever, brain jumping from one thing to the next like a June bug in heat tap-dancing on a sizzling hot stove."

I know that Cappy's not overly concerned about Auggie's lack of computation skills. Just the opposite. Cappy loves to read in the newspaper that Americans are getting worse in math every year, since it means big money for his gambling business through making losing customers into what he terms a "renewable resource."

"I honestly don't think I'm getting back into the business, Cappy," I say. "School starts in two weeks."

Ray comes over with our drinks and Cappy waves good-bye. "Okay. Great to see you, Ray Ray. Send my regards to your family." He quickly heads away from us and toward the door.

"How do you know Cappy?" I ask. "Or rather, *Walter*." I finally release my stifled giggle. Just goes to show you, at some point every mother with a newborn babe on her lap is confident that she can beat the odds.

"Old friend of my dad's," says Ray, and removes his jacket. "But I think the question is more like, how do *you* know Walter?" He says this in a tone indicating that Cappy is not exactly the type of person you'd want as your child's guidance counselor.

"We used to hang out together at the track," I say.

Ray appears surprised that I would freely choose to associate with Cappy, as if I'm not living up to his expectations to be a member in good standing of polite society.

Just then, Gwen and Jane come bursting in with another friend from high school, Megan. They giggle as they introduce themselves and make no secret of the fact that they're checking out Ray and find his dark good looks appealing. Gwen indicates her approval by nudging me with her elbow, and Jane says loud enough so that everyone can hear, "You didn't tell us he has *muscles*." She openly stares at his fitted shirt. "Nautilus?" asks Jane the Jock.

"Naw." Ray makes it sound as if exercise machines are for badminton players. "Free weights."

Jane's lips part as if she's just been told he's the best kisser in the State of Ohio.

While those two talk weights and repetitions, Gwen says to me under her breath, "You didn't tell me what a sexy mouth he has."

"I guess I never really noticed." I study Ray's mouth as he enthralls Jane with a detailed explanation of his workout routine. Yeah, I suppose it's sexy, with full lips and sort of pouty at the corners. He proceeds to tell a funny story about the gym where he lifts weights. Ray is definitely easy to like. He's entertaining and able to make conversation with anyone. But I guess the real question tonight is, do I love him? And that's something for which I'm having a harder time devising a formula.

The girls are full of questions and gossip, and talk over and under each other a mile a minute. Fortunately Jane seems to have more or less recovered from the shock of her father moving out. When I look up at the clock above the counter it's a little after six and I realize that Bernard is going to kill me if we're late and his ham ends up drying out.

As we walk out the door Gwen comes chasing after me. "Hey, Hallie, I almost forgot. Megan wants me to ask you if it's okay if she goes out with Craig." Only it sounds more like Megan is *already* going out with Craig and simply wants to know if I mind.

"But isn't she leaving for Wellesley soon?" I ask.

Gwen gives me a look that says, *What has* that *got to do with anything?* And Ray gives me a stare that says, *Who is this guy and what does he have to do with* you?

"Sure. I mean, why would I mind?" I try to sound casual. Only what I really want to know is, if Craig doesn't want a long-distance relationship, which is what we'd *both said,* then why is he going out with *her* right before they both leave for colleges at least a thousand miles apart?

"Be sure to call me tomorrow." Gwen tosses me a playful smile.

As we walk toward the car, Craig's black Audi pulls into the parking space right in front of ours. I suppose I shouldn't care that he's here to meet Megan. I mean, Ray is really good-looking and doesn't have any weird tattoos or strange mannerisms that would embarrass me. However, for some reason I wish they hadn't run into each other, at least not tonight.

"Hey, Hallie," Craig calls out, and comes over.

"This is Ray." I introduce him to Craig. "A friend from school."

The guys shake hands and Craig says, "Aren't you staying at the pizza parlor? Gwen's organized a party since lots of people are leaving for college soon."

"Uh, no, we're having dinner back at the house," I say.

Ray obviously recognizes the name Craig from Gwen's recent conversation and puts his arm around me in a proprietary way.

"Okay, then I guess I'll see you around," says Craig. He looks at Ray's brand-new white Thunderbird with the tinted windows, raised back end, and chrome hubcaps and says, "Nice ride," which obviously pleases its owner. But I know that Craig considers the car impractical and flashy and doesn't really mean this as a compliment. It looks chopped and channeled, which is what we used to say about the juiced-up muscle cars of the cigarettes-dangling-from-their-lips, drag-racing motorheads who parked in the back of the high school lot.

However, Ray accepts the remark as praise and returns the tribute, the same way women do about each other's outfits, by asking Craig about the suspension on his Audi.

And although the exchange appears friendly enough, when Ray and I get into the car he asks, "Who is *that* dopey guy? Is he the one your friend was just asking about?"

"Yeah," I say. "Just an old boyfriend."

"Then how come you didn't introduce me as your *new* boyfriend?" Ray acts slightly miffed.

"I don't know," I say, though that's not entirely true. "I mean, *are* you my boyfriend?"

"Yes," he says, and to prove it he gives me a very serious kiss. Then he adds, "I drove all the way out here to see you, didn't I?"

"Yeah," I say, and feel as if I should be awarding him mileage points the way the airlines do.

Chapter
Seventy-three

DINNER TURNS OUT TO BE PERFECT IN EVERY WAY. RAY EVEN HAS a third helping of the ham with pineapple and maraschino cherries. "It's just like my grandmother makes," he tells Bernard, who beams with satisfaction.

"Hallie did all the cooking, really," Bernard lies. "I just supervised, you know, adding a pinch of sage here and there."

When the chocolate torte is served, Ray says, "It looks really great, but I'm too full. Maybe I'll have some later."

Bernard appears momentarily horrified. "Oh, no! You *must* try it. We made it from scratch. I'll cut you a tiny sliver." He doesn't give Ray a chance to protest and within seconds there's an enormous slice of chocolate torte on a Haviland dessert plate. Ray easily devours it.

All throughout the meal I'm afraid to look any of them in the eye for fear that I'll either start laughing, wondering if Ray is actually falling under the romantic spell of Bernard's menu, or else go into a full panic about what lies ahead.

After helping to clear the table, Ray and I head back toward the summerhouse. Off to the west the sun is settling onto the horizon, splashing the sky with orange. And the air is fragrant with the aroma of late summer, the sweet scent of new-mown grass and thickly laden trees.

Only I'm much too distracted to enjoy the results of all my hard work in making the yard look nice. Instead I'm discovering what is meant by The Gallows Walk. Maybe this is a mistake. It feels as if I'm approaching the edge of something, about to take a plunge or make a permanent departure.

"Cool pond," says Ray, oblivious to my anguish.

"Yeah," I agree. The water is illuminated by dozens of soft blue lights hidden under the various ledges. Even on a dark night it's possible to catch glimpses of the fish gliding among the water lilies and see the way the water mirrors the overhanging fern trees and the gentle sway of the colorful Japanese irises growing along the banks. A few bullfrogs have already moved in and their *ribbits* add a much-needed bass section to the usual chorus of crickets.

I'm tempted to grab one of the irises and perform a quick round of "He loves me, he loves me not." It's not too late to change my mind. No. I have to get this over with. I can't go through another semester worrying about sex all the time. Though if I *am* a sex maniac, perhaps forging ahead will only make matters worse . . . I hadn't considered that. However, I decide instead to concentrate on Cappy's advice to the faint of heart when shooting craps: He who is afraid to throw the dice will never make seven or eleven on the first roll.

"You live with some interesting people," says Ray.

But I can't tell if he means this in a good way or a bad way. Ray's parents have lots of businessmen and their wives for friends and somehow I don't think he means "interesting" in the same sense of the word.

"Things certainly never get boring around here," I admit.

The minute we're inside the summerhouse, Ray begins to kiss

me, and eventually I have to gulp for air. "Wait a second." I push on his shoulders.

Olivia has given me some freesia-scented Diptyque candles to light. But my hands are shaking so much that it takes me a while to get the match to stay on the wicks long enough to catch. And if I can't steady myself enough to light a candle, I can't imagine opening a condom.

When Ray pulls me down on the bed I'm convinced that my heart will explode and shatter into tiny fragments like a dandelion going to seed.

It sounds as if the music committee has finally come to an agreement, or more likely, Bernard has prevailed. A suite from his favorite Jason Vieaux guitar CD drifts into the room from the miniature speakers hidden behind vases on the shelves.

Ray wriggles his tongue in my ear for a moment before removing my top. When he goes to unclasp my bra it feels more like I'm being prepared for an X ray rather than to have sex for the first time.

"This is a little weird," I say.

"Oh sorry. Let me take off my stuff." Ray jumps up and sheds his clothes as if he's going swimming.

"I'm cold," I say.

We climb under the comforter and that's a little better. He kisses me and moves his mouth down to my neck and makes some noises like a whale clearing out its blowhole. He then proceeds to place his cock in my hand, unzip my jeans, and slide his hands down the back of my underwear. I don't feel like a desirable woman so much as a big pile of poker chips being gathered up by a greedy gambler.

I decide that I may as well just get the whole thing over with as fast as possible. Besides, Craig is probably with Megan by now. Not that I care or anything. But why should they be the only ones to have a date on a Saturday night?

After taking off my jeans myself, I retrieve the condom box from under the bed. My fingers are trembling as I tear open a packet. I hope that the condom's facing in the right direction as I begin rolling it on. However, I loose my grip and it flies off like a rocket on the Fourth of July.

This is definitely a sign. From God, from my mother, Mr. Spock, I don't know, but definitely from somewhere. And I'm sure Brandt would agree.

"This isn't going to work," I say.

"Don't worry," Ray pulls me onto the bed. "I'll pull out in time."

"No," I say.

"Then we'll get another one," he says. "I have some in my wallet."

"No, Ray, I mean this, us. I—I can't. . . ."

"Damn it, Hallie, I drove over two hours to get here. You *said* that you were ready."

"Well, I made a *mistake*." I feel like apologizing but at the same time I'm not exactly sure that he deserves one. "I mean, maybe we could just do the usual stuff."

Ray angrily pulls on his clothes. "There's no point in staying over. I'm sick of you and your little games. And I'm playing golf with my dad and my uncle at eight in the morning."

I sit on the edge of the bed, with the comforter wrapped around me, and silently watch Ray head for the door.

"Still saving yourself because you think you're so special? Well, you're nothing special that I can see. You're just a tease. So long!" he says with an air of finality. It's difficult to make that thin door slam but Ray manages to do so. The next noise I hear is gravel shooting out from under tires, and a squeal as he turns onto the road and guns the engine.

The candles continue to flicker and I feel so alone. Not child alone, the kind that can mostly be cured by going inside for the comfort of the familiar. But grown-up alone. The real thing. I slowly pull on my clothes and wonder what went wrong. An enormous emptiness has opened on all sides of me, and outside the branches clutch at one another and cast crazy dark shadows on the walls while the rustling leaves sound as if they're whispering secrets I'll never know.

The slowest hour of my life is ticking by when I hear a voice come from out of the darkness. "Having a séance in there?"

Chapter
Seventy-four

For a moment I stare at the tall handsome young man silhouetted in the doorway, his broad shoulders outlined by a yellow T-shirt, and it feels as if I'm staring into a mirage.

"Craig?" I call out. "What are *you* doing here?"

He smiles at me, that familiar half smile I know so well. "I leave for Minnesota in the morning. All the guys are going up early to put an addition onto the frat house. And then lacrosse practice starts Tuesday. Just thought I'd drop in and say good-bye."

"At midnight?"

"Since when did *you* start going to bed early?" he jokes.

Only I have a feeling this is more than a coincidence. "One of them called you." The music suddenly switches to Rostropovich playing Schumann on the cello, the CD that Bernard keeps on his dresser in the bedroom. "Bernard!" I say.

"Yup."

I chuckle at the thought of Bernard trying to put his proposition as delicately as possible. "And what did he *say* exactly? That Hallie the black widow spider just chased another perfectly good date away?"

"Nooo, not exactly," says Craig.

One thing is for sure, Bernard and I are going to have a little review of the chain of command when it comes to organizing my love life. On the other hand, I have to give him credit—even though he doesn't like the idea of me going all the way, at least he's decided to take charge of quality control.

"Uh, can I come in?" asks Craig.

"Sorry, sure." I open the door the rest of the way. "I thought you were out with Megan."

"Megan? Yeah, she was at the pizza parlor. But I've known Megan since nursery school. And she's leaving for Wellesley in a few days."

"Oh. Gwen said that Megan wants to date you."

Craig shakes his head to indicate that whether this may or may not be the case, it's not going to happen. "Speaking of dates, where's your boyfriend with the love machine?"

"Gone fishing." I turn away and stare out into the darkness. "Craig, do you get nervous when you're about to, you know, make love to a woman?" I ask.

"A little," he says.

But I'm guessing that he's lying to make me feel better.

"I mean, a guy hopes that everything works okay," he continues. "And you want to sort of impress a girl. You worry about what she thinks."

We sit down on the daybed together and he reaches his arm around me. Only it feels like old friends. "Remember when we tried to sleep in my bed together after the prom?" I ask.

"Yeah," he says. "That was pretty funny. But it was nice. I think about that night a lot. I mean, the whole thing—the dance, watching the sunrise, the party afterward, Gil directing traffic with flares and wearing a Day-Glo orange rain suit so he wouldn't get run over.

Bernard's *huevos rancheros* and *vaya con Dios* tomato juice. He must have used an entire case of Tabasco sauce!"

We both laugh at the memory of it all, but something in his tone makes me feel very tender toward him and I snuggle in a bit closer.

"It sure seems as if life was a lot simpler back then," he says.

"It was definitely less expensive," I joke. And we laugh just a little, like an old couple that finds humor in something not necessarily because it's funny so much as because we remember doing it together.

With his fingertips he traces the lines of my palm and I suddenly feel wide-awake. Craig leans over me and his breath is sweet and familiar as he kisses me in that gentle yet thrilling way. The kiss grows and blossoms like one of Bernard's musical overtures. We melt into each other's lips for a long time, until everything within me is alive and stirring. Only this time I'm not crippled by apprehension. Yes, he's leaving the next day. But I've recently learned that there are moments when questioning the future too much can ruin the present.

"I miss you," he whispers, and runs his hand underneath my shirt and around my waist.

"Mmmm." I kiss him in return and place my hand on the front of his jeans. I remember back to the first time I touched him there and how unsure I was. And now I'm very sure. I start to take off my shirt, but he stops me.

"No, let me," he says. He delicately removes my clothes as if they're petals on a flower and then runs his hands over my hips and across my stomach. "You've gotten sexier," he says. "Less halfback and more Helen of Troy."

"It's my first time," I say, remembering Olivia's warning.

"I'll go slow," he says. "And if it hurts or you change your mind, then we'll stop."

"We should use something," I say.

"We will. But relax and let me worry about that."

He kisses me again, this time on the neck and shoulders, and we touch, making a detailed inventory of each other's bodies and the multiple possibilities for pleasure. And I suddenly feel certain that I really do want more. For a moment it seems as if our passion is an insatiable thirst.

Craig leans over and moves up and down so that we're almost having sex but he's not quite inside of me. Then he jumps up, grabs his jeans, and produces a condom with the deftness of a magician. Within seconds he's back on top of me and our hearts beat hungrily right up against each other.

We kiss and he moves his hips so they're above mine. "Okay, now tell me if it hurts," he says.

I can feel him start to sink inside me and it's strange, like nothing I've ever experienced. "It's all right."

Only suddenly it feels as if he's hit a fence. "Wait!" I say, and take a deep breath. "Okay, go." Only I sound more like the starter for the hundred-yard dash.

There's a sharp pain and for a second it seems as if all the clocks in the world have stopped. But just as suddenly it's over and he's deep within me. Oh my gosh. I did it. We lie like that, not moving for a moment, and kiss. Then I start to giggle.

"What?" he says.

"We're having sex," I say. "Don't you think that's funny?"

"Yeah, it's hilarious," he says. "Why don't we call some people?" Then he starts to move up and down slightly.

"Whoa," I yelp.

"You want to stop?"

"No. It's just really, really different, you know?"

"I'm coming," he says, and makes one final thrust.

But I don't feel anything different happening as he scrunches up his face and then pulls out. Craig flops down next to me and exhales deeply.

"The next time will be really nice for you," he assures me. "I promise."

And I can't help but wonder if he means the next time in general, or the next time with him.

Craig gently runs his fingertips across my midsection. Then he sits on the edge of the bed and removes the condom. Afterward we crawl under the covers and get close like ribs in corduroy and whisper and giggle. The music went off at some point and all that can be heard is the occasional breeze shuffling the leaves and the tap of a tree branch against the window.

"How do you feel?" he asks.

"Okay," I say.

"Do you want to, you know, come?" he asks.

"No, that's all right."

"You're funny." He hugs me tight.

"Why's that?"

"Because when you have all your clothes on you're such a loud-mouth. But when you're naked you get all shy."

I start to defend myself but Craig puts his lips over my mouth and kisses me. Then he runs his hand up my thigh and gently moves his finger back and forth inside of me. For a moment it's as if he's touching the center of my longing. A sharp intake of air. And suddenly a sense of release and surrender courses through my entire body, as if sinking into a hot bath. We lie quietly for a moment so that our breathing seems to fill the room.

After a while I turn to him and whisper, "I'm glad that you stopped by."

"Me too," says Craig. His voice is a soft passionate breath, more like his soul talking. "No matter what happens, I'll always love you."

I think about what that means exactly, specifically the word *happens*. Does he mean if we meet and marry other people? Or if one of us should die in a horrible car crash? Eventually I decide it's probably the way you tell your parents and other relatives that you love them because you're bound to them by countless invisible threads.

"I love you too," I say. But he's asleep.

Sleep doesn't come as easily for me. The candles have burned out and the room is dark except for strands of silver moonlight that spill across the wooden floorboards. Through the windows the flowers look like brightly colored birds that have settled down to sleep in the grass, safe in the palm of night. And up above, the stars form a great fresco across the ceiling of the universe.

An occasional involuntary tremble rushes through me as I think back on what just happened, which is more like a scene out of a dream. For a long while I lie awake enjoying the sweet taste left by his kisses, until the slow-moving moon passes my window on its way up to the heavens and I feel myself drifting into Craig's breathing and the soft thump of his heartbeat. Something unseen and beautiful came from his soul into mine, where he took my secret and then he gave me his in return. And I finally feel quieted, as if freezing cold water has been poured over a raging fever.

Chapter
Seventy-five

I AWAKE IN A SOFT HALO OF GOLDEN LIGHT AND CRAIG IS STILL asleep next to me, with his mouth slightly open and his rumpled butterscotch hair all shimmery against the white pillowcase. It's one of those late-summer mornings where the early sky glows in a cathedral of anticipation.

Walking across the damp grass in my bare feet I feel like a diver coming up from the deep ocean, having to readjust to the level of oxygen in the air and practice breathing. Bernard's tiger lilies are in full bloom and droplets of water roll across the curved leaves like beads of mercury. Wet blades of grass are stuck in the wings of Olivia's cupid statue so that he appears to be part Chia pet. However I give him a thumbs-up for a job well done.

Gil, Olivia, and Ottavio are seated around the dining room table having breakfast, while Bernard rushes to and from the kitchen.

As my eyes adjust to the dimness of the indoors I realize there's an extra body at the table. And because I'm still in another world it takes a nanosecond to place her.

"Mom!" I practically shout as I enter the dining room. "Oh my God, what are *you* doing here?"

My mother looks puzzled by my reaction, since she regularly pops in to say hello, even more so since the girls arrived.

"I've come to visit my oldest daughter. And these darling children, of course." The little girls reach out their arms to her like kittens chasing a ball of yarn. They must be able to sense the diaper-changing gene in her DNA helix.

Gigi is perched on Mom's lap slurping up spoonfuls of yogurt while Rose sits in her highchair being fed by Rocky. Though he was trained to assist paraplegics, there seems to be a certain amount of crossover with young children. Whereas Gigi is a little bit afraid of Rocky, Rose acts as if he's the best nanny in the world. It's going to be a miracle if the two of them don't end up living in the top of a tree together. After Rocky finishes feeding Rose he takes off, I assume to get ready for church, since it's Sunday. His former owner may have been an alcoholic, but she was a regular churchgoer. And as soon as Rocky hears those bells on Sunday morning he hops to it. Or as Bernard likes to say, turns into Pavlov's chimp.

"Actually, I do have some news this morning," my mother tells me. "I went to the doctor yesterday, and we're having twins!"

Apparently she told everyone else before I arrived because they've already absorbed the information and look to me for a reaction. "Oh my gosh," I do a quick calculation. "Ten kids and two parents—you'll have enough for a sweatshop!" Financial problems solved!

"Two babies are better than one," says Bernard, beaming at the little girls.

"Right. I meant, 'Congratulations.' " But I feel as if I'm floating in a distant place where time touches eternity and that if I were to drop a china bowl right now it wouldn't make a noise when it shattered. Suddenly I see and hear people talking but am unable to make out exactly what is being said. They all sound very far away, as if they're calling into a thick fog.

A knock at the front door brings me back to earth. Especially when I turn and see Craig's parents on the opposite side of the screen door. "Mr. and Mrs. Larkin. What are *you* doing here? I mean, please come in."

"We were worried about Craig," his mother explains as they enter the dining room. "He didn't come home last night."

"And his car is in your driveway," says Mr. Larkin. "So I assume he spent the night here and everything is all right."

Haven't they ever heard of *phones*? I guess this is what Craig means about the extra pressure of being an only child. Your folks hunt you down in person like a posse, even when you're almost twenty.

However, my mother also appears concerned. Any report of a missing child can't fail to snag her sympathy and interest, even if said "child" is approaching middle age.

"Craig fell asleep here," I explain, well aware that my mother is taking an interest in the conversation. "We were working on . . . actually, *he* was working on . . . well, the pond."

Gil and Bernard both give me an *Oh really* look, which, if they were somewhat younger, could be translated to: *liar, liar, pants on fire.*

Fortunately it's at this moment that the "missing child" strolls in. And I'm relieved to see that he had the good sense to put on his jeans, T-shirt, and shoes. Even though he looks like the same old Craig, it's as if I'm seeing a completely different person. I mean, we slept together! This makes me suddenly worry that everyone in the room is also going to be able to tell that something has changed between us, and so I quickly look away from him.

Bernard of course can't get to the stereo fast enough to put on "Hello Young Lovers" from *The King and I,* but everyone else is too preoccupied to notice that anything has changed between us. Olivia starts telling Craig's parents how wonderfully creative the new pond is. It shouldn't take her more than a few minutes to gracefully segue into her position on US government sanctions against Cuba.

Gil goes to the front hall and digs out the leaf for the dining room table. Ottavio runs around pouring coffee and tea for everyone. And Bernard heads back into the kitchen, where he's firing up eggs and waffles and only the bread machine knows what else. He continues his mischievousness by putting a big bowl of fresh strawberries in front of my place at the table.

"Thank you, Puppetmaster," I say, and pick up a fork. Suddenly I'm starving. I know that smoking pot gives you the munchies but I'd never heard the same thing said about sex.

The Larkins haven't been inside the house before and it's easy to see by the way they glance around and nudge each other that they're surprised by some of the more elaborate furnishings. "What a beautiful highboy!" exclaims Mrs. Larkin.

"*Virgin* spruce." Bernard gives me a covert wink.

Olivia shoots him a look.

"I thought it was *fruit*wood," I say with mock surprise.

Bernard ignores us both. He goes over to Rose, who is now bouncing in Ottavio's lap and says, "Who wants Lillian Russell?" The faces of both Gigi and Rose break into big smiles. Then from behind his back Bernard produces a plate of two half cantaloupes filled with vanilla ice cream placed side by side—a culinary tribute to the voluptuous stage star of the early twentieth century.

Mr. and Mrs. Larkin glance at each other as if they're not sure whether to call a photographer to capture the happiest little girls in Cosgrove County, or else phone Social Services for using breakfast as a lesson in female anatomy.

Meantime Craig takes the seat next to me, and having forgotten to get a clean glass from the kitchen, he casually picks up mine, finishes my orange juice, and then refills it from the pitcher in the middle of the table. Everyone else is too busy talking to notice, but I do, and he notices that I notice. We give each other a secret smile acknowledging that we have recently been *that close,* and are thereby authorized to share germs.

The next person to knock on the door is Officer Rich. He lumbers into the room. "Hiya, folks, mind if I join you?"

Now, what is *he* doing here? I happen to know that I can't get arrested for having sex, at least so long as I didn't charge for it. But *what* is going on? A post-virginity party? It reminds me of the first day I went to school with my period—feeling as if everybody in the entire world could tell that something was different.

However, Bernard seems to be the only one attuned to my anxiety. He holds up a big pitcher of tomato juice with a celery stalk in it and asks, "Does anyone care for a *virgin Bloody Mary?*" Only he's looking right at me as he says the words.

Gil returns from the hall closet with *another* leaf for the table. "The more the merrier!"

Ottavio lifts Rose onto Olivia's lap and goes into the kitchen for *another* mug of coffee, though he's obviously delighted at the prospect of an impromptu brunch party. Ottavio is happiest when there's a mob of people sitting around a table with lots of good food. I sneak into the living room and begin playing "They Say It's Wonderful" from the Ethel Merman disco album. Bernard is the only one who notices the change in background music. He's so startled by Ethel's sudden burst of vibrato that he accidentally drops the teakettle into the sink, and this gives me some measure of revenge for his smugness and double entendres.

"Did you expect me to take all your crap *lying down,*" I whisper as Bernard hurtles past me toward the stereo.

Sliding his sizable bulk into the last empty seat, Officer Rich takes a swig of coffee and beams at all of us. "Well, Hallie," he announces, "it would appear that you've solved my pothole problem."

Chapter
Seventy-six

"What did *I* do?" I have absolutely no idea what Officer Rich is talking about.

"Valueland is being charged with tax evasion and has been forced to shut its doors, and I mean *permanently*," he answers. "It turns out that Kunckle's crew has been bringing in goods from Canada that were originally manufactured in the Far East and sticking MADE IN AMERICA labels onto them. The shipping documents were then altered for US Customs.

"Another step toward ending child labor!" cries a delighted Olivia. "But how does this involve potholes?"

"Hallie noticed the delivery trucks when she and Bernard were out late one night—or rather, early one morning," says Officer Rich. "So I staked out Valueland for a few weeks and it turned out to be a nightly occurrence."

I can see my mother's eyebrows shooting skyward and Bernard

looking worried, so I quickly jump in. "When we left early for that antiques show in Pittsburgh, I mean, Philadelphia. It must have been about 3 A.M."

"Oh, of course," Bernard energetically agrees. "The *antiques show.*"

"Anyway," continues Officer Rich, "the day before I'd been telling Hallie how the back roads between here and Valueland were constantly getting ripped up. When she next ran into me at our weekly poker game and said how she'd seen some large trucks, the kind intended for highway travel, she figured that they must be causing the potholes."

Now it's Mr. and Mrs. Larkin's turn to look intrigued when they hear my name mentioned in conjunction with a poker game.

"So the trucks were pulling into Valueland to unload," explains Officer Rich. "And five in the morning is an unusual time to be unpacking a truck around here."

"Yeah, but I only told you I thought I knew where the potholes were coming from," I remind him. "You went off and figured out the tax evasion stuff."

"Actually, the state revenue officer took care of that when I told him about the shipments in the middle of the night. Valueland isn't the first store to attempt this sort of label switcheroo," says Officer Rich. "Though I'm surprised that Edwin Kunckle would be involved in such a sleazy operation."

Mr. Larkin harrumphs in a way that indicates he's not *at all* surprised that Edwin Kunckle would be involved in something like this. "There's a good example of a man who'd rather reign in hell than serve in heaven."

"Milton!" exclaims Olivia, obviously thrilled to have another person at the table with a stanza to suit every occasion.

"Will he go to jail?" I'm hoping yes; after almost putting Herb out of business he deserves it. What a creep. I'd love to see how those stupid blue silk ascots look with an orange jumpsuit.

Officer Rich shakes his head. "Sorry, but he's already out on bail. And of course he's employed the most expensive lawyers in Cleveland to work on the case round the clock. But the *big* news," he turns to me, "is that you're going to get a five-thousand-dollar reward!"

"No kidding?" I must be dreaming. First I have the best night of my life with Craig and now, after losing the design contest and throwing the poker game, I'm still getting some money. That will pay for the tuition gap second semester and so I won't have to quit for a year and work full-time! It's as if the odds have suddenly and mysteriously shifted in my favor. And a good thing too, since I'd been starting to think that perhaps my luck was finally running out.

"That's wonderful," says my mother, who attended the Every-Bit-Helps School of Finance.

And as much as I can really use the money, it crosses my mind that I'm not really entitled to it, at least all of it. "But *you're* the one who figured out the tax evasion!" I say to Officer Rich.

"The money is for tips that help crack a case, and you were the one who provided the tip, Hallie." Officer Rich is firm. "Besides, I can't take any of the money. I'm in law enforcement. It's specifically for good citizenship."

"Cool!" I say. And who would have imagined that the words *good citizenship* would ever be used in conjunction with *my* name!

Craig raises "our" orange juice glass in toast fashion and gives me a proud smile.

His parents appear impressed too, as if you shouldn't judge a person just because they wear torn jeans with a Mr. Bubble T-shirt and play poker.

"Maybe you can use the money to go on a trip," suggests Bernard. "To historic Williamsburg, *Virginia*. Or better yet, the *Virgin* Islands."

"Just be sure and go to the *British* Virgin Islands." Olivia is back on message. "They have a social welfare system and take care of the people who work hard their entire lives. Unlike America, which more often than not heartlessly casts aside her human resources."

There's *another* knock at the door and Gil goes to answer it. Who's left, I wonder? Maybe it's Dr. Just Call Me Dick from the high school coming to tell me that there's been a mistake and I never graduated after all.

Chapter
Seventy-seven

GIL RETURNS TO THE TABLE WITH CAPPY, SMARTLY TURNED OUT in neatly pressed white pants, plaid shirt, maroon linen sport jacket, and wearing his good-luck boating cap at a jaunty angle. He politely removes his cap upon entering the dining room and holds it in front of his chest as if "The Star-Spangled Banner" is about to begin playing.

Until now I've managed to keep my old gambling life and my new life with the Stocktons separate. Bernard has heard about Cappy, but he's never met him. However, as soon as I introduce my old track crony, Bernard graciously offers him coffee and breakfast.

It's obvious that Officer Rich and also Mr. Larkin *do* know Cappy, and hold a negative opinion regarding his line of business. And though they don't say anything, I can tell that they'd rather he didn't stay. Cappy doesn't make any trouble around town and so the

Morality Police tend to leave him alone, because the truth is that a lot of local doctors and lawyers and businessmen use his services all the time. However, it's understood that Cappy's supposed to stay on his own turf, meaning the track and his office down at Bob's, or else Officer Rich might be interested in offering him some free lodging.

Cappy is no doubt aware that his presence may not be desired all around and politely refuses the offer of breakfast and also Bernard's chair at the table. "Thanks, but I just need to talk to Hallie for a minute and I'll be on my way." He looks around the table and nods to everyone and shoots a horse trader's glance into the kitchen. "Where's Ray Ray?" he asks me.

"Gone Gone," I tell him. "We sort of broke up."

"Who's Ray Ray?" asks Officer Rich, apparently interested in anyone who might also be of interest to the local bookie.

"Raymond Vincent Bolliteri Junior." Cappy's tone is heavy with disapproval, suggesting that he and Officer Rich aren't in such different businesses after all.

The name Raymond Bolliteri certainly gets the attention of Craig's dad, who sits straight up in his chair. "Raymond Bolliteri *Senior* is the head of the most powerful crime family in the Midwest," he explains for the benefit of assembled company, including me.

Holy shit, I almost slept with a mafioso-in-training. He certainly didn't *talk* or *act* like any of those hoods on TV. How was I supposed to know? Oh my gosh, if Ray had stayed over last night I might have had to start wearing makeup and big hair and maybe even high heels!

"They have huge money-laundering operations all over the state," continues Mr. Larkin. "In fact, well, I probably shouldn't tell you this, but Valueland was one of their laundries. Ed Kunckle is only the front man."

"Oh good heavens!" says my mother. Women in their childbearing years are often the first to connect a financial windfall for offspring with potential harm to offspring.

"Don't worry," says Mr. Larkin. "That's why they use people like Ed Kunckle. The store disappears, he gets paid off, cuts a deal to stay out of prison, spreads some money around for a new library and a day-care center, and the local paper prints that Kunckle was embezzled by his accountants."

"You almost slept with a mobster!" blurts out Craig, echoing my own thoughts. But out *loud*!

My mother's jaw drops an inch at the words *slept with* and then another inch for *mobster*. And for a split second it's hard to tell whether engaging in premarital sex trumps being on a Mafia hit list in her parental playbook.

"Hallie would have of course reformed him," interjects Bernard. "The way Sarah Brown converted Sky Masterson in *Guys and Dolls*."

Craig's announcement about my dating history appears to pique Mrs. Larkin's curiosity as well, if one can judge a person's interest in something by the way their palms fly up to their cheeks and stare at the party in question.

Meantime Cappy lets out a low but satisfied chuckle, the way he does when the favorite starts out too strong and the experts know it's going to drop back to last place in the final furlong but the gullible bettors are cheering their hearts out.

Fortunately I'm saved by the bells of Our Lady of Perpetual Sanctity, which start clanging out an earsplitting "What a Friend You Have in Jesus" to call the faithful to worship. Rocky comes bounding through the dining room dressed in his suit and tie.

Craig's parents have never seen Rocky before. In fact, by the looks on their faces it's safe to say they've never seen *any* chimpanzee wearing a three-piece suit.

"He certainly looks excited about going to church today," exclaims Gil.

"I should think so," says Olivia. "Rocky's converted Lulu to Catholicism. Now that they've settled on being friends they attend Mass together every Sunday."

The news of a chimp taking a dog to church doesn't surprise Gil, because he's lived with the Stocktons long enough to know that this could be considered one of the more boring things to happen around here. The Stocktons live in capital letters, is the way Gil likes to explain it. However, it's probably a good thing that Craig's parents don't know that the "Lulu" being spoken of is a Great Dane.

"They're off to pray to the *Virgin* Mary," adds Bernard, no doubt for my benefit.

But I no longer mind his teasing. This particular ending has been lost in a crowd of wonderful new beginnings.

Rocky heads out the front door, and Cappy, after politely saying his good-byes, follows him. There's no doubt in my mind that Cappy is already working on ways to make a couple bucks off the chimp, like betting some of his pals down at the pool hall a C-note that there's a monkey attending Mass over at Our Lady right this very minute.

Just as Cappy exits, Herb from the drugstore enters with a pleased look on his face and a big cardboard box under his arm. He stands at the head of the table and announces, "Hallie, I can't thank you enough for helping to close down Valueland. I was planning to call it quits after Labor Day and close the store."

"Then next time deal me some cards that I can use," I say.

"I'm being serious, for once," insists Herb. "They've only been shut for two days and I'm busier than a lesbian in a hardware store at closing time."

"*What* did you just say?" I can't believe my ears. Herb is not exactly known for being the most gay-friendly of all my friends.

But Herb only laughs. "Bernard taught me that one. I just love it. And my kids think I'm really cool when I surprise them with these bonbons."

My mother and the Larkins appear puzzled.

However, Olivia politely clears up the confusion without embarrassing Herb. "Ah yes, perhaps someday Hallie can write a book containing all of Bernard's *bon mots.*"

Herb places the large box down on the floor. "There's enough toothpaste and shampoo and stuff in here to last you through the holidays."

I glance over at the open carton to make sure there aren't boxes of condoms or pregnancy tests on top.

"And if you give me your address at school, I'll ship you paper products and microwave food," promises a joyous Herb.

"Now that's an offer I'm not going to refuse," I say. Between the reward money and the Herb pipeline I may not even have to take out much more in loans this year. At least assuming that I can win a few games of hearts every now and then.

Chapter
Seventy-eight

WHEN WE'VE ALL FINISHED EATING, BERNARD GOES TO THE stereo and puts on "I Enjoy Being a Girl" from Rodgers and Hammerstein's *Flower Drum Song* so he can show off the choreography he's been teaching to the girls. The pediatrician said that lots of movement is good for the development of their muscles and bones, and Bernard of course interpreted this to mean dance lessons.

Rose is very enthusiastic about dancing and the minute any sort of music is turned on she begins flouncing around. Little Gigi can only wave her arms, but she does a fine job of it and practically keeps time with the music.

"Isadora Duncan had a divine revelation that she could free people from their shackles through dance," Olivia explains to the assembled crowd. "Bertie believes the same to be true for curing rickets."

Bernard turns to my mother and places a reassuring hand on

her elbow. "Although Isadora *was* slightly hostile to the idea of marriage, she always believed in motherhood."

"They do have a way of winning your heart." Mom smiles at the girls while holding a hand on her midriff, where she's starting to show with the expected twins.

"I'm going to install a swimming pool next summer and you must bring *all* the children over," Bernard says to my mother.

A pool? This is news to Gil and me. We both give Bernard a quizzical look.

"It seems a shame to let my experience with swimming go to waste," continues Bernard.

"I agree that all children should learn to swim at an early age," says my mother in her *Safety First* tone of voice.

Gil mouths "water ballet" at me and puts his hands above his head as if forming the flame of a candle atop a cake and we both crack up.

After the recital is over, Craig and I walk back to the summerhouse so he can get his car keys. He's in a hurry to go home and finish packing and hit the road. It's a long drive back to his campus in Minnesota.

Above the orchard the clouds are high in the sky and windswept, as if someone has run a comb through them. Apples are dropping off the sagging trees and the lawn is no longer the emerald green of spring. Petals from the daylilies lie curled up on the walk like so many scattered bits of paper.

But the yard has been restored to its enchanted status, where fairies are free to nestle like birds in all of its nooks and crannies. Butterflies with wings of yellow and blue satin hover near the edge of the pond. Back here you wouldn't know if it was the sixteenth century or the twenty-first.

However, my own world is changing like the sky at daybreak.

Craig and I face each other to say good-bye. He takes my hands in his and gazes at me with those luminous green eyes. "So we'll stay in touch."

"Definitely," I quickly agree. "And visit whenever possible."

"Absolutely," he says. "But not be . . ."

"Not be exclusive," I finish for him.

As much as we both might like the situation to be different at this moment, and not have busy lives playing out eleven hundred miles apart, we agree that it's better to leave things as they are rather than be consumed by a bonfire of broken promises later on.

Yes, the devil had won another easy hand in God's poker game. But what if freedom itself is currently my true heart's desire? And that my future is out there right now, waiting for me in far-off places. Because I have a hunch that things will only get better. And that life is indeed a good gamble.

Heart's Desire

a reader's guide

Laura Pedersen

A CONVERSATION WITH
LAURA PEDERSEN

Julie Sciandra and **Laura Pedersen** have been friends since their teenage days in Buffalo, New York, and can talk for hours about anything, though most conversations inevitably turn to snow and bowling.

Julie Sciandra: When are you finally going to tell us the name of Hallie's mother?

Laura Pedersen: She's just Mom. Mom is devoted to her family, has hopes and aspirations for her children, but she also worries about them.

JS: What's your favorite part of writing a novel?

LP: In real life I'm entertained most by exasperation—when a person we care about is doing something ill-advised and there's the urge to try and rescue the situation, but it can't work for whatever reason, and so frustrated bystanders have to release that energy by yelling, joking, baking a pie, running, or whatever their thing happens to be. This usually occurs when Bernard is upset by the actions of his socially and sexually progressive mother, only he can't really stop her because a) he has no right to, and b) at some level he knows that she's usually right. So he acts out instead.

JS: This book seems to be mostly about love—searching for it, finding it, and in some cases losing it.

LP: Hallie is almost eighteen, and after you finish rebelling against your folks, live through the SATs, and get into college, it seems as if that's usually next on the list.

JS: Did you borrow any of Hallie's trials and tribulations from your own love life?

LP: I probably borrowed more for the older characters because I was in a tree or on a bike until I was around seventeen and didn't have serious boyfriends until my twenties. In the Midwest in the 1970s and early '80s there wasn't this rush to grow up—it was the end of a long recession, one that had basically lasted throughout our entire childhoods. People still didn't have money to spare and the media wasn't bombarding us with products and images. I played touch football and street hockey with kids in my neighborhood. In high school I had a boyfriend who was captain of the lacrosse team, and Hallie's boyfriend Craig plays lacrosse, so I guess I'm guilty there. But I don't know that much about sports and thus am heavily dependent on my limited knowledge of what equipment goes with what game.

JS: What did you borrow from your own experiences for the older characters?

LP: When I was growing up most couples stayed together—they'd be like Officer Rich and his wife, Hallie's folks, or Gwen's parents. I was the only one of my friends whose parents were divorced, and that was after twenty-three years of marriage. So I probably developed a more questioning nature toward romance: How do you know when it's right? What goes wrong and splits people up? I went at it more from the scientific side: What if you get married and then meet the true love of your life five minutes after the wedding? It's all fascinating to me, the importance of timing, how people meet—at parties, through friends, at work. And how they break up—with a huge fight, a growing drift, a civilized chat. Yet as much as I want to be a cynic, I'm a romantic at heart, believing in true love and all that Hallmark malarkey.

JS: Is that why you got married?

LP: I married a few months before turning thirty and that was definitely the right age for me. Anything earlier would probably have been a mistake. During your twenties is a good time to try everything, before the mailbox is filled with envelopes from the insurance company and under "doctor" in your address book there are several different names and numbers. I've been married for ten years now and don't anticipate a midlife crisis. But if I do have one I'm pretty sure it will involve smoke jumping—you know, parachuting out of planes to extinguish forest fires. I've always wanted to do that.

JS: Hallie always seems to be struggling to earn money. Where does that comes from?

LP: It's one of the things that makes me want to become a politician—that and the millions of children in this country without medical insurance. The cost of getting a good education is way too high and discriminatory toward people in lower income brackets. Most of my friends had jobs after school, on weekends, and during the summer. Heather worked at a department store, Mary was at CVS, Debbie was a camp counselor, Paul rode the garbage truck, Mike had a paper route, and I worked at a donut shop, among other places. All the girls baby-sat and the boys did yard work. Yet the money we labored hard to earn barely made a dent in our tuition costs. And that was twenty years ago!

JS: There hasn't been a reference to a sitting president or a real-time current event in any of your books. Is there a particular year in which *Heart's Desire* takes place?

LP: I've tried to make it seem like the present at whatever time you're reading the book. There are gadgets such as computers with cameras and the Internet that tie it to the early twenty-first century, but I'm trying to avoid an exact year. Life and death don't change that much, and the same with gardens, cooking, and the four seasons. Also the passions, disappointments, hopes, and humiliations of the heart remain pretty much the same. And it would be a sad day if first-graders stopped telling booger jokes.

JS: Rocky the dipsomaniacal chimpanzee has proved to be an extremely popular character. Do you know any alcoholic chimpanzees in real life?

LP: My husband is from South Africa, and when we were there visiting I met a monkey that had belonged to a sailor and had become a very bad alcoholic. The sailor had died and the monkey was taken in by a primate refuge that worked to get him off the sauce, though he remained one angry monkey. Otherwise I've read about special monkeys trained to help paraplegics. I took some literary license with Rocky because chimpanzees don't perform this type of home health care that I'm aware of. But I worked with a chimpanzee named Chippy on a TV show, and so I was familiar with his size, movements, and expressions, and I thought I could describe him easily enough. Plus I couldn't see doing a Dian Fossey and moving in with a gorilla colony in Rwanda for a year just to write a book chapter. Chimpanzees are usually the ones you see acting in movies, and so I think this will be an entertaining element in the big-screen version of *Heart's Desire*. Remind me to find out how much Chippy is charging these days.

JS: You live in Manhattan and haven't been in school in twenty years, so how do you write about teenagers currently living in the Midwest?

LP: Much of it is based on having grown up in a small town outside of Buffalo, New York, which had more in common with Nebraska than New York City, or at least it did back then. We had gardens with plenty of vegetables, church ladies who carried plastic shopping bags of knitting around, a firemen's picnic, the county fair, and all the stuff from a 1950s musical. Nowadays I tutor at an after-school center in East Harlem, and this helps keep me up-to-date on popular music, clothes, and candy. Believe me, if it weren't for the kids at Booker T. Washington Learning Center I would *not* know the value of a Yu-Gi-Oh! card or what a "hoodie" sweatshirt is. Fortunately old comic book characters like Spider-Man and Batman keep coming back in style, and so those are usually safe. Then there are the ten-ton backpacks being wheeled around by first-graders who look as if they should be heading off to the airport rather than school. My gosh, we didn't have homework until third grade, and even then it wasn't much. You could usually stick it in your pocket.

JS: And the question everyone always asks: *How* do you know so much about gambling?

LP: Oh, that. When I was growing up holiday gatherings were comprised of a half-dozen adults and me, the only child. Occasionally we'd play Parcheesi but it was usually a long night of poker. My mother taught me your basic stud games when I was five and so I'd sit on a phone book and play, bet, and deal along with everyone else. They were merciless. I remember being yelled at to hold up my cards the way you'd tell another seven-year-old to stop flinging peas. At the time my uncle was a police reporter in Buffalo and the official Damon Runyon of the family, complete with colorful phrasing and a gun strapped to his leg. When I was eleven he took me to the racetrack over in Fort Erie, Canada, which I found quite fascinating, and so after that I would ride my bike over there. It was always fun to bicycle over the Peace Bridge. There was a narrow cement path that went downhill as you approached the Canadian side, and usually some construction along the way, so I would consider whether it was preferable to be run over by a truck or plunge into the swirling Niagara River several hundred feet below and then go over the falls, possibly the first person to do so on a bicycle. Counting cards at blackjack was a natural next step since you could get pretty good odds back then if a place didn't use lots of decks. And then I learned even more about probability while trading options on the floor of the stock exchange. However, I was always terrible at math in school. I only came to life when you put a real dollar sign in front of the problem.

JS: So what's next?

LP: I just finished the third installment of the Hallie Palmer series, *Full House,* and am working on the fourth and probably final book.

JS: Give us hints.

LP: In *Full House* Hallie must return home due to a tragedy in her own family. For her it's basically the year I think most of us experience at some point where life becomes not so much about us anymore—when diplomacy enters our psyche in a big way. For example, for many people it's when they have their first serious relationship, and for others it's when they have a child. In the final book Hallie leaves the seventy-five-mile area that has always been her world and heads out into the wild blue yonder.

JS: Is it like a soap opera where she discovers a lost twin?

LP: Definitely not. There are enough twins in that family. But I think the ending will be a big surprise to those who've read the entire series.

JS: When you travel around the country doing readings and signings, have you noticed that restaurants *claim* to serve Buffalo-style chicken wings but they're not at all like Buffalo wings?

LP: I've been a vegetarian for a long time, but I can say with authority that they certainly don't look as good as Buffalo wings.

They're not nearly as large and oftentimes don't include the blue cheese sauce. Furthermore, Buffalo has better pizza than most places, and we don't get any credit for that. You know what else? People don't believe me when I tell them that Buffalonians put snowblowers in their wills.

JS: People don't believe me when I tell them my family owned a bowling alley.

LP: If they saw you do that backward-between-the-legs throw they'd change their minds in a hurry. Or play foosball.

JS: I guess we're getting off track. So why do you like writing?

LP: Watching the news every night will make you think the world isn't a good place. It certainly has its problems, but I find there's a tremendous generosity of spirit in most people and a desire to make things better. I enjoy celebrating that. I'm hopeful about the future. I also believe that if the ship you're after doesn't come sailing into the harbor, then sometimes you have to borrow a rowboat and paddle out to it.

JS: Was there any main point you were hoping to get across in *Heart's Desire*?

LP: It's a story about things lost and things found—the ebb and flow that is an intrinsic part of nature and also creates the tapestry of our lives. My only regret is not to have said anything about fire safety, especially having grown up in a place where old kerosene heaters regularly burned down wooden houses in fifty minutes flat.

JS: Fire safety? Like a seminar from Officer Rich, the way he warns the local kids about blowing off their fingers with firecrackers?

LP: Not exactly. It's just that I enjoy candles and feature them in the book. But these days you can buy floating candles that sit in a bowl of water. This way if you leave the room and forget about them you never have to worry about starting a fire. I highly recommend floating candles for everyone.

JS: You've officially turned into your mother.

LP: If that's true then I won't finish the next book because I'll be too busy making citizen's arrests of people smoking in malls and government office buildings.

Reading Group Questions and Topics for Discussion

1. Hallie believes that she's fallen in love with Auggie after a brief meeting. Is there such a thing as love at first sight?

2. Do you have a set of criteria for "the right one," characteristics that you know you really like in a person, or do you just go by how you feel when you meet someone and then spend a bit of time together?

3. Brandt points out that most species are not monogamous. Into which category do you think humans fall? Are we meant to mate for life, be serially monogamous, or just date various people? Or does it depend on the individuals and the relationship?

4. At the beginning of the book Hallie observes that many couples seem to divorce when their kids leave for college. Do you think that people wanting to get divorced should try and stay together until their children are at least teenagers?

5. Can your significant other also be your best friend? Is it necessary to have a good friend with whom you're not engaged in a physical relationship in order to talk about certain things?

6. Hallie's mother believes that Louise has taken up with a bad crowd of friends and that this is to blame for her recent wayward behavior. Is it fair to judge people by the company they choose to keep, or should you be able to view them strictly as individuals? Would you worry if you had a teenage daughter hanging around with older guys who drove fast cars?

7. Hallie and Brandt have known each other a long time, and it appears that they might start a relationship. Has there ever been a person you really like and have known for a long time, but never considered for a relationship? What makes for "chemistry" between two people, where they both want more than friendship?

8. Hallie is having what she deems to be a good experience at college, but it sounds as if only a fraction of her time is devoted to actual learning. What percentage of high school and/or college would you say is about academics and what percentage is about other things such as learning how to be a friend, have a relationship, and basically be a human being?

9. Craig and Hallie agreed not to be exclusive while attending colleges so far away from each other. Based on your experiences, can long-distance relationships work?

10. Brandt and Louise choose abstinence when it comes to premarital sex. Is this the best option for all young people, or does it depend on the teenager? Should parents, teachers, and counselors be trying to steer teens toward abstinence, or should they provide all the information and let them decide what's right? If you had a teenage son or daughter what route would you want him or her to take?

11. What are the pros and cons of marrying the only person with whom you ever plan on having a serious physical relationship?

12. Every once in a while we're surprised to hear someone we thought was heterosexual announce a lifestyle change. In the book, Gil briefly considers being with a woman after a long same-sex relationship. Do you know people who have questioned their sexual preferences, and if so, do you think the urge to do so came on suddenly or had been on their minds for a while, only they may have been worried about sharing the information?

13. Ottavio wants to marry and Olivia doesn't. Whose side are you on? Would you mind if one of your children, parents, or grandparents was living with a significant other?

14. Is it true that you always remember your first kiss and/or the first time you enter into a serious physical relationship? Do people make too big a deal about first times or are they really special?

15. Hallie's parents have a lot of kids to keep track of. If you're a teenager, do your parents know much about your *real* life? How might they answer if you were to ask them? If you're older and you think back, did your parents know much about what was really going on when you were sixteen or seventeen? And if you have teenagers now, do you think you know much about their relationships?

16. Occasionally Hallie is forthcoming about her fears and concerns but usually lets them bubble inside for a long time. On the other hand, Bernard is happy to unburden himself to basically anyone willing to listen. Do you tend to discuss your problems with others or keep them to yourself? Is either way healthier, is there a happy medium, or does it depend on the person?

17. As you get older, has your view on love changed at all? Are you more hopeful or more cynical about romance than you were a few years ago?

18. Do you think people usually break up because they feel that one of them has changed, or because they find they didn't really

know the other person as well as they thought? Or is there another cause you see happening a lot, such as meeting someone else?

19. Can the brain be saying one thing about a person while the heart is saying another? Why do you think we sometimes make bad choices for partners? And is this a learning curve so that as you get older your selection process improves? If a friend told you that he or she loved someone who didn't love that person back, what would be your advice?

20. Bernard goes through a very bad time after splitting up with Gil. Have you ever had a bad breakup? What helped you through it? Did you learn anything that ended up being useful later on?

21. What do you think is the most important element in a successful relationship?

Please turn the page for an exciting preview
of Laura Pedersen's next novel,
the sequel to *Heart's Desire*.

Full
House

By the second week of January everyone is finally finished dropping and adding classes, changing majors, joining ski club, and breaking off relationships that had been allowed to drift through the holidays. It was easier to coast the extra few weeks to avoid changing plans, returning long-ago-purchased gifts, and general all-around misery. It's a brand-new year. A fresh start. And when you're eighteen, the possibilities seem endless.

The biggest fraternity on campus holds a keg party Saturday night and welcomes all comers as long as they can produce a fake ID along with twenty bucks to be paid in cash at the door. Since my roommate Suzy has this huge crush on the treasurer, she convinces Robin and me to be her accomplices in searching for ways to drive the manhunt in a forward direction.

The frat house is a box-shaped building with dark brown vinyl siding that looks as if it could be the back part of a church where the priests live, were it not for the large Greek letters carved out of wood and pounded in between the second and third floors. Also, it's practically new. Craig had explained to me that the tradition of the dilapidated *Animal House*–style fraternity house had ended a decade ago when insurance companies started discontinuing policies to buildings that no longer measured up to all the fire codes. So even though the furniture on the inside might have springs popping out of the cushions, or be nonexistent, the structure itself has to be sound.

We pay our cover charge on the front steps, and a guy wearing a multicolored jester's hat uses a stamp to emblazon the backs of our hands with big purple beavers. In the strobe-lit entrance hall Billy Joel's "We Didn't Start the Fire" is blaring from speakers that seem to be everywhere. Meantime the jacked-up bass causes the wooden floor to thump so hard it feels as if there's a heartbeat in each foot. The couches are pushed back to the walls and the ceiling of the large living room is hung with dozens of strings of chili pepper lights that cast a crazy quilt of patterns onto the walls and guests.

The next hour consists of a shouted exchange with this junior in the art department named Josh whom I had a crush on the entire first semester of my freshman year, while he didn't even know I was alive. Only the problem is that now, after so much fantasizing about our nonexistent relationship, as well as several beers, I'm experiencing difficulty separating the real conversation we're finally engaged in right now from all the imaginary ones I had with him last fall. For instance, Josh looks surprised when I talk about having nine brothers and sisters, whereas I'm thinking we covered that *months* ago. Furthermore, I'm desperately trying to act interested in everything that Josh is telling me about where he's from and what he's studying even though I already know all this from asking around and looking up his campus profile on the Internet. I may be majoring in graphic arts, but like most college women I minor in stalking.

Finally he asks me to dance. Only I can't help but wonder if it's his way of ending the conversation and working toward making an exit, alone. Nonetheless, Josh and I move toward the area in front of the fireplace where throngs of intoxicated students dance to Jason

Mraz's "I'll Do Anything." I'm probably reading too much into the situation, as usual, but it's as if every line in the song has a double, or even triple, meaning. And when Josh pulls me close I realize that if he puts his arms around me we're headed for more than just dancing.

"*Hall-ie . . .*" I hear my name echoing somewhere within the swirl of music, shouts, laughter, and a gauzy but pleasant alcoholic haze.

It can't be. It *cannot* be the voice that boomerangs through the garden at the Stocktons' and calls me into dinner at the end of the day.

Sure enough, Bernard is *pardonnez-moi*-ing his way through the gyrating, closely packed crowd, carefully ducking and maneuvering so as not to disturb any of the headgear with beer cans attached to the top and plastic tubes running into the mouths of thirsty party-goers.

It must be two o'clock in the morning and the party is by now in full swing, with at least a hundred people wildly dancing to "I Melt with You."

Oh no—could there have been another breakup with Gil? Tell me it isn't so! Or worse, maybe something terrible has happened to Olivia and Ottavio on their trip to Italy. A plane crash?

"I've been looking everywhere for you!" Bernard cups his hands around his mouth to form a makeshift bullhorn. "Come on—we have to go!"

"What?" I can hardly hear over the music. On top of that Bernard doesn't so much as say hello to the young man attached to my midsection, when normally he is so well mannered.

"Your father had a heart attack!" he shouts in the general direction of my left ear. "We have to go *now*!"

Josh steps back, and now that I'm a solitary human form again Bernard uses the opportunity to grab me by the arm and pull me toward the door. It takes a moment to get through a crowd of rowdy (translate: drunk) women just arriving and claiming to have paid earlier. The heavyset doorman, who happens to be a linebacker on the football team, is effectively blocking their entrance and shouting, "Show me your beavers!"

Bernard looks questioningly at me. "Hand stamp," I explain. But it's too loud to hear anything, and so I put mine up to his face and he nods that he now understands.

Once we're outside Bernard continues to yell as if still competing with the music. "Gil is waiting in the car with the girls. It must be a mile from here—there isn't any place to park on campus. In fact, I've been to so many different parties tonight I don't even know where I am anymore." Bernard stops and looks searchingly up and down the street.

"What did you park in front of?" I holler back, though it's quiet now but for a few shouts coming from a late-night snowball fight across the quad.

"There was some sort of sculpture out front—it looked like a giant toadstool."

"That's the science building," I say. "It's supposed to be a molecule or an amoeba or something along those lines."

I hurry Bernard in the correct direction and the cold air clears my head slightly. "Is it serious?" I ask Bernard.

"I'm not sure. Louise phoned." Only now we've been jogging for a few minutes and it's not so easy to catch our breath. "You-can-call-her-from-the-car."

I easily locate the maroon Volvo that Bernard recently traded for his antique silver Alfa Romeo waiting across from the science building with its engine running, the exhaust puffing a cloud of gray smoke into the cold winter air.

The girls are asleep in their car seats in the back and I quickly climb between them while Bernard dives into the passenger side. The moment I pull the door closed Gil shoves a cell phone in my ear and then puts the car into gear so that we jump away from the curb.

Louise is frantic on the other end of the line. "Hallie? Is that you?"

"Yeah," I exhale heavily.

"*Thank God* they found you! *Please* go to the hospital right away and tell me what's going on. I'm stuck here with the kids. And every time the phone rings I practically faint. Relatives are calling. There are people I've never even heard of—an Uncle Ernie called from somewhere in the West Indies."

"That's Dad's uncle," I explain. "Our great-uncle. Only I thought he lived on a houseboat near San Diego."

"I'm so worried, Hallie." Louise sounds as if she's starting to cry, and that it's not for the first time over the past few hours. "I don't know what happened. I woke up and the paramedics were flying down the stairs with Dad on a stretcher and Mom threw a coat over her nightgown and yelled at me to watch the kids. Reggie's been screaming bloody murder. I finally gave him a bottle of regular milk. It'll probably kill him. But at least he shut up. Tell Bernard and Gil that I'm sorry to have woken them up and everything, but I didn't know what else to do."

"No, it's fine." I'm suddenly feeling incredibly sober.

"I finally got hold of Eric about an hour ago," reports Louise. "He's taking a bus from Indiana that leaves late tonight and arrives in the morning."

"I'll go to the hospital, find out what's going on, and then call you right back." I click off the phone and let my head tip over backward.

"Don't worry," says Gil. "The new hospital has a terrific cardiac unit—state of the art."

"How old is your dad?" asks Bernard.

"Both my parents are thirty-nine," I say. It's easy to remember because I just have to add nineteen to whatever Eric's age is at any given time.

"Oh, that's *young*," says Bernard. "He'll be fine. They can do quadruple bypasses and even replace valves and aortas with pig parts. And if your heart can't be fixed then they just throw it away and paste in a whole new one."

About the Author

LAURA PEDERSEN grew up near Buffalo, New York, and now lives in Manhattan, where she volunteers at the Booker T. Washington Learning Center in East Harlem.

Visit her website at www.LauraPedersenBooks.com.